"In my career, having reviewed over 1,200 novels, I can honestly say . . . I have never read *anything* quite like this. Think *Misery* meets *Gone Girl*. Landon Beach delivers a special, unforgettable, jaw-dropping reading experience that readers won't soon forget. *Narrator* is a masterpiece."

**—The Real Book Spy**

"Landon Beach's *Narrator* is an engaging and remarkably accurate dive into the life of a professional voice actor, while delivering twists and turns that will leave you on the edge of your seat. Compelling from start to finish. You won't be able to put it down!"

**— J. Michael Collins, award-winning voice actor, coach, demo producer, and scriptwriter**

"Electric. Powerful. Original. Reads like a movie, exploding towards a breathless climax that readers won't ever forget."

**—Chris Hauty, national bestselling author of *Deep State, Savage Road,* and *Storm Rising***

"*Narrator* is an intellectual labyrinth that Landon Beach navigates with evocative prose and twist after compelling twist. Imagine Stephen King's *Misery* rendered by M.C. Escher. Plan on reading this one straight through to the dazzling end."

**—Bryan Gruley, Edgar-nominated author of the Starvation Lake trilogy**

"*Narrator* has everything: a peek behind the curtain (in this instance, into the commingled world of publishing and audiobooks), characters who are compelling and provoking (sometimes both at once), and a twisting, turning plot that will keep you guessing—and then second-guessing. Dynamic and audacious, *Narrator* is a triumph."

**—Christopher Rosow, #1 *Wall Street Journal*, Apple Books, and Amazon bestselling author of the Ben Porter series**

"Landon Beach created a one-of-a-kind, twisting, gut-wrenching tale that kept me guessing until the very end. Expertly crafted, and a unique, highly recommended read!"

**—Mike Houtz, author of award-winning DARK SPIRAL DOWN and co-host of The CREW Reviews**

"With *Narrator*, Landon Beach has fashioned a singularly spectacular tale. At once harrowing and hypnotic, with a complex protagonist in Shawn Frost who defies genre conventions, and a duo of genuinely terrifying villains, *Narrator* is a descent into obsession and madness that will leave you exhilarated and disturbed in equal measure. This one will stick with you long after the final page."

**—Sean Cameron, co-host of The CREW Reviews**

"With a meticulously researched and engrossing plot that twists and turns and deepens with the flip of each page, *Narrator* is as ambitious as it is enjoyable. Thriller fans who have not yet discovered Landon Beach are in for an exhilarating ride. Be warned, you're going to lose sleep."

**—C.E. Albanese, award-winning author of DRONE KINGS and co-host of The CREW Reviews**

"With its sharply written dialogue and inner introspection, perfectly placed pop-cultural references, and twists that are guaranteed to blindside you, *Narrator* is wonderfully inventive and will keep you guessing until the end. As a veteran-narrator-turned-thriller-writer, I found this book spoke to me on many levels. The fine detail of an audiobook narrator's process is spot-on; not surprising, given that Beach's narrator is one of the best in the biz. Highly recommend you pick up this book…or even better, the audiobook."

**—Nick Sullivan, veteran audiobook narrator and author of The Deep Series**

"Instant immersion and nonstop thrills won't let you put *Narrator* down or press pause. Landon Beach takes us into the mind of the titular talent, offering clever and well-researched glimpses inside both the booth and industry. And the audiobook—read by Scott Brick, the quintessential synonym for the title— makes for a mellifluously meta must-listen."

**—P.J. Ochlan, acclaimed actor, Audie Award-winning narrator, and producer**

"Landon Beach's *Narrator* is gripping, breath-taking, compulsive reading. His plot and characterizations are spot on. He captures the life of a narrator perfectly. I planned to read for an hour, and I didn't put it down until I'd finished the entire book. I've read more thrillers than is healthy, but I've never read anything like this. I now have to read every one of Landon Beach's books. This thriller delivers in spades!"

**—Daniela Acitelli, actress, professional audiobook narrator, and host of The Narrator's Cup of Joe**

"What a meta ride *Narrator* is! A twisty, turny, tense look at a job I've always considered (aside from fatigued vocal cords every now and then) rather benign. Beach has me rethinking my booth security… My only complaint is that the protagonist isn't female because I want to narrate this book!"

**—Hillary Huber, award-winning audiobook narrator**

"In this 'artist comeback story turned Hitchcock thriller,' award-winning actor/audiobook narrator Shawn Frost gets pulled into the nightmarish world of overzealous fans, recurring personal demons and the challenge of separating literal fact from nefarious fiction. The book alone is fantastic, but with Scott Brick's seductive narration, you're guaranteed to be kept hanging on his every word."

**—Sean Pratt, actor, award-winning audiobook narrator, and coach**

"A twisty, psychological thriller. Kept me guessing to the very last page."

—Robert Dugoni, *New York Times* Bestselling Author of the Tracy Crosswhite Series

"Thrills on the page suddenly become life and death in *Narrator*. Shawn Frost goes from telling stories behind the mic to living a story he can only hope won't be his last. Author Landon Beach has taken a deep dive into the world of the people who bring your audiobooks to life in this twisty adventure you won't be able to put down."

—Christina Rooney, Grammy-nominated audiobook director

"Landon Beach's *Narrator* will make your hair stand on end and give you goose bumps. This entire thriller is a viscerally wild rollercoaster ride—complete with mind-blowing twists you won't see coming. And *Narrator*'s conclusion will leave you breathless. Beach's insight into narrating is so accurate and realistic I felt like Shawn Frost *must* be someone I know. This is a narrator's life…right up until the murder and mayhem, anyway."

—Suzanne Elise Freeman, actor and award-winning audiobook narrator

"What a thrill ride. Who would have thought reading a book about a guy reading a book would be such a psychological roller coaster ride!"

—Kevin Allen, WKJC FM 104.7

"Just wow! The audiobook industry will never be the same. Beach has created an intense, immersive thread that you will not be able to put down. It's a doozy of a thriller that will leave you gasping for air."

—Dan Musselman, Director of Studio Production, Penguin Random House Audio (retired)

"Voice acting becomes life & death in Landon Beach's *Narrator*, and I'm hanging on every word of this twisted thriller! Raw, real, and psychotically brilliant—I couldn't put it down. I'll never feel safe in my recording booth again…"

**—Anne Ganguzza, Award-winning Voice Actor, Director, and Producer**

"Every voice actor is going to re-think their job (and job security) after reading *Narrator*! Landon Beach strikes visceral chords and pulls the wires tight on this thriller!"

**—Mary Lynn Wissner, Award-winning Casting Director and founder of Voices Voicecasting**

"A fantastic and fun look into what we narrators do for a living! And I'm putting a lock on my recording booth door..."

**—Ray Porter, actor and award-winning audiobook narrator**

# NARRATOR

Landon Beach

Landon Beach
Visit my website at landonbeachbooks.com

Printed in the United States of America

First Printing: May 2022
Landon Beach Books

ISBN-13 978-1-7322578-8-7

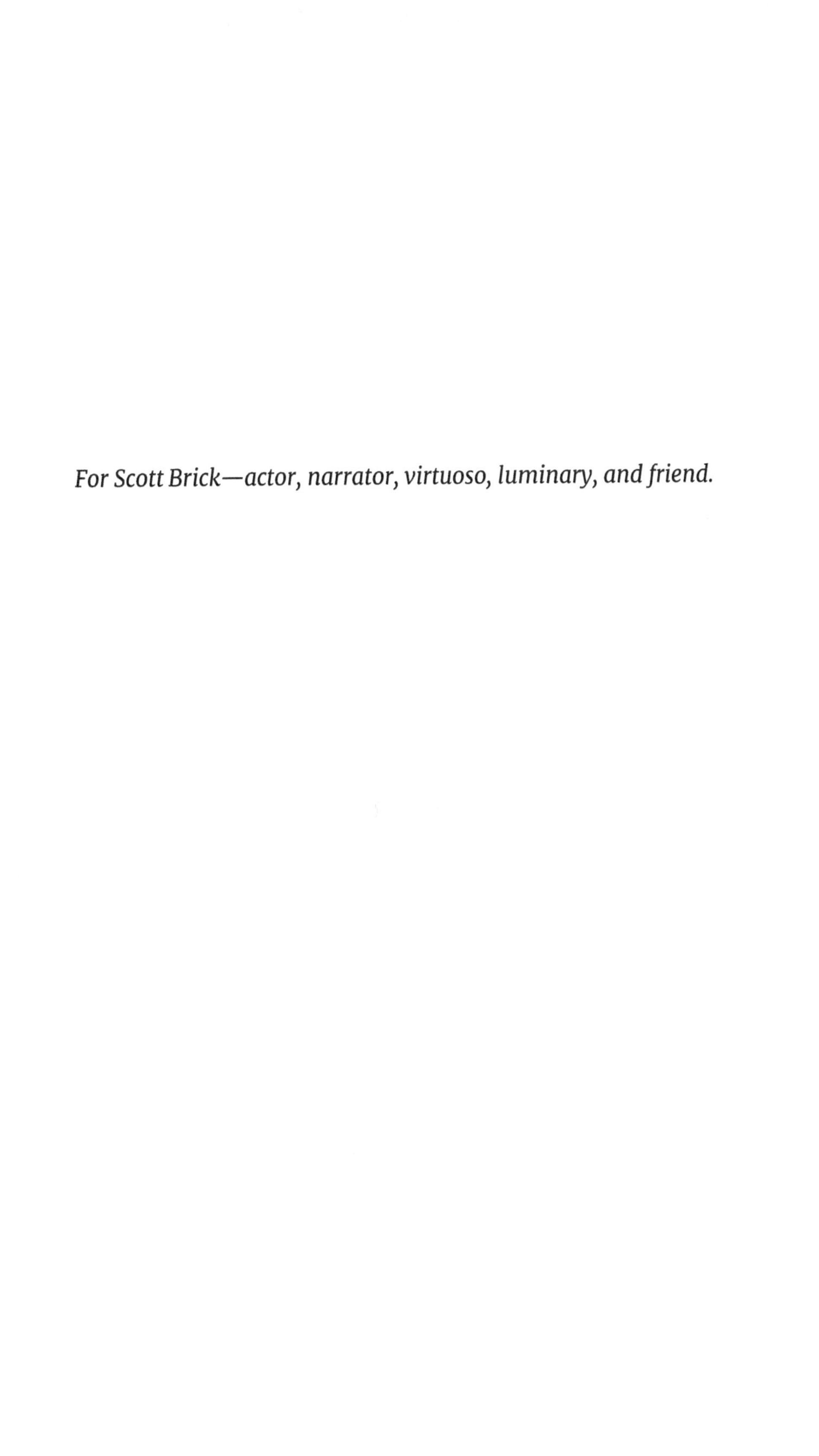

*For Scott Brick—actor, narrator, virtuoso, luminary, and friend.*

# NARRATOR

# OVERTURE

*from* "They Are Not Long"

They are not long, the days of wine and roses:
    Out of a misty dream
Our path emerges for a while, then closes
    Within a dream.

—Ernest Dowson


*from* "Annabel Lee"

For the moon never beams, without bringing me dreams
    Of the beautiful Annabel Lee;
And the stars never rise, but I feel the bright eyes
    Of the beautiful Annabel Lee;
And so, all the night-tide, I lie down by the side
    Of my darling—my darling—my life and my bride,
    In her sepulchre there by the sea—
    In her tomb by the sounding sea.

—Edgar Allan Poe


"You're my number-one fan."

—Paul Sheldon, *Misery*


*"Step carefully, Nick, step very carefully."*

—Nick Dunne, *Gone Girl*


"She never gets old.  Marci can't be real.  She never gets old."

—John Nash, *A Beautiful Mind*

"And you were such an apt pupil! What fun you two must have had, playing games with me! Why me? Why did he pick on me?!!...And the necklace. Carlotta's necklace. That was your mistake, Judy. One shouldn't keep souvenirs of a killing. You shouldn't have been that sentimental."

—Scottie Ferguson, *Vertigo*


*from* "The Continuity of Parks"

"Through the blood galloping in his ears came the woman's words: first a blue parlor, then a gallery, then a carpeted stairway. At the top, two doors. No one in the first bedroom, no one in the second. The door of the salon, and then the knife in his hand, the light from the great windows, the high back of an armchair covered in green velvet, the head of the man in the chair reading a novel."

—Julio Cortázar

# PART I

## Research and Narrating

# 1

## Carmel-by-the-Sea, September 2022

Why do authors have to kill off characters we love?  I, Shawn Frost, sit in my darkened recording booth and stare at the final paragraph of the novel I am narrating. Almost there. Finish it. Finish it right. Finish it with a flourish.

But I can't. Not right now.

For I am crying. The main character, Nehemiah Stone, died two pages ago in a self-sacrifice that I had not seen coming. The book, *The Paris Sanction*, is author M. Scott Sala's fourth Nehemiah Stone thriller, which I have waited patiently for two years for the chance to narrate. Five years ago, Simon & Schuster thought I was the perfect narrator for the job when they contacted my agent, David Killian, whom I affectionately refer to as "Killy." At that point in my career, the beginning of it, I was reading mid-list mysteries, a handful of Christmas-themed romances that always had a dog and a character that needed saving, and *zero* thrillers—especially from any top-tier talent. But, I had built a loyal following in addition to my fan base that stemmed from my two-time Tony

Award-winning writing and acting career—before the spectacular fall occurred that almost ended my life. In any case, Killy heard that thriller legend M. Scott Sala was shopping around book one of a planned decade-long series featuring a new protagonist, Nehemiah Stone, who was, and Killy quoted Sala's agent, *'The Cain to Sala's Abel, longtime protagonist Billy Rollins.'* It was big news because Sala, who had become a legend in part due to Hall of Fame audiobook narrator *Michael Hunnie's* narration of all twenty of Billy Rollins's adventures, was looking for a different narrator for his new series. Have you guessed my feelings for Michael Hunnie yet?

Every rivalry has history, and ours is no different.

I'm the new guy, and he's the legend.

Now, the audiobook narrator community that I am a part of is one of the nicest, closest-knit, and most supportive communities that you will ever find, and I'm invested in it. You won't find the kind of mentoring and giving that takes place in our community in other acting circles. However, the profession is not immune from being vicious, cutthroat, and unforgiving, and you better have some grit and chutzpah to survive. And we do have our disagreements: You should read a book before you narrate it; you should *never* read a book before you narrate it. That kind of stuff. However, there is one thing that, minus one person, we all unanimously agree on: We all *hate* Michael Hunnie. To be fair, he is an extraordinary talent. In fact, Hunnie's voice is the homophone to his last name— pure, smooth, golden honey, and it will forever be attached to Sala's most enduring character, the loveable drifter Billy Rollins. But. Even though Hunnie, by the point I was chosen for the new series, had already accumulated more Best Male Narrator Audies than he had fingers on his right hand, Sala reasoned that for Nehemiah Stone, he needed a deeper, naturally coarser voice for the character. Stone was the dark side of Billy Rollins, and the books would not be globe-trotting adventures with Billy getting laid every hundred pages and having his faults illuminated by the comedic foil of Boykins Wrathbone, an ex-con who was drunk for most of each outing.

No, Nehemiah Stone was a vigilante with an impenetrable veneer and a sledgehammer for a fist. He had an ex-wife whom he couldn't seem to get out of his life, he liked fast cars and fast boats, and he enjoyed an Islay scotch now and again. There was no partner, no best friend, no sentimentality, and nothing clean about anything in Nehemiah's life—except for his ability to work outside of the law and bring justice to hopeless cases. Rarely were the stakes larger than this, and the beauty of the novels was that they didn't have to be. One climbed onboard a Nehemiah Stone novel for Nehemiah Stone, plain and simple.

And so, Killy told me that he had been on the lookout for the perfect vehicle to put me in the spotlight where he could raise my profile so I could start to compete with Hunnie and other narrators for top books. I remember saying, *'I'll never get that series, but go ahead and give the publisher my demo.'* This was met with a stern, *'Let me do the figuring, okay, Shawn?'* from Killy. *'I sent it over a month ago—and met with M. Scott Sala. The reason that I'm* here, *in your home right now, is to tell you that you got the job.'*

After feeling the initial rush that accompanies the news of landing a major gig, I was left with questions. Did I get the job because the publisher, Sala, and Sala's agent loved my demo? Was it because of my theater accolades or the success of the works I had already narrated? Or was it because of Killy's power?

The answer...

Mostly because of Killy's power.

And so began the climb to the top of the audiobook world. Most people in the business ended up agreeing that I was the perfect fit for the series, and, after book one became a runaway bestseller—better than the ten previous Billy Rollins thrillers—I signed on for the rest of the series. After that, it was one book a year until two years ago when, for the first time since the series started, Killy came over for dinner and told me that the fourth book had been delayed indefinitely.

Sala couldn't get past the first third and was caught up in writing the screenplay for the ninth Billy Rollins film, which would soon start production and eventually join the first eight on Netflix. The series—addictive and huge budget—had already won numerous Golden Globes and featured Adam Driver, sporting an unforgettable mullet, as Billy Rollins and Cedric the Entertainer as Boykins Wrathbone, and fans were clamoring for *'like fifty more of them, bruh.'*

By this time, I was narrating other top thrillers, but my *favorite* character, the one my eyes still got big for when the manuscript arrived, was Nehemiah Stone. I should also mention that narrating the series has been my best-paying job *ever* since leaving New York. In the audiobook world, performing a series is the very definition of financial security.

And so I waited and waited. Months went by, and then *years*.

Then, finally, on a cool September morning, Killy rang my doorbell at 7 a.m. and delivered the manuscript for the spectacularly overdue novel *The Paris Sanction*. I was immediately thrown off because Killy had never delivered a manuscript before; Simon & Schuster usually handled it, and the book was always sent via a secure file-sharing application because they trusted me. But this novel was delivered via a company iPad. Once Killy placed it in my hand, he immediately called his contact at the publishing house and said that I had possession of the novel. Then, Killy and I did a page count with the contact. The new safeguards didn't bother me. However, the strangest change to my usual process was that I was to perform the book cold. It should have been an unmistakable hint that something was up, but I loved the series so much, and it had been two years since I'd performed the last one. I figured this was just an added precaution so that details about the novel would not leak before the release. Hell, we had six more novels to go after this one.

What had impressed me the most was that Simon & Schuster had hired someone to do the usual cold-bastard work of reading the novel and providing notes in the actual document—pronunciation keys for strange words, highlights of who was speaking when there was an extended back and forth with no dialog tags, etc. Of course, by this time, I had my own research team, and they had been eagerly awaiting Sala's new Nehemiah Stone thriller. Confused, pissed, disappointed—you name it—they were not happy with the arrangement when I called them.

*'Someone went to a lot of trouble here, Killy,'* I said to my antsy agent. *'Is there something I should know about this one?'*

When David Killian wants to be as unreachable as Nehemiah Stone, he has an uncanny way of turning his normally friendly brown eyes into two of the cruelest daggers that I have ever seen. And, at that moment, Killy's eyes could have sliced me up for chum. *'Not that I'm aware of. Publisher is just being careful. Now, get after it. S & S needs it in a week.'*

And now, with one paragraph left in the book, I decide that if Killy was here right now, I'd at least attempt to rip off the head that rested on my mega-agent's six-foot-four-inch frame.

Killy had known. Hell, they all must have known that this was my beloved character's swan song. But…*why* was it his swan song?

Looking back now, I had become suspicious in the last twenty pages. Nehemiah had never been under such pressure. The character he had been called to save in this edition was an orphan named Kara—who was only known as that: Kara—for the entire novel. But the stakes were more than just Nehemiah helping Kara find her biological family. That would have been too easy of a challenge for Nehemiah Stone to conquer in a book that had taken two years to reach my booth. No, the twist was delivered with a master stroke by Sala midway through part two. Nehemiah and Kara discovered that one of the orphanages in Paris that she had grown up in was a front for an elite group of five assassins who, for the right price, would sanction political opponents who got in the way of keeping France's elite socialist party in power. The top floor of the enormous, decrepit three-story orphanage, which the orphans were never allowed to see, was, in fact, the business offices and training center for the assassins.

By the time I turned the page to start the final chapter, Nehemiah had done away with four of the assassins, but the best of them, a man known only as "Reich," was still very much alive and now hunting Kara and Nehemiah in an office building where they had run to after Nehemiah killed assassin number four but not before the assassin had shot Nehemiah through the right shoulder, rendering his shooting arm useless. I gasped at that point and clicked my tally counter to signal that I was re-reading the lines so that the post-production crew could delete the gasp. Nehemiah Stone had been injured before, but never like this. It was just before midnight, and the building was empty save for the three of them; there would be no help. They raced up the stairs, floor after floor of close calls.

With Reich closing in on the rooftop, Nehemiah hugged Kara goodbye and got her safely into a corner stairwell, where she headed downstairs to shelter. Reich was around a service structure and had not seen Kara's escape. He sprinted around the building and found a waiting Nehemiah Stone who, in classic M. Scott Sala prose, *clotheslined* Reich with his good arm. Certain that Nehemiah had regained the initiative and would soon finish off the assassin, I slouched in my chair, looked at the ceiling, and exhaled into the claustrophobic air of the booth.

I clicked my tally counter because of the exhalation and sat back up, my eyes tiptoeing down until they found the correct spot on the page.

And now, my performance came back to me as I struggled to hold back more tears:

*With his left hand, Nehemiah pulled out his Bowie knife from the large black sheath on his waistband. He went down to one knee, already pulling the knife back, ready to drive it through the heart of Reich. It would be a righteous kill, a necessary kill, a needed kill for him. The blade, a silver moonbeam against the starry night, continued to descend toward the open target on the ground below. Down, down, dow—*

*Suddenly, as if powered up by an overwhelming energy source, a collision of particles that would have outlined his features in neon, Reich's body twisted, and Nehemiah's knife plummeted into the empty space where its target had been a second ago.*

*Unable to stop his momentum, Nehemiah continued his insidious downward arc until the knife point struck the rooftop's concrete floor. The energy from the impact transferred from the knife handle into Nehemiah's wrist, which made a sick crunch as he felt it dislocate in a rush of smoldering heat. The physical pain overcame his sensory message from his brain to his hand, which told his hand to hold on to the weapon. He dropped the knife.*

*And now, Reich, with one swift motion, took his own knife out and drove it into Nehemiah's stomach...*

I shake my head, which takes me out of my memory of the performance. I search the booth for a tissue box, but I have never needed one for the ending of a Nehemiah Stone novel before. I would be starting a *New York Times* bestselling romance novelist's newest tear-jerker after supper tonight and had planned on grabbing the tissue box then; she always got me crying—and probably every other reader—within the first chapter when some horrible offering of life's unfair outcomes befalls a sweet, innocent person who leaves life prematurely and forces the main character to start a journey of discovery and healing by going through hell. I knew it would happen, welcomed it, really—who doesn't love a good, cleansing cry in the privacy of a place like the booth? But now? At the moment when I should be smiling at how Nehemiah Stone has once again "taken the garbage out" (another M. Scott Sala trademark phrase) and thus resumed his slow drift across the U.S. *à la* David Banner in *The Incredible Hulk* TV show? Before starting the final chapter, I even queued up "The Lonely Man" theme from the show, which is my tradition after finishing Nehemiah Stone's latest adventure. It signifies the end of another journey with my favorite character to narrate and helps me transition from a state of sadness—each ending is like losing a friend for an indefinite amount of time—to a state of anticipation for the day when the next installment of Nehemiah Stone's life shows up from Simon & Schuster— the *lonely man* returning to my life.

Now, I knew that day was never coming because M. Scott Sala has taken Nehemiah Stone away from me. He's dead, Kara is on the run, and Reich is after her.

My eyes well up again.

I yell, "Who in the *hell* is going to save her now?"

Tears burst from my eyes, and between sobs, I get out, "God damn you, Killy. You knew. You *knew*. And you didn't even warn me."

A few minutes pass, and I regain control and wipe my eyes with the shirtsleeve of my ten-year-old Monterey Jazz Festival shirt—another tradition that will now die; I've worn it the last day of recording for every single Stone thriller.

The word "thriller" makes my stomach turn.

Let's get something straight. I am a pacifist. I have never and *will never* own a gun, don't believe in violence—especially hunting or hurting other human beings—and I'm of the mind that if someone up the road in Silicon Valley created a chip that, when inserted into our brains, brought about harmony and world peace…I'd kind of be okay with it. Except I wouldn't. There's a catch to my utopian dreams: I love thrillers and could never give them up. Murder, destroying shit, affairs, knives in backs, raids, secret missions, guns with silencers—count me in for all of it. Just because I believe in the concept of world peace and John Lennon's *Imagine* doesn't mean that I'm not human. I just prefer to work these things out and experience them in a fake world, hoping that I never see them, let alone go there myself in the real world. As I've narrated books, I've thought about what I would do in certain situations, but I just can't see myself being violent beyond my language, which, as you can see, goes south when I feel surprised, stressed, or off-balance. Seriously, I think I would run at the first sight of a knife. And getting robbed? Yeah, I'm the guy who can't get his wallet out of his pocket and the rings off his fingers fast enough to hand them over and wish the thief a long and happy life.

Anyway, I'm mercifully letting my mind wander right now because of the shake-up that just occurred in my sanctuary. I mean, I'm a massive fan of the series and a good friend to Nehemiah, but the financial impact of this series ending prematurely is hitting me hard, too.

I just lost my favorite job.

I try some breathing exercises to calm down. Inhale for four seconds, hold the breath for four more, and then exhale for four. I repeat the cycle five times.

It doesn't do shit.

I stare back at the screen. The last paragraph waits for me. I don't want to finish this novel. The book is sort of like the famous "Dream Season" in my all-time favorite sitcom *Dallas*. It might be the best one, but I want Nehemiah Stone to come back like Bobby Ewing right about now. Sala could have one of Nehemiah's old flings wake up and hear the shower running, walk in to investigate, open the door, and witness Nehemiah turn around while saying, "Good morning."

Forget it, Frost. It's not happening.

I check my watch to make sure it's tight around my wrist. I like to use hand gestures when I narrate, and a loose-fitting piece of jewelry can make enough noise to screw up the recording. I lean forward, my mouth perhaps only two inches from the microphone. I've decided to read the final lines of Nehemiah Stone's life in an eerie whisper while cursing M. Scott Sala with my hands.

The spectrum of lights danced in Kara's glasses as she ran past a café and into the heart of Paris. She was sure that Nehemiah was behind her, perhaps about to catch up, or perhaps he was taking a different route. Either way, he had told her not to stop and not to look back. *"Just get to the apartment, lock the door, and if I'm not there in ten minutes, call the police. Do not let anyone in. Now, get going."* They were the last words he had said to her before she took off down the back stairwell. Now, with every pounding step, she felt her heartbeat match the force of each impact. She gritted her teeth and focused on the blocks ahead. Everything would be fine. Everything would be *just* fine.

"No, it won't!" I yell.

I sit for a moment in silence.

Dude, no one hears you.

I turn off my recording system and hang my head. Five years, and it's all over. He's gone. And you are one of only a handful of people who know. Dear God, what will Sala's fans think? Will they forgive me for narrating it? Is there a way I can warn them?

I laugh at my question. That would be against the rules. You are the narrator, and you do not spoil books for fans. But, damnit, why do I have to suffer for the next few weeks? I take a drink of warm tea to keep my vocal cords lubricated and reconsider my position. Well, at least I don't have to wait any longer than that. There have been books that I finished three months ahead of a release; I couldn't imagine having to wait that long for this book. At least I can thank Killy for holding this one off until I had only a week to finish *The Paris Sanction* before Simon & Schuster prepared it to be released to the world. The publication date— shoot, that should have been another warning sign. It was three weeks away. S & S was going to have to leverage its resources to get it ready that fast. Wait a minute. What about the paperback proof copies that would have gone out to bookstores and reviewers months ago? Did S & S not do it this time? It is almost unfathomable to think so. Killy will know, and I'll ask him.

The butterflies return to my stomach, and my mind starts to race. Nehemiah Stone is dead. How can I start the romance novel tonight? I won't be able to read it, I'll be crying so much. Put it off until tomorrow. It's time to regroup. I'll call Jo, and we'll go out. No, we'll stay in. I need her right now. I have to tell her about the book. It's the only way I can explain what kind of shape I'm in. I need a drink—something stronger, perhaps? No. No, no, no, no, no—no. Don't even think about it.

I look around, and it feels like the walls of the booth are compressing as if I'm in the trash compactor scene in *Star Wars*. *"Get on top of it!" said Han Solo. "I'm trying!" replied Princess Leia.*

Get me *out* of this booth.

I grasp the handle, push the door open, and fall to my basement floor— always been a tad bit dramatic, but, seriously, every ounce of energy has been sucked out of me. Books, films, and, above all, plays do this to me: I live and die with the main character—he or she is a friend, a goddamn good friend—and if something happens to him or her, then count me out for a few hours. You might think it silly, but when I'm in the grasp of a master artist, I feel like I'm in whatever medium I'm experiencing—the ordinary world disappears. That's art. That's my life.

I lie there, gasping for air. My legs will not move. Reaching for my cell phone, which is on the coffee table just a few feet away—*never* have it in the booth with me—my last recorded lines of the book play through my head:

**She gritted her teeth and focused on the blocks ahead. Everything would be fine. Everything would be** just *fine.*

I want to lie here longer. But, my legs come back to life like Reich's body, and I snatch my cell phone. I thumb the phone until it unlocks, and then I swipe the screen to my favorites.

Jo…Killy?

Wait, there is another option. I see the name of my best friend and fellow audiobook narrator Corie Woods below Killy's. My breathing slows, and I start to calm down. Have to call Corie. Corie will understand.

I change my mind.

I exit my favorites and bring up Jenna's number. I dial her—probably not the best thing to do, but, hey, there are people out there doing worse things.

# 2

## New York City, March 2023

I sit at the well-appointed table in the back right corner, farthest away from the glimmering stage, where the austere and beloved Executive Director of the Audies, Mariel W. Sissel, approaches the podium and adjusts the microphone to accommodate for her nearly six-foot, lithe frame. The blue sequins from her dinner dress sparkle in the spotlight, and her emerald eyes glow like safety beacons, welcoming the weary space traveler home. I'm hyper-focused on details, but this is exactly what I need to be doing right now to calm my nerves, for *the* moment of the evening has arrived. Mariel is going to announce the final three and most prestigious audiobook awards of the evening: Best Female Narrator, Best Male Narrator, and Audiobook of the Year. My palms are moist, and I feel a channel of sweat running down the middle of my back. It's a good sign. I felt the same way when I won my Tony Awards. This night feels different, though. Killy says I've never had a better chance at Best Male Narrator. I know that my work this year has been superior to my work last year—can't tell if it's because of the material or the fact that my relationship with Jo has never been better, or if I just got into a groove with my work. Or if seeing Jenna is doing something to me.

Keep it together, Frost.

Mariel speaks. "I have been informed by the wonderful staff here that the room's temperature has been maintained at a consistent sixty-eight degrees so far this evening."

I listen as the room goes pin-drop quiet. Mariel pauses. There are quizzical glances around my table that say, *"What's going on?" "What the hell?" "Why'd she mention that?" "Um, Mariel?"* As if in answer to the chorus of possible questions floating in my overstuffed noggin', Corie, seated on the other side of Jo, starts to clap. And because Corie starts to clap, I start to clap. Corie is my safety valve—has been for the past five years. He knows what this night means to me.

Our clapping catches on quickly, thank God, and soon the room fills with polite applause…for the room temperature. I stop clapping and reach for my iced tea. The other glasses on the white lace tablecloth have just been refilled with either red or white wine, and there are heavy, empty Collins glasses by a few place settings from happy hour beforehand. I eye them all, reminiscing of the days when I could partake. If I reach for Jo's glass of wine…

No. Focus, man. This is the moment you have worked for since changing careers to save your life. My hand closes around the condensation sweating on the glass, and the cool water droplets give my warm palm instant relief. I take a measured sip, whatever that means. I made a restroom break half an hour ago and am not worried about holding my iced tea. What I *am* worried about is having a dry mouth and not being able to deliver an acceptance speech on stage if I win the big one tonight.

I raise the glass to my mouth again as the applause dies down.

My proud and paternal figure, mega-agent extraordinaire (his description, not mine), David Killian, eyes me from directly across the table. Killy's eyes are a bit glazed, but they are still sharp enough to command my full attention. And right now, after all of our years together, I know what Killy's eyes are saying to me. *"Be calm. Take your sip and put the glass down."*

I do it.

Then, Killy takes a sip from his glass of red wine and breaks eye contact, focusing on his fourth wife's delicate neck, which Killy uses his other hand to give a soothing rub.

Then, I feel the smooth hand of Jo massage my right hand, the pads of her fingertips moving back and forth across my wrist's underside tendons. I know, it sounds like it would make my hand twitch, but it doesn't. It calms me like a tall glass of scotch used to. I swallow, which is difficult because of my dress shirt's buttoned collar. I never wear a collared shirt in the booth. Most days, it's jeans, a t-shirt, and socks—no shoes. I once recorded an entire book while naked—deserted island survival tale, you know, *"Wilson! Wilson!"* and all that shit. Gave a convincing performance, but I'll never do it again. There is such a thing as becoming too comfortable with being nude all day.

But tonight, I'm in a dark, tailored suit that Jo purchased for the occasion. *'It's your first nomination for Best Male Narrator, and you are going to look the part, buster,'* she said. My green tie is in honor of St. Patrick's Day, which is a few days away. Jo also picked it out for the psychological angle, *'A win tonight, and you'll be a shoo-in for the Hall of Fame. And then, my dearest, you'll be in the money.'* Of the two of us, she is definitely more the entertainer-piranha. I'm more lax and let the audiobooks come to me. *'Huh, easy for you to say, Tony winner,'* she needled. *'Some of us still have to fight for our roles, and when you haven't won a major award like you have, then there is such a thing as bad publicity, sweetheart.'* I know she is right. I find it ironic that the Audies are held in New York because it is the city where I became a cutthroat and vicious playwright and actor before the incident; now, I do my recording almost exclusively in my home in Carmel. I have used studios before, but they were all in L.A.

Jo is always looking for ways to get her thirty-nine-year-old self into a hot new stage production. This is what I am more accustomed to. That is, before I joined the audiobook community. I was hungry, like Jo, jockeying and angling for any position to get me a role—especially when I was just starting out after being asked to leave early from The Julliard School. The official word from the school was, *'Shawn is taking a break for family reasons, which we completely support. The entire staff looks forward to his return and the continuation of guiding him in the pursuit of growing his craft.'* The unofficial word was that I had clashed with two of my professors and had become intolerable during the grueling sessions. The unofficial word was closer to the truth.

I never returned.

If it sounds like I'm a bit into myself, it's because, well, I am. Who in the entertainment business isn't? As David Niven once wrote, *"To be an actor it is essential to be an egomaniac, otherwise it just doesn't work."* The master of wit and charm was right. However, a colleague of mine once said that being famous as an audiobook narrator was like saying you're the tallest midget in a room. Anyway, I don't think I'm into myself in a bad way; I used to be into myself because I wanted fame. That line of thinking led to awards, more money than I knew what to do with, power and the means to sculpt and maintain my celebrity status, and, eventually, terror.

Now, I care about my work, love the community that I am a part of, and know that if I lose my work, I'm likely to become interested in myself again—for all the wrong reasons. And I'm scared shitless that I won't be long for the world if that happens. The beast is always there, right under the surface, ready to emerge if I give him a chance. My psychologist, Dr. Roman I. Baker—"Bake"—told me that, and I believe the bearded sonofabitch.

Bake could not make it to the ceremony tonight, but my parents, John and Kim, and my older sister, Nicole, were able to. They're sitting at our table a few seats over from Killy's wife. I told them when they arrived yesterday at JFK that their coming meant a lot to me—and it does. Mom and Nicole are wearing new dresses they bought for the ceremony, but Dad has on his same old outfit of khaki slacks, a brown blazer with leather elbow patches, a white shirt with buttons on the collar, and the only tie he's ever owned, a red knit one—you know, the kind with the square bottom? You'd think the professor was ready to conduct class, but you'd be wrong. John Daniel Frost has been an electrician in our small hometown of Shelter Harbor, Michigan, for the past 40 years. He got the blazer off a clearance rack before I was born and in a department store that is long gone—he loves to tell me the story of how he spotted it. I don't care one bit that his clothes don't fit the occasion. He's here. He showed up. He's got my back like he always has, and I love him.

The room becomes silent again, and Mariel, whom I know to be an introvert by nature, grips the lectern and then releases it, her fingers spread wide.

She got thrown off by the applause. Probably had her words all set and then watched them float away as the clapping started.

Mariel manages a grin and continues, "Well, I think I should quit while I'm ahead."

That's it! Get back in the fight! I relax, focusing on being a telepathic cheerleader to help Mariel get through.

"But no, that was just too ripe of a setup." She pauses. "The room's temperature may be cool, but things are about to *heat up*."

There are a few cheers. We know it's unoriginal, but this woman could say, "Hi, Shawn," and I would bow down and kiss her feet. She's that good of a person and friend.

Killy gives a mocking laugh and shakes his head. He can be a dick. Then, he spills his drink on the table. Karma in action.

I watch as a staff member wearing a crisp uniform of black slacks, a white blouse, and a gold nametag with black lettering spelling "Karen" walks over with a forgiving smile and efficiently wipes up the wine, opens a new bottle, and refills

Killy's glass. As quickly as she appeared, Karen gracefully retreats to the shadows on the perimeter of the large hall. She and the other staff members must have been here all night, but, until now, I haven't noticed them.

Mariel proceeds to announce the Best Female Narrator, and it is no surprise. Courtney Tyson, the narrator deemed "The Second Coming of Bahni Turpin" by *AudioFile Magazine*, has won her second Audie of the night. Her reading of Billy Dee Williams's autobiography *Lando and the Cape of Many Colors* has dazzled since its release ten months ago on the 42nd anniversary of the release of *The Empire Strikes Back*. The fact that Billy Dee has hired a woman to read his autobiography has broken new ground. Traditionally, a man would be hired to read another man's autobiography, but rumor had it that when Billy Dee heard Courtney Tyson's voice, he said to his publisher, *'Who says Courtney can't narrate my book?'*

The formal announcement was made at a Recorded Books press conference that I attended, and I watched as Courtney and Billy Dee walked onto the stage hand-in-hand. The legendary actor—wearing a crimson cape around his jet black button-down shirt—announced to the adoring crowd assembled at the Waldorf Astoria, *'No one's got my swagger.'* Then, he looked at Courtney. *'And no narrator has her swagger.'* The crowd erupted, and Courtney, with her red blouse and black scarf complementing Billy Dee's classy style, accepted the mic delicately from the author and added, *'The project was irresistible as I have long been a fan of this beautiful man, his talents, and his unparalleled career.'* She paused, giving Billy Dee a sweet kiss on his cheek, and then said, *'I would now like to deliver the first few lines of the book.'* Along with me, the capacity crowd went silent in an instant as if Billy Dee had raised his cane and, with one wave, put the group under a magic spell. Courtney opened the proof copy of the book she had in her hands, swallowed, and then said, *"When you're up against the Darth Vaders of the world, sometimes all you can do is grab a cape, wear it the best you can, and hope you have friends with good timing. Well, I've stared down my share of Darth Vaders, worn many capes, and now, eighty-plus years into my trip across the galaxy of Earth, I've been fortunate enough and—"* she looked at him out of the corner of her eyes and smiled; his iconic grin widened—*"I've had a lot of special friends with expedient timing. I've lived a rich and blessed life, old buddies, and I refuse to accept that I'm slowing down, but while there's still some life left in my hyperdrive, I figure the time has come to reflect back on the times I've had and the wonderful human beings I met along the way."* Courtney closed the book with a resounding *THUMP!* We all clapped, whistled, and cheered for two minutes straight. And the greatest treat of all was when Courtney put the mic back under Billy Dee's mouth, and he winked and said, *'Beautiful. Who wrote those words?'* which unleashed a wave of laughter—so much for me that I went into a coughing fit—and as it finally died down, he gave her a knowing look and asked, *'And who might you be?'* I lost it at that point. Billy Dee is one of my heroes—always wanted to work with him. Perhaps, there's still time.

And now, coming across the stage, aided by his cane, is Billy Dee Williams himself. There is no cape but rather a crimson tuxedo jacket over a white shirt with a black tie. He reaches Mariel, gives her a hug and then a kiss on both cheeks—he does this slowly, not because he's older, but it's the refined style of a man whose every movement warrants attention. They await Courtney as she makes her way through the maze of tables, finally reaching the stairs to the stage. She takes them and strides across the stage, stopping just a few feet short of Billy Dee.

I hold my breath, wondering what they have planned. Winning Best Male Narrator is the furthest thing from my mind.

Billy Dee takes the microphone from Mariel, looks out at us—we audiobook people tend to be an anxious crowd—looks at Courtney, and holds out his hand for hers. She gives it to him, and I think, *"Oh my God, it's going to happen!"*

And then it does.

Billy Dee kisses Courtney's hand and says into the microphone, "Welcome, Courtney."

I stand up and start hopping up and down. I am soon joined on my feet by the rest of the crowd, and the applause goes on for what seems like *years*.

Eventually, the noise dies down, and Courtney gives a short speech. As much as I love Courtney, I remember none of what she says. My eyes are transfixed on Billy Dee, who looms large to the side of one of our most celebrated narrators. And then, as if the Hollywood actor brought a Hollywood ending with him, the pair walk hand-in-hand off stage.

Immediately, I'm lost in my thoughts—being ten years old and going to see *The Empire Strikes Back* a dozen times with my friends in the spring of 1997 when they released the special editions, which meant a lot to my generation because, as my father informed me, you have to see the *Star Wars* movies in the theater. Up until that point, I had only seen the trilogy on the small screen via our family's VHS player. But, Dad—a man who was not a film aficionado and had very little interest in art—was absolutely right. Before I went with my friends, Dad took me to see *A New Hope* on opening night and then *Empire*; there was something different about him that night in the theater, as if he was reliving some of the best memories that he ever had. He liked to remind me that the films came out when he was in high school, which, to him, was the perfect time. When the lights came up after the credits, he was looking away from me, and I swore he was wiping away tears. Never asked him about it, but I left the theater those nights thinking that anything was possible in life. I look at my dad now. His eyes are zeroed in on Billy Dee as Billy Dee breaks from Courtney after another hug and kiss and is escorted to a side entrance. I told Dad that the legend might show up tonight, and now that he has been able to see him here makes me feel good. I wanted this part of the night for him. As Billy Dee disappears through the doorway, Dad looks back at me and gives me a simple yet knowing nod.

My nerves are bundles of popcorn kernels, ready to pop. I wish I could leave right now and go back to that spring and escape into the darkened theater. Man, that spring. Halcyon days, not a care in the world. I wonder where my *Star Wars* t-shirt, the one that I wore every time I went to the theater back then, ended up. I had it until…

Killy's "Unbelievable!  Un*fucking* believable.  Never see anything like that again!" stirs me awake.

And suddenly, I'm aware of where I'm at again and that *the* moment of my fairly new career may be just a minute away.  Jo has a firm grasp on my hand now, the gentle massaging has ceased, and my nerves are at *Threat Level Midnight*—big fan of *The Office*.

Mariel, probably still in awe of the moment herself, takes a sip of water and then taps on the microphone.  "Just wanted to see if it still worked after *that*."

The crowd bursts into laughter, and then drinks are raised in an unspoken toast to the highlight of the night so far.

As glasses are refilled by Karen along with a host of efficient staff members, Dad takes a drink from his can of beer—wouldn't ever pour it in a glass—gives me a thumbs up, and then turns his attention toward the stage.  He's excited for me, but it's not the same way he was at the Tony Awards years ago.  I understand why.  Mom blows me a kiss and winks, then joins Dad in looking at the podium. Nicole gives me a fist pump and a look of determination.  I nod back like I know what in the hell I'm doing.

It gets quiet.  Really quiet.  I mean Tiger-is-putting-for-another-Green-Jacket type of quiet.  I swallow.  Mariel starts to announce the nominees for Best Male Narrator.

I look to Killy for reassurance, but he just raises an eyebrow at me from behind his designer glasses.

"The following group of men has been nominated for excellence in narration over the past year.  As with Courtney and the other wonderful female narrator nominees, each of these talented individuals possesses a unique, authentic voice that invites us into the story he tells.  The nominees are—"

On the massive screen behind Mariel, a split image appears.  On the left: a professional headshot of Crassus Dynasty, an old friend who records exclusively science fiction novels.  On the right: the audiobook cover of Andy Weir's newest *Beyond Rigel*, read by Dynasty.

"—Crassus Dynasty."

Loud applause.

If Crassus wins, I'll be okay.  He won two years ago, but that man deserves every award he's ever won.  His work on *Beyond Rigel* was superb; I listened to the audiobook twice—hey, I'm a sci-fi nerd, and I love all of Andy's books, call him "Father Andy," and could listen to Crassus all day.

The clapping fades, and a new split image appears on the screen.  This one is of Desmond Jay Webster, who has been nicknamed this generation's James Earl Jones.  Whoever said that is right on, and if D.J. wins, then I've got no issues.  It's his first nomination.  I look over at him and see him wiping his forehead before taking a sip of wine.  He's nervous.

I know the feeling.

Last year when I received my first nomination for a thriller I'd performed, I couldn't eat a thing at dinner.  Now, I see Sir Kenneth Branagh, who is sitting right next to D.J., give him a quick supportive shoulder rub and wink.  No matter who wins, I've got to catch up with them at the after-party.  D.J.'s performance in Branagh's *Othello* audiobook, a project that Sir Ken had wanted to produce for years since he starred in his own film version…Jesus, when was it, the mid-90s?...well, a long time ago, rated R, I had an older friend who worked at our town's one video store who snuck it out of there for me.  Johnny Gifford—solid citizen right there, haven't seen him for years.

Where was I?  Oh, right.  D.J.'s narration.  Well, the audiobook was the very pinnacle of Shakespearean art, and D.J.'s performance in the title role was magnificent.  I hear they're all in talks to perform the actual play and tour if they can work around Hiddleston's (who was the perfect Iago) shooting schedule of yet another Marvel film. In the industry—other than Corie—I'm probably closest to D.J. since we were both actors before we became narrators. The right-hand side of the screen is dominated by the *Othello* audiobook cover, all black with blood-red letters.

Mariel says, "Desmond Jay Webster."

Again, huge applause.

This time, it takes a little bit longer for the noise to subside, which gives me more time to think about the next two nominees: he-who-shall-not-be-named…and me.

Then, Mariel names him as his split image appears on the screen behind her. "Michael Hunnie."

Polite applause would be one way to put it—the clenched-teeth variety.

While hosting the Oscars, Bob Hope once poked fun at the nominees for Best Actor in a Leading Role and their rivalries. He said that each man was saying to himself in his head, '*Let it be me, let it be me. But, it if can't be me…not* him.' Hunnie is a great talent, perhaps the smoothest voice in the business—seductive, layered, original. And he deserves his nomination for the image that is displayed on the right side of the screen: the audiobook cover of Prada Zane's surprise runaway bestseller, '*Night, Dear Brother.* This thing had *Crawdad* buzz, sales, and legs that continued to stretch. So, like everyone else, I listened to it, and, like always, Hunnie's performance elevated the prose—especially the main character, a psychologist turned serial killer named Gregory Hymnal. I even gifted the audiobook to my own shrink, Bake. He listened to it, and we used a few of our sessions to deconstruct how Hymnal could have possessed so many public and private selves. Well, Hunnie's a bore and a weasel and a backstabbing sonofabitch. They can't give the award to him again tonight. Just can't.

I look to Killy again. This time he raises both eyebrows at me and then turns away.

Mariel says—I swear she's looking right at me—"And, Shawn Frost."

And it's my turn for the screen.  A picture, one that I don't mind, of me leaning forward with my hands clasped together while wearing a black V-neck sweater appears on the right-hand side of the screen.  I'm sort of smiling in it.

Jo squeezes my hand.  Hard.

On the other side of the screen is the cover of the controversial audiobook that ended Nehemiah Stone's journey, *The Paris Sanction.*  I can't look at it too long because of the gloomy memories—think about the girl Kara all of the time and wonder if she is still running from the wicked villain Reich.  I've had nightmares that he was in my own house and that I had nothing to fight him with.  A few times, I've woken up screaming for Nehemiah's help—scared the hell out of Jo.

And now I hear the clapping.  It prompts me to give a humble grin, and I exchange variations of this expression as everyone around our table turns toward me and gives me a smile while clapping.

Then, the noise dissipates, and it is time to announce the winner.  You would think that I'd be ruminating about my speech or wondering what it would be like to have my name called as the winner, but what's on my mind now is how I felt last year when I didn't win.  Call it a defense mechanism, lowering expectations so as not to be crushed if it doesn't happen, or some kind of fatalistic self-sabotage.  Whatever.  If Bake was here, he could explain exactly what was going on inside me right now and what the precise, scientific name was for it—all behind his all-knowing Goldblum glasses.

Mariel steps aside as the spotlight finds—dear Lord, it was rumored that he might be here tonight, but I can't believe it—*Tom Hanks.*  The place erupts, and I'm put at ease as the majesty of Hanks's presence seemingly makes everyone forget the award that is just about to be announced.  Fine with me; I'm on the razor's edge.  Probably not fine with attention-hound Mister Michael Hunnie, three tables over.

Hanks gets behind the podium and adjusts the microphone.  He is every bit the "Aw shucks, folks," down-to-earth man in person that he is on screen.  He gives Mariel his signature grin of appreciation, and she uses her hands to try and quiet the crowd.  He's not an audiobook narrator, but he is also no stranger to performing characters from behind a microphone.  I would be happy to receive my Audie from him if my number is called.

Killy is bouncing in his seat.  He knows Hanks and has vacationed with him.  I wonder if he or Hanks knows whose name is on the card inside of the envelope that Hanks will open.  Speaking of the envelope, where is it?

My question is answered as Hanks reaches down and pulls up one of his pant legs.  Jesus, he's wearing cowboy boots.

He pulls an envelope from his boot, and with perfect timing—before the audience can react—he snaps to attention behind the podium and says into the microphone, "There's—an—envelope—in—mah—*boot*!"

The crowd delivers a standing ovation—led by Killy.

Woody the Cowboy has now joined the evening.

Mariel hunches over, she's laughing so hard, and I can tell Hanks enjoys his joke as he laughs along with everyone else.  If my name gets called, it will be the perfect evening.

I take the scene in and wonder when we'll all sit down.  The crowd shows no sign of weakening, and the applause goes on.  Thirty seconds later, even my dad is still on his feet.

Then, Hanks calms the audience down with a few pleas, and we all take our seats once more.

Once the room is quiet, he wastes no time and says, "And the Audie goes to…"

He opens the envelope.

"Michael Hunnie."

# 3

## Los Angeles, June 2023

I arrive at the office of my counselor, Roman I. Baker, Ph.D., at just after four-thirty in the afternoon. Summer in L.A.—usually mild, airy, and pleasant. But today, it's steamy, smoggy, sweaty, and irritated-eyes-and-struggle-to-take-a-breath muggy hot caused by the winds blowing up from Mexico, which is rare, but there you have it. It's also Friday, and I both want to be here and don't want to be here. Bake's guidance, delivered at intermittent intervals before the Audies, helped keep me focused on my work and also helped me understand my life so far. The recurring sessions for the past three months after my defeat at the hands, well, *voice*, of Michael Hunnie have given me some of my old juice back and pushed me to get past the disappointment of that evening.

I climb the stairs to the second floor, where Bake's small-but-cozy sanctuary of privacy is, and open the door to the waiting room. There, I'm met by Portia, Bake's administrative assistant. She's told me that she doesn't mind being referred to as a secretary, but it's an antiquated term. Bake likes it. I don't.

"Early today," she says.

I say, "Working on the new me," which is the line I use, at some point, every time we see each other.

Here it comes.

She shakes her head and rolls her eyes. Pretty sure she loathes the sight of me.

I sign in—she tells me that I don't have any forms to update, thank God—grab a Blow Pop from the bowl next to the clipboard and hand sanitizer, and then take a seat in my usual spot: the far corner of an L-shaped couch next to the room's only window. Sitting so that I have a view of the outside world has become more important to me since I became an audiobook narrator. On good days, the booth is an area of solitude, focus, creativity, and comfort for me; on bad days, the booth is a claustrophobic, sweaty, solitary confinement cell. I've said, *'Here come the booth sweats,'* on more than one occasion, I promise you. Also, having booth hair and booth butt are real things. Corie also believes in having afflictions such as booth legs, booth neck, and booth eyes. I agree with him. Naturally, we haven't been able to stop ourselves at just those. He texted me the other day that his "booth toe" was acting up again, and I replied that I had a severe case of "booth dick" that was making it challenging to work.

Anyway, I want to see the world every chance I get when I'm out of my professional workspace. Portia has never asked me why I sit in the exact same spot every time I come to see Bake for an appointment. I really don't care. She used to say, *'He'll see you soon,'* as a soothing precursor to what, I'm sure she knows, goes on behind the heavy oak door of Bake's office. There is a noise-masking machine that hums just outside the door, so I don't know if she's ever heard my sobs when Doctor Roman I. Baker introduced me to a part of myself I didn't want to know but *needed* to know. She may have heard a few of my outbursts where I sounded like there were only a handful of words in my vocabulary— profane words used as different parts of speech. In the theater, my descriptions would be considered lazy writing; in a shifty psychologist's inner realm, I consider those purging exclamations a thing of genius. It's been a while since I delivered one of those heaters, but sometimes the man pushes me beyond what I think is reasonable. Moving on, there's another door next to Portia's station that leads to a hallway that has a bathroom and a rear exit down a back flight of stairs. I once hid in the restroom for fifteen minutes during an early session. Not the best idea.

I sink into the couch, and it still feels good. Portia is talking on her cell phone behind the plexiglass window, which is now closed, and the only sound in the room is the noise machine. I remove the wrapper from my Blow Pop and take a lick of the sweetness—grape today. Always have a sucker when I come in here; the outer layer of candy is tasty, but that's just a warm-up. The gum in the middle is what it's all about.

Where will Bake and I go today? Lately, he's been trying to help me unpack what exactly happened at the Audies, which, I guess if I believe him, has been the cause of my sadness.

It has taken us three months to narrow it down to that specific night. My fault. I was blocking him. But now I'm all in because the cracks in my sanity are getting wider. I'm behind on recording, I'm seeing Jenna more often—and I think Jo is getting suspicious—and I have an idea for a new play. None of this is good, not even the idea for the play.

I look outside for two seconds—just another sunny day in L.A.—and then get out my phone and do what everybody else does, start scrolling through something. For me, it's my Instagram feed. There's gourmet cooking videos, Broadway ads for upcoming shows, golden retrievers doing a variety of adorable things—I saw one yesterday where a cat was snuggled up next to one—a ton of Detroit Tigers-themed ads and videos, and my tiny house feed. I cannot stop looking at how cozy each home is and how each design gets the most out of each space. If you live alone like I do, a tiny house has everything that you need, except for, in my case, a recording booth. I think of my 5,000-square-foot oceanfront home in Carmel and feel embarrassed. I do not need a house that big. After a few scrolls, I stop.

Something else I am supposed to be working on is my cell phone addiction, but it's a challenge. I never have it with me in the booth, but, to be honest, I'm on it every moment I am out of the booth. And I know that ninety-five percent of the time, I don't need to be on it. Bake says that my unhealthy attachment stems from the need to constantly numb myself from any feeling about not being a playwright anymore. Free time is not good for me. Every time I get a sliver of it, I think about New York City and what my life used to be. Then, I become morose and lonely. If I don't get to my phone for escape by then, the real demons will come out of the shadows and drag me away. So, here I sit, looking at a log cabin tiny home with a bright orange fire in the fireplace and stacked wood nearby—which, right now, I want to light and watch that tiny log home burn to the ground.

I hear the sound of Dr. Baker's office door swinging open—the creaky hinges need some WD-40—and I look up from the screen and stop my sadistic daydream. There he is. Roman Ingraham Baker, Ph.D.—Teva sandals, brown corduroy slacks, tattered navy blue cardigan, white t-shirt, full black beard only betrayed by a gray goatee, and thinning black hair pulled back into a messy ponytail. He never changes. My phone slips out of my hands and lands on the couch cushions. I'll pick it up in a minute.

In Doctor Baker's right hand is a coffee mug with a faded University of Southern California logo on it, and his black-plastic-framed glasses hang from one of his cardigan's upper pockets. His smile is as welcoming as Patrick Duffey's in a Hallmark Christmas movie, and I've always described him to Jo as having the perceived warmth of a bearded Mandy Patinkin, the discerning and quirky nature of Jeff Goldblum, and the humor and range of Jeff Daniels. Yes, I always use famous actors and actresses for my descriptions—it's my life…well, it used to be my life. I prefer to use theater actors and actresses, but, as painful as this is to admit, many people don't know who I'm talking about.  The screen continues to dominate.  Not to say that film actors and actresses can't do well on the stage or vice versa.  But, I'll try and prove my point.  If I said that someone looked like Frank Langella in the magnificent production of *The Father*, I would get, at best, a strange reaction.  This is because they probably know who Frank Langella is but would think I had made a mistake since Sir Anthony Hopkins played the lead in the film version of *The Father*.  However, I would be referencing Langella's Tony Award-winning portrayal in the Broadway production five years earlier.  How Langella was never cast in the film is still beyond me.  Did anyone associated with the film *see* his stage performance?  Well, Sir Anthony won the Oscar, and he *is* a legend, and everyone thinks he is the father, but I don't.

I know.  This all reeks of theater snobbery.  I get it.  But someone needs to stand up for live performance where you can't hide behind multiple takes, editing tricks, and camera angles!  Why are movie stars larger than life?  Robert Mitchum wondered the same thing when he asked his wife, *'Dorothy, why do they think I'm such a big deal?  You know me as well as anyone, and you don't give a shit.  So why do they care?'*  And, perhaps, Dorothy gave the answer that has stood the test of time, *'Mitch, it's because when you're up there on the screen, they're smaller than your nostril.'*  She's right.  And that's something the stage can never compete with.  I admit that I'm guilty of caring more about movie stars than TV stars, probably for Dorothy's answer.  However, streaming, long-form TV shows on big-screen TVs at home are now changing this.  But, back to the stage.  If you've acted in plays or been to plays, then you know that there is nothing like live, in-the-moment art that unfolds before your eyes.  The curtain comes up, and the show's on.  No going back.  No do-overs until the next performance.  Any experience where you can't push the pause button is infinitely better than the experience where you can—Shawn Frost Entertainment Rule #1.

Because of the theater, I don't worry about perfection in the booth.  I did when I started recording my first audiobook but soon realized that the technology

I had available to me was making it seem like I could reach perfection. And so I was doing take after take of each line. Not good. This is why I've never used the punch and roll method; I'd never finish a book. Sure, I make mistakes and correct them, and sometimes I'll try something different for a section, but reaching perfection? No. That is an illusion. Again, my theater experience guided me back to what I should have been focusing on, and that was concentrating on my overall performance instead of sweating each line. Better yet, if I can connect to a character like I did with Nehemiah Stone and discover his truth, then that's about as good as it gets.

And now I'm thinking about the loss of my job again—and how I lost the Audie to Michael Hunnie. Great job, Frost.

Anyway, I read that Spielberg would direct an actor in a particular scene by telling him something like, *'Remember how Rick looks when he says to Sam, 'Stop it, you know what I want to hear,' in* Casablanca? *Give me that."* Genius, assuming that the actor *has seen* the film—the original, black and white version, not the 1988 colorized version that Ted Turner presented on cable television that Killy told me about. It used to be a given that every actor *had* seen *Casablanca*, but now—

"C'mon back, Shawn," Bake says.

I follow him in but not before watching the good doctor exchange a pleasant glance with Portia. I've always wondered about them. Is there something more going on between the hippie psychologist and the keeper of his appointments? I don't know and shouldn't care. It's none of my business, but thinking about it keeps my mind distracted for a few more moments before Bake starts peeling off the bandages, and I have to look inward. In our first session, I tried to counter Doctor Baker's *'Look inward, young man. Look inward,'* with an ingratiating smile and the words, *'Go west, young man. Go west.'* It gained me an extra ten seconds of procrastination as he laughed in an accommodating way. But then the laughing stopped, and I had to look inward. I haven't told him to "Go west" since.

I almost kick the noise-masking machine on my way into his office. Not to stay stuck on the annoying creaky hinges, but during my last visit, I asked him why I could still hear the hinges but could not hear what he and his previous appointment were talking about. Yes, I have tried to eavesdrop. He told me in a kind of master-schooling-the-apprentice way that his ambient noise machine matched the frequency levels of human speech, which is why I couldn't hear what he and his client were talking about. Makes sense, but I'm still not convinced that the Echo-sized machine can drown the sounds of my few ugly cries and bombastic eruptions.

The door closes behind me, and I imagine Portia walking over to the couch and taking a snooze while I'm in here suffering. It's happened before. I don't know how he allows it, but I suppose if there's not an appointment after mine, then what is the harm in a little afternoon siesta to recharge the batteries for the final few hours of the day? Well, I only caught her conked out on the couch because I leave the office the same way I come in—never worry about someone recognizing me because I always wear sunglasses and my Detroit Tigers ballcap. Bake also has another exit at the far end of his therapy room where a client can leave without being seen at all by the next victim. The door opens into the hallway—the one with the bathroom and back door. I wonder who he had in here before me today as I plop down in a pool lounger with soft, black cushions. He's also got a recliner and a couch in here, but I always go for the pool lounger. Something about lying back in it helps me to open up, at least when I want to open up.

"And how is Mister Frost today?" he asks.

I don't know why he does that—he calls me Shawn when he invites me back and then switches to my last name when we start the session. But, watch, he'll call me "Shawn" the rest of the way.

"I'm present," I say, taking off my sunglasses.

He smiles. "Sure are, Shawn."

See!

"No playing today, huh?"

He crosses his legs and puts on his glasses. "It's your hour."

I hate it. He's right. I need to get better. I say, "Okay," let it hang in the air for a few seconds, and then follow up with, "The last time I was here, I felt like we had distilled some of my pain down to my loss three months ago."

He flips through a few pages of his legal pad, stops, reads for a few seconds, and then looks up at me. "We did." He takes a pen out of one of his cardigan's pockets and writes something on the page. After stopping, he taps the pad with the point of his pen a few times. "At the end of our last session, we agreed that it might be a good idea for you to write down some of your feelings if you happened to think about that night before our next session." His eyes rise up from their focus on the paper and meet mine. "So, have you given that night any more thought since then?"

The truth is that I have—can't get it out of my mind. What I liked about our agreement was that I wasn't forced to think about that night. Now, Bake has me meditating every day, and all sorts of thoughts enter my mind then, but I never felt forced to revisit that night, which is something that I appreciate about Bake's methods.

"I have."

His eyes scan my hands, my pockets, the floor next to the pool lounger. "Write anything down?"

"No."

"Okay," he says with his usual drink-green-tea-all-day calmness. "Want to talk about your thoughts?"

I say, "No."

He leans forward. I know he's about to push me, but I continue and say, "But I have to."

He reclines. "Want to do it like we have in the past?"

Even though I've been seeing him for years now, he still asks me this question. I suppose it's because he wonders the same thing I do: "Will I ever be able to discuss my thoughts without using the system we came up with when, after the first few sessions, I realized that I was getting nowhere due to my inability to open up. Some of it was because of denial and shame, but most of it was an innate defense mechanism where I could not directly express any negative feelings about myself or take ownership for any wrongdoing or any pain I may have caused others and myself. Looking back, that's how bad I was when I started therapy. I can process my thoughts, but, imagine this, a playwright can't come up with the words to communicate to his shrink. So, what Bake means by, *Want to do it like we have in the past?'* is, after those first few wasted sessions, we invented a way for me to detach a level and discuss my thoughts. What I do is take any event that has happened in my own life, remove myself from the first person point of view, and then pretend that I am a third-person narrator who is able to get inside the head of the main character, Shawn Frost, and relay that story to Dr. Baker. After we struck gold in session three, when I narrated a story about Shawn Frost being introduced to cocaine for the first time at a party thrown by his so-called close friend, legendary hedge fund manager Morton L. Jamie, in Jamie's multi-million-dollar Manhattan home, we discovered that after the story had been delivered, I was then able to talk about my feelings and thoughts. Hence, I think Bake believes one day that I won't need my storytelling gadget/crutch/method—whatever the hell it is. I want to believe it too, but even after all of my work, it seems like that breakthrough is still a ways off.

After I became an audiobook narrator, I asked him if he had ever listened to an audiobook before, and he told me that he hadn't—explained to me that he was a "purist," meaning he only read hardcover editions of books and those books were almost exclusively non-fiction. I inquired to learn what slice of fiction he read, but he wouldn't answer. Killy had arranged my treatment with Bake, so I asked Killy to try and find out. I'm not a theater or literary snob, but it comforts me to know what authors a person reads for leisure. Killy was harsh, *We just got you a second chance at life! Don't piss it away by demanding things of your counselor. Shut the fuck up and let him help you. Do you know how in-demand this guy is?'* So, I dropped the topic, but right before I go into my narration during a session, I always wonder if Doctor Roman I. Baker has ever listened to one of the books that *I* have narrated. Or, if after listening to me, it has turned him even more off to audiobooks.

"Yes, let's stick with our method," I answer. I've been sucking away at my Blow Pop, and my tongue just licked over the first grainy spot of bubble gum. Bake has worn me down, and I've worn down the grape candy. I'm going to have to talk for a while now, so I put the entire sucker in my mouth and gnaw until I've removed the gum from the white stick.

Bake holds out a trash can for me, and I throw the stick in. For a few seconds, I enjoy the mixture of gum and grape candy, but then the candy disappears, and all I'm left with is my pink chew. I blow a bubble.

*POP!*

I wink at Bake.

He turns to a fresh page and readies his pen. He crosses his legs the other way and seems to relax. Maybe he does like my narration and has listened to every single M. Scott Sala novel ever written. But if that is true, then he has heard the voice of Michael Hunnie, the man I am going to tell a story about.

I keep with my routine and adjust my chair so that I'm facing a wall with a picture that Doctor Baker hangs for each of our sessions. The picture that usually hangs on the wall, one of a gorgeous cathedral in autumn with the leaves at the full peak of their color, is on the floor underneath the photo he has put up for me. I lie back in the chair, close my eyes, take five deep breaths, access the memory, and then open my eyes and focus on the picture of a microphone on a wooden desk in an empty recording booth. I start.

✱ ✱ ✱

Michael Hunnie may have been five-foot-one inches tall in his polished black leather dress shoes from Barney's, but at this precise moment, he *towered* over all other audiobook narrators, towered over New York City, towered over the world. With a stride reminiscent of an Olympic rower on a glass-surfaced lake, Hunnie approached the stage to receive the most coveted Audie award in his legendary career, an honor he knew better than anyone in the business: Best Male Narrator—his 9th time receiving the award.

The cameras followed his compact frame but, eventually, as they always did, soon zoomed in on his iconic look. His thick, black locks with credentialed wisps of gray had been combed, blown dry, and then gelled into a permanent windswept appearance as if he were forever standing on Malibu beach, looking out at the Pacific. His beard was lavish and trimmed in such a manner that the audience might have believed that he had been born with it.

His tuxedo was classic black—a tailored Ralph Lauren that nearly achieved the impossible feat of disguising his recent burst in girth. His eyes were sharp, never nervous, never drowsy, just ice cold blue daggers that, when met, said, "You don't call Michael Hunnie. Michael Hunnie calls you." He passed by the table closest to the stage where Brick, Fraley, Porter, Freeman, and Vance sat. Hunnie glided past them, keeping his eyes on the Executive Director, Mariel W. Sissel, and screen legend Tom Hanks.

At the far back corner table, Shawn Frost sat in stunned silence. All of his hard work, both professionally and personally, that had gone into this moment, which was supposed to be *his* moment, now seemed all for nothing. He had lost to Hunnie—the man with the magic voice. Gone were Frost's nerves, and gone was his confidence. Every glass of alcohol on the table seemed to turn into the face of a beautiful woman with a dark complexion and red lips that now spoke to him, *"It's okay. Have a sip and relax. The ceremony will soon be over, and you can have a full glass of me or more at the after-party."*

"Okay," Frost whispered to the glass.

"What was that?" his girlfriend, Jo Mansfield, asked.

Frost quickly dipped his napkin in his glass of ice water and then began to dab it across his face. "Nothing, nothing," Frost said.

Jo began to rub his back and moved closer, whispering into his ear, "I'm sorry, Shawn. You deserved this award. Not him."

He heard her but kept dabbing. Then, his eyes caught his best friend Corie Woods staring at him.

Corie mouthed, "Sorry, man. You okay?"

Frost tried to move his mouth muscles, but they would not respond. He suspected others—his father, mother, sister, Killy—were probably looking at him now, but all he could see was Corie's face.

The clapping faded, and the words, "Thank you, Mariel, Tom," spoken by Hunnie drew Frost out of his trance, and his eyes glossed over the other seated members at his table until he focused on the podium.

Hunnie had the Audie trophy in his hand and was standing behind the microphone, which he had lowered to account for his height. Hanks and Mariel had moved several yards behind him and off to the right, now in the stage shadows.

"And many thanks to the Audio Publishers Association for what I think you will all agree has been a most pleasant evening."

There was polite applause; Frost was not contributing. His hands were on his thighs, the fingers of both hands slowly clawing his pants as if trying to slice the material and then make a shredded mess out of his thighs.

"And to my fellow finalists—"

*Oh, no, you don't!* Frost thought.

"—my congratulations." Hunnie searched the crowd and found his first target. "Crassus, I listened to your reading of Andy's latest when I was on my way to Acapulco to research for an upcoming project, and I must tell you, I did not feel like I was in an airplane." He rubbed his beard. "I felt like I was in a spaceship traveling…*Beyond Rigel*."

More applause, and Crassus nodded his thanks while Hunnie searched for his next victim.

*Don't act like you don't know where we're all seated*, Frost thought.

"What's he doing?" Jo asked Frost.

It was normal and polite for Hunnie to congratulate the other finalists, but to single them out and heap praise on each of them individually was to subversively rub their faces in his accomplishment. At least that was what Shawn Frost thought. "I don't know," he said to Jo.

Hunnie found D.J. and shook his head in disbelief. Then, the shit-eating grin to top all shit-eating grins in the world appeared on Hunnie's face as he said, "And D.J., I'll never listen to *Othello* by anyone else." He pointed to Sir Kenneth Branagh. "Please don't hurt me, Sir Ken, even though I'm quite certain that you both think I'm Iago right now." Branagh gave a full smile and clapped as others around the table joined in—even D.J.

*He's so humble*, Frost thought. *Why couldn't at least he have won!*

Thunderous applause. *I think they all wanted D.J. to win tonight.*

"You're next," Jo said, pinching Frost's arm.

"And, finally, Mister Shawn Frost—"

*Why in the* hell *is he saying* Mister?

The loud clapping silenced his inner thoughts and took away his pain as Frost realized that others in the room were proud of him, respected him, and even some of them had been pulling for him.

"—what is there to say?" The moment of positivity vanished. Hunnie's eyes bore into Frost's skull, and Hunnie's voice lost the playfulness used with the first two finalists and became serious—the kind he always used when a beloved character died in a book he was narrating.

"That BOOK. What," he said, pausing, "an extraordinary talent." The applause picked back up and then intensified. There were tears in the eyes of Frost's parents, his sister. Corie rubbed his eyes. Killy—well, Killy flipped Michael Hunnie off and threw back the rest of his wine.

Frost felt pain, embarrassment, suffering—and hate.

*This was supposed to be* my *night.*

The room quieted, and Hunnie continued. "But, I think Shawn would agree with me that when you receive *any* book by M. Scott Sala, especially a series-*ending* novel like *The Paris Sanction*, it's difficult not to rise to the occasion."

Hunnie didn't wait for his zinger to Frost to hit home. That would happen later.

"However, there is no other person on earth, including me, who could have performed Nehemiah Stone's final chapter any better than *you.*"

If there were any applause, Shawn Frost didn't hear them. He only heard the scattering of "Hmmm"s and "Mmmmm"s as if a preacher had just delivered a thought-provoking ending to a sermon that had the congregation stirring in wonder.

"What we four gentlemen have in common is our dedication to the work. It is all about the work. And. Working—on the work." Hunnie gave a laugh. "We could all start calling it 'WOW.'" Polite laughter all around.

Frost hated the sound of it.

"Nah," Hunnie said, rubbing his perfect beard and then dismissing the cheesy acronym with a wave of his miniature arm. "That's stupid."

Louder laughter.

Frost was grinding his teeth.

The room went silent again, and Hunnie finished with, "Okay, enough. I am honored to be in their company and yours—for a *ninth* time." He bowed.


"Sonofabitch!" I yell in Roman I. Baker's office.

And, like that, I'm back. My cheeks are wet as if the retelling of that night has caused me to become a method actor for my own emotions. The picture on the wall of the microphone is blurry.

Instead of slinging more mud at Hunnie, I say, "I used to run the hundred in ten flat. I'll be back with the whole fire department!"

And I know what just happened—and so does Bake. When I reach my breaking point, the point where I cry and feel that I have no way out of something—trapped, cornered, fated, whatever you want to call it—I pull from my favorite disaster film of the 1970s, *The Towering Inferno*. Right before Robert Wagner, a man having an affair in his posh skyscraper suite, takes off into the flames in a doomed attempt to get help, he delivers the words, the ones I just said, to his mistress. Then, he runs into a room with a wet towel over his head, becomes engulfed by the flames, and, well, *heee gone.*

That's where I'm at right now.

I feel a hand on my shoulder, and it is Bake's. He's holding out a box of tissues for me in his other hand. When he first heard me yell the lines out, we had to break down what happened for the rest of the session. Now, we don't need to talk about it when it happens.

I grab a few tissues, and he scoots back across the room to his original position.

After I wipe my eyes and blow my nose, the room becomes quiet for a few seconds. Then, I turn my pool lounger toward him, so I can make eye contact, and lie back down.

Bake watches me get settled and then starts in with, "You want to start, or should we wait a few more minutes?"

"We can start." I pause. "I'm glad I went there."

"Brave," says Bake. "So, what is it about the win that still bothers you and has you feeling helpless?"

"It's been a long haul to get where I am right now."

"It has been."

"Narrating audiobooks has helped me turn it around, and I like performing them." I pause again. We're in a valley with uneven terrain here.

"But," Bake prods.

I decide to give a little. "I guess I'm more competitive than I thought I was. In New York, it didn't feel like competition."

"What did it feel like?"

"Like I was just waking up every day and working on my craft—writing plays, searching for complex characters with multiple dimensions, and trying to create an overwhelming, emotional experience for an audience of theatergoers." I swallow, then lick my dry lips. I always have lip balm with me in the booth and usually keep a small tube of it in my pocket wherever I go. I'm in sweatpants with no pockets today and left the balm at home—know exactly where it is. "It felt collaborative, not competitive." I swallow again. "It felt right."

My eyes remain shut, but I hear Bake's chair moan, and I envision him leaning back into his *let-me-enlighten-you-now pose*.

"Do you think the reason that you didn't feel competitive was because you were on top? Late twenties, already two Tonys—"

He stops, and I can sense that he is reaching back for something—something poignant, yet not embarrassing and not distracting to take me away from our work together.

"—'The Boy Wonder of Broadway,' wasn't it?"

He's referring to the headline that appeared in the *New York Times* and *Wall Street Journal* on the same day, which *was* and *remains* a statistical impossibility. And yet it happened. "It was," I say. In fact, when that article came out, of the forty-one Broadway theaters that exist, *all forty-one* wanted to book my next play. This includes even the Gershwin Theatre, which is the largest Broadway theater and has been home to the musical *Wicked* since 2003; but, for me, the theater was actually considering finding a new home for *Wicked* while my show had its run.

Doesn't matter. Didn't happen. It was crazy to begin with. My play wasn't a musical.

More creaking from the chair, he's leaning forward now—always does when he gently drives home a point. "The other playwrights were competing. Doors opened and stayed open for you, theaters filled, and reviews of your work were positive. Your string of hits kept the bubble filled, and it kept people lining up to kiss your ass. It didn't feel like you were competing because you were winning, Shawn. You were insulated, which is an enviable place to be. No matter what people say, everyone yearns for security."

"Then it ended."

It's silent for a few beats—long enough for me to hear his gigantic cat, Snuggles, purring. Fat fella must be right under the lounger. What's he all happy about?

"You got back up," he says. "Now, you're performing at a high level in a different entertainment discipline. And—you've got security again. Audiobooks are booming. Didn't you tell me last time that they'll remain popular because people still commute? And, if I may add, everyone that has a phone with an audiobook app can now take Corie Woods, Crassus Dynasty, D.J. Webster, Michael Hunnie, and Shawn Frost with them pretty much wherever they go. People are multi-tasking more than ever; they can exercise, trim the bushes, and clean the house while experiencing a book. We're greedy and will always take two for one over one for one."

"I don't know anyone who has ever said, 'I'm planning on opening a bottle of wine, sitting by the fire, and listening to Shawn Frost tonight.'"

Another creak. He's leaning back again. I open my eyes, confirm it, and look up at his face.

He purses his lips and sighs—then says, "But performing at a high level is not enough, is it?"

And for the first time since I've been coming to this man to take my pain away, I realize that he's right. Being a finalist, in anything, is a failure. "Because I'm competitive and want to be the best again. That what you're saying?"

"You are chasing something that will never satisfy you, my friend. Even if you win."

I give a weak laugh. "Words spoken by my father."

"After the Audie Awards?"

"No," I say. "In the New York-Presbyterian Lower Manhattan Hospital." I look away from him and close my eyes again. "After I had the accidental overdose."

"And, yet, you're not chasing the top dollar either, right?"

He's correct. I told him a few sessions ago that the real money in voice acting is working for Disney or narrating documentaries. Even narrating top-product commercials pays big. With audiobooks, I get paid less for more time. "True," I say. "Narrating books is the closest I can get to the stage at this point. I don't think I'd last long doing any other voice work." However, let's not get carried away here. I *am* in it to make money, and a major series just ended out of the blue.

"It's more about legacy," Bake says.

"What's that mean?"

"It means that once you narrate a book, you are part of something that is as close to permanent as possible. There will always be new commercials for Tide or Walmart with different voice actors. But, there's only one, and will probably only ever be *one*, narrator for M. Scott Sala's Nehemiah Stone series."

"Unless society cancels me twenty years from now and they get someone to re-record all of the books."

"Society doesn't cancel people, Shawn. People cancel people. And there are too many different people with too many different views to realistically cancel a performer like you."

"If I become a serial killer?"

"You'll be canceled.  Hell, I'll cancel your ass."

There's a knock at the door.  Portia.

Portia, Portia, Portia.

Marcia, Marcia, Marcia.

She does this on occasion—interrupts my session with Bake.  Aren't there privacy rules?  I watch as he gets up and walks to the door.  Then, he opens it enough for a shaft of light from the waiting room to beam in.

I angle my head, and now I can see who it is.  Yep, Portia.  I hear the noise-masking machine as she and Bake talk.  Their chat goes on for half a minute, and then he closes the door.

On the way back to his throne, he gives me the same apologetic smile he always does and says in a grave voice, "Sorry, Shawn."

He knows what he's done is rude—apologized about it before.  I am paying the bastard a ton of money.  But routines are hard to break, so, instead of arguing, we go into our Pavlov's Dog routine—me as Pavlov, Bake as the dog.  I hold out my hand, and he gives me another Blow Pop.  The gum in my mouth is stale enough not to keep it around and mix it with the replacement.  I spit it into my hand; Bake holds out the trashcan, and I toss the gum in.  Nothing else is said about Portia's interruption.

After a few licks, I say, "So my competitive nature is driving some of my sorrow, and if I'm not careful, I am in danger of relapsing."  I point at him with my sucker.  "Back to the needle, right?"

He presses both of his palms together and holds his welded hands underneath his chin.  "Sometimes, I think I should keep you for a double session and give you another sucker."

"How do I not let my competitiveness set me back?"

"The good news is that your challenge is not unique.  A lot of people who find success early in life think the rest of their existence is just varying levels of failure when, in reality, they continue to do well. But, because it isn't what they started out with, they get down, and many self-sabotage until there's nothing left."

"What's the bad news?"

He takes his glasses off and hangs them back on the same pocket as before. "Once you've been number one, it's not easy being anything lower than that."

I throw my hands up. "Where do I start?"

"Forget rankings and forget awards. Don't chase money. Chase *quality* in your craft."

Is he nuts?

A timer goes off on his watch, and he silences it.

The session is over. Damn, we were getting somewhere today.

"For next week?" I ask.

He scribbles something down while saying, "Think about the things you have some control over in your audiobook narration—like your routine, your craft. Focus on what aspects you'd like to improve, and let's talk about them next time." He finishes and puts the pen down on the pad.

I nod and swing my feet over the edge of the pool lounger. As I go to stand up, I hear a screech and pull my feet off the ground.

Bake's gargantuan cat trots away toward the sanctuary of the office's desk.

"Sorry," I say, standing up.

Bake nods.

I use my sucker to point again, this time at his back door—seen enough of Portia for today.

He smiles and opens it for me, and I head out.

As I descend the back flight of stairs, I sense something different in my step—a little pep, a little hope. I think I'll go home and see if the feeling stays with me in the booth. The thriller I'm supposed to be working on isn't bad. In fact, I like the author. It's just not M. Scott Sala writing about Nehemiah Stone. But I can adjust. I can move on. Plus, I've got Bake, and he's never not delivered.

I exit onto the back street.  It's darker out now, but, as I often forget, being cooped up in a booth with no windows all day, when the sun disappears on a cloudy day in L.A., it's like someone has turned off the lights—depressing West Coast Gotham kind of excrement.  All the more motivation to get home and get in the booth.  Who wants to be outside in this?

"Hey, Shawn!"

I peer around and see a hand wave from the open window of a car across the street.

Who is that?

The male voice sounds welcoming, and I can see that he's got a smile on his face underneath a Dodgers ballcap.  Anyone who wears that hat is a friend of mine.  Yes, I'm a Detroit Tigers fan for life, but since I moved out here, I've adopted the Dodgers as my team away from home.

I cross the street.

Still can't make out who is in the car, but the radio is on, and…it's Bossa Nova.

My favorite.

I reach the open window—still no idea who it is.

"Hey," I say.

"Hey," the man says back.

Then, I feel my arm being held against the car.  There's a hot feeling in my shoulder, then my chest, then it's all throughout my body.

I'm starting to slide down the side of the car—going to lose consciousness…

Before I do, I hear, "Time to take a little ride."

Where in the hell am I?

*What* is going on?

The first thing I notice is the smell—like I'm being smothered by a thousand mildewed army blankets.  I remember blacking out but nothing after that until now.  How long was I out?  Is there anyone else with me right now?

As I try to open my eyes, the summative question moves to the front of the classroom of my brain: What happened?

My eyes blink open.  It's dark.

Okay, calm down, Frost.

I'm in a dark, musty-smelling room.  I'm lying down.  What is this—a bed?  There's a pillow behind my head, and I have what feels like a heavy wool blanket over me, but it's damp, making it feel like one of those new "heavy blankets" that Jo recently purchased for me.  Some kind of psychological trick where I feel comfortable because it simulates being back in the safety and security of the womb.  That's how heavy and claustrophobic I feel in this thing right now.  I try to lift my arms up, but it's no good.  The blanket is too heavy.  However, I am able to rub my fingers on the surface below me—there's no sheet—and it feels like canvas. My ass is hanging lower than my feet and head. I tiptoe my hands across the surface, away from both sides of my body, and they reach a frame. My movements are sluggish, and it's taking more effort than usual to do something this simple. Have I been drugged? Am I still drugged?

I stretch my feet, and my heels reach a part of the frame. I'm convinced that I'm on a cot, and a small one at that—no room to maneuver. But, the fact that I was able to move my hands and feet momentarily puts me at ease; minus the weight of the blanket, I'm not restrained in any way. At least, I think I'm not. There could be straps across my legs and chest.

Time to see if I can get an arm free.

I move my right hand and then, with considerable effort, my right forearm over the frame. Free of the weight of the blanket, I let my arm drop.

My hand reaches the floor, and I tap it with my fingers—ice-cold and hard. I sweep my fingers across the surface—gritty. I'm going with concrete.

My eyes seem to be adjusting to the darkness, but there is absolutely no light in the room and no light coming into the room. My eyes sweep what I assume to be the walls and see no windows or the outline of a door. Then, I turn my head and focus on where I would guess that the walls would meet the floor. There is no telltale line of light that would signify a doorway or where another adjoining room or hallway might be.

Am I asleep, caught in a nightmare? Was my session with Bake too much? Did I faint in his office, and the part about leaving his office and heading across the street to the car was the beginning of my dream?

After another great exertion, I bring my right arm back up onto the cot and rest. Jesus, even that small move has caused me to start breathing heavily. And it is difficult with this blanket on my chest!

I stare up at what I think is the ceiling, but, hell, maybe the ceiling is only a few feet above me and is lowering to eventually flatten me and the cot.

Okay, calm yourself down. In a minute, I'm going to get this blanket off and get up and—

My phone! I can use the flashlight on it to see where I am.

It would be in my right pocket.

I slide my hand over and feel for it over my pocket. My fingers push on the blue jean fabric and sink into my thigh.

There's nothing in my right pocket.

I do the same with my left hand.

Nothing in my left pocket.

Where is it? Am I lying on it? I slip my hands as far underneath my butt as I can. No phone there.

I slide my back side to side, trying to feel anything hard or irregular that might be my phone.

Nothing.

Where did I have it last?

At Bake's. But *where* at Bake's?

I lie motionless and close my eyes, trying to recall the last time I remember having it…

…in my car on the way to Dr. Baker's because I called Jo…in my hand as I walked up the stairs to the second floor because I was reading a text from Corie…in my pocket before I entered the office…I sat down on the couch and took it out to scroll while I waited…I dropped it on one of the couch's cushions…I picked it—

I stop and open my eyes.

I don't think I picked it up. I close my eyes again and concentrate.

After a minute of seeing red and white colors—like fat laser beams—and explosions of orange globes in the middle of star fields, I open my eyes again.

I can't remember.  Maybe I picked it up.  Or, wait a minute, did Portia hand it to Dr. Baker when she interrupted the end of our session?  Did he give it to me as I headed out?

Maybe.

Well, then where is it?

I decide it's time to sit up.  I need answers, and being alone—am I alone?—in this dark room is making me uncomfortable.

I bring my hands up near my chin, where the edge of the heavy blanket is. The first thing I've got to do is get this thing off of my chest.  After taking three calming breaths, I push upward, like I'm bench pressing my body weight in one of the exclusive New York City fitness clubs I used to go to before a night of partying.  Before the dark times, before the—

God, this blanket's weight is substantial.  Things are not adding up, but I continue to press.  I'm starting to breathe as if the amount of air that my lungs need can only be acquired by sucking through a plastic restaurant straw.

Finally, I get the blanket to a height where my elbows are a few inches above my chest, and, with a gasp, I push it in the direction of my thighs.

It goes, but the majority lands short and uncomfortably on top of my genitals. I let out a moan as my arms drop on top of my chest.  As the pain starts to recede and my breathing becomes easier, my hands discover something that makes me start to sweat with fear.

Over my shirt is a strap, perhaps six inches wide—feels smooth, like leather—which disappears into the canvas of the cot on both sides of my chest. There is no buckle or loose end.  I try to sit up, thinking the strap might not be tight.

It is.  I can't sit up.

My legs.

I try to spread them; I can't, for I feel another strap against both thighs, just above the knees.

My breathing picks up. This is no dream. I swallow.

I am strapped down to a cot in a pitch-black room that has a concrete floor.

What in the hell is going on?

I want to struggle—use all of my energy to break through these straps like the Incredible Hulk. Then, I can survey the room; maybe my cell phone is somewhere on the floor. I clench my fists around the chest strap and grit my teeth. My brain is signaling that it's fight or flight time, and I'm ready to shred this restraint with my bare hands; one by one, the switches in my mental fuse box are being switched on. It's like in the original *Jurassic Park* movie when Laura Dern is resetting the power to the park by pushing the buttons for each individual section, moving down toward the last button. Well, my anger button just got pushed, and I come to life as the adrenaline courses throughout my body. I wish I could see my eyes right now because I'm sure they're like bat-shit-Jack-Nicholson-Captain-Insano-crazy eyes right now. I am grinding my teeth, and then I think of the mouthguard my dentist keeps recommending for me to wear at night so that I don't destroy my smile. Night grinding has been a problem since I left New York.

And, as if the Laura Dern inside my head not only stops turning systems on but also starts turning the systems off that she had just turned on, I let go of the strap, and my hands come down to rest on the cot once more. I open my mouth and try to stretch my face muscles to ease the pain from my grinding. My dentist has, perhaps, just saved me from getting myself into an even worse position.

"Unwise, Frost. You might tip the cot over, and then you might be screwed," I say out loud.

The best move here is to not try and break free until I know more about my situation. Then, a thought starts to form in my mind.

"Don't go there," I say.

I go there.

What if I had some kind of accident and I'm now restrained so that I don't move?  But why would I be on a cot?  My God.  What if I'm so pumped full of drugs to ease the pain that I just think I'm on a cot in a room that is totally dark.  What if I'm just about to have surgery?

Or…

Am I dreaming all of this?  Was my session with Bake so penetrating that I fainted outside of his office, and I'm home now and will wake up soon?

Why am I so tired?  I bring my right hand to my face and give it a pretty good slap.  Nothing changes other than my right cheek hurting.

I need answers!

Well, I could call out—haven't done it yet.  I clear my throat and yell, "Help!  Is anyone there?  My name is Shawn Frost.  I'm right here and need assistance!"

There seems to be an echo, so I have to be inside some sort of room, right?

I start to hyperventilate, always do it when I'm about to lose it.  Why isn't anyone answering me?

I lose it.

"Hey!  I'm Shawn fucking Frost, and I'm in here!  Where in the *fuck* am I?  HELP!"

My neck begins to throb, and I realize that during the last few shouts, I lifted my head off the pillow and bellowed as if addressing someone standing at the foot of the cot, facing me.  I exhale and lie my head back.  My throat is sore now too because I—Let. It. Rip—especially the *'HELP.'*

"Well, that was pointless," I say aloud and then swallow.

My right arm and hand return to the strip of canvas between my right hip and the hard frame.  After that, there is no sound again in the room except for my breathing, which is starting to slow.  I vow to count to one hundred and see if anyone shows up.  Then, I'll either yell again or try and go back to sleep or continue to see this nightmare out to the end and maybe wake up on Bake's couch with a cold cloth on my head and a vomit bucket on the floor next to the couch.

There is also another option. I could try and pull a Richard Matheson here and attempt to transport myself somewhere, preferably my bed at home—maybe, like, three months ago right after the Audie Awards so I could re-live those wasted 12 weeks and be in a different place right now. Of course, *Somewhere in Time* was not the original title of the book. No, that was for the movie. See? Screen dominates. No, the title of the book, *Bid Time Return*, was from my original stomping ground, the stage. The words come from Act III, Scene II of Shakespeare's *Richard III*. The lines are, *"O, call back yesterday, bid time return, / And thou shalt have twelve thousand / fighting men!"* And right now, how I wish I could call back yesterday and bid—

*"You have all overbid! Erase the bids, please,"* says Mr. Bob Barker in my head, as if my wish to cheat time has already failed.

Next to me on Contestant's Row are Corie, Killy…and *Michael Hunnie*. Barker stares into my eyes, a father embarrassed with his son. *"Shawn, go lower than—"*

Get out of my head, *The Price is Right!*

The whole scene disappears from my mind, and it's back to time travel. Let's see, what were the exact words Matheson's character Richard Collier used in *Somewhere in Time?*

For the moment, I can't remember. But why?

Then, it comes to me. I'm focusing on the wrong time period. I have to go back further. I have to get this right. I settle on the night after I won my first Tony. Yes, the night my flawed mentor, I. Stanley Hirsch, pulled me aside at one of the after-parties and said that corporate raider Morton L. Jamie wanted to meet me. If I can just return to that night and speak with myself alone for 5 minutes— maybe pull myself into a restroom, lock the door, and say, *'When Stanley approaches you later, don't go with him to see Jamie. In fact, never meet Jamie.'* If I can do that, then I know I can make everything right. I swear it.

I remember Collier's line. Time to try it.

I close my eyes—

A sound!  Like a big shop broom being pushed across the garage floor.

I open my eyes.  Approximately five feet from the foot of my cot, I see a vertical line of light that keeps widening as…as a door swings open.

The sound stops.  The door is all the way open, and the rectangle of light coming from what appears to be a hallway outside of the door nearly blinds me. But a figure steps into the doorway, blocking most of the light.

He's large, the top of his head perhaps six inches from the top of the doorway.  I can't make out his face, but he's got shoulder-length hair.

"Hello," he says in a heavy, rich tone while entering the room.

Before I can speak, he says, "Big light," and then flips a switch.

Like a hibernating bear who hasn't seen the sun for six months, my eyes see a yellow sheet for a few seconds, and then the scene saunters into focus.

Then I utter the words that I swore I would never write in any of my plays: "Oh. My. God."

I am indeed strapped to a cot…

In a homemade recording studio.

# 5

My eyes scan from wall to wall. If I had to guess, I'm in a twenty-foot-by-twenty-foot room, which is way too big for the recording studio this man has tried to turn it into.

Yes, by the way, I'm scared out of my mind, but concentrating on my surroundings is the only thing keeping me from weeping right now. Well, that and trying to play tough guy, which I suck at.

The ceiling is eight feet high, like in the house I grew up in, and the room feels smaller because of it. I guess I'm used to the ten and twelve-foot ceilings in the house I live in now. On the far side of the room, two drafting chairs are pulled up to a wooden desk, and the desk has some recording equipment on it—computer, monitor…can't see the rest—and there's a mic with a pop screen secured to a shock mount and mic stand. A toilet is next to the table.

I crane my neck back to see what's in the space behind me. It's empty except for a round shower head coming out of the ceiling with a metal grate in the floor below it. And other than the grate and a few metal rings that appear to be countersunk into the ground—one by the grate, one by the desk, and one by the toilet—the entire floor is concrete. My cot is approximately four feet from the wall opposite the one with the desk. That's it.

"Who are you?" I ask, my heartbeat picking back up again. I struggle against the straps. "What in the hell is going on?"

"Save your strength, Shawn," he says. "Tightened the straps myself, and that cot is bolted to the floor. Goin' nowhere, know what I mean?" This time, his tone is colder, a bit more clipped.

I continue to wage my war against the straps and the cot—adrenaline's got me convinced that I possess the power to rip the cot from the floor housings, burst through the straps, and tear this psychopath apart. I know, I know, I said I hate conflict, but at this moment, I happen to be very *pro*-conflict. As I fight, I say, "I said, who in the fuck are you?"

He just watches and gives an amused laugh as my left hand slips off the chest strap and whacks me in the chin.

I twist two or three more times—the heavy blanket falls off the cot—and then stop struggling. He's right; there's no way I am getting out of these straps, which are leather, by the way.

"That's better," he says and pulls out one of the two chairs and sits down facing me.

I expect him to start explaining my situation to me, but he says nothing and just stares at the cot. So, I use my remaining energy to quickly study the room again. If I can ever *get loose* and there is something in here I can use as a weapon, I want to know where it's located so I can find it in the dark if necessary.

I complete my survey. Well, this sucks. I've got two options—one decent, one crappy. Decent: I could use the power cord as a garotte. Crappy: I could use the mic stand as a bat.

"Know it's not what you're used to, bigun," he says, looking around the room, "but she'll get the job done. Want you comfy," he smiles, "but not *too* comfy."

I rest my head on the pillow for a beat and then lift it and twist my neck so I can get a better look at this guy.

He's big—got thick arms coming out of a tight, black-colored polo shirt, glasses with hefty, brown-colored plastic rims—can't tell the color of his eyes— brown handlebar mustache, shoulder-length brown hair—might be a wig—jeans, black belt, and some kind of work boots. Maybe Wolverine, like my dad still wears to work every day. His waist is tight, no flab hanging over his pants.

Yelling and struggling are not working, and it's time to try a different approach. I've got "charm offensive," "logical presentation," and "under-promise & over-deliver" in my arsenal. I decide on a blend of all three. "Okay, let's start over," I say. "You know I'm Shawn Frost." My eyes lock onto the desk and recording equipment for a few seconds. "And you know I'm an audiobook narrator."

He nods, then sits back, crosses his legs, and rubs his chin.

"It appears that you want me to record something. Right?"

"Yessir," he says.

I wouldn't say hick, but good old country boy wouldn't be too far from the mark. I'll try to reach him with just a slight adjustment to my speech—no mocking, just an attempt to connect. Be subtle, Frost. Don't fuck it up.

"Okay, now that we've got that settled. I need to straight-up know where we stand or somethin' of that nature. What's up with the straps? Can't think of any bad blood I've got with anyone, especially you—who, I swear, I've never laid eyes on before. Just want to get back to my house. What do I have to do to make things square? You and I work something out, man-to-man, you know. I wanna make it right." I debate whether I should push it any further.

You're tied up, Frost! Go for it. I hold his eyes in mine and give him a stare that I hope conveys a sense of *my word is as strong as a fresh plank of hickory.* I ask, "You help me out, bossman?" I am proud of myself, said it without seeming to beg but was in no way standoffish. The question is: Will he work with me?

He squints at me and says nothing.

He didn't buy it, and now I'm certain that he thinks I'm a politician who changes his words and accents when visiting different parts of the country.

"What do you think this is?" he asks.

"I—"

"Some kind of negotiation?" he says, cutting me off.

"Well, you haven't told me what this i—"

"This is this, sir. This. Is. This. You're not negotiating anything. Can't believe you started in that way, and I thought once you were done strugglin', we were makin' some progress."

He stands up.

Oh, God, don't leave. Suddenly, I'm very thirsty. "I'm…I'm sorry. That didn't come out right. I'm stressed out, okay? Please—can we start over? I'll listen. Just—just tell me what you want."

He walks over to me—heavy footsteps on the concrete—and stops by my head, about a foot away from the cot. "I'll be back, and we'll try this again."

He starts to turn, and my instinct to survive overrides my good sense. I reach out and grab one of his legs. "Please don't g—"

It's all I get out as he turns, leans over, and punches me in the face. He's so fast that I can't even get a hand up to protect myself. Couple that with the fact that I have never been hit before, and I'm immediately a pilgrim in an unknown country. There are messages sent to my brain, telling it that something awful has happened.

The first pain starts as a dull pulsating wave coming from somewhere inside my left cheek. Then, I can't see—black with a crimson starfield. The stars turn white. My left eye is watering, so I've got a blind waterfall going on. My head vibrates as if someone were strumming it like a guitar. Then, my right eye regains its vision.

He's blurry, but he's still standing over me. I put my hands in front of my face; he's not getting another clean shot.

Nothing happens.

The adrenaline starts to wear off, and the pain increases. I blink with both eyes, and now, through blurry tears, my left eye is coming back around.

"Don't ever touch me again," he says. "Got it…*bossman?*"

He turns and walks away.

I watch as the lights go out and the door closes. I'm in the dark again, but now, in addition to my aching face, I've got another problem.

I just pissed myself.


I have no idea how long it has been when he returns. I know that I've slept and what was a warm, comfortable swaddle of urine has turned into a cold, wet diaper.

He turns on the light and sits down in the chair. For a moment, there are no words, and then he reaches over and flushes the toilet. "Next time, use that instead of your drawers."

There are many things I want to say, but after his last visit, I've got a half-shut eye and throbbing head to remind me not to say any of it. I finally reply with, "Okay." Then, I decide to feel my injury.

Instant, piercing, and radiating pain—like a bowl full of angry red ants have been overturned on the left side of my face and have no way out of the bowl. They bite…and bite.

I pull my hand away. No way I'm touching it again. No way I'm asking for ice. And there's no way I'm speaking unless asked a question. You're in serious trouble, Frost. My chin starts to quiver, and I try to hide my shaking hand underneath my leg. I'm going to die. I just know it.

"Yeah, sorry about the shiner. Shouldn't have walloped you so hard. Big boss upstairs is angry with me."

I grit my teeth, trying to get my vibrating chin under control. Calm down! Think logically. You're getting information. Use it.

So, this is at least a two-person abduction team, this guy works for someone else, and if he's speaking to me in the literal sense, then there's an upstairs to this place, which means I could be in some kind of basement or in a room that is at ground level. My guess would be that since there's no window in here, there's only one escape route—either up a flight of stairs or in an elevator.

Yeah, my escape chances don't look good right now, and I'm basically down to one eye.

Stop it!

Keep thinking everything through.

They want me to record something for them. Why? If it's my voice, then there are a thousand YouTube videos of me speaking that they can listen to for free. And, if they want professional recordings, then the audiobooks aren't that expensive. Just by the looks of this place, they've dropped enough money on the equipment alone to pay for all of my audiobooks. And why me? I'm known, but there are many more famous and accomplished narrators than me. Are they going to make me record something and blackmail me with it? I can't imagine what it could be. I purposely hang my political hat on the door outside of the booth before I enter and rarely wear it when I'm out of the booth—about a million voices on both sides of the spectrum that are louder and more passionate than mine. If I do get a political piece to narrate that I'm comfortable with, whether I agree with it or not, I always make sure that I don't comment on the work through my narration. That's where the trouble starts: too many emotions to juggle. Perhaps Heston was right when he said that actors and writers make their livings off their imaginations and feelings, and, therefore, they put a great deal of faith in them and, hence, rely on their emotions when making intellectual decisions, which is not a wise move. However, that is not to say that I don't have my line drawn in the sand of what I will and will not record. But, I've always kept the specifics of where that line is to myself and Killy. This guy, and whoever the hell "Big Boss Upstairs" is, could never know it.

And.

Even if I do record what they want, what is the endgame here? I've seen this man's face, and that is *never* a good sign for the kidnapped. I've narrated enough mystery and thriller novels to know that.

"It's okay," I lie. "Everything good now with you and Big Boss?"

He rubs his chin and studies me. A few more seconds pass, and he nods, saying, "Big Boss, Big Boss."

"I'm sorry, did I say something wrong?"

"Not at all. Big Boss and I are fine," he says. "I can hear that your voice isn't screwed up, so I'm thankful for that. Verrrrry thankful."

"Me too," I say.

"So, you wanna hear about the equipment you'll be usin'?"

I don't, but I'm in no position to object right now. Also, I can't see everything that is on the table. "Sure."

"Got you a good room with a door that seals well. Computer over there with extension cords from it to the monitor and keyboard. No fan noise," he says proudly. "Got a peripheral drive with loads of space; Big Boss wanted to have a backup drive, so we don't lose nothin'. Bought you a large-diaphragm condenser mic. You can see it's set in a shock mount, and we got you a solid stand."

He looks at the pop screen and itches his head. "Can't remember what that thing is called, but I know it's supposed to help the recording."

I can't resist. "It's a pop screen," I say.

He snaps his fingers. "That's the ticket." He stands up and flicks it. "Online site said somethin' about p's and f's and stuff. Don't know what it means, but I'm sure you do."

Okay, if this isn't an act, this is not the guy who wants my voice recorded. He's the muscle.

"Cable here that connects your mic to," he says, pausing to lean over the table, "your M Box Mini…two, is it? Well—" he chuckles, "—I'll just go with M Box. And this—"

He has his back to me, so I can't see what he's doing.

"—is a nice set of headphones." He turns around, and in his hands is a pair of studio headphones. "Cost us over a hundred bucks for these. Waste of money if you ask me." He puts them down and points to the drafting chair that is pulled up flush with the desk. "Pretty comfortable chair for you. Gonna be puttin' in some hours sittin' in it. Heard that some of your fellow narrators sit on exercise balls in their booths, but that's…well, we ain't doin' that." He sits back down in the other chair.

On one hand, they've done their homework and put a lot into their preparation; they definitely know some aspects of the process. On the other hand, they'll never get a good recording in here. First, the room is too large with too many hard reflective surfaces. There is absolutely no sound dampening material anywhere, which means that any sound is going to echo like crazy—the noise floor in this room will be off the charts. Killy would die of a heart attack if he saw this place.

So, apparently, these guys aren't worried about the quality of the recording, and that scares me because they went to an awful amount of trouble to set up this cell-studio and kidnap me. I look around once more. It would have been nice to have acoustic foam panels lining the walls like my studio at home has. Carpet on the floor, walls, or ceiling would make this room quieter. Hell, you could even hang blankets, quilts, and heavy curtains along the walls. Or, better yet, construct a wooden frame and enclose it with those things, making a room within a room. But that's all irrelevant anyway. I want to tell him, *Who gives a shit that you've got extension cords that run from the computer to the monitor and keyboard to keep the fan noise away from the mic. You've got a* toilet *in here!*" Instead, I say, "Can I ask what the project is?"

"We'll get you that tomorrow. Any questions about the equipment?"

I shake my head 'no.' Hurts like hell.

"I'm also supposed to ask you if we forgot anything." He crosses his legs. "Well?"

"No, should be a good place to work."

At this, he says, "Hmmm," and stands up.

Okay, what does *hmmm* mean?

His eyes glance around the room and then steady up on mine. He walks over and stops near the cot like he did before. "You sure?" he asks.

Now, it is my right eye that dances around the room. Of course, I should mention the complete lack of noise dampening material, but I want the recording to be shitty, my only way to fight back right now. Plus, if the recording is bad, they might still need me to record the material again. This keeps me alive and buys me more time to come up with a plan. I stare up at him. "None that I can think of. You've got everything I need to perform a recording." It's not a lie. I do have everything I need to make a recording. I just don't have everything I need to make a *good* recording.

"That so?" he asks.

Before I can answer, he swings at my stomach and connects.

It knocks the wind out of me, and because of my thin midsection, it feels like his fist has gone all the way through and reached my backbone. The cot's canvas gives in the area where he hit, and my head comes off the pillow but is jerked back because the chest strap does its job and does not allow my entire upper body to rise up. I hold my stomach with both hands and gasp for air as he takes a few steps back.

"I tell you, man, it's going to be a lot easier on you if we are honest with each other. You didn't mention the lack of sound dampening material. Heck, you didn't even mention the toilet. 'Course, this means that you were ready to start recording without the proper setup. And now I've gotta go upstairs and tell Big

Boss that you ain't serious about your work. It's a shame, man. I was hoping that you'd ask me to properly set up the room. Don't know what this is gonna mean now."

I try to get out words, but I still can't breathe. I'm actually reaching out my right arm and opening and closing my right hand in a plea.

He stops by the door and looks back at me. "Shit, I was gonna go upstairs and get you some food and water. Then, I was going to let you take a bathroom break." He shakes his head. "Sorry about the punch, but you gotta learn, Shawn."

Hearing him say my name sickens me. I feel the first normal breath come, and the air feels cool, thick, and fulfilling.

He points at my stomach. "That's where I was supposed to hit you the first time." He exhales.

I still can't get a word out.

"I know what yer thinkin', bubba. I'm the enforcer and might not be in on the entire plan, right? Well, you're wrong. I'm more than that, but you need to get one thing straight: I'm the only chance you've got of seein' the inside of your house in Carmel again."

I can finally hear a wheezing sound come out of my mouth, and I say, almost in a whisper, "I'm sorry."

"That's soundin' better, but I don't know if I believe you. Well, I need to get upstairs. Big Boss also said that if you answered my question about the recording equipment honestly, then I could have you strip out of those clothes, and we'd wash 'em for you—got a pair of sweatpants and a sweatshirt you could wear while you worked. Huh—suppose that's off the table now."

My eyes start to water, and I shout, "Please! I wanted to mention the condition of the room, but I didn't know if that would get me beaten like I was ungrateful or something. I'm scared out of my mind here, and I just want to go home."

He starts to turn away.

"Please, please reconsider. I'll work with you and Big Boss. Hell, I don't even know your name, and that doesn't sit well with me because we're in this together. I mean, you want a recording, right? Well, if I'm so beat up and can't record, then we both don't get what we want."

Then, he swivels his head around and gives a short laugh back at me. "You don't know the half of what's going on here." He flicks off the lights and closes the door, plunging me back into total darkness.

How am I ever going to get out of here alive?

# 6

This time it's the lights that wake me up.

"Mornin'," he says, closing the door.

Like I would know what time it is. My pants are wet again, a cold wet—must have urinated while I was asleep. I wait a few moments until my anger subsides. Let's try and start the new day or night off right; I'm starving, have to defecate, and I can't handle any more punches. My left eye must be starting to swell shut because all I see out of it is a blurry slit of light, and any body movement makes my stomach feel like an alien just burst out of it. "Good morning," I say back.

He has nothing with him. No change of clothes, no food, no water, no sound dampening material. Maybe some or all of it is out in the hallway, and I just have to be good. Earlier, I thought about trying to escape when I got unstrapped, but now, I'm in no position to fight. Maybe in a few days.

Bide your time, Frost. Play the game.

He sits down. "We ready to start over?"

Zero hesitation from me. "Yes."

"All right," he says. "Talked to Big Boss, and we're willing to give you a second chance."

"Thank you."

"But, from here on out, you gotta play by our rules.  Understand?"

"Done," I reply.

"Okay," he says while lifting his head as if to peer down on my cot, "looks like you've wet yourself again."

"Sorry."

I see him shake his head.

Please don't hit me again.

"So, here's what we're gonna do."  He stands up and opens the door.

I look into the hallway to see if anything I need is out there, but he blocks my view as he enters the doorway.  I hear a clang, like metal on metal, as he reaches over to the right of the doorway.

He returns with what looks like a medieval breastplate—a steel tank top of armor that is in two pieces, a front and a back.  A heavy-duty chain, one that might be used to anchor a large ship, hangs from a molded eye that comes out from the breastplate's bottom left-hand corner.

Oh, sweet Jesus.

"This here's a breastplate that we call 'the vest.'  I'll have you put it on whenever you record, eat, shower, or use the toilet."  He points at the three places on the floor I noticed before—one by the desk, one by the shower, and one by the toilet.  "Three heavy rings, there, there, and there.  I'll chain you in so you won't be able to move very much; when you sit on the chair at the desk or on the toilet, you'll be able to stand up, and when you stand underneath the shower, you'll be able to slide a few inches to the right or left, or forward or backward.  Don't want you gettin' any ideas 'bout escapin'.  Understand?"

I barely get out, "Yes."  My chin is starting to quiver again, and I feel queasy.  If they want me to record while chained to the floor, I won't be able to move *at all*.  Also, "the vest" will give any recording a tinny sound.  Do they know that?

He sits in the chair and runs his hands along the breastplate, taps it a few times with his meaty fingers.  "And just so we're clear," he says, looking at the armor and not at me, "if you do try something, Big Boss says we're going to have to visit Jo…and Jenna. Yeah, we know all about your affair. Be a shame if that had to come out while you're with us." He shrugs. "Or if any harm should come to them. Ya know?"

My God, they know about my personal life. Jo, not Jo…and Jenna. Who are these sickos? I'll never be able to live with myself if I cause anyone else harm; I immediately cancel my escape plans. "I don't want anyone hurt," I say, pleading.

"Us either," he replies. "Believe me, Shawn, us either."

The added stress has my insides churning, and I know that if I don't sit on the toilet soon, I will have to empty my bowels right here on the cot. "I really have to use the restroom," I get out. Large, hot tears are streaming down my face.

"Not a problem," he says. "After you go, we'll get you showered up and then fed." He pauses, still looking at the armor. "That work?"

I try to speak, but my chin is vibrating so much that all I can do is nod.


It's maybe an hour later, no clue if I'm right, and all I can say is that I'm doing better—still aching, still scared, but my basic needs have been met. When you have to use the restroom as much as I did, you quickly get over wearing a breastplate and being chained to a ring on the floor. Likewise, when the entire area around your private parts is soaked with urine, you also get over being chained up under a shower head with freezing water. I was only given a bar of soap, but I made it work.

After the shower, I was able to towel off and put on a brand new gray sweatsuit and white socks, no underwear. My captor sprayed and wiped my cot while I was chained by the desk, eating the first food I'd had in who knows how long. Two peanut butter and jelly sandwiches, a banana, and a bottle of water— no dessert. I haven't had a PB&J in years, and I didn't mind the crunchy peanut butter, but grape jelly is not my favorite. I wish he would have put raspberry jam on it.  Anyway, I devoured all of it, but that wasn't the best part.  When he saw that I only had a little water left, he mercifully gave me three white tablets of aspirin.

I was also able to get a better measure of my captor.  Without shoes, I'm a hair under six feet tall; when he stood next to me, I estimated that with his work boots on (which ended up being Wolverine brand, by the way—still got a sharp writer's eye), he was around six inches taller than me, so perhaps somewhere in the neighborhood of six-five without boots.  Large cruiser.  Confirmed his eyes were brown—wasn't sure I had been accurate earlier when he slugged me both times.

Also—and this may mean nothing—I am absolutely certain that I saw him walk across the doorway with a slight limp in his left leg.  He'd gone out to retrieve and bring in my food and must have thought that he had closed the door behind him; he's always careful not to let me see what is out there or what he does out there.  Anyway, he closed the door every other time he went out—while I sat on the throne, while I showered, and while he retrieved my new clothes.  But, after he chained me up to the ring by the table, he must have forgotten when he went to fetch my food because the door was wide open, and I saw him limp across the doorway to what I presumed was a table that was just out of sight.  When he returned with the tray of food, he limped into the doorway, suddenly stopped, looked at the door, looked at me—I had already turned toward the desk, but I've got good peripheral vision—and then walked normally over to the desk.  I acted surprised when he approached the table like I didn't notice that he had entered the room, which I think he bought because he seemed to relax and proceed as if nothing had happened.  So, now I've got my profile: Six-five male, weighs maybe two-thirty, trim waist, huge shoulders and arms, brown shoulder-length hair, brown eyes, thick glasses, brown handlebar stache, a slight limp in the left leg, and talks like a good old southern boy.  As I reviewed the profile while I ate, I realized the futility of it all: There's nothing I can do with this information.

He just finished strapping me in and putting the heavy blanket back on me. The room feels colder than earlier, and I'm shivering.

"Not bad at all," he says. "You behave like that, and we'll be just fine."

"Thank you for allowing me to go to the bathroom, to clean up, for the meal, and for the aspirin," I say. "Since I drank a full bottle of water, how do I let you know when I need to go to the bathroom again?"

He points at the corner of the ceiling up from near the foot of my cot. There's a small black square angled down at the room—a camera. Was it always there? I can't remember.

"We'll know, but, again, there are rules. After one bottle of water at lunch, you get one restroom break between that and the next meal, so choose wisely. If you start asking for more, the bottle of fresh water will disappear, and I'll bring you a mug that you'll have to dip in the bowl over there for your water." He sees my eyes look at the toilet in horror. "Don't wanna go there, right? So, make sure you've really got to go."

I am in hell. Whatever I did to put myself here, I will beg for forgiveness. Please, God, deliver me from here. Funny. I haven't been to church since I left home for college. Why am I suddenly becoming religious again? You know the answer, Frost: It's because some guy just threatened you with drinking toilet water.

He continues. "Now, during the morning, after breakfast, you'll be able to go as many times as you need while you are recording because we know that you need water." He laughs to himself. "What was the shit you said in that interview? Right, 'The most important thing that an audiobook narrator needs is water because the lair—"

He searches for the word. *Larynx*, dipshit.

"—liari, well, whatever the hell it's called 'is a muscle, and it fails without water.' Well, sir, I got my own opinions about that, but Big Boss says you're right. So, as long as you don't break our rules, you'll have plenty of water in the mornin' while you're doin' your thing. At night, after supper, I'll come in one time around 8 p.m., and you'll take your bathroom break then. And that will be it for the night because I'll be getting you up at 4 a.m. every day, so you can start recording at 4:30. You'll work from then until around 1 p.m. when lunch will be served. Then, you rest in the afternoon and after dinner. Want you fresh every mornin'. Big Boss says you try to get between 2 and 3…" He pauses, searching for the words.

I say, "Finished recording hours."

He nods. "Yessir, thank you. Between 2 and 3 finished recording hours a day. Well, we want to be at *four* per day and think the schedule we've come up with will do 'er."

"Can I ask what time it is right now?" I feel like I have to know. We can't be starting anytime soon if he is going to put up any sound dampening material. He's not wearing a watch, but a watch-band-sized area of the skin around his left wrist is ghost white, so I know he's used to wearing one.

"Let's just say that what you had was dinner."

Okay, so we're starting tomorrow morning. "Are you going to—"

"Put up sound dampening material?" he says, cutting me off. "Yes. Don't worry, though, you're gonna sleep right through it."

I swallow. What in the hell does that mean?

He must see that I am nervous again. "You got nothin' to worry 'bout, man. You're recording tomorrow morning, so we ain't gonna hurt ya."

That means drugs. I'm going to be drugged. Can I fight it off? Maybe for a little bit, but what good would that do? He's going to eventually wear me down and stick me with a needle or force the pills down my throat. Pick your battles, Frost. You need to lose this one before it's fought. Right now, just stay alive. The only thing I can say is, "All right."

"Want to talk about the job?"

I don't, but then I reconsider. The recording they want me to do might give me something to focus on, something to center me. I've already got the parameters for my work hours, 4:30 a.m. to 1 p.m.  Maybe having the assignment will give me purpose, which could keep me alive.  The film, *The Edge*, bursts into my mind from some forgotten realm of my gray matter.  When the rich billionaire, Charles, played by Sir Anthony Hopkins, is stranded in the wilderness with his wife's lover Bob, played by Alec Baldwin, Charles tells Bob that most people who are in their position *"die of shame."*  That line never made sense to me until now.  I can't imagine what they want me to record for them, but I decide that knowing is better than not knowing at this point.  "Yes," I answer.

He takes a metal flask from his back pocket, unscrews the lid, and takes a sip.

My mouth starts to water.  I want to get ripped.  Right.  Now.  Give me the flask so I can make my suffering vanish, if only for a few hours.  Let me get so soused that I vomit all over this cot.  Maybe I can get some to spill onto the floor.  Let him clean *that* up.

He smacks his lips and sees me eying the flask.  "Oh, sorry, bubba.  I know how much you like the kickin' chicken.  Very rude of me to do that in front of you."  He puts it in his back pocket.  "First, are there any questions ya have 'fore I go over what you'll be recordin' for us?"

All I can think about is the booze.  Was it Wild Turkey in the flask?  Or is he lying?  Was it Jack?  Jim?  Johnny?  "No," I finally say.

"Good, good," he whispers, staring at the floor.  He continues to gaze for at least another thirty seconds.

What is he thinking about?  C'mon, start talking.  He doesn't, and now I'm starting to think about the drugs they're going to give me.  Then, an idea comes to mind.  I consider it for a few beats and decide to go forward—no way it could make things worse.

"I doubt you're going to give me your real name, but do you have a name that I can call you?"

His eyes shoot up from the floor.

Weren't expecting that were you, *bubba?*

"I mean, if we're going to be working together on a recording, I think it would be a good idea to have names, don't you? And you've already got mine."

Using the index finger and thumb of his right hand, he begins to stroke his mustache. His dark brown eyes are welded to mine, but then I break off because it's hard to keep my neck turned that far to the right. Plus, I can't see much out of my left eye. I now stare at the ceiling and await his answer.

"You like my boots?" he asks.

I turn my head back toward him. "Yeah, sturdy. Wolverine, right?"

He smirks. "Same as your daddy wears over in Shelter Harbor, Michigan, right?"

I immediately turn my head and bore my eyes into the ceiling. Dad. These assholes know everything.

"You angry? Shouldn't be. How many interviews have you given over the years sayin' how he has always stuck by you and supported you even though he was blue-collar, which I admire, and you were an artist? What, he's been with that electric company for over forty years now, right? Information's out there, maaynnn. Just got to watch a few of your interviews. You sure do like to yap."

I close my eyes. Why did he have to bring Dad into this? Look, I love my mom, sister, Jo, Corie, sometimes Killy, my high school teacher Ray Jarold, and some other friends, but the one person I cannot go on without is John Daniel Frost. And this malicious monster sitting across the room from me right now is right, I've mentioned my dad in about every interview I've ever given. My father and I are about as different as you come, but even though he did not understand my drive to make the performing arts my living, that man gave me everything he had, from love, to encouragement, to unconditional support, to money, to the most valuable of all things in life: time. He never missed a play. Privately, my mother told me that they should have invented fidget toys about fifty years earlier because Dad could not sit still, but that old warrior soldiered on and sat through every performance, and he was the first one to stand when the standing ovations started; I know, because I always knew where he sat. If this guy threatens my dad again, all bets might be off.

He claps his hands together once as if he is a politician who's just stolen a good idea and is ready to get down to work. "Shawn, I ain't gonna give you my real name. But, I do agree with you. Should provide ya with a name you can call me." He leans back and crosses his legs, then pulls the flask out and takes a long pull. "You can call me 'Wolverine.'"

It's obvious, and it reminds me of Dad; it's also easy to remember. Michigan is "The Wolverine State," so I decide to focus on that instead of my father. I stare at him, determination, not cockiness, in my eyes. "Wolverine it is."

"Done deal, man." He takes another pull.

Suddenly, a voice echoes through the room. "That's enough."

I look to Wolverine for guidance and see him glance up at the square camera in the corner—must have a speaker too.

Wolverine secures the cap to his flask and stows it. "That was Big Boss," he says. "Guess he don't want me drinkin' anymore today."

And I've got at least one of my answers. Big boss is a man. I assumed it was so but needed to confirm it. Why? I have no idea. I guess if I ever get out of here, then I'll have a place to start with the police. I take a breath in, hold it, and exhale. So, at least two men are holding me captive.

He rises and heads for the door. "I'll grab a bit of the project material for you to look over, and we can chew the fat."

I try to imagine what they want me to record, but my mind is filled with thoughts of how I might escape. Getting free of the straps is a non-starter. I've tried, and I can't loosen them. Also, there is absolutely nothing I could swipe off the recording table that would allow me to cut either strap. Plus, I'm being monitored. They'll see what I'm doing. Even if I got free, I have no way out of the room because it's locked from the outside.

I hear papers being shuffled by Wolverine in the hallway. Wolverine…he's my only chance. If I was chained to the ring by the table and sitting in the chair, I could use a piece of the recording equipment, maybe the M Box, to smash him over the head and knock him out. If that was successful, I could get his keys—

Shit. I would need him to fall perfectly—like *straight down* to the floor. The only slack in the chain I have is enough for me to stand up. If he fell away from the table, I don't know if I could pull him close enough to get his keys and unlock myself. And time is everything at that point because Big Brother Boss is going to see what happens and probably rush downstairs to help Wolverine, in which case I am screwed. This eliminates the strangle-Wolverine-with-the-computer-cord option too. I have to be able to knock him out—can't do that with the mic stand—grab his keys, unlock myself, and then…who knows what? There's a hallway outside the door, and another man is supposedly upstairs—doesn't give me much to work with, which is why I'm so hesitant to try it.

Don't get ahead of yourself, Frost. You're doing well by plotting how you might get free, but this may be your no-win-Kobayashi-Maru test. What I would give right now to watch *Star Trek* while fully baked.

Wolverine trudges back in with a stack of paper that has a small binder clip holding the sheets together. He sits back down and lofts the stack onto the desk.

*SMACK!*

"After I fill you in a bit, Big Boss wants you to read that packet." He puts his elbows on his knees and folds his hands as if he's a disappointed basketball coach sitting on one of the locker room's benches at half-time, trying to figure out what went wrong with the full-court press. "You wanna read it from there or at the table?" he asks.

My chance! I've eaten; I'm clothed; they haven't drugged me yet; I've been able to rest; this could be it. I read somewhere that after being in captivity for more than 48 hours, your chances for escape are cut in half.

Actually, I just made that up. Freaking out here, folks.

"The table, if possible," I answer.

He gives me a thumbs up.

"So, it's like this, Shawn. You're Big Boss's favorite narrator. I know, I know, you haven't been in the game for too long, but he freakin' loves your work, man. You ain't mine. No offense, I think you're good, but I got my own tastes."

I'm sure you do.

"What he wants from you is in two parts." He pats the packet with his large, pudgy fingers. "First, he's got a list of things he'd like you to record—short sayings and stuff, won't take long. Second, he wants you to record the novel he's written. I read it already, and it's *good*. I mean like go out and howl at the moon good."

That translates to me as fuck-a-woodpile, splinters-in-your-dick bad.

"Can I ask questions?"

"Sure, bubba."

"How long is the book?"

He leans back and brings his hands behind his head. "Pretty long, I guess."

"Sorry," I say. "I mean, how many words is the manuscript?"

Wolverine looks like he's sitting on Santa's lap and has just been asked what his IQ is.

The ceiling microphone saves him. "A hundred and two thousand words," Big Boss's voice projects into the room.

So, it's a book that, when printed, would be between three and four-hundred pages, depending on the type they use. When I started my career, Corie told me that narrators usually speak about 9,400 words per hour when they record. Killy had me timed, and I'm a bit faster, but not by much—maybe 9,600 words per hour. This means that the finished audiobook will be somewhere in the vicinity of eleven hours. Since it takes me approximately two hours of recording to get one finished hour, Big Boss's abortion of a novel will take me around twenty-two hours to record. If I work the hours he says I'll be working, 4:30 a.m. to 1 p.m., then I could be done in three days, but probably four.

Okay, four days, Frost.

"Thank you," I say to the camera.

"Like I was sayin', pretty long book. Intense as hell, though." Wolverine taps the packet once more. "Probably wonderin' why we're having you do this, right?"

The thought had never occurred to me.

"Once you see the list of short stuff he wants you to record, you'll understand why. As for the thriller—well, dagummit, I just gave away what kind it was now, didn't I? Huh. Well, yeah, it's a thriller all righty." He points at the ceiling. "Big Boss wrote it, and *I think* he should try to get an agent and get it published, but he's pretty private. Won't listen to me."

I wonder why.

"But, see, he wants it narrated so he can listen to it, and the only person in this world he wants it narrated by is you, Mister Shawn Frost. Says he'll never go public with anything that you record so long as you never talk about what took place here. It's all in the packet."

"How do you both know that people aren't looking for me right now and will find this place soon?"

Wolverine chuckles. "Oh, I'm sure they're lookin' for you, might even be worried about you, but, Shawn, they're never going to find this place."

His words have a ring of finality to them like he poured a bucket of ice water on my red-hot plans to escape. I am now living every audiobook narrator's nightmare—having a psychotic fan kidnap you and force you to read something he or she wrote.

And yet, I feel somewhat hopeful. I'll record some short sayings, whatever they may be, then an amateurish thriller novel, swear that I'll tell no one about this place, and maybe be out of here in less than a week. Everyone has a bad week now and then.  For Christ's sake, there are *entire weeks* that I don't remember when it got bad in New York City.

"May I read through the packet now?"

Five minutes pass.  I've got the vest on, and I sit in the desk chair while Wolverine chains and locks me to the stainless-steel floor ring.

"There we go," he says and then sits down next to me.  He passes me the packet.

The cover is blank except for this line, centered and halfway down the page:

THE S.F. PROJECT

I flip the page…

Oh, no.

# 7

The page that I stare at has the heading:

MATERIAL FOR SHAWN TO RECORD

Underneath it, is a list.

1. Happy Birthday Song to "Big Boss"

2. "Congratulations, sir."

3. In a female tone:  "That's the best I've ever had."

4. "You da man!"

5. The Lord's Prayer

6. The bottom of the 10th inning in Game 6 of the 1986 World Series

7. "Good morning."

8. "Good afternoon."

9. "Good evening."

10. "Good night."

11. "I'll see you in the morning.  Rest well, my friend."

12. "Good to see you!"

13. "Many thanks.  You're too kind."

14. "You can do this.  I believe in you."

15. Poem – " The Suitor" by: Jane Kenyon

16. The days of the week

17. The months of the year

18. In a male and a female voice, "You're looking very hot today."

19. "I hate Michael Hunnie."

20. "I hate Crassus Dynasty."

21. "I hate D. J. Webster."

22. "I love Julliard!"

23. "I am a drug addict."

24. "M. Scott Sala has zero talent."

25. "Let's shoot up."

26. "I don't always drink beer, but when I do, I prefer Dos Equis.  Stay thirsty, my friends."

27. Macbeth's "Tomorrow" soliloquy

28. "I'm a Republican."

29. "I'm a Democrat."

30. Big Boss's song: "Coke in the Backseat"

*Bonus: Any imitations of political figures, sports heroes, actors, actresses, or other famous people.

"Pretty easy, right?" Wolverine asks.

I continue to study the list.

Not that I should attempt to do so, but I am unable to gain any insight into who "Big Boss" is from the contents of this list.  I mean, *weird* left the building a long time ago in my present predicament, but this list is all over the place.  Don't worry.  We'll get to why I thought, *oh, no*, in just a minute.

I quickly sort most of the items into the following seven categories: Affirmation, Sexual/Ego, Greeting/Connecting, Performance, Dissing, Personal Attacks, and Political.  A few random items like the days of the week and the months of the year don't fit into a category, and then there's Big Boss's song "Coke in the Backseat."  Suffice to say, this song, along with the personal attacks and the sexual statements that these maniacs want me to perform, are the items that brought out the *oh, no* in me. And why the statements dissing my colleagues? As soon as I think it, I come up with the answer: They want you to read these first so that they can leverage the blackmail card if I don't read the novel.

And, about that novel, nothing here gives me any kind of clue as to what I'll be recording tomorrow. For instance, you tell me the thriller novel that comes out of the following combination: The bottom of the 10th inning in Game 6 of the 1986 World Series + Jane Kenyon's poem "The Suitor" + Happy Birthday + The Lord's Prayer + "That's the best I've ever had" + "I'm a Republican" + "Coke in the Backseat."

I got nothin'.

And, if this man is going to have me shoot arrows at M. Scott Sala, the best thriller writer on the planet, then…

"You hear me, Shawn?"

Right. He asked me if these would be easy to perform. "Ah, I think this is manageable," I say.

"Told ya."

"A few questions, if I may?"

He grins, gives me a pat on the shoulder, which rattles my armor a bit, and sits back—relaxing as if he hasn't a care in the world. "Shoot, yeah, man."

I want to say no to any of the impersonations. Yes, I can do some, but I want to avoid this at all costs. Imitation is the sincerest form of flattery—except when it's not, and, in the entertainment business, you better be safe and secure in your position when you jump into that end of the pool. And right now, my career as an audiobook narrator is far from being secure. Of course, the horrible things they want me to say about other narrators and my go-to author won't help either, but I think I would have a better chance of having Killy explain to their agents that I was in a life-and-death situation and forced to read those statements. He could say the same about an imitation, but people are finicky about hearing someone else imitate them.  However, I'm in no position to bargain yet or ask about not doing the impersonations.  I'll start with what I *can* do.

"Twenty-eight of these will only take me about fifteen minutes to record total."

He nods as if he'd calculated this years beforehand.

"But, the World Series game and the song," I pause, barely able to say it without laughing, "'Coke in the Backseat'—"

"One of my favorites that he's written."

Jesus, he's written more?  Part of me wants to know the other titles *right now*, but I press on, ignoring the fact that Wolverine interrupts me any time he wants to, which doesn't happen to Shawn Frost in the real world.  "Yes, catchy title."

"Ain't it?"

Shut the hell up!

"Quite.  For the game, does Big Boss want play-by-play or commentary?  And, for the song, how long is it?  Does he want me to sing it or just read the lyrics?"

He pulls out a folded piece of paper from his shirt pocket.  "Let's see, he thought you might have a few questions."

"Don't mean to interrupt, but can he just answer through the speaker?"

Wolverine peeks over the top of the paper, which he's unfolded now, but doesn't say anything.

I think it's a fair question, and, well, perhaps I am tired of being interrupted and can't help myself.  Either way, he's not answering, just eyeing me.  Now, all sorts of thoughts start to go through my mind.  Is Big Boss always watching and listening?  What if he's not?  Does that change my escape plan in any way?

"He'll answer you," the voice from the ceiling pipes in.

"Thank ye, Big Boss," Wolverine says, miming the tipping of a cap.  His eyes disappear behind the paper.  "Let's see here.  Yup.  He wants you to do play-by-play for the game and to get excited—" he holds up the index finger on his right hand—"one: when the wild pitch occurs and—" he adds the middle finger—"two: when the ball goes through that guy's legs."

Of course, I know what he's talking about. Even though I'm a Tigers and Dodgers fan, I love baseball. And anyone who knows baseball knows about the '86 World Series. True, I was born a few months after that game took place, but when I got hooked on baseball in Little League, and we lost a game we should have won, I let my emotions get the better of me. So, my father took me home and told me about Game 6 between the Mets and the Red Sox. *"When you lose a game like* that, *then you can let your emotions loose. Until then, it's only Little League. Enjoy the game and work on* your *game,"* he said to me. Of course, he was right, and, after determining that I was not very athletic a few years later, I decided to put my energy into something I was good at: reading and writing plays. Later, when YouTube came around, I found that game and watched it with Dad. The agony of defeat and the ecstasy of victory. No other way to put it.

To have me lend my voice to that inning now was absurd. One, Vin Scully called that game. That should be enough for anyone, let alone this psycho. Two, I have no idea how this man plans to use my recording, but if it is to re-open an old wound with Red Sox Nation, then that is sick and cruel; my career would definitely take a hit. All I can hope for is that Big Boss is some kind of a die-hard Mets fan who wants to relive a fond memory through the voice of his favorite narrator. I seem to remember Paul Haggis saying that at one time in his career, every film that he went to see that *he* wished *he* had made was penned by Lawrence Kasdan. Or something like that. The part I remember word-for-word was when Haggis said this about Kasdan, *"I am so glad to see him working again; his voice has been missed."* Why do I remember that part? Because those words make me wonder if anyone will ever voice similar sentiments about me in regard to my playwrighting if I ever return to the theater.

"I'll do my best," I lie. "Now, what about the song?"

He starts to bounce in his chair. "Turn the page, bubba."

I do…

And there it is:

**"Coke in the Backseat"**

I start to read, but Wolverine takes the packet from me. "You're gonna perform this way better'n me, but let me give you the beat." He clears his throat.

No, don't.

"Here Eyeee go."

I blink in disbelief; I don't think he noticed.


*"I got coke in the backseat, coke in the backseat*
*Rollin' down the highway, rollin' down the highway,*

*Coke in the backseat, coke in the backseat*
*Bitches, nuns, and pastors,*
*Bitches, nuns, and pastorssss…*

*Like that coke in backseat, coke in the backseat*
*Rollin' down the highway, rollin' down the highway*

*When the Police come, when the Police come*
*don't get caught, don't get caught*
*don't you dare get caught.*
*DON'T. GET. CAUGHT with theeeeee*
*coke in the backseat, coke in the backseat*

*Rollin' down the highway, rollin' down the highway*
*With that coke in the backseat, coke in the backseat…*

*I lost you once, lost you once*
*But want you back, want you back,*

*So if you want me, want me*
*I'll be waitin' in my car with the…*
*COKE.  IN. THE. BACKSEAT."*

He exhales, smacking the packet with the back of his hand in triumph.  "Who weeeee."  Wipes his forehead.  "Well, there you have it.  Got good movement and great lyrics.  Hope I gave ya a good sense of the beat."

"You certainly did," I say.  I attempt to hide deep down, rooms within rooms within rooms of my inner thoughts, what I think about my captor's song: the most amateurish, ridiculous, and worthless creation I've ever heard.

And, yet—I could, by a miracle, somehow see this going viral and making a miscreant like Big Boss an overnight sensation.  I could also envision that fame disappearing after more garbage came out after that one *hit*.  Seeing the thread into the future, you could see Big Boss at a music convention shooting the breeze with an artist who looks at Big Boss with a questioning glance and says, *"And, who are you?"*  And Big Boss would reply, *"I'm—"* Shit.  What would his name be?  Damn it, *Big Boss* might actually be appropriate.  Let's go with it.  *"I'm Big Boss. You know, 'Coke In The Backseat'?"*  And the artist would reply with a knowing grin, *"Oh, yeah, yeah, yeah.  I remember."*

I give Wolverine my most professional tone of acknowledgment and say, "I think I've got enough to go on for my reading tomorrow."

*"Readin'* tomorrow?  You gonna sing it tomorrow mornin'."

"Right."  Again, professional.

"Good deal," he says, handing the packet back to me.  "On the next page, you'll find the beginning of the book's notes.  Big Boss wanted you to read through it so that ya knew all the twists and turns and stuff—heard you like to know whodunit from the get-go."

I give a weak nod. Why did I ever grant interviews about my process? Stop it. What's happening now is so beyond normal. If being kidnapped was normal, no one would ever do interviews.

"Anyway, you'll have the whole book tomorrow." He stands up. "Gonna take me a break out in the hall." Wolverine peers up at the camera. "Where I *won't* be drinkin'." He looks back at me over his shoulder. "Be back in about fifteen minutes to collect the packet and get you tucked in for the night."

Almost forgot about the drugs they're going to give me to get me to sleep.

He enters the hallway and locks the door.

I go to turn the page but stop when I hear, "Don't mind him. He's just a big buffoon." I turn my head and stare up at the camera.

Is this a test? Is he trying to get me to talk bad about Wolverine? If I do, will Wolverine burst in and beat me. I decide to ignore what Big Boss has just said and return to the packet.

"I hope you enjoy the book," the voice says.

I flip the page…

And it's blank—with the exception of one word:

**NARRATOR**

I turn to the next page and begin to read.

## NARRATOR Notes

## Overview

A female mega-author, Stacey Groff, has written a novel titled *Converging Affairs* as both a tribute and a dig to her longtime, legendary audiobook narrator and on-again, off-again lover, Robbie Bernstein. However, Stacey's publicist, Kurt Boar, who became lovers with Stacey during her relationship with Robbie, has grown to hate her because of her eventual rejection of his romantic overtures to make their relationship exclusive because she still had feelings for Robbie. She has also roused Kurt's rage because of her lack of appreciation for all of the work he has done to turn her into a publishing phenomenon. Hence, Kurt plans to kill Stacey and Robbie Bernstein and make it look like a murder-suicide—and he plans to do this in the most devious way possible.

And his plans come from the plot of Stacey's novel *Converging Affairs*.

**<u>Stacey's Novel</u>**

In Stacey's novel, *Converging Affairs*, the main character, an audiobook narrator named Bernie Hopkins (a nod to Robbie Bernstein), is murdered in his booth at the precise moment that the audiobook narrator, Zach Zane, *in the book Bernie is performing*, titled *The Audiobook Admirer*, is murdered in *his* booth.  The murderer in *The Audiobook Admirer* is a crazed, obsessed fan named Wiley Diamond.  (Wiley is another dark, inside joke as there was a wacko fan by the name of Will Drucker who was arrested for stalking Robbie Bernstein.)  Anyway, Wiley Diamond's fan letters & e-mails to Zach have gone unanswered for years, and Wiley is out for revenge.  Wiley has gotten a job as an electrician, moved to Zach's city, Portland, Oregon, staked out Zach's home, and eventually (through an elaborate plan) cut the power to Zach's house.  Wiley, as an electrician, then shows up to help restore power to Zach's home.  Zach is grateful and lets the murderer in.  Once inside, Zach graciously gives Wiley a tour of the home as the good and decent electrician claims that he needs to check various outlets before looking at the fuse box.  The tour ends at Zach's booth.  As Zach enters to show Wiley the outlets inside the booth, Wiley stabs Zach to death.

In *Converging Affairs*, Bernie's next-door neighbor, Evelyn Chill, whom he has slept with on occasion over the past few months in a casual relationship, approaches Bernie about taking the next step and becoming an official couple.  When Bernie says no, and breaks it off, she enters his house and puts a listening device in the new booth in his basement.  While they were dating, she read the proof copy of *The Audiobook Admirer* and knows how it ends.  Because she misses his voice, she listens as he records in his booth, hoping that they'll one day get back together again once Bernie recognizes the error of his ways.  But, one day, she sees him enter his home with an attractive female whom she doesn't know.  Two days later, the female comes over again.  Convinced now that they will never again be a couple, Evelyn decides that if she can't have Bernie, then no one can.  That evening, she listens as he records *The Audiobook Admirer*.  While she listens, the plan for the perfect murder forms in her mind.  She still has a key that she secretly made for Bernie's front door, so she has a way into the house.  She listens as Bernie records the book.  When he gets to the part where Wiley cuts power to Zach's house and shows up, she makes her way over to Bernie's, enters through the front door, and shoots him in his booth just as he's reading about Wiley killing Zach in Zach's booth.  The novel ends with a huge funeral for Bernie, Evelyn is put in an insane asylum, and the award-winning novelist and ex-wife of Bernie, Sadie Green (Stacey Groff's nod to herself), jets off to Bermuda.

### How Kurt Boar uses *Converging Affairs* and his knowledge of Stacey and Robbie's past to plot his revenge:

Stacey Groff and Robbie Bernstein have been friends for years and occasional lovers; she's been to Robbie's house, stayed over on multiple occasions, there have been dinners, covert trips to rich locales such as the French Riviera, the Swiss Alps, etc.  The bottom line is that

Kurt knows that it would not be a surprise that Stacey would be at Robbie's house.

Kurt has gained access to Robbie's house because every year, Robbie throws a massive party for all of his publishing world contacts.  One particular party, a few years back, Stacey and Kurt were in town that weekend—their own affair was in full bloom at that point—and were invited over.  Oblivious to Stacey's betrayal of him with Kurt, Robbie gives Kurt a V.I.P. tour of his legendary house.  During the showcase, Kurt observes that Robbie's recording studio is in a walk-in closet off one of the main floor's bedrooms.  Hence, Kurt thinks that Robbie has only one booth.  Later on, when he reads Stacey's novel *Converging Affairs*, he finds it amusing that, to remove it a step from reality, she gives her main character Bernie two booths—one in a living room closet that he no longer uses and one in the basement that is brand new.  The other reason she has done this, he thinks, is an inside joke.  She used to poke fun at Robbie because of his walk-in-closet booth, saying he needed to upgrade, but Robbie always refused.  In fact, to drive her point home, she gives Bernie a state-of-the-art booth in a basement that is to die for—wet bar, lounge, bookshelves, leather couch, reading chair, pool table, home theater.

In any event, Kurt believes that Robbie still has only one studio, and this will be a key point because, in the time since Kurt toured his house and Stacey and Robbie had a falling out, Robbie has had a luxury recording studio built in his basement.

So, Kurt knows Robbie's recording schedule, and when Robbie starts to record *Converging Affairs*, Kurt pays him a visit. Robbie suspects nothing; he never knew of Stacey's affair with Kurt. Robbie welcomes Kurt in, and they spend an evening catching up. At this point, Robbie still splits time between the basement studio and the one in his guest room closet; he performs one book in his basement booth and a different book in his guest room closet booth. In the spirit of nostalgia, he plans to record *Converging Affairs* in his guest room closet booth; he knows that Stacey has written this book with him in mind, and it's the last book he will narrate for her. During the visit, Robbie heads upstairs for a few minutes, and Kurt goes to work. First, he notices that Robbie still does not have a security system; there are no cameras or alarms anywhere in the house. He places listening devices in Robbie's living room, guest bedroom, and, of course, the closet booth. The evening ends, and Kurt drives down the street, parks, and tests his listening devices: He can hear everything in all three locations.

A few days later, Kurt arranges for Stacey to be in town for a book event. She arrives and checks into a hotel. One day later, Kurt listens as Robbie continues to record *Converging Affairs*. Robbie's getting near the end, and then, a bit out of character for him, Robbie decides to try and finish the audiobook that night. Kurt accelerates his plans. He has a fake note sent from Robbie to Stacey inviting her over to his house. In it, Kurt, writing as Robbie, tells her not to call but to please show up alone at 8 p.m.—he wants to apologize to her in person and be forgiven. He has a health update to share with her and alludes to the fact that this might be the last time they're able to see each other. He also says that he will finish the recording tonight.

Stacey buys it and heads to his house to arrive at the appointed hour.

## **Climax & Resolution**

Kurt listens as Robbie records in his closet booth.  Then, from his car that is parked down the street from Robbie's house, Kurt sees Stacey turn onto the long street leading to Robbie's.  Perfect.

He turns off his listening device; a minute later, perhaps, out of a bit of spite, Robbie decides to leave the closet recording booth and heads down to his new basement booth to finish the book.  He knows that he'll have to process the audio on the back end to account for the acoustical differences between the two rooms but doesn't care.

Kurt approaches the house from the backyard; Stacey's car is still coming down the street.  When he used the bathroom the other night, he left the window unlocked and removed the screen.  To his delight, Robbie has not noticed it, and Kurt opens the window and enters the house.  From the bathroom closet, he reaches under a stack of towels and gets out the material he stowed there the other night: a plastic jumpsuit with plastic gloves and a plastic shower cap, rope, a revolver, one of Robbie's steak knives, and a handkerchief.  He had a backpack on when he visited Robbie earlier in the week—said it was typical office-on-the-run stuff.  Laptop, tablet, etc.  About an hour ago, he walked up to the front door wearing a disguise and placed a note on the front door that says: It's unlocked, like we used to do to the front door with the cabin in Colorado.  C'mon in.  Love, Robbie.

Kurt runs through the house in his stockinged feet and unlocks the front door.  Then, from the front window, he sees Stacey pulling up.  He hides, dressed in his plastic covering outfit—with the rope, handkerchief, and steak knife in his pocket and the revolver in his right hand.  At this point, we learn that Kurt was previously married to a criminologist; he knows how to stage a murder-suicide.

Stacey enters through the door.  Before she is able to scream, Kurt's hand goes over her mouth, and he binds and gags her to a kitchen chair.  He puts the revolver in his pocket and takes out the steak knife.  Then, smiling, he heads for the guest bedroom…and the closet booth.

Kurt rips open the booth door, ready to stab Robbie—but the booth is empty.  Dumbfounded, Kurt backs out of the booth.  Where in the hell is Robbie?

Downstairs, Robbie takes a breather from the booth and exits into his luxurious basement.  He heads for the wet bar.  Only a few more pages to read in the book, but he's thirsty.  As he reaches the bar, he stops dead in his tracks.  He hears footsteps on the floor above.

Someone is in his house!

He freaks out and looks for a weapon.  Nothing.  He considers a cue stick, but it's too long, he's too clumsy, and he sucks at pool anyway.  So, he grabs the only thing that has any weight that he can swing: a bottle of red wine—and an expensive one at that.  He tiptoes up the stairs.

Kurt hears the footsteps and turns the chair to face the door to the basement.  Then, he hides.

Robbie slowly opens the door...
...and sees Stacey tied up and gagged.

Her eyes open wide, and she screams into the rag.  He doesn't understand her but starts running toward her, but...

...behind him comes Kurt with the knife!

Stacey screams and struggles even more, her eyes almost popping out of their sockets.

Robbie starts to turn, but it's too late.  Kurt stabs Robbie in the upper back, but Robbie's adrenaline rush allows him to block and fight off Kurt's second swing with the knife.  They struggle, and the revolver drops to the floor.

They roll over and knock the chair over, and Stacey tumbles to the ground.  Kurt makes another swing with the knife, and this time, it pierces Robbie's right shoulder.

Stacey breaks free!  She scrambles across the floor and picks up the revolver.  Kurt sees her and gets off of Robbie, who writhes in pain.

She turns and...

…pulls the trigger at Kurt, who is in a mid-air leap with the knife pulled back over his head, ready to swing it down into her.

Kurt falls on top of her, dead.

Robbie and Stacey embrace.  They call the police, and sirens can be heard as the book ends.

I turn the page and see:


The End


Idiotic.  No one writes "The End" anymore.  Exhaling, I lay the packet down and then rub my eyes.

What in the world did I just read?  Not that bad of an outline.  Well thought out, and I like the end even though I've got chills thinking about my own studio at home and the horrible imaginings of what could happen.  The book-within-a-book-within-a-book premise is exciting, complex—and will be hard to pull off. The danger present in any story, regardless of the medium, is that there are too many plotlines or too many character names, which causes the reader or viewer to become, at best, overwhelmed or, at worst, confused.  Many a fine storyteller has fallen prey to the enticing falsehood that complexity equals quality or high art.  Complexity *paired* with clarity and style is the desired outcome.  And that seems to be what *Narrator* is attempting to achieve.  Style?  Iffy, at this point; I haven't seen the finished prose.  Complexity?  It's there.  Clarity?  From my study of the outline, Big Boss has placed about every classic trap along the path that the story's intelligibility could get snared in and become a wounded animal, waiting to get clubbed on the head and taken out of its misery.  In the hands of an amateur writer, as I believe my captor to be, this is the most likely scenario, and—it pains me to say this—not even *Michael Hunnie* could save this book.  However, I would be lying if I said that *Narrator* didn't interest me.

Wait a minute.  Frost, you are *chained* to a desk in a cell-studio about to be drugged.  You are living the horror right now, you idiot.

The voice from the ceiling says, "Well, do you like the story?"

Hell no, I don't *like* it!  I realize that there is no good answer here.  Even if I do like the outline, it's one thing to map out a story with notes; it's another to make it come alive over the course of one hundred thousand words.  There's only one honest word that is coming to mind, and so I say it.  "Curious."

There is a moment of silence, and then the door opens.  Wolverine enters.  "So, you got through it, huh?"

"Yeah," I say, almost in a whisper.

He walks behind me, and I suppose he'll be unlocking me n—

I feel the instant pain of the needle being jabbed into my shoulder.  Before I can yell, the room goes out of focus, and that's the last thing I remember.

I hear the door open and assume it's 4:30 the next morning. I'm groggy but nothing more than the usual start-of-the-day stiffness. The sliver of light from the hallway grows larger. I hear the *click* of the light switch being flipped, and the flash blinds me for a few seconds as my eyes acclimate to the first light they have seen in hours. I rub my shoulder while this is happening and feel a little bit of soreness but far less than a tetanus shot leaves behind. Whatever Wolverine stuck me in the shoulder with has worn off, or at least I think it has worn off—I'll know more when I stand up.

The ugly monstrosity comes into view, but my gaze instantly shifts away from him to the walls, then the ceiling, and then the floor. Whoa. These men work fast. The entire room, minus the concrete around the floor drain beneath the shower, has been fitted with sound dampening material. Tan-colored carpet has been crudely thrown on the floor and affixed to the ceiling; the walls are covered in a mix of acoustic foam, carpet, and thick drapes; the desk is now shielded with blankets and towels. It still isn't a perfect studio to perform in, but they'll get a much more professional recording now.

"Impressed, bubba?" Wolverine asks as he brings in the packet once again and lays it on top of the crimson-colored towel covering the few feet of desk in front of the computer screen.

"You and Big Boss are efficient." My eyes are fully adjusted, and I now become aware of my bladder. "I need to urinate."

"I bet!" he says.

"What's that mean?"

"You've been out for thirty-two hours." He approaches with the vest and chain. "Appreciate the compliment, but we're not that fast, my narrator friend."

So, an entire day has passed. The thought of the two of them working on the room while I slept makes my mind go to places it shouldn't. I shiver.

He sees me. "You cold?"

"No, just have to use the bathroom." I try to squirm just a little bit closer to the head of the cot; he sometimes tightens the chest strap before realizing that he needs to be loosening it, and it has made my underarms sore. "And I'm starving. Is it 4:30 in the morning?"

"On the nose. You got a lot of work to do today."

I use the restroom, and then he brings in a plate of food plus two bottles of water and a cup of hot tea. Beyond the basic sustenance needed to carry on, the water and tea put me at ease. I need to preserve my voice.

He removes the napkin, revealing a plate of eggs, bacon, and toast. I devour everything.

The first bottle of water goes down fast, and then I sip on the tea while leafing through the packet. Wolverine prepares the equipment and adjusts the microphone so I can sit straight up in the chair and speak into the mic.

"Way I figure it, from what you said the other day, we should be through everything except the book by our stopping point this afternoon. You'll start on the book tomorrow mornin'."

I nod. The faster, the better. "Do you think I could read the manuscript this afternoon?"

He scratches his head. "But you already read the outline."

"I know, but I'd like to get a feel for the actual book. Is that okay?"

The voice pipes in from the ceiling. "I want you to read it cold, Shawn."

The tone tells me that there is no way I am changing Big Boss's mind. "No problem. I've done it before."

"I know you have," Big Boss's voice replies.

From a recording perspective, the morning's work will be straightforward. The only challenge will be the song, which I hope to get in the first run. I feel uncomfortable reading most of the items they've given me, but a timeline of sorts has been established, made a shade grayer by the fact that they pumped something into me to knock me out for over thirty hours. Whatever that is, it can't be good for me to receive doses of it day after day. I resolve myself to the fact that I am going to have to record well but fast. The sooner I have a chance to get out of here, the better.

What makes me the most uneasy is that they know so much: my parents, Jo, Jenna, where I live, my routines, my interview answers, including the admission that I've read some work cold before. All of this has me spooked—not about what will happen during the recording but what my life will be like after they have what they want and I get out of here. Will I spend the rest of my life looking over my shoulder? Will I be afraid to leave my house? Will I be so paranoid that I do a three hundred and sixty-degree check of my surroundings every time before exiting my car? Upon leaving one of my favorite restaurants after dinner? As unpredictable as some of my time in this recording cell has been, the next few days seem to feel like they will be more of a routine, which gives me a spot of comfort. However, I know that I must never get to the point where being strapped and chained down here becomes more comfortable than what I might face if I get out of here. If I let that happen, I'm done for.

To be honest, I narrate most of my thrillers cold. I like to be surprised and let my emotion affect my performance—except when it's M. Scott Sala killing off Nehemiah Stone. This doesn't mean that I don't go back and revise my performance where necessary. It's more akin to the spirit of writing the first draft of a play. Your goal is to take the storm that has been gathering inside of yourself for weeks and months and then empty that hurricane onto the page. Reading a thriller cold is the only way I have found to capture that authentic feeling of immediacy, the bursts of energy as I experience the story much like listeners will when they start the finished audiobook months after I record it. The only difference is that when I'm writing, I am aware of what type of storm I'm getting into; when I'm narrating, it's the anticipation of the storm that drives me. Trust between me and an author is essential on this point. When trust has been established, I know that I can trust myself and my own creative decisions in the booth when I read his or her work. I want listeners to be so engrossed that when the last word of the book reaches their ears, they can say, *"That really happened."* So, what was I doing by asking for the manuscript ahead of time? As sick as it sounds, even to myself, I was attempting to establish trust. Even though I have seen the outline, I don't have any conviction that I will be able to give a performance that will satisfy Big Boss and his mountain man jail guard. Something tells me that my voice alone will not carry the day. As Corie Woods once told me, *'Your voice will never book you a job. It's what you can do with your voice to make a book come alive that will book you a job.'* I wish Corie was here right now. Together, we could take out Wolverine and get out of here. Many people see Corie as the kind, loving, and gentle man who spoils his boyfriend Matt every chance he gets. But Matt and I have seen Corie in a bar fight—he is the lion in winter. There was also a second reason that I asked for the manuscript. Since I've been in this shit hole, there has been no sight or mention of books or lined paper, pens, and pencils. I will happily sit down at the desk, chained to the floor while wearing the vest, if I can read or at least write. Hence, I also asked to see the manuscript so that I would have something to do this afternoon.

In one sense, I'm looking forward to 1 p.m. because I'll be done recording all of this ridiculous material; in another sense, I'm dreading 1 p.m. because I don't want to spend an afternoon strapped to my cot.

Wolverine finishes with his adjustments. But, I have a concern: the toilet. Not mine but one that must be nearby—like it's on the other side of the wall that is behind my own toilet. Then again, it might be a dream, but I swear that I must have been close to awake a few times over the past 32 hours because I heard a toilet flush, and, if I heard it right, the sound was loud enough to affect any recording that would be done in this room. Who used the toilet? Had to be either Big Boss or Wolverine—slipped next door to use it during the time that they were installing the sound dampening material in this room.

Bottom line: I don't want to have to re-record anything because someone flushes a toilet next door. Should I tell them this? I decide to put the chips on the table.

"This setup will work," I say to Wolverine. "But I have a concern."

He sits down in the chair next to mine. "And what would that be?"

"Is there a toilet on the other side of this wall?"

He narrows his eyes.

I've touched something in him. He may think that he's got an impressive poker face, but I know when a question has surprised him now, which makes me feel like I've got some control here. However, I can't tell if he's nervous, angry, or dumbfounded by my question as in *There is no toilet on the other side, Shawn. What in the hell are you talking about?'*

"Where'd that question come from?"

"I thought I heard a flushing noise earlier and didn't want anything to disrupt the recording today."

His face becomes a sheet of granite, nothing moving except his eyes, which shift side to side once. A prop manager from one of my plays used to start every one of his feedback statements with, *'In my humble opinion…'* Well, in *my* humble opinion, I think he's nervous.

"When did you *think* you heard it?"

"When I was asleep," I say. Hey, I'm being honest.

He considers my statement for a moment.

Big Boss weighs in from above. "There is, Shawn. We used it while we were finishing your room over the past day. You don't have to worry about any interruptions while you work."

So, I was right.

Wolverine looks like he wants to ask follow-up questions, but Big Boss says, "Everything is secure. Now, let's get to work."

Wolverine nods up at the camera, and I take a sip of tea. Interesting way to phrase it: *'Everything is secure.'* I file his statement away; I'll give it some more thought later. Right now, I realize that the recording is about to get started, which triggers my instincts to follow my normal routine. I don't do vocal exercises before a session. Corie swears by them—humming, breathing, some light scales, and using his hands to stretch his face—and I heard that Michael Hunnie has a forty-five-minute program he goes through before each session. Maybe I should, but, *in my very humble opinion*, I've never needed them. Perhaps, in ten years, I'll regret it. Perhaps, in three days, I'll be dead.

What I focus on is throat maintenance. To me, that is where you keep or lose your voice. And right now, I only have one of the necessary three ingredients in my full routine in front of me: water. The hot tea is nice, but I'm not a big tea guy. Some of my fellow narrators are. The other two items are a bottle of Ice Drops breath drops, spearmint flavor, which I purchase by the case from Amazon, and a tube of Burt's Bees lip balm. Corie doesn't do tea either, but he constantly flushes water down his throat like I do and uses Binaca instead of Ice Drops and Blistex instead of Burt's Bees. To each their own. The breath drops eliminate mouth noises, and the balm keeps one's lips from drying out and becoming chapped. On my first day of recording, I rubbed my lips with my stick of Burt's Bees every few pages. Then, later, when I listened to my performance, the air went out of my balloon when I realized that my constant rubbing had made my lips smack. I called up Corie, and, being the veteran narrator that he was, he told me to only dab the stick on my bottom and top lips. Problem solved. After that, I consulted him on everything before recording. As usual, I thought I knew more than anyone else, and it cost me—just like it did in New York City.

So, do I ask for the two other products or not? I know I can get by with just water, and I'll drink the tea as long as they keep bringing it, but I'm so used to using the other items that I'm afraid not having them will throw off my performance. Again, I'm trying to give myself the best chance at getting it recorded in one shot. I know that is unrealistic; even the best narrators make mistakes reading and have to make corrections. Then, again, they aren't being drugged and chained.

I decide to ask. Besides, these guys have obviously listened to all of my interviews—bastards know my routine. "Would it be possible for me to have some lip balm and mouth drops?"

Wolverine chuckles and then looks up at the camera. "Okay, so I owe you." His eyes return to me. "We had a bet about whether you'd ask for the other two items. I lost."

Glad I'm so damn amusing to you guys. Where is Corie when I need him?

Wolverine goes out in the hall and returns with a handful of bottles of Ice Drops and a tube of Burt's Bees lip balm. "Now you're set, right?"

He hands me the headphones, and I put them on. They are not as high quality as the ones I wear at home, but there's enough cushion so as not to make my ears feel like someone is pinching them after two hours. I say into the microphone:

## This is Shawn Frost, and this is a test of my new headphones.

The headphones will work. Pretty good neutral sound. Not too bassy. But what do I care? I'm just looking the part and won't be focused on pronunciations, microphone technique, and subtle things with my voice like I usually would when I don my Princess Leia buns. No, I'm reading all of this stuff straight through, don't give a flip about my performance or the quality of the recording. If anything, I hope that wearing the headphones gives me a daily stretch of quiet, removing me a bit from the situation I'm in.

Wolverine gives me a thumbs up and says, "Headphones good, man?"

Ugh. Even with the headphones on, I can still hear his annoying voice. "All good," I reply.

He smiles and settles in.

It's going to be difficult to maintain any kind of posture that doesn't end up giving me a sore neck and back. In my booth back at home, I have my notes, the screen, the text, and my microphone all set at eye level. Here? I don't have any notes, and *nothing* else is level. The crummy wooden stand for the binder is too bulky, and I have to lean forward to read the text.

Tough hand to play.

Okay, Frost, let's get this over with.

I take a sip of tea and open the packet to the page with my first recording material. I glance at the first item:


## 1.  Happy Birthday Song to "Big Boss"


I take a sip of water.

I put one drop of Ice Drops into my mouth.

I dab the lip balm a few times on my top lip, then my bottom lip.

"Ready," I say.

He nods.

And I begin to sing "Happy Birthday" to a man I've never met, who is holding me hostage and has watched me be beaten and pee my pants.

# 10

I'm back on the cot, strapped down tighter than Gulliver. As expected, I finished everything but the novel in this morning's session. Inside, I cringed when reading the suggestive material. Outwardly, I wept when the ball went through Buckner's legs, and for pretty much the entire time I read the Kenyon poem, which are the only parts I had to re-record—got them both on the third try. I almost lost my composure when I read the tag line from the Dos Equis commercial because it reminded me of the Saturday afternoons of watching college football with Corie and Matt and smiling every time *the most interesting man in the world* came on during a commercial break…and laughing again when we bought more beer because of the commercial. If Satan has returned to earth, then he has to work somewhere in either advertising or cell phone research and development.

I got through Macbeth's soliloquy and the knife-in-the-back statements directed toward my entertainment colleagues without any trouble. The days of the week and months of the year bored me to no end, but probably my proudest moment of the morning came when I let myself go in singing, "Coke in the Backseat." Now, as I thought it would, the song plays inside my head.

It's probably around three in the afternoon. I had two PB&Js and a banana for lunch, along with another bottle of water. Then, I showered, and now I'm in a black sweatsuit while my gray one is being washed.  I haven't seen my own clothes since Wolverine collected them from me to wash them.  The fresh socks feel good on my feet.  They must have bought this sweatsuit and pair of socks right before abducting me because they are stiff, creased, and haven't been washed—smell like a used dryer sheet, though, just like the gray ones did.  I didn't mention that earlier?  Well, I'm stressed.

The lights are still on, so I assume Wolverine will be back at some point to turn them off.  I glance over at the camera.  At least I have some way to communicate with someone when I'm alone.  Even if Big Boss isn't always monitoring me, the fact that he might be gives me some comfort.  He only chimed in a few times during the morning recording.  You guessed right; it was when I had to re-record material because I was crying.  My eyes are sore because the first crying spell must have lasted a few minutes.  I couldn't stop.  Looking back, the first tears broke loose because of what I was reading—I still feel bad for Bill Buckner to this day—but then I started to think about Dad and my situation, and the floodgates opened.  'Twas a cleansing cry, though, and after that, I didn't get hit again until the poem.  Not as wet of a cry that time—more of a cry about the poem's message: what it feels like to come out of a long depression.  I empathized with the speaker because I've been there before, but also, I can see it happening again once I get the hell out of this place.

Other than the insane and uninspired lyrics of "Coke in the Backseat" running through my mind, I am wondering what this afternoon and the following afternoons will hold for me.  I don't need to do any more talking—my voice needs rest after that long of a recording session—but would enjoy something, anyth—

Well, not *anything*, but something to stave off the boredom.  Something to keep my mind busy so that I'm not lip-synching a stupid song about cocaine or thinking about how my life is going to end in a few days once I'm done with the recording.

And then there is another thing that could occur if I'm strapped in this cot with the lights on for five hours in the afternoon each day: I might start to replay scenes from my life and second guess certain things. Dr. Roman I. Baker— remember him?—said to be wary of doing this too often. It's healthy to look back on one's follies and try to come to peace with what is and what is not in one's control, but to quote the good and righteous doctor, *'To over-reflect, Shawn, could prove fatal for a man of the arts such as yourself. You thrive when your brain is given license to create in a focused manner toward an end product—a play, a novel, a performance. You become paralyzed when your brain becomes consumed with the what-ifs of your past. What if I did this instead of that? What if that opportunity had never come my way? What if a different one had? You'll suffocate, wither, become a coward, and eventually self-destruct.'*

"Well, Bake, if I can't find something to do these next few afternoons, then I'm in trouble." The words are out of my mouth for a few seconds, and I realize that I have said them out loud. Hope Big Boss or Wolverine didn't hear them, but if they did, I mean, they know everything else about me, so they probably know that I regularly see Dr. Baker. Would they understand? They don't seem like the counseling type. I know, I know, that's a horrible thing to think because there is no "counseling type." In fact, I withdraw my statement; if there were ever two men who needed someone like Roman I. Baker to get inside their heads and untangle the balls of string that wound themselves to the point where they thought kidnapping an audiobook narrator was a humane and good idea, then Big Boss and Wolverine are those two men.

Thinking of Dr. Baker makes me wonder how the search for Shawn Frost is shaping up across California. Undoubtedly, they found my phone. Are they following any leads? Were there any leads? Is a detective, wearing a bad suit and followed by a S.W.A.T. team, about to break in here and rescue me?

The door starts to open, and my spirits soar for a few seconds…Bring me *Thanos*!

…then Wolverine's body appears in the doorway, and my head rests back against the pillow. I stare blankly at the carpeted ceiling, wishing some of the threads would start to grow like vines and come down, intertwine, and rip these straps off of me. Then, the tentacle could grow in size and strength and strangle Wolverine. I could control it like Doc Ock.

"Afternoon, sir."

"Good afternoon." I turn my head to the right. Don't see anything in his hands.

He closes the door behind him. "How's the throat?"

I go back to focusing on the ceiling and wishing for it to come alive. "Throat's fine."

He pulls up a chair, closer than ever before, and crosses his legs. I can see the bottom of his boots—clean, but there's mud mixed with grass along the sides of his soles and a spray pattern of mud splattered across the leather sides. The mud looks fresh and wet, definitely not dried. It's the first time his boots have been dirty, and it makes me wonder what the terrain is outside. I suppose you can have mud and grass pretty much anywhere, especially after it rains, but, for some reason, the amount of it makes me think that I'm not in California anymore. Another question I have is: Why are his boots dirty all of a sudden? They've been clean as a whistle since I first saw him. It's obvious he went outside, but…ah, I'm going nowhere with my Sherlockian investigation fast.

"That's good. Big day tomorrow."

I turn away and close my eyes. "Yes."

"'Bout that, I got somethin' that ya might like."

You've got terminal cancer and will die tonight? Big Boss has decided to call it all off, and I'm free? John Lennon and George Harrison have come back to life? Lisa Kron wants to collaborate with me on a play? There will be a Broadway revival this year of Marsha Norman's *'Night, Mother*? Lin-Manuel Miranda *and* Tony Kushner called? "And what's that?" I ask.

"Big Boss don't want you doin' no imitations. You did so well today that he wants you to start recordin' *Narrator* first thing tomorrow mornin'.'"

At this point, I have to celebrate even the tiniest win, and this is one of them. But, do it with humility, Frost. "That's awfully generous of him. I was lying here wondering if we might jump right in."

"Yeppers. I'll warn you, though, he's picky. Wants it done to his standards, know what I mean?"

"Guess I'm lucky that I'm his favorite narrator."

"Well, true, but the—"

"Wolverine, that's enough," says the voice of Big Boss from the ceiling.

What was he going to say? I search Wolverine's face for answers, but the only read I can get is a flash of embarrassment.

"No problem," he says up at the speaker.

I want to probe but resist. First the muddy boots, and now he's getting cut off before revealing something to me. Wait it out, Frost. Survive and advance, then use that run-the-hundred-in-ten-flat speed to escape and return with the whole fire department.

I almost laugh out loud at my thought. The things that have taken place in the last few minutes are throwing me off and stressing me out. What would Dr. Baker tell me to do to calm myself back down? First: breathe. I take a few breaths. Next: try to bring whatever situation you're in back on familiar turf. Well, that's next to impossible. However, we were just talking about how I was Big Boss's favorite narrator. There may be an opportunity here. "Wolverine, who is your favorite narrator?"

A sly grin forms. "Oh, you don't wanna know. *Believe me*, you don't wanna know."

"C'mon. I know it isn't me." I give him a charming laugh. "Seriously, who is it?"

He rubs his chin, which is now covered in brown stubble. "Tell you what, when you finish the book, I'll let you know."

I feel deflated as he sits up and regains his mask. My moment has passed. I feel a shift of sorts has occurred and wish that I knew why. "So, what's the schedule for the rest of the afternoon before dinnertime and sleep?" Might as well ask. He hasn't brought anything for me to read and no writing material either.

"Big Boss wants to ask you some questions before the recording. Now, he's heard all of your interview answers before, but since it's his book that you're going to be performing, he wants to talk it through with you."

"Is he coming down?"

"Nah, he'll be asking the questions through the speaker."

"Why didn't we do this the other day?"

"It's a fair question. Answer is, we didn't know how it would go this mornin'. Now that we do, he wants to kind of have an exclusive with you 'fore you get started."

My answers are going to be the same as in all of the interviews you criminals have watched. This is a waste of time…but wait. At least this gives me something to do. I would rather sit and talk about narrating than about anything else Wolverine and Big Boss could have me doing. And, I might be able to steer the conversation back toward what Wolverine was going to say before Big Boss cut him off. "I'd like that," I say.

Wolverine hits his right knee in delight. "How about that! I knew you was gonna agree, Shawn." He angles his head up at the speaker. "See, Big Boss? I just knew it." He stands up and says to me, "Be right back with a bonus, sir."

Bonus? Will I get paper? A pen? Some more tea? Adrenaline courses through my body; any unknown at this point automatically heightens my awareness. I start to fidget.

He departs the room and is gone for what seems like a year as I sweat and watch the doorway. I can't see him, but I hear his feet shuffling.

"Relax, Shawn," the voice from the ceiling commands.

I register his suggestion and realize once again that whatever they have planned, it's out of my control. I inhale, hold it for a few seconds, exhale, and then rest my eyes, trying to forget about the *bonus*. Concentrating on something work-related has always helped me in the past, and my ability to do it now pays off again. I alleviate some of my anxiety by pondering what questions Big Boss will ask me. We've already covered some of the usual interview questions, like my routine and how long it takes to record a book. My guess is that he'll ask me for specifics about my craft since I'm about to work on *his* book. These questions won't be difficult to handle.

I hear the door shut, and my momentary relief vanishes. I open my eyes and jerk my head over to get a look at Wolverine. If I had a machine that measured anxiety hooked up to me right now, it would be beeping and chirping like mad— maybe even a digital message that scrolled across a monitor's screen reading: OVERLOAD.

Wolverine is holding two boxes—a large box with a smaller shoebox on top. On the shoebox, I can see the unmistakable swoosh on the side. Am I getting a pair of Nikes? But what about the bottom box?

He sets the boxes down on the table.

I'm so nervous, I start talking. "Let me guess: Lakers jersey and shorts and Nike basketball shoes?"

Wolverine says, "Ha! Don't you wish."

And for the first time, I hear laughing coming from the speaker. My chin starts to vibrate.

He takes the shoe box and sets it down on another part of the table. Smirking, he glances back at me and then opens the larger box. From it, he pulls out a heavy-duty chain that is attached to two shackles…

Shackles that go around someone's wrists.

My wrists.

# 11

oth of my wrists are now shackled and chained to the floor. I cannot move my arms. During the times that I've been free from the cot, I did not think to look under it in detail. I knew it was secured to the floor, and that's all that mattered. But if I had looked more closely, then I might have seen the two stainless-steel rings countersunk into the floor underneath the foot of the bed, similar to the rings in the other locations across the room. I've been told by Wolverine that the chain runs up from the ring on the right side of the cot, through the shackle around my right wrist, across my body and through the shackle around my left wrist, and then down to the ring underneath the left side of the cot.

His ultimatum before chaining me up was, *Let me do this without any problems, and you won't get hit.* It was enough of a threat for me to go limp and let him chain me down.

"There we are," he says, standing back up from the foot of the cot.

"I don't understand. Have I done something wrong?" I ask.

"Naw, naw, naw," Wolverine says. "Just need to have your arms secure for your bonus, that's all."

What is going on? Why do they need my arms secure? I'm just about to be interviewed about audiobook recording, for Christ's sake!

He takes the shoebox from the table and pulls up a chair next to my cot.

"Please, Wolverine. Whatever I've done. I—I…"

He opens the box and shows me the contents.

I swallow. It's a terror of a different kind.

"See? Whatchu all worried about?" he says. "We thought this would make you a little happy. Ya know, pick up the spirits and all that stuff."

He sets the box down on the carpet and pulls out a length of rubber tubing and a syringe.

"Mixed up a dose for you out in the hall. Not a big one, just a little nip to help you relax."

It's heroin. I am helpless to prevent what is about to happen. My only hope is that it doesn't have the dreaded "F" word in it, in which case these might be the final breaths that I ever take on this earth. Mom, Dad, Nicole, Jo, Corie, Killy, I tried—

He wraps the tubing around my right arm, finds a vein, and then injects the liquid into my body.

Within seconds, I feel the familiar rush; the momentary elimination of pain and suffering overrides the area of my brain that is saying, *Your situation is now worse.*' The euphoria comes on strong, and my body feels like liquid. I wait. Will I live? Keep breathing. As long as you can breathe, you're alive, Frost. Now, breathe, Goddamnit!

I keep breathing. After some time has passed, I close my eyes, knowing that I'll make it…but also knowing that I'm hooked on heroin again. I'll feel good for a little while longer, and then my mental functioning will get foggy, which is why I don't understand why Big Boss wants to interview me right now.

"See, not a lot, Shawn. Just a smidge. We know you've had your troubles with this before, so, don't wanna overdo it, know what I'm sayin'? Stuff I just put in you is pure. Cost us plenty, but we can't have you divin' six feet under on us now, can we?"

Thanks for telling me *after* you shot me up with that shit.  "What about the interview?"

"Oh, we'll get to that.  You just relax right now, bubba."

I wake up to the sound of the door opening—starting to be my alarm clock.  The lights are still on, so my eyes adjust faster, at least I think they do.  Wolverine enters with a tray of food and a cup of tea, and two bottles of water.

"Know what you're thinkin', sir," he says.  "It's six p.m.  Had yourself a nice little high and a couple hours in the sack."  He sets the tray on the table and then walks over to me while carrying the vest.  "Any crazy dreams?  I never tried any of that junk, cold beer and whiskey are as far as I get, but I hear you can have wacko dreams."

I feel okay but have to urinate again.  "None that I can recall," I answer him.  "Can we hurry it up?  I need to pee."

"Sure thing," he says, winking.

I use the restroom and eat everything on my plate.  Same as before: two PB&Js and a banana.  After I chug the two bottles of water, I start in on the tea.

He sits on the chair next to mine and just watches me.

I turn toward him.  "Why did you do that to me?"

He frowns, and it's the worst kind: a frown of pity.  "All part of the deal."

I give him the most honest stare I can muster.  Our faces are about two feet apart.  "I'm not leaving here, am I?"

"I can't answer that."

We don't say anything for a while but maintain eye contact—me with my right eye and the half I can see out of with my left.

I am now more determined than ever to get out of here the first chance I get.  A few more doses of heroin, especially if they give me more each time, and my priority will shift from escaping to doing anything they want in order to get my next fix. I want to cry. It's how it works. They'll own me, and they know it. In fact, I'm already thinking about my next dose.

He breaks eye contact first and says, "Ready for your interview?" as he gets up and stretches.

"What? I thought that was just part of the setup for what you did to me earlier."

"Oh, hell no. Big Boss is anxious to speak with you now that you're back in your right mind. Let's get you another bathroom break and then get you back on the cot."

Wolverine tightens the last of the straps. The chain and shackles are on the floor at the foot of the bed. Next, he puts the heavy blanket on top of me so that the only thing showing is my neck and head. "Okay, we'll do the interview now, give you one more restroom break, and then put you to sleep. Huge morning tomorrow." He heads toward the door. "I'll close up to give you and Big Boss some privacy. Be out in the hall if you need anything; just tell him, and he'll give me a holler."

He exits and, for the first time, turns off the lights over my bed but leaves on the lights over the desk. I lie in the shadows and wait.

"Ready?" the voice says from the ceiling.

"I assume you heard everything we talked about?"

"I did."

"Look, I'm going to give you my best effort tomorrow." It's a half-lie. "But I have to ask, since you are the one in charge here: Why would you want to kill me? I've never seen you, I'm never going to see Wolverine again, I've done everything you've asked of me so far, and I'm going to narrate your entire book. Can't you just let me go after it's done, and we'll all just go on with our lives? I mean, if I'm your favorite audiobook narrator, then don't you want me to be able to keep narrating books?"

"Let's focus on the interview, Shawn."

"Okay, but would you please consider what I just said? I've got people in my life. I've got more to do. I don't want it to end like this." I'm trying not to plead, but the time for holding cards has passed.

"The first thing I'd like to know is what goes through your mind when you receive a new manuscript—like mine tomorrow?"

I'm on the verge of breaking. Tears are welling up in my eyes, and my chin is starting to vibrate. I pinch my thighs, trying to stay strong.

"Don't go soft on me now, Shawn," Big Boss says. "If you can't answer, then I might have Wolverine come in and loosen your lips. Understand?"

Don't make the situation any worse, Frost. You don't want another beating. Man the fuck up right now and answer his questions. I pull my right arm out from underneath the heavy blanket and carefully wipe the tears from my eyes. Then, I sniff and wipe my nose. "Yeah, sorry about that. Can you repeat the question, please?"

He does.

Now, answer him. Just get through the night, and maybe you'll have your chance tomorrow after recording. "It is exciting to get a book from a major author who is going to sell hundreds of thousands of copies and know that no one else has read it yet. I've always considered it an honor."

"And *my* book?"

"I've never worked with you before."

"I thought you'd be excited to perform my book after reading the outline the other day."

"It has some potential, but I'll have to see what the prose looks like tomorrow. I wish you would let me see the manuscript tonight." Never hurts to ask again. Seriously, what in God's name do I have to lose at this point?

"I want you to be *surprised* by the prose. *Mesmerized* by the prose. I want you to experience how rich and achingly beautiful it is—during every *moment* of recording."

"Are you certain that I'm starting tomorrow morning?"

"Yes. Why wouldn't you be?"

"I mean…this afternoon's event has me wondering about a lot of things."

"Wolverine has already told you the schedule. We are going to stick by it."

"Okay," I say.

"As the director of this project, I've worked hard to create a controlled and rich environment so that you can go anywhere creatively that you want to. I'm anxious to see you respond to the material, and I want to see you take risks that you normally would not take, Shawn." He lets the last sentence hang in the air for a few seconds and then follows it with, "I've given you a gift that you'll never get again."

This entire setup is insane. This *man* is insane. He hasn't posed a question, but I have one of my own. "What's the gift?" I ask, feeling the tightness in the straps and the weight of the blanket.

"Complete isolation from any other responsibilities. The opportunity to focus on nothing but the work."

I don't say anything back. In one small way, he's right. There are no outside distractions here. In every other way, he's wrong. All the distractions are inside—inside this cell and inside my head. I'm being held prisoner. End of discussion.

"Now, for my book, will you be doing different voices or not?"

Okay, he wants answers? I'll give him an earful. "No. I don't do that. And I don't cast parts in my head."

"Why not?"

"Not my style. If I cast a part in my head, then I get too wrapped up in who *that character* is and not the one in the book. It's also difficult for me to put on a voice for over eleven hours. I tried it once and found that it wasn't in my skill set. Some narrators can, but, as I'm sure you know, we usually fall into one of two categories: those who do voices and those who don't."

"Corie Woods does both."

"Well, Corie is an exception and has the rare ability to do both."

"What can you do tomorrow?"

He knows the answer to this already—and it doesn't matter. "What I can do, though, is play an attitude. I won't go for an imitation, but I'm usually able to capture the cadence of a character after a few pages with them. What matters the most is that the listener knows who is speaking at all times." I pause, hoping to lend weight to my next statement. "It all depends on the partner I'm working with."

"Go on," the voice from above says.

"Well, if I'm with a strong writer, then I don't have to do as much because the words do the work. I can take a great book and, perhaps, make it a little better with my performance. However, I can't make a bad book good. It's impossible. Hence, if I'm with a weak writer, then I have to do more work." I pause again before saying, "Usually, I'm not with a weak writer or one that has too many weaknesses." What I won't tell him is that it takes just as much effort to narrate an awful book as it does to narrate a great book. If the book is lacking in any way, then I have to use every skill I have to elevate the material; if it's a great book, then I have to be at my best in order to perform at the level of the text.

"How about me?"

I won't be elevating anything you wrote. "I'm hoping that you're strong. The outline was serviceable, but that has never been an indication to me if the author can excite and be exacting with his or her prose."

"There he is. That's the Shawn Frost I wanted for this job. You sound more and more like an audiobook guru every day. Given any more thought about writing a 'how to' book for narrators?"

"That's going to be difficult to do if I don't get out of here, right?"

"And the wit to boot! You could have a chapter with common rookie mistakes and even a quiz at the end of that chapter. Maybe a question like this:

Would you record if you had a glass that was half-full of water in the booth with you?"

I say nothing.

"Well…what's the answer, mister expert?"

"Of course not.  Any open container will change the sound in the booth—you'd get an echo."

"Bravo!"

Don't forget the chapter on how to systematically hunt down, disembowel, hang upside down, and machine gun to death any crazed fans who kidnap you.

"You really need to write it, Shawn.  Anyway, what's your plan for tomorrow?"

"What do you mean?"

"How will you go about playing attitudes, capturing cadences, and so forth?"

"My position has always been that, in an audiobook, readers want to be guided by the narrator.  I have to point them in the direction that will help them think and feel what the author wants them to think and feel.  There's work to be done on every page, every line.  I try not to be neutral in successive sentences—always attempting to bring something to the story.  My intuition will be a powerful ally tomorrow."  Notice how epic I made that last sentence sound?  My lord, it is killing me to do this interview because it means *nothing*.  However, I'm an extrovert, and the fact that conversation has been hard to come by the past few days is overriding the fact that I am conversing with someone who ordered heroin pumped into my veins around 3 hours ago.

"What about characters?  Have you thought at all about Stacey, Robbie, and Kurt?"

"As you know—"

"Don't say that," he says, cutting me off. "Answer like I don't know anything about you."

Fuck you. "Sure," I say. "In terms of your characters, I've got an advantage tomorrow. I always perform like I'm the main character, so since Robbie is an audiobook narrator, I'll slip into the role easily but also adapt myself to who Robbie is and play off of the differences between him and me. If Stacey and Kurt are who I think they are, then I've met dozens of people in the entertainment business that are like them. They should be fun to play if you've written them in a way that makes them distinct from the supporting roles. Since you won't give me anything more than the outline, I'll be looking for indicators about each of their backgrounds—geographic location, any accents, what kind of home they grew up in, how smart they are, and how intuitive they are. Anything like that. Additionally, I'll see what kind of narrator you have and make my adjustments based on that. For instance, I may shift the narrator's posture based on which character he is watching. It's all about subtlety and imagination."

Being a playwright has also helped me as a narrator. For instance, if this novel was a play and I was an actor playing Robbie, I'd only be focused on his character—his background, his arc, his total story. But, as an audiobook narrator of this novel, I have to focus on these aspects for Robbie, Stacey, Kurt, and other characters. Since I was a director in the theater, I already know how to do this, and so, when I prep for an audiobook, I approach it like a director first and an actor second. Won't be the case here because I've got to perform *Narrator* cold, but thinking about my process is helping me stay sane right now—and helping me get through this ridiculous interview.

"How do you know my narrator is a male?"

"Look, there's no rule about it. The narrator could be male or female. I've just found that if the author is male, then usually the narrator is male or tells the story from a male perspective."

"Pretty good assumption. Punctuation?"

"I'll dishonor it whenever I believe it helps the narrating of the story. Remember, in human speech, punctuation doesn't exist. Punctuation marks are visual cues that you are providing to the readers of your novel as you attempt to approximate the way humans speak.  And you have to do it.  I don't.  My job is to turn those visual cues into oral cues, and so there's a ton that I won't honor tomorrow."  I sigh.  Yes, I'm trying to be an asshole here, but this is a battle I feel I can win—and I need a win.  "I just hope you don't have a ton of 'he said' and 'she said' in there—really interrupts the read.  I'll throw them away immediately.  Remember, I'll always be trying to fulfill the *intent* of your writing, whatever that may be."

"I understand what you're saying, but I have a lot of exclamation points in the novel.  And I *want them* honored, which means raising your voice.  Can you handle that?"

"I'll raise my voice if I think the situation calls for it, but when I see an exclamation point, I don't automatically think about volume."

"What do you think about?"

"*Emphasis*.  Sometimes that means shouting in the booth.  Sometimes that means that I adjust my pitch or shorten or elongate a word, and other times it means that I'll put in a pause between sentences.  I've got to have that freedom tomorrow."  Like I said, I have to win here.

"I'll have to hear what you sound like tomorrow."

It's not a win, but it's not a loss either.  "Fair enough," I say.  And, no, it isn't.  Plus, none of this matters anyway.  If I don't connect with the text, then it will show in my performance.  And, even though this guy's story is about an audiobook narrator, I've already decided to check out.  The challenge will be to not appear that I am checked out when I start narrating tomorrow.  Something he doesn't know, though, is that I'm saying some of this stuff to throw him off about what I'll be doing to ruin the book.  I'm going to actually attempt to honor the majority of his punctuation and *read* the book rather than *narrate* it.  There's a difference, which I doubt he'll pick up on, but *I'll know it*, which will help me feel like I have some sort of control.  This is the key to survival at this point.  Oh, what's the difference between reading and narrating?  Reading is a cold-bastard-sober-robot-like-focused attempt to get all of the *words* right.  Narrating is using my artistic gifts and skill to *share a story* with other human beings, and I believe it is the purest form of storytelling and the oldest art form we have—people sitting around the fire, sharing tales.  If I had kids, I'd take them camping all of the time just to be able to do *that*.  On occasion, Jo and I talked about having kids together, but our careers won out each time.  For some reason, I feel guilty about that.  Anyway, one thing is for certain: This inhumane person whom I am talking to through a speaker in the ceiling right now does not deserve *any* narrating.

"We will not be providing you with any props or costumes."

"I'll do my best without them."

"You really think they help, don't you?"

"I do.  When I narrated a mountain climbing scene that took place in freezing temperatures in M. Scott Sala's *The Alps Assassination*, I cranked the A/C so that I could wear a knit cap and gloves in my booth.  Sala also mailed me an ice ax to keep in there for the entire recording.  I know my performance was better because of those elements."

"I don't think you need them for this project.  You're narrating a story about a narrator in his booth, right?"

"Sweatsuit and socks will have to do.  And…you've got *plenty* of props in this booth for me to draw from."

"Eighty percent of the manuscript is written from a third-person close point of view, anchored to the protagonist, Robbie Bernstein.  The other twenty percent is written in close third from the point of view of the antagonist, Kurt Boar.  Can you handle this the same way you did in *The Paris Sanction*?  Reich was menacing."

What he's talking about is something I do sometimes when I'm recording.  My mouth is usually around six inches away from the mic, but sometimes when a selection is written in close third, which means that we get more access to a particular character's thoughts, then I'll bring my mouth to within three inches of the mic and lower my volume. This is one of the subtleties that I can achieve while narrating that I could never explore on the stage; there's a difference between performing Shakespeare in front of over 1,200 people in the August Wilson Theatre and narrating the inner thoughts of a character inside my booth. Third-person close allows for more intimacy. As he says, I did this for Reich, which *freaked* listeners out. I took a creative risk, and it paid off. Can't do it every time, or the decision risks becoming procedure, which diminishes its effect. This is probably the best example I can give as to why narrating is a science *and* an art. My experience, acting background, and method all go into the artistic decisions I make using my intuition. More science has always equaled less art—perhaps not in output, but definitely inside each creation. Science also has the ability to diminish previous works of art; think about how many novels and films wouldn't work today in a cell phone and surveillance camera world.

I digress. Now, will Big Boss's villain publicist, *Kurt Boar*—not a fan of his character names—warrant that I make the same creative decision that I made in *The Paris Sanction*? Doubtful. However, this is what my captor wants, and I have to continue to play the game. "No problem," I say. "I can do the same for Kurt." But, this doesn't mean that I don't have my own game in mind. Starting tomorrow, I'm going to do my best to covertly sabotage his main character. My version of being a pissed-off barista giving his rude customer decaf coffee instead of regular goes like this: I usually slouch when I read scumbag characters because it helps me to add authenticity to their characters. As difficult as it will be tomorrow, wearing a vest and chained to the floor, I plan on slouching whenever I read about Robbie Buffoon Bernstein. And, since eighty percent of the book is from Master Robbie's point of view, I'm going to be doing a lot of slouching.

"That's the right answer. I want you committed, Shawn. Treat every line as if it is happening to you."

Not going to be difficult considering the circumstances I find myself in. Every line *is* happening to me. Right here in this dungeon of a studio. And, the sonofabitch just used my own line against me. "That's my plan." However, he just opened himself up, and I'm going to ask again about the toilet next door. "I'm going to need the right conditions tomorrow, though."

"You already know the recording conditions."

"I'm talking about the toilet flushing in the room next to this one. I can't have that happening in the middle of the recording tomorrow. Sometimes, an interruption like that makes me shut things down for a few hours, even a day." I am lying. I can narrate through a hurricane if need be, but I have to make it seem like I'm a fragile artist here. Am I going to mention how I think "the vest" and the chain will affect the recording? No. I'll see if he brings it up. I am certain that I moved when I recorded the initial material, but they never stopped me.

"There won't be any interruptions when you record tomorrow morning, Shawn."

Do I push it and talk about Wolverine's boots? Frost, they're shooting you up with heroin. Yes, do it. "How come Wolverine's boots had mud all over them? Are we in the country somewhere or in the woods? Been getting a lot of rain?"

"This is *my* interview, Shawn."

"C'mon, you're in complete control here. I'm not going anywhere. At least give me a quadrant of the U.S. to work with. Northwest? Midwest? Southeast? Or are we still in the Golden State?"

"Aren't you going to thank me?"

The bastard isn't budging. "For what?"

"That *Narrator* is a thriller and not a science fiction novel?"

I don't care what kind of novel it is! Just tell me where I'm at. "I'm not sure I follow," I lie.

"Yes, you do."

I do.  Corie Woods narrates the occasional science fiction novel and has told me about having to work very closely with the author when made-up words appear.  In one novel alone, he had to learn how to pronounce 74 words that the author had completely made up.  *It's a lot,'* he said, *'but nowhere near the* Dune *series. Herbert made up* 498 words *in the first book, and there are like over* 2,000 words *that have been created now in the series.  No thanks.'*

"I am thankful," I say.

"Good," Big Boss says.  "Don't ask about your location again."

"Why not?  What does it matter to you?"  I wave my arm in a circle, motioning to the entirety of the room.  "Does it look like I'm getting out of here?"

"Shawn, aren't you jealous of all the movie stars performing animated characters for Disney?  Doesn't it just piss you off when a famous actor performs an audiobook and everyone swoons?  Shouldn't audiobooks only be read by audiobook narrators?  I mean, c'mon, the film stars are already famous on the screen.  The writers are famous on the page.  You and your fellow narrators should be famous in the ear."

He's trying to mind-fuck me now.  I'm not giving in.  "It's all about the bucks, sir, and famous actors and actresses sell more.  But, audiobooks are part of the book business and not the film business, so there is not much crossover."

"And when there is?"

"Then we welcome all performers."

"How about the advances in A.I.?  Ever worry that your voice will be deep faked?"

"So out of my control that I don't even give it a second thought."

"There's that fantastic wit again.  I love how quickly you react."  He pauses. "Any more questions about the recording tomorrow before I call in Wolverine and he tucks you in for a long goodnight?"

"Here's something you don't know: Sometimes, in the booth, I pretend that I'm narrating the story to my girlfriend, and I bring up a picture of her on the computer screen." I pause. My mouth is dry, and my throat is getting sore from talking. I'll need water soon. "I am aware that you know who she is. To help me concentrate tomorrow, I wonder if you could print out a picture of Jo so that I can tape it to the screen. I know you were impressed with what I did this morning, but I'm being honest with you when I say I barely made it through. I need to have something to focus my attention."

There are around thirty seconds of silence before I hear, "We'll see what we can do."

It's a sliver of light, but at least it's something. "Thank you."

"Anything else?"

"Just one more about the story. Can you tell me what the characters, primarily Stacey, Robbie, and Kurt, say about each other? Even if you read me a few lines in this regard, it would help inform my performance. I could think about it tonight."

"I don't know what they say about each other. Who cares?"

"I—"

The voice cuts me off. "I think we're done."

A few seconds later, Wolverine opens the door and enters.

His boots are wiped clean.

"Heard you had a productive chat, feller."

I'm too tired to say anything more, so I nod.

He gets me over to the bathroom one last time, I get a quick sip of water, and then I'm back in the cot, strapped down. A needle goes smoothly into my shoulder, and I fade away.


The next morning, I awake when Wolverine comes in with my breakfast. I use the bathroom, eat all of my food again, suck down the water, and start sipping on my tea. Then, he brings in a piece of paper and a roll of Scotch tape from the hallway.

"Got a picture for ya.  Big Boss said you explained to him that it might help today."  He leans over in front of me; I can't see the picture.  "Well, sir, I am *your* guy.  Anything to make this morning's work go better."

I want to see her—need to see her.  So far, she's just been in my mind, and I wonder if I've somehow distorted what she looks like.  I need something concrete in front of me so I can center myself.  Seeing Jo will do that.

"All right," he says.  "Bingo."

He moves away.

There is a large picture taped to the screen.

It is not a picture of Jo.

It is a picture of Jenna.

"You goddamn sonsabitches!"

# 12

I try to reach out and rip the picture off the screen, but my arms are chained in a way that I can only get up to my forearms past the table edge, which is enough to be able to hold onto the manuscript.

The picture is still feet away from my outstretched fingers.

"He, he, he," laughs Wolverine. "That man upstairs has a twisted sense of humor sometimes." He sits down next to me. "Now, if you do well in the first hour, I'll take that picture down. But if you don't, she 'gon stay up there the rest of the mornin'."

In one quick move, he grabs my chin and turns my head toward him. I've never seen his eyes so intense. I could struggle, but all he has to do is move his hand down to my neck…and *squeeze*. "Also, man, don't be swearin' like that. Don't appreciate hearin' you take the lord's name in vain. Understand?" He nods my head for me and releases my chin.

And now I've made my situation even worse.

"I'll go get the manuscript now."

Wolverine exits the room. Any hope of establishing a working routine in this room has just vanished. Not only do I fear for my life, but I just had one of my *captors* claim some sort of *moral high ground* over me. Now that my arms are chained, I can't even gesture with them, which has always aided my performance.

I know that if I move too much the chains will rattle and spoil the recording, and I don't know what they'll do to me if that happens today. The pressure is on. Being chained to the floor in the vest was bad enough, but now, I am doubting whether I will be able to concentrate enough to even read the manuscript. I start to hyperventilate; I have no way of escape. When will it be the afternoon? Then, I can at least have my shot.

No! That is what they want you to do. You're going to have to fight today, Frost. I take a sip of tea and look at Jenna. What a mistake.

"Here we are," Wolverine says, placing a large, 3-ring binder in front of me.

So, we're going old-school. Fine by me. Publishers usually send me books digitally these days, and I read them on my iPad. But sometimes, I will request a physical copy—still like the *feel* of a book.

I open the binder. There's only a title page and a page with a quotation on it before the story starts.

You can do it. Go into your routine, then get lost in this sucker. It will be over before you know it.

I clear my throat and take a sip of water.

I put one drop of Ice Drops into my mouth.

I dab the lip balm a few times on my top lip, then my bottom lip.

"Ready to start," I say to Wolverine.

He gives me a pat on the shoulder and then directs his attention to the ceiling microphone and says, "We got a famous narrator down here ready to start recording a bigtime thriller novel."

There is a pause—enough of one for me to turn and look up at the ceiling microphone too.

"Proceed," the voice from above finally says.

"Yee-haw, bigun," Wolverine says. "It's 'go time.'"

I read the title into the microphone:

Narrator

I flip the page.

I read the quotation:

"We tell ourselves stories in order to live."
—Joan Didion, *The White Album*

Wolverine nods in approval.

The room is absolutely silent.

I flip the page.

Chapter 1
San Francisco
*Present Day*

To say that Robbie Bernstein was an audiobook narrator was to say that he was a performer of the first magnitude.  An occasional bore at parties?  Yes, but isn't everyone?

I pause the recording.

"Somethin' wrong, bubba?" Wolverine asks.

"I thought you said this was third-person close?" I say to the ceiling microphone.

There is silence.  Wolverine looks like a bank robber who forgot the money on the way out.

"This starts in third-person omniscient."

Finally, Big Boss says, "Don't worry about it.  Continue."

I go through my routine again: sip, drop, dab, dab—dab, dab.

But what mattered most now was that *Robbie Bernstein* was at the end of his storied career, and surprises in his lavish life were about to sprout like mushroom clouds during a nuclear fu

It says "nuclear fucking holocaust."

"What's wrong this time, man?" Wolverine says.

"*What's wrong?*" I say. "Saying that word won't be blasphemy, but it's the mother of all swear words." I eyeball him. "And I prefer not to get punished again."

He laughs. "Aw, geez. This is the manuscript. You're fine, buddy. Let 'er rip. Right, Big Boss?"

"Yes," the voice says from above. "Narrate it *exactly* as I have written it, *Shawn.*"

The book is much worse than I thought. *Achingly beautiful prose*, my ass. I already hate Robbie Bernstein—and I'm an *audiobook narrator*. I take a sip of tea and then start again at the beginning of the sentence.

But what mattered most now was that *Robbie Bernstein* was at the end of his storied career, and surprises in his lavish life were about to sprout like mushroom clouds during a nuclear fucking holocaust.

I go on like this for another three hours, suffering through what has to be the worst book I have ever narrated. It seems every single page has a shift in narration. Third-person close, then third-person omniscient, then third-person close…and even a few pages of *first-person* narration. No, no, this is not the master craftsman in his workshop. This is an abhorrent display of writing, which helps me to understand why I've been kidnapped. *Narrator* would have never made it past an agent's desk.

But, I understand that I have to make it through the entire book, so I try about every ten pages to latch on to Robbie Bernstein, see him as a fellow brother in the profession, perhaps even a stand-in for my best friend, Corie Woods. It's difficult. Stacey should have left Robbie long ago, and there is no way she should be writing the novel *Converging Affairs* as a tribute to him. I can completely see the dig angle, but there is nothing redeeming about this man. In fact, I just performed my first Kurt Boar chapter, and I like *him* more than Robbie. I believe I've not shown my hand so far, but when you know that another dose of heroin is headed for your veins after lunch, you tend not to have a clear mind. The only evidence that I can rely on that tells me my captors have not picked up on my distaste for Robbie is that they haven't stopped me yet.

We had a break after those three straight hours, and then I went on for another three. A second break, and now I've been narrating for just over an hour. The end is in sight, and I'm surprised by my stamina. However, I am sore everywhere from keeping my body and arms still. Wolverine has been good about making sure that I constantly have enough water. In a way, I like making him unchain me so I can take a long, power-stream piss every now and then.

I flip the page, go through my routine, and then say:


## Stacey had stayed out of the publishing house's politics—


There is an em dash after "politics," one of the few em dashes that I have come across in the manuscript, and I decide to honor the punctuation choice, which means I take a longer pause. Here, as I do many times when performing a book, my mind fills in the rest of the sentence with what I think it should be before I read what the writer has actually written.  In this case, my mind tells me the end should be: *that was her mega-agent's job, to cajole the men and women who held the levers of power into thinking that the once-in-a-generation book deserved a commensurate price tag.*

Almost simultaneously, I am able to see what the writer has actually put on the page—a skill I've developed through centuries in the booth.  Okay, I'm exaggerating, but my ass bears the scars from my wars in that tiny room.  I even gained fifteen pounds once for more cushion—my body pulled a bait and switch on me, cushion went to my gut and not my rear.  Anyway, here is what Big Boss concluded the sentence with: *it was beyond her caring or control.*

Like hell it was.  And now, I do something that I occasionally do when reading a manuscript: I narrate *what I think* the sentence should end with.


—that was her mega-agent's job, to cajole the men and women who held the levers of power into thinking that the once-in-a-generation book deserved a commensurate price tag.


And I'm ready for either Big Boss or Wolverine to stop me.

Nothing happens.  Curious, but I think I know what occurred.  I continue reading a few more lines.  As I do, I look out of the corner of my eye and can see that Wolverine has the glaze-eyed, 10,000-yard stare going on.  I was right.

We've been at this for hours.  Many times, when you've read a book for that long, your mind will start to wander—especially if you reach a dull section like the one I'm reading now: publishing house politics, Kurt's prowess as a publicist, internal bickering about the book's cover…you get the point.  I'm definitely thinking about other things while I read this drivel.

In any event, it looks like Big Boss and Wolverine have glazed right over the improvement I just made to the manuscript, which pains me to know that I've helped in any way. However, I'm being forced to narrate this, I'm bored, and it's impossible for me to suspend all of the habits that have been forged in the crucible of my booth. Okay, okay, I'll knock off the narrator-warrior parallel.

The next line I read is:


**Kurt was being Kurt, and it pissed her off so bad.**


I want to laugh out loud. Perhaps, even the thought of laughing affected my reading, and I expect Big Boss to stop me and have me read the line again. Wouldn't be the first time an author has done this. Even M. Scott Sala contacted me once to let me know how he wanted a particular line read. I listened to him…and then ignored what he had said. That's the thing about authors sometimes: They think that because they wrote the book, they also know how to *perform* it. When an author gives me a line reading over the phone or over Zoom, I usually say in an even tone, while thoughtfully rubbing my chin, "Well, that's definitely one way to deliver it."

Big Boss stays silent, and I continue.

A half-a-dozen more lines come and go, and then I narrate:


**Kurt's handling of the novel *Sacred Stone* by fantasy writer T. Jasmin Oracle had sent shivers through the publishing house when the book underperformed. With the publication of *Converging Affairs* right around the corner, the book that *had* to hit it big, Kurt's boss had been forced to reaffirm the house's confidence in Kurt during a damage-repair interview. When asked, "How are the pre-sale numbers shaping up? Kurt Boar is still handling the launch, correct?" Kurt's boss gave a knowing smile and replied, "Teddy Roosevelt once said, 'Speak**

softly and carry a big stick.' Well, I can tell you, when it comes to promoting books, believe me, Kurt Boar has a big stick."

As my sense of humor overrides my sense of self-preservation, I start to laugh…

…but turn it into a cough, which necessitates a sip of water and the repeat of my recording routine.

There is no reaction at all from Wolverine or Big Boss as I dab my lip balm on my lips. I have survived to narrate some more.

I look at the next lines. Surely, they are about Kurt's boss's regret of turning what is meant to be a complimentary phrase about Kurt's ability as a publicist into an unintended allusion to the size of Kurt's penis.

No such luck. He actually doubles down on the insinuation, for the next line reads:

And like a wave from one of T. Jasmin Oracle's magicians' wands, all was right in the publishing house once more.

Big Boss has been blinded by using a famous quote to perform the heavy lifting that his prose could not without realizing the context in which he has used the quote. Thankfully, there will never be people who read this book, but if there were, then, perhaps, a select few would be taken in by the Roosevelt quote and Merlin's magic to think that Kurt Boar, master publicist, had a firm grasp on the promotion's tiller—Jesus! Now, I'm doing it!—whereas the rest of us would see sticks, wands, and Kurt's member.

The next paragraph wanders into the territory of why Kurt is unreadable, why Stacey should maintain healthy boundaries, and, yet, why she can't quite avoid the magnetism of his charm—a skill he wields with ease as a publicist and one he leverages with bravado as a lover. It's atrocious writing and doesn't follow what had been established in the preceding paragraphs, but at least it gives me a momentary reprieve from Kurt's log of firewood. For heaven's sake, I can't stop. When Big Boss wrote about Kurt's confidence in the sack, I knew I was done. This is the best example I can give you as to why it is difficult for writers to narrate. Normally, I would pause in the booth at this point, get my laughs and insults out of my system, and then go back to performing.

No such luck in this environment. I continue to push through.

A few pages later, I read:


**But Stacey knew who she was, which was to say she knew who she thought she was before being invited into Kurt Boar's bed again.**


Oh, no. He's returning to Kurt's equipment. Maybe he *did* know what he was doing with the Roosevelt quote. I sense an overly described sex scene coming up. Give me streng—

The toilet in the adjoining room flushes.

I pause and casually look over at Wolverine, but all I catch is a glimpse of his wide-open eyes—like he's about to be ripped apart by a pack of raptors—before he's up and running for the door. What is going o—

The toilet flushes again, and I take off my headphones.

The door to my room is wide open, and I can hear a door being opened down the hall.

Then, as soon as it opens, I hear Wolverine yell in a menacing tone, "Oh no, you don't!"

This is followed by a loud reply of, "Fuck you!" from a man's voice. It is so deafening and visceral that I can't determine whether I know or don't know who the owner of the voice is. Then, I hear the sounds of a struggle. Punches, someone being thrown up against a door, then a scream of pain—and I think it's from Wolverine.  I hear a few footsteps in the hall and then bodies hitting the ground like someone just got tackled out there.

More struggling, but the other man yells, "Shawn!  Shawn!  Get out of here! They're never letting us out!"

This time, the words are clearer, and I swallow, shaking in horror as I become aware of who is speaking.

The voice that is calling out to me is one of the most recognizable male voices in the world—in the rarefied lane of Richard Burton and James Earl Jones.  The voice belongs to…

Michael Hunnie.

# 13

"Michael!" I shout and then pull on my chains—so hard that the shackles start to chafe my skin.

I hear struggling again, punches, and cries of pain. There is a huge crash like a table just got knocked over.

"Shawn! Help me!" Michael screams.

I pull even harder on my chains, but there is no way I'm getting free. "I can't get loose, Michael!"

Are those footsteps I hear now, like someone running toward them? A being flashes in front of the doorway and is gone. Big Boss?

"Shawwwwwwwn!"

It is the last word I hear before there is a *CRACK!* that echoes through the hallway.

There is silence for a beat. Then, I hear what sounds like a body being dragged away.

My voice breaks. "No…" then turns to rage. "Michael! Leave him alone!"

There is no reply.

Just more of the dragging sound, getting quieter and quieter. My guess is someone—either Wolverine or Big Boss—is dragging him away from my door, which means that there could be an exit at that end of the hallway. The human being that flashed across the open doorway was coming from the opposite direction, so there must be an exit on that side.

I'm no weapons expert, but I've heard a gunshot before, and the *CRACK!* sounded like one to me. Is Michael dead? Why did they have him here too? And what was Michael's plan to get us out? He obviously knew I was in here. How long has he been down here with me? It was only the other day that I first heard the toilet flush. Was that him and not Wolverine or Big Boss?

I try to imagine what his plan was. First, he must have been restrained in the room next to me but broke free somehow. He couldn't have been chained because there is no way to break loose from those. So, maybe he was strapped down to a cot like me. In terms of keeping him quiet, there are only two options. One: He was gagged somehow, maybe with duct tape over his mouth or a bandanna. But, that would mean that his arms had to be strapped down too because he could remove the gag if his arms and hands were free. Two: He was threatened that if he made any noise, they would hurt or kill me.

Either way, he got free. Now, what would his move be? I'm guessing he flushed the toilet to get Wolverine's attention. Then, Michael hid on the other side of the door and waited for him. From my recollection, as soon as the door opened, the scuffle started. Then what? Michael fought his way into the hall and most likely saw my door open and started yelling. Wolverine and Michael continued to fight, knocked over a table, and then someone—had to be Big Boss—came flying down the hallway, sped past my open doorway, and shot Michael. It couldn't have been Wolverine who shot him because Wolverine isn't armed and has never been since I've been here.

Now, the question becomes: Is Michael Hunnie dead?

I listen.

The dragging has stopped, and now I hear what sounds like a table being stood back up and then items being placed on top of it. The clanging and banging are loud, so I can't tell if a door has been opened at the far end of the hallway and

Michael's body taken through the doorway. Whoever is cleaning up the hallway is making a hell of a lot of noise.

I decide to try and get a response from Michael again. I cannot believe he is being held captive along with me. "Michael! It's Shawn! Are you okay?"

The noise in the hallway stops, and the door to my cell is slammed shut.

I sit still, concentrating, trying to hear anything that might let me know what is going on. There is nothing.

Perhaps a half-hour passes by, and the door to my cell opens. In steps Wolverine. He has a loaded syringe in his right hand, and I notice that he's changed his clothes. There is a huge bruise on the left side of his face. If Michael went down, at least he got in one square hit.

"What's going on?" I ask. "Please tell me that Michael is alive."

He doesn't answer as he continues to approach my seat with calm, even strides—no panic or weariness, he just keeps on coming straight at me.

"Wolverine!"

"Shhh," he says and sits down next to me.

I struggle against my chains.

"Shhh, shhh, shhh, shhh," he continues. Without warning, he grabs my sweatshirt collar and pulls the sweatshirt over my left shoulder and down to my elbow. With an iron grip around my bicep, he steadies my arm and inserts the needle into my shoulder. "There, there, bubba. Done recordin' for the day."

I think I say something back to him in anger, but I blackout before knowing for sure if I said anything at all.

I wake up, strapped down and chained to my cot. The lights are on, and Wolverine is seated next to me. His bruise is gone. How can that be? Wait a minute! One of his eyes is blue—the bluest shade I've seen since Paul Newman's. He must be wearing brown contacts to hide his real eye color! I'm on to you, sir. Blue eyes, a slight limp in the left leg.

Shit.  Or are his real eyes brown in color, and he's just toying with me.  Or are his eyes neither blue nor brown in color, and he's mixing it up to confuse me even more?

It doesn't matter right now.  There is a rubber tube around my upper arm.

"Evenin', sir."  He finds a vein and injects me with heroin.  "Happy time, man."

I hit my high, and everything seems right for the moment.  Zero pain.  Zero bad memories.  Then, I hear my own voice come down from the speaker in the ceiling.  I am narrating the first chapter of *Narrator*.  I sound *good*.  Maybe this book isn't all that bad.

It's the drugs.  C'mon, fight, Frost.

"Big Boss wants you to listen to your work before you start in again tomorrow.  We couldn't be happier with how it's gone."

From the speaker, I hear myself say:

**The first surprise in Monsieur Bernstein's morning came at the roundabout waking hour of nine a.m., when morning chores are long past due and morning coffee calls like a disregarded muse to the artist-in-residence.**

Stop listening and concentrate.  Form the sentence in your brain before you say it.  *Where is Michael Hunnie?*  There, you've got it.  I turn my head toward Wolverine.

"Your eyes are lookin' cheery-wacko, man.  You feelin' the rush?"

"Where is Michael Hunnie?"

He grins at me.  "Who?"

I swallow.  He's making fun of me, I'm sure of it.  "*Where* is Michael Hunnie?"

"Michael Hunnie?  The greatest audiobook narrator ever?"  He gives me a pat on my shoulder.  "No offense, Shawn."

"Yes, Michael Hunnie, the audiobook narrator who fought with you in the hall?"

His laugh is so boisterous and silly, and the brown sugar is doing its job on me that I join in and laugh.

"Man, that's a humdinger if I ever heard one. The stuff I've been pumpin' into you *must* be good. There's no one down here but you, sir. Now, between you and me," he whispers as if Big Boss won't hear, "Michael Hunnie is my favorite narrator, always has been, always will be, and if he was down here, you can bet your doped-up butt that you wouldn't be. Too high profile for us to borrow from society for a few days. You readin' me?"

It makes sense, and he's right: I am *gone* and shouldn't be trying to make any kind of conversation right now. I'll have to wait until the morning. "I read you," I say.

"Good, now you have yourself a nice little trippy, and I'll bring in some dinner after a while. For right now, just concentrate on your performance. We'll be hittin' it hard and heavy tomorrow."

I watch as he takes his chair and places it next to the one I use for narrating. He gives me a thumbs-up, turns out the lights, and leaves the room.

From the speaker, I now hear myself say:

The phone call from Stacey, his ex-lover of a thousand nights, had thrown Robbie Bernstein back into the cauldron of "what if" potion. What if they had had a child together? What if he hadn't gotten scared when she mentioned the word *marriage*? What *if* their nights together on the beach in St. Thomas had stretched another few days?

The words start to fade, and the bright lasers and brilliantly-colored balloons appear behind the shade of my eyelids. I'm floating, hand-in-hand with Bing Bong from *Inside Out*, over the chasm where, moments ago, Shawn Frost Reality Island fell into the darkness. I think I say, "Don't worry, we're clear of any danger, Bing Bong," before slipping away.

I wake up. Wolverine is right next to me again. His eyes are back to being brown. Did I dream that one was blue? Don't know. I'm groggy. He gets me up, and we do the bathroom routine. There is no sitting down at the desk; I stand up from the toilet, and Wolverine hands me my dinner—a glassful of thick goop from a blender. Tastes like peanut butter and chocolate, so I'm fine with it. He leads me back to the cot, straps me down, and injects a needle into my right shoulder. For the first time, I'm unsure about what might have happened with Michael Hunnie. Was I doped up? Was he really down here? I know what I said about how everyone hates him, but the truth is…he *is* the best. And…

He's my favorite narrator.

Michael Hunnie might be dead.

I hope my favorite narrator is not dead.

All I know is that…why are my eyes so heavy?

Michael Hunnie.

Is it possible that…I can't hold my eyes open.

No! Fight it, Frost.

Michael Hunnie.

What's going on?

Wait. May…maybe…

"Good mornin', good MORNIN'!" Wolverine says, entering the room and flipping on the lights. I expect the normal routine of bathroom, breakfast, hydration, and then recording. I want to talk about Michael. I am also starting to get the itch for another fix. It's not the worst that it's ever been, but I'm starting to think about it more, which is bad news for me.

I get to use the bathroom, but then I'm taken back over and strapped down to the bed. My arms are also chained to the floor.

"Aren't we recording this morning?"

"We are," he says, walking out of the room for a few seconds and then returning.

He has a loaded syringe and rubber tubing.

My breathing gets shallow because my body wants the drug, but I'm also confused. "I thought that was only in the afternoons?"

"Oh, this here is nuthin'. Just a little quarter dose to get you up and movin'."

I've never narrated while under the influence. "I don't know what I'll be able to do after I've had it," I say as he ties the rubber tube around my arm and looks for a vein.

"We got faith, man."

He injects me.

I awake in the dark once more, oblivious to the time. What did he give me? I felt the rush at first but then something else. My mind is foggy, and with the room as pitch black as it was when I first woke up down here, it is impossible to get my bearings. My body is also achy.

I concentrate on my breathing. Control what you can control, Frost. I inhale for four beats, hold it for four beats, and then exhale it for four beats. I complete four cycles of this, and it does calm me a bit, but what bothers me is that I can't remember what happened from the time Wolverine injected me until moments ago when I woke up. I squeeze my eyes shut as if this exertion will bring everything into focus.

It does not.

I relax my eyes and realize that I tensed up too much while trying to recall what happened because now I feel like someone has just strummed a set of guitar strings in my brain. This is only temporary, though, because I am now aware of my sore, empty stomach. My mouth is dry, and I know I'm dehydrated, but I am hungry like I've never been before.

How long have I been out?

I can't even remember if I had water after Wolverine shot me up. He's been pretty good about getting me what I need. The human body can absorb one liter of water per hour, but during the first hour that you are awake, your body can absorb two liters of water since you are dehydrated after a night of sleep. He started with plastic water bottles but got annoyed with how many trips he was taking. So, he took my advice and brought in a gallon jug of water. I drank half of it to start the day, and he refilled it twice throughout the morning.

I lick my lips and try to work up some saliva in my mouth so that I can swallow. As I do this, a sick feeling comes over me—a realization that makes me not want to try and swallow.

Do it. You have to know.

I swallow…

The pain is immense.

Say something. I say, "Shawn Fr—" and that is all the further I get. My voice is hoarse, and I haven't felt anything like this since I narrated for thirteen hours straight on my first book and woke up the next day with no voice. I panicked and called Corie, who scolded me with, *'You dumbass, you're going to kill your voice, dear brother. Our profession is a marathon, not a sprint, and you have to take care of your biggest asset.'*

I close my eyes and go through four cycles of my breathing routine. Bake gave me this trick to help calm myself down. Sweet Jesus, if I ever get out of this nightmare, he is going to earn his pay.

I sniffle. *Ouch!* I haven't felt that kind of pain since…

My God. Some of what happened is coming back to me. I remember sitting next to Wolverine and narrating. He's…he's rubbing my back? *'That left eye don't hurt no more, does it, bubba?'* I reply, *'Shit no, brother!'* Now we're laughing. There's a five-gallon bucket on the floor in front of the chair, and I'm pissing into it. Now he's passing me a full jug of water. *'Drink up, and then whip that snake out whenever you need to. I'll take care of the bucket. We're gettin' efficient, Shawn!'* Now he's placing a piece of paper on top of the towel, pouring white powder out of what looks like a sugar packet that is too big to be a sugar packet. He's waving a plastic straw through the air as if conducting a symphony. Then he changes posture and points with it at the small pile of white powder—a magician who just cast a spell. He hands me the straw, and I sniff. I narrate. I make noise with the chains…and don't care that I do.

Do I remember any of the lines that I narrated? At the moment, no. Wait a minute, is Michael Hunnie sitting on a chair next to us now? Was the fight earlier one big joke they played on me? Is *Michael Hunnie* behind all of this? No, it can't be. What would he gain by having me kidnapped, tortured, and forced to narrate a horrible book? Nothing I can think of. Now Hunnie has disappeared, and so has the chair he was sitting on. I am aware that there is someone else in the room while I'm recording, but I can't make out who it is. He's standing at the door watching. Big Boss? Bing Bong? No earthly clue.

Then, a recording situation—not a line—comes back to me. I just finished a sentence that ran on for *eight pages*. Big Boss's voice says, *'Ha! That's my Faulkner section.'* I hear myself saying, *'This is not Faulkner. You are not Faulkner. Your name will never be in the same sentence, page, or book as Faulkner.'* Is there punishment doled out due to my rebellious spirit? No. I must have merely thought those words.

It's later, and Big Boss is screaming at me. *'Do the different voices, Shawn!'* And I'm crying, and I can't stop crying. I sob and reply, *'I can only be me.'* He yells, *'Stop crying!'* I say, *'I can't.'*

It's later still, and I'm floating again.  I pause from recording and say with absolute conviction, *'This is the most important and beautiful book I have ever performed—an instant classic.'*  Wolverine is clapping, and I'm recording again.  But, the effect of whatever combo of drugs that they're giving me is wearing off, and I suddenly become aware once again of the nightmare I'm in.  I lean on Langella like I have my entire playwrighting career.  *'Focus!  Leverage the day's events into one's evening performance.  Let it feed your presentation.  Goddammit, Shawn, learn the lines, know what they mean, and mean them when you say them!'*  I'm breaking.  I stop reading the manuscript and yell at the top of my lungs, *'I used to run the hundred in ten flat!  I'll be back with the whole fire department!'*  Big Boss slaps me, then injects me.  I'm reading again.  Then the magic straw wand is out, and I'm sniffing and narrating, narrating and sniffing.  And, that's it.

I open my eyes, and darkness is all I see now.  If it *was* Michael who yelled, *'Shawn!  Shawn!  Get out of here!  They're never letting us out!'* then he was right; if *I* said those things to myself as some sort of way to cope with the trauma I am experiencing, then *I* was right.  I am going to die here, and there's so much I've never said to the people I love.  I wasn't ready.  I—

The moment overwhelms me.  My chin shakes, and I sob.

A few minutes later, I cease sobbing as a line pops into my head.


**"The hell with nostalgia," Robbie said, exiting his closet studio.  "I'm going to finish this in the basement booth and expunge both this novel and Stacey Groff from my life."**


And I realize that I had *finished* narrating the book.

The door opens, and Wolverine enters.  He whistles the tune of Carole King's *It's Too Late* as he turns on the lights.

I fight to adjust my eyes as fast as possible.  I can see him going for a chair, and then he comes into focus as he approaches the bed.

Two loaded syringes are in his huge right hand, along with the rubber tubing.

"Been a pleasure workin' with ya, bubba," he says, pulling up a chair.

My brain sends my body an all caps, bold-faced message on my nervous system's superhighway that reads: *DEATH IS IMMINENT. FIGHT, FROST!* My body goes into all-out panic mode, and I devote every ounce of energy to trying to break free. I'm gonna pull a Sloth here from *The Goonies* and rip these motherfuckin' chains out and strangle this bastard to death. Then, I'm gonna head upstairs and plunge these syringes into Big Boss's flesh and watch him squirm before I kill *him*.

And so I pull on the chains while contorting my body in every direction I can. I scream and sling insults out of my mouth that would ex-communicate me from the civilized world. I think I'm getting the chains loose…

My arms drop, and I gasp for breath; Wolverine sits peacefully on his chair and says, "Damn."

He ties the rubber band around my arm.

"No! I don't want to die!" I scream.

He picks back up with his whistling, finds the nice big blue vein of mine that he's been using, and inserts the needle.

The rush comes on like a red-hot locomotive. Euphoria. Madness. Wolverine is moving his hand toward my shoulder with the second syringe…

# PART II

~~Strikethrough~~

# 14

## Santa Monica, June 2023

"Your full name, please?" the nurse at the UCLA Santa Monica Medical Center check-in counter says.

"Joann Mansfield," I say. C'mon, I was here last night—well, the emergency room anyway.

She types it in, presses enter, and then squints at her computer screen. "Right, you visited yesterday. Not my shift." She looks up at me. "Let me check with nurse Dee and see if he's allowed visitors right now."

She slides out from behind the desk and then shuffles down the hall.

They told me last night that visiting hours started at 8:00 a.m., and it's 8:02 a.m. I choose not to say anything and take a seat and start sipping on my coffee. The hot liquid is soothing and strong. I need it. My smartwatch beeps, and it's a message—I reached my exercise goal for the day. Big surprise. After getting almost no sleep last night, I took a run this morning to clear my head. The past ten hours have been a relief and a nightmare.

The hallway is empty and quiet, which is a change from last night, with lots of screaming, crying, confusion, disappointment—you name it. I'm nervous to see Shawn—the *real* Shawn Frost. I'm still trying to make sense of the person I saw strapped down to the hospital bed last night. He was Shawn Frost in name, but that was not the man I have been dating for the past two years.

The nurse comes out of a room at the far end of the hall and starts her long journey toward me. She appears to be in no hurry.

Will he be able to speak to me today? Will he even be coherent? The things he was shouting last night…

The nurse returns to her station, but before she sits down in her rolling chair, she says, "You can see him now, Ms. Mansfield. Last room on the right. You'll see his name." She pauses, as if she's weighing the option of saying something more to me. "You were here last night, so you know that…" Her voice trails off.

That my famous audiobook narrator boyfriend, a recovering heroin addict, has had a relapse and was out of his mind last night? Yes. That he's going to go through hell as he fights withdrawal? Yes. That no one knows where in the hell he's been the past week? Yes.

Again.

However, it's never been this bad. He's disappeared for a few days before but not ever for a week. And never because he was using heroin again. Looking back, I can't say I'm totally surprised. He lost his favorite and money-making character, and he lost at the Audies.

Yeah, feeling a bit guilty, like I should have seen this coming and helped him. But, we haven't seen a lot of each other since New York. Still, that's no excuse.

"Yes," I say.

She gives me a sympathetic and knowing nod. Working in this ward, she must give them all of the time. And both of us know that part of her nod is an acknowledgment of the fact that most of the residents in the rooms that line this hallway will be dead within a year, six months, maybe sooner. They'll be dead because this kind of addiction is the hardest to beat.

Before I entered high school, my father showed me the film *Days of Wine and Roses*. It was the first time I ever saw what being addicted to a drug could do to someone's life. The lines, *"It's a lottery, Joe. And you lost,"* are running through my mind right now.

Speaking of movies, I remember screening *Apocalypse Now* in a collegiate film course. At the immediate conclusion of *Apocalypse Now*, my professor kept the lights off in the auditorium, and we all sat in the darkness for a few minutes. I wanted to whisper to a fellow classmate, but my mind was so disturbed by what I had just witnessed that all I could think about was the film and what everything in it meant. Then, the doors at the rear of the auditorium opened, and my professor stood in one of the two doorways and said, *'Class is dismissed.'* As we all shuffled out, he and his graduate assistant handed us a program of white paper that had the credits for the film written in black ink. It was then that I realized that there had been no end credits and thought it odd. Had I ever seen a film that did not have end credits? I didn't think so. The next class, my professor came in and told us that what we had experienced was what Francis Ford Coppola had been able to execute for the first few screenings of the film until the studio made him insert an end credit sequence. He went on to explain, *'So, my lovely intellectual sponges, if film is the most powerful medium ever invented for swaying opinions and* Apocalypse *is the greatest anti-war film ever made, and Coppola had the undivided attention of his audience, in a voluntary experience—no one was made to pay money to see the film in the theater, right?—and, after the film, he engineered a singular moment of reflection by keeping the theaters dark and eliminating the end credit sequence, a sequence which has always been a psychological cue for audiences to return to reality, how successful has he been in the past thirty years of eliminating war?'* At that point, we all scrolled through our memories, counting the number of conflicts that had occurred in the past three decades around the world—the number recalled depending on the quality of our social studies classes and our own knowledge of history. When he had given us enough time to think on it, he said, *'So, you all believe that your generation is destined for greatness, you're all activists that are going to improve the human condition and leave the world better than you found it. Your generation will be the one to. Get. It. Right. This is noble, and I wish you well on your journey. I'm sweating alongside you right now and will cheer you on one day from the bleachers when I've left the field. But, in this pursuit, like anyone who has ever tried to change society, you need to know what you're up against. And that is what older generations owe you as you start. Well, ladies and gentlemen,'* he said as he scanned the room, making eye contact with as many people as possible. Then, he displayed the words *Apocalypse Now* on the screen, held up one of the programs he had passed out in class, and said, *'Thirty plus years ago. There are your real odds.'* And he walked out of class.

Those words, *'There are your real odds,'* echo through my mind as I give a quick stare of acknowledgment back at the nurse and then take my first steps toward Shawn's room. After being clean for five-plus years, what caused him to go off the rails? And now, what are his real odds of recovering? But, from what the P.I. that David Killian hired to find him told us back during the first twenty-four hours that Shawn went missing, the larger questions for me are as follows: *How long has he been hiding his relapse?* and *How did I not see it?*

I pause outside of his room. The horror of what I saw and heard last night has not left me, and I suspect that it won't. "He hurt you. He's not himself. But, you love him," I say. "He's alive. Start there." I open the door and enter. The overhead lights are off, but a butter-yellow shaft of sunlight streams down through the window and illuminates a rectangular section of the white blanket draped across Shawn's body. A nurse, nurse Dee I presume, is by his bedside and giving his shoulder a pat. His head is turned toward her face; he has not heard me come in.

"Look who is here," she says to Shawn.

He slowly rotates his head until he sees me.

I'm still not used to seeing him with a week-old beard—it comes in thicker than I imagined it would.

"Jo," he whispers. I didn't hear much of my name but know what he said by the way he moved his lips, the 'O' making them end in a kiss.

She motions me to stay where I'm at so that we can speak before I approach Shawn.

"I'll be right back, Shawn," she says to him. "Going to tell her how well you're doing today."

"Okay," he whispers back.

I give him a wave.

He doesn't wave back, but he moves his cheek muscles, looks like with some difficulty, into something that resembles a smile, and then closes his eyes. Well, his right eye anyway; the left eye is pretty much swollen shut.

"Hi, I'm nurse Dee," she says. "Let's back up just a touch closer to the door."

"I'm Jo Mansfield, Shawn's girlfriend," I reply, following her lead back to the door.

We stop, and she glances back at Shawn. His eyes are still closed.

"He's still sedated, so you won't be able to talk much with him. But, as you just saw, he is coherent enough to know that people are in the room. Someone from the Laguna Treatment Hospital will be here at nine-thirty to pick him up."

She's whispering, and I don't think that there is any way that Shawn can hear her. "I was here last night," I whisper back.

"I know. My friend, nurse Tammy told me." Her eyes get big. "Rough night."

"It was. Tammy was a Godsend. I can't believe how calm she was throughout the whole thing."

"Just another day in this wing," Dee says. "Unfortunately."

She's not being crass or trite. She's being honest—an honesty born of repeated exposure to an ugliness that most people have never witnessed and will never witness. I wouldn't last a day working here. "I don't know where to begin."

"It's okay. Most people don't. This your first time seeing him or anyone like this?"

"Yes."

"During my turnover with Tammy this morning, I learned that his parents and sister were at the hospital in New York the last time this happened. They're flying in later this morning, right?"

I nod. I've only met Shawn's parents twice: Christmas last year—we flew to Detroit, cold as hell—and at the Audies.

"I'm picking them up at LAX in a few hours. Then, we'll head over to Laguna."

"And his agent…"

"David Killian."

"Yes, thanks. Tammy told me that he said he'd be coming over this morning too."

"He called me half an hour ago. Should be here anytime."

"Good. Just wanted to confirm who was coming so I could direct the flow of visitors. Any time something like this happens, it's important that the patient sees people that care for him and that he trusts. I read your statement last night where you made a list."

"David and I are the only ones who will be visiting him here this morning. His best friend, Corie Woods, and Corie's boyfriend Matt will see him over at Laguna."

"That's fine. The staff at Laguna will work with Shawn to see what he's comfortable with and arrange the in-person visits if he's up to it. The next few days will be tough as he goes through their detox program." She turns back toward him for a second. "He's going to continue to experience awful withdrawal symptoms."

"Like the nausea, sweating, and shaking?"

"This morning, we added abdominal pain."

I can feel tears starting to form in my eyes. I look over her shoulder at him resting. "How long?"

"We're using medicine to help him right now, and therapy will start over at Laguna. But, to answer your question, withdrawal symptoms usually start six to twelve hours after the last dose, with the symptoms peaking 1 to 3 days after. In a week or so, the symptoms will start to subside. With how he was when Mr. Killian found him last night, we estimate that he's in the peak period right now." She puts a reassuring hand on my shoulder. "The Laguna facility is wonderful, though, so hang in there. Normally, Shawn would have been taken straight there, but the symptoms he was exhibiting last night necessitated that he be brought here first."

"Not everyone in his hallway is going to Laguna, though, right?"

There is a hint of a frown as she says, "Not everyone can afford it. I'll step outside and give you some time. Press the call button by his bed if you need anything."

She moves past me and exits.

I walk over and give him a kiss on the forehead before sitting down in the chair beside his bed.

He turns his head and opens his right eye. The left eye is pink and purple and puffy and difficult to look at. "Hi," he says.

"Hi."

He reaches his left hand out, and I take it in mine.

"Jo—"

His voice is now above a whisper.

"—I don't know what I said last night, but I'm sorry if I scared you—you and Killy, right? You're the only ones I remember."

I squeeze his hand. "Yes, we were both here."

"Okay. We have to move fast if we're going to catch who did this to me." He looks down at my smartwatch. "My phone. My phone is one piece to the puzzle. I don't know for sure, but I think I had it on me when I left Doctor Baker's office after I finished an appointment with him. If we can go back and track—"

A tear escapes my left eye and travels down my cheek. Even in this diminished state, he still has an energy about him that pulls people in. It's one of his gifts. But I can't let that charisma influence me right now. "Shawn, we found your phone."

He closes his eye. "Thank God. We need to get a detective on it. I'm sure that Bake has cameras on the outside of his building. I know I was close to the building when they took me."

I wasn't sure what he would say, but he has now confirmed the worst. I didn't want to believe it when the detective sat David Killian and me down a day after Shawn had disappeared, but after last night and what Shawn just said, I know the detective was right.

"Shawn?"

"Yes, my love, what is it?"

I put my other hand on top of his and hold his hand between my hands. "You're sick, sweetie, and we're going to get you some help."

"What? I don't know what you mean. I was kidnapped and drugged on purpose. It looks like I've had a relapse, but you have to believe me, Jo."

Time to be real, and this breaks my heart. "You saw Doctor Baker last week?"

"Yes. Absolutely I did. Talked a ton of stuff through. Why are you asking me this?"

I watch the fingers on his right hand start to dance on the blanket. There's sweat beading on his forehead. Is he lying, or does he not understand? I look into his eyes, and I honestly can't tell.

But one thing is certain.

"Shawn, we called Doctor Baker. You haven't seen him for the past month."

# 15

I watch as my boyfriend goes through a cycle of the breathing exercise he introduced me to as a result of his sessions with his psychologist—his *real* psychologist. He inhales for four seconds, holds his breath for four seconds, and then exhales for four seconds. We've done this routine together many times before: ten minutes when we wake up in the morning, five minutes before having sex, five minutes before making a big decision, five minutes before exercising, five minutes before going to sleep, and so forth. He's attempting to calm his mind. I just hit him with something big. I've waited four days to do it, so I'm anxious to see how he responds. I won't follow up with *By the way, who is Jenna?*' yet, but you better believe it's on my mind. And I already know the answer. He's injured me. He's betrayed my trust.

"Of course, I've seen him," he says. "Didn't you just hear me? I think I left my phone there."

He chose to continue the lie. How long has he been lying to me? And, how many things has he been lying to me about? I let go of his left hand and take a sip of my coffee. He now starts a routine of grabbing his blanket and then releasing it as if a hand grip exerciser is in his grasp.

The door opens, and nurse Dee ushers in the tall, muscular form of David Killian. Good. Some backup will help here, and Killian doesn't mince his words.

"Everything okay?" Nurse Dee asks.

I look at Shawn, and he nods.

Nurse Dee exits, and Killian pulls up a chair next to me and sits down.

He looks better than last night. I've never seen David Killian look so disheveled as he did when I arrived here just before eleven—jogging pants and running shoes with vomit on them, a torn t-shirt from his altercation with Shawn, and no designer glasses. This morning is more of what I'm used to. Expensive loafers, tan dress slacks, collared shirt, gold rings on his huge, immaculately-manicured brown hands, and black designer glasses. I can see he's touched up his hair and whiskers overnight, and now there is a never-ending, perfect five o'clock shadow that covers his face and head. He's wearing a hint of cologne. He has a commanding presence of relief and security, a vibe that announces to the room, *'Order has been restored.'* He takes a drink of his own coffee—the small cup looks ridiculous in his hand—and sets the cup down on the windowsill.

Shawn starts in. "Killy, I'm sorry about last night. I didn't mean to go after you. I don't even know how I got near Pacific Palisades. I know I was on something, but I didn't mean to go after you. I was out of my goddamned head."

Killian peers into Shawn's eyes.

"I just told him that we know he hasn't seen Doctor Baker in a month," I say.

"Killy, that's insane. I—"

"Shut up. Right now," Killian cuts him off. He isn't yelling, but his words carry the weight of a yell. I'd shut the hell up. "You're in a mess, and I'm going to try and get you out of it. Against all odds, your disappearance and reemergence haven't made the news. And I'm going to fight to keep it that way. In a little bit, you're going over *quietly* to the Laguna facility where you're going to detox." He crosses his big legs. "Now, about your psychologist—"

"I saw him last week!"

"Do you know where the police found your phone?" He doesn't wait for Shawn's answer. "In a second-floor apartment rented by a one Jeffrey Calliope. Name ring a bell? How about his drug-dealer nickname? *Doctor Baker.*"

I see it in Shawn's eyes. He's caught.

Killian leans in. "The real Roman I. Baker, who you are supposed to be seeing, told us you canceled the last two appointments. After seeing you for years, he didn't think anything was wrong since you told him you were late on an audiobook deadline. He's been worried about you since you disappeared last week, like everyone in your life has. I phoned him this morning and told him you were still alive. He'll be working with the Laguna staff, and you better pour your fucking heart out to that man. You hear me?"

Shawn looks down and fixates his gaze on the portion of the blanket covering his feet.

Killian isn't done, and there is no way I'm cutting in right now. "The detective I hired and the police went to Calliope's drug den—upscale apartment complex a few blocks from here, near Memorial Park—and found your phone underneath a couch that Calliope's girlfriend, Portia, was passed out on when they busted down the door. *Doctor* Baker tried to get away through a rear entrance, but the police caught him on the stairs. With the paraphernalia they found in that apartment, he's going away for a long time." Killian reaches back, grabs his coffee cup, and takes a big gulp.

I take a sip of mine.

Killian puts his back while saying, "I don't even know where to start with you. How long have you been using?"

Shawn shrugs.

"Don't give me that shrugging garbage! Your *life* is on the line. Your *career* is on the line."

I'm not into the good cop bad cop routine—not into routines, period, except for the breathing deal—but Shawn could use a little light here. "Shawn, we need to know. This is serious."

He makes eye contact with me, then braves a stare at Killian. Enough time passes for me to take another drink. "A few weeks after the Audies."

"So, a couple of months," Killian says. "Now I'm hearing the truth because that's pretty much what Calliope told the police when they sweated the sonofabitch. It also matches the story the detective was putting together when he reviewed your phone's location for the past few months and your credit card record. I sat with him and watched on a huge screen in his office like I was watching some damned video game, as your phone traveled back and forth to L.A. since March. First few times were in your car, weren't they?"

Shawn can't look at him.

"He switched the screen and showed me the gas station purchases on your credit card, like a little trail of breadcrumbs along the PCH. Then, you started flying as you became more addicted, right."

"Forty-seven-minute flight, about an hour and seven minutes gate to gate, beats over six hours in the car," Shawn says, still not looking at either of us.

"Calliope must have lived up to his nickname. I didn't understand why you didn't drive ten minutes into Monterey to get your stuff."

"I didn't start out using heroin when I first went down there. Just some weed and a little coke. Heard about the guy when I was in L.A. a year ago recording a book. The sound engineer casually mentioned that he got his stuff from 'The Best Doctor in Santa Monica.'" He turns toward us. "It was only when I started shooting up that I began flying down. I knew from New York that eventually, I would have to find a dealer closer because I'd start needing it more often. Baker was ready to set me up with someone he knew in Monterey."

I can see the pain in his face as he admits this. He's a master at hiding things, but I learned today that when he's caught, he doesn't continue the charade. On some level, I can work with someone like that.

Killian peers up at the ceiling. "What in the hell were you thinking?"

Shawn grits his teeth and says, "But there were two men who kidnapped me!"

But, he's also human and can only admit his guilt for so long. He just pulled one of his favorite moves that he uses with me when we get into arguments that he starts losing. Misdirection.

Killian shakes his head. "Listen, man, you have been on some harsh shit for months now. I don't know how I could have missed it. Looking back last night, I should have picked up on the fact that you were wearing long-sleeved t-shirts every time I saw you and that you canceled a few of our Zoom calls. But you were still functioning enough to record, and I didn't think anything else was up. So, I own that. But, you have got to let this crazy story go. If the press or any bloggers get a hold of it, you are finished, my friend."

"I was in a cell, pissing myself, and forced to narrate—"

"Bullshit!" Killian explodes. "You were on some five or six-day bender in some godforsaken place, which we'll probably never know about, doing heroin and whatever else the toxicology report shows."

"They shot me up repeatedly with some kind of tranquilizer."

Killian exhales. "Right, to put you to sleep so that you could wake up rested and record an audiobook about an audiobook narrator who almost gets killed in his booth or his house or whatever you shouted last night. Nonsense." He exhales again. "Now, I'm with you; you shot up all kinds of dope wherever you were and haven't been right in the head for a week. You got socked in the face and the stomach, and who knows what's up with your wrists. Bottom line: Somebody roughed you the hell up. From what the police told me, this kind of stuff happens all the time, but you know what the difference is? Most people don't make it out. They die. Do you know how lucky you are to even be alive?"

"Killy, they had Michael Hunnie. I swear it."

Killian laughs. "I must say that *that* won the award for the most ridiculous thing you said last evening." He pauses. "Well, that and you yelling, 'Killy, there's coke in the backseat' right before you threw up on me."

I almost laugh. I had never heard my boyfriend rap before last night.

"It's tru—"

"No. It's not." He laughs again. "I can't believe I did this, but you know what I did for you last night after we had you admitted here and sedated? Well, the first thing I did when I got home was throw away my clothes that you puked all over. Then, I took a shower. And while I was drying off, I delivered a profanity-laced monologue in my bathroom about how my client, in a drug-induced rage, had just told me that the best audiobook narrator in the world, one that had recently beaten him for Best Male Narrator, the one and only, Michael Hunnie, had been in a prison cell next to him and had made a valiant effort to escape. It was so outrageous that after I slipped into my pajamas, robe, and slippers, I called Hunnie's agent last night, made up some excuse about me wondering if Michael had any new deals coming up or any gossip about M. Scott Sala, which he's always good for. Of course, he did, and then I slid in my question about where Michael was right now. Know what he said? He told me that Michael was away at his cabin retreat in Utah, outside of St. George. Goes there every June for a month alone—doesn't even take his girlfriend—wants to be by himself with no distractions and no contact. Every July first, he returns to L.A. for the 4th of July festivities and then starts work again on July 6th. He's done this for two decades now. He asked me about you, and I lied my ass off. Told him you were still a bit down after the Stone series ended."

Killian reaches over and wraps his left hand around Shawn's left forearm; he avoids the wrist because it has scrapes and bruises—the doctors couldn't determine what they were from. I admit it is interesting that he has similar marks on both wrists, but the underground L.A. drug culture, including Santa-no-it-doesn't-happen-around-here-because-rent-costs-too-much-Monica, is known for all kinds of brutality, and the detective and police who worked Shawn's case told us that being chained up and beaten are things that have happened before. They didn't find any chains at Calliope's crack house, but they did find heavy-duty cable ties, rope, handcuffs, needles, syringes, rubber tubing, handguns, shotguns, knives, machetes, bundles of cash, and enough cocaine, weed, and heroin to trip half the city's residents. It scares me to imagine what happened to him over the past week. In any event, Killian enclosing Shawn's forearm in his hand is not an aggressive gesture but rather one reserved, I suspect, for a long-time friend who is in pain as well. Killian is larger than life, but he has always had a soft spot in his heart for Shawn. Like me. It's hard not to. He's so damned vulnerable and likable. "Shawn, I'm your agent, and I'm your friend. Michael Hunnie was not with you in some basement cell complex the past few days because *you weren't* in some basement cell complex the past few days." Killian swallows, glances at the ground, and then bores his eyes into Shawn's right eye, which is glassy now. I can always tell when Shawn is going to cry. The major tell is when his chin starts to vibrate—like it is right now. "We're going to get you into Laguna. You're going to get clean. I'm going to surround you with people who love you. Your parents and sister are on their way. Corie and Matt will be there too. And, of course, Jo, who never left your side last night until the hospital staff kicked us out. Dr. Baker is going to help you figure out what happened, and then, when you're ready, we'll talk about getting you working again."

And that does it. Shawn not only sobs but sobs so hard that moans accompany the irregular breaths and flood of tears. I start crying, putting aside my anger and disbelief for the moment.

Killian releases Shawn's forearm, grabs his coffee cup, and stands. "I'll check with the nurse to see if the Laguna transport is on its way yet." He gives my shoulder a rub, which is a lot for David Killian.

"Thanks, David," I say.

He exits, and Shawn and I cry until we both reach the point where a body simply cannot produce any more tears, and breathing becomes regular again. I hand him a few tissues and then wipe my eyes with another handful.

I kiss him on the forehead and sit back down.

"If they had my phone and checked the numbers I've called and who I've texted, then I'm sure you know…"

He can't finish the sentence.

"About Jenna?"

He nods.

"Yes. They questioned her, and she told them that she had been seeing you for the past few months. Even let them search her house without a warrant because she was so concerned."

"And you're still here?" He starts to cry again.

"We've shared a lot," I say.

"Oh, Jo, don't leave me. Please? I screwed up. I *am* screwed up right now, but if you let me work things out at the clinic and get my mind right, sort through what's real and what's not, then I want to repair what I've done. I. Don't. Love. Her. I fell apart after I lost in March, and I need to find out why that happened." He grabs the blanket with both hands and squeezes like he's trying to crush two beer cans. "Oh, please don't give up on me, Jo. I still love you—"

His voice is breaking again.

"—more than ever."

And I know that he does. But I can't commit to anything right now—not without answers. I want to unload on him, but I can't. Perhaps later, but not right now—not when this talented, broken man needs to see some light. "I promise that we'll talk after detox, okay?"

He nods three times quickly and tries to say something, but all Shawn Frost can do is sob.

*3 Weeks Later...*

# 16

## Carmel-by-the-Sea

I am clean and back home.  No real other way to put it—it's what my life has become at this moment in time.  I report my drug status: clean.  And I report my location: home.  Everything for me, and I mean everything, starts with those two markers.  Once those are established, I check in with the rest of myself and proceed accordingly each second, each hour, each day.  It's been a helluva three weeks since I woke up in a hospital and had Jo and Killy peer into my brain.

It's a quarter past eight in the evening, and Jo and I are seated in separate Adirondack chairs on my back deck, about to observe one of the most stunning sights that the earth has to offer: a cloudless, orange sunset over the vast Pacific blue.  The end of June marks the latest that sunsets occur in Carmel-by-the-Sea, but here on July 6th, the sun still sets around 8:30, and the glow keeps the horizon lit for some time after.  The march toward earlier and earlier sunsets has begun, reaching the earliest setting time around 4:50 p.m. in early December and then climbing later and later toward summer.  Why do I know these details?  One, because I live here. Two, because when you are clean, you have a lot more time each day to think about matters like what time the sun sets and what time it rises and how many times you urinate during the day.

Jo is drinking coffee; I'm drinking tea.

"I'm glad you came over tonight," I say.

"I wanted to say what I had to say in person. Thank you for being understanding."

Over dinner—Mediterranean salad, warm bread dipped in olive oil, water with a twist of lemon—she ended our relationship. I can't blame her. I shattered the trust we had between us, and I betrayed her and the loving bond we shared—the relationship that we had built. I hurt her.

Do I want her back immediately? Yes. But it's over. And I have no feelings of anger or frustration toward her, only regret. She could have left the moment she found out about Jenna, but instead, she stuck with me through rehab and attended some of my counseling sessions with Dr. Baker. I discovered why I ran to Jenna when things went south months ago, and now Jo understands why too. I was jealous of Jo. She got to be an actress. At first, I was able to keep the spirit of the theater alive in myself by watching her perform. Then, after a while, I grew to resent it. Each conversation, each opening night, and each time I ran lines with her, I was reminded that, because of my addiction, I was no longer able to be a part of that world.

I was also intimidated by Jo because of how good an actress she was—still is. She admitted that she was somewhat intimidated by me but that she found our conversations about the stage invigorating and enriching. I suppose I hid my resentment well. And Jo was sympathetic throughout our entire relationship, always asking, *'Are you okay talking about this?'* I said I was. In the beginning, I meant it. But at some point, I did realize that even the mere mention of the theater was chewing me up; at that point, my answers became lies.

However, our newfound clarity of why things happened the way they did does not change the fact that I ran into the arms and eventually into the bed of another woman and have to face the consequences. Not wanting to take responsibility for my actions was a major theme unearthed through the past few weeks of intensive counseling—we're talking two to three sessions per day; Bake was a lion. By the way, Jenna ended our…well, whatever we were, a day after I completed detox. She figured that I was in a safe enough environment for her to pull the plug without me falling off the wagon again. She did not want to wait and risk initiating another relapse if she told me when I was back on my own, found a box of my things that I had apparently left at her place on my front porch when Corie drove me home a few days ago. I never opened it—threw it immediately in the trash. Thoughtful as she believed she was being, she assigned herself too much importance in my life. I was relieved when she cut me off early.

Jo is another matter. I want things to be like they were before I screwed up, but those days are gone. History. I can't bring them back. Knowing that we'll be moving on without each other has been crushing to accept. But, tonight's discussion was not a surprise. We had actually talked about the relationship ending in the last few sessions at Laguna with Bake. Tonight was more of a formality. It still hurts.

"Exquisite, isn't it?" I say, raising my cup of tea toward the setting sun.

"You haven't seen a sunset until you've seen it here," she says. "Isn't that the line you gave me when we first met?"

"Might have been. I seem to have lost the ability to come up with even simple statements like that now."

"The ones that were honest will come back."

An important part of the last few weeks with everyone—Dr. Baker, Jo, Killy, my parents, my sister, Corie, and Matt—was trying to sort through the past few months, separating the truths from the lies. No surprise, the majority of my lies were either covering up my recent relapse with heroin or my affair with Jenna.

The truths were easy to identify. I still loved Jo, my parents, my sister, Corie, Matt, and even Killy. I do not love Bake, but I respect him and love what he has done for me. My relapse has been totally on me. We eventually had a session that covered many of the topics that I lied about covering with Jeffrey-Calliope-as-Dr. Baker in the session in L.A. before I was abducted. Truth is stranger than…well, you know the goddamned saying. I had been given the chance to reinvent myself. In some ways, the internet and social media make the world seem a lot smaller than it actually is. New York City and L.A. are different galaxies—different energies and different speeds. But if you can't make it in one, you might be able to make it in the other. I am living proof that it is possible. Talk about being humbled—almost no one knew who I was when I arrived in L.A. Big in the theater does not equal big in Hollywood. And being big in Hollywood definitely does not equal being big in the theater. Had to get that in there. L.A. is an enigma anyway. You've got extreme wealth right around the corner from devastating poverty, and drug addicts huddled on the sidewalk as a procession of Ferraris, Teslas, Porsches, and Lamborghinis pass by on the street.

Crazy.

In any event, narrating was safe for me. Narrating kept me clean.

Until it didn't.

I always dreamed of returning to the theater and thought narrating was just a detour on the road back to what I really loved. And it was an attractive detour. Just me in a booth—a safe vacuum-like environment that kept the creative juices flowing and kept me out of the milieu that was triggering me to gamble my life every day. Then, the unexpected happened. I realized that I loved narrating—and became competitive.

Anyway, some of the most difficult matters to sort out were the events surrounding the kidnapping that I reported in my sessions with Dr. Baker. The task of trying to separate what *did* and what *did not* happen proved impossible for me to do. I eventually took a lie detector test, with Killy and Jo present, and passed. I swear at least some of it happened, but everyone, including me to some degree, believes that my delusions came from being on an epic bender which I am lucky to have survived.

Where does my narrating career go from here? I don't know.

Earlier this evening, I asked Jo if she thought that there might be even the slightest possibility that the kidnapping happened. After a lengthy pause, she answered, *'That's a tough one.'* And she is the only person to give me that answer. It's a hard "no" from everyone else, and I can't blame them. However, almost every night, I wake up sweating, hearing Michael Hunnie's voice crying out to me for help. I can also detail every aspect of Wolverine and the cell I was in. I even drew detailed sketches at Laguna and have them with me here at the house. Corie had a stretch a few years ago when he was heavy into Buddhism—tried to rope me in, but I declined. As I attempted to make sense of my memories, a phrase uttered often by Corie in those days came back to me. *'The mind is like water. When it's turbulent, it's difficult to see. When it's calm, everything becomes clear.'* No idea who said it, but I can tell you this: the surface water of my mind looks like a polished silver plate when it comes to everything except the kidnapping. *That* particular area of water is still a mountain range of waves formed by a Category 5 hurricane with the longest name in hurricane naming history: Narrator Big Boss Wolverine. Maybe Corie was on to something. Then again, Corie once got inebriated before performing a chapter of a book where the main character was drunk—tried to pass it off as "method narrating." Total disaster, almost got him fired. I think he just hated the book.

Dr. Baker has affirmed my feelings and concerns, and he can't explain the lie detector test, but Killy is right: There's no investigation to start. Absolutely nothing to go on. Begrudgingly, I have come to accept the fact that Michael Hunnie is alive, which means I'll continue to compete against him in the audiobook world. I am going to have to let the rest go, but, as a favor to me, Killy had additional alarm sensors put in my house while I was at the clinic—glass break sensors, motion detectors, and even alarms on the windows upstairs. I feel more secure at home than ever before. Cameras everywhere—each feed accessible by the touch of a button on my smartphone. What a world. And yet, I hope the nightmares go away soon. Bake's got me on Xanax, so there's that.

I look into my cup. Only a few sips left. I wonder how much coffee is in Jo's mug. It's kind of her to believe that I'll regain my wit at some point. I'm not so sure. "Think so?" I ask.

She takes a sip—a final sip by the way she tips the mug back. "Yeah. I do."

Her coffee is done, which means we're at the end of our evening. There aren't any more delays to engineer. Before everything went to hell, our next logical destination after sitting out here was always inside to sit by the fireplace, feel the warmth, and deliver words of endearment to each other—some of my best lines ever emerged because of those moments—and then disrobe.

"You were being truthful about seeing sunsets from here—elevates the experience. I'll miss seeing them in this way." She sets her mug on the glass table next to her chair. Still taking in the bright glow on the horizon, she says, "I'll miss *you*, Shawn."

Forever is a long time. I do not want to push, but I have to see if there is an opening—even if it is far off in the future. I still love her. "You don't think you'll ever come here again? To my house?"

She makes eye contact with me, which, I'm happy to report, is with both of my eyes. But after a quick lock, like a *tap*, she gazes back out at the miles of Pacific indigo. "I don't know if we can ever just carry on platonically. And I don't mean that in a harmful way."

"I know you don't."

"To be honest, I'm hoping that the play has a long run. That would make it easier for both of us."

She's talking about a new play that will start running Off-Broadway in a little over a month. She's headed out next week for readings, workshops, and rehearsals. When she auditioned for the part, we discussed the possibility of living in an apartment together in Greenwich Village while the show ran. I had also talked it over with Dr. Baker in one of our final sessions before I started canceling appointments with him; if she got the part, then my temporary move to New York City would be a test run to see if I could handle being back in the environment without slipping into my old destructive habits. I would still be recording audiobooks at a local studio, but I would be back in the center of the theater universe. Bake had agreed to one Zoom therapy session every other day for the first few weeks that I would be there.

For me, to travel to New York City now would be a disaster. Even I know that. And Jo and I are done. There is no reason for me to go anymore.

"You may be right. I won't be tempted to drive over." Her house is in Monterey, which is a ten-minute drive from my place. She's been a member of the Monterey theater community for almost a decade now. She also acts in plays in Los Angeles, which is five hours to the south, but this is her first time acting in New York City in over five years.

She stands up, her body a dreamy silhouette against the darkening sky. "Thank you for tonight, Shawn."

And now, the weight of the evening has finally settled on my shoulders. She's leaving, maybe forever—it's over. Of all the statements I want to make, the ending of what was once a relationship that I believed would get me to the altar relegates me to utter the words, "I'll see you out," as I stand up.

But then, as I feel a cool breeze touch my face, I realize I have one more thing to say. "Jo, maybe it didn't happen."

Her eyes are glassy, and she gives me a few nods of understanding.

Why I felt the need to make that statement right now is beyond my comprehension. It's not like it was going to save our relationship. Perhaps it's part of the healing process, and maybe I believe what I just said to her.

Maybe I don't.

We embrace, and I'm glad it is here and not out by her car.  This is the place where we shared our first kiss.  This is the place where we waxed poetic about our new life together.  This is where I felt closer to my old self and the theater.  This is where I told her that becoming an audiobook narrator was never the endgame for me, just an artistic placeholder before I returned to New York City and Broadway and revitalized my career as a playwright and actor.  But then, I grew to love the art of narrating, and I wasn't so sure, and I told her this.  And then got good.  And then I lost.

Then I became lost.

And now, I am hoping that I do not become a lost cause.

We break our embrace.  We're both crying—probably for some of the same reasons and probably for different ones as well.

I wipe my eyes and open the sliding glass door.  She enters, and I follow.

We arrive outside my front door, and the air is pure, the scent sweet.  Each full breath in the dying sunlight seems to signal a new possibility.  If you have never experienced a summer evening in Carmel-by-the-Sea, then you must, at least once in your lifetime.  And this is coming from a native of Michigan where, believe me, we get summer right.

Jo unlocks her car, opens the door, and turns, noticing that I've taken a few steps back.  Know thyself, right?  Well, if I felt her body against mine and smelled her wonderful perfume, I would not let go.  I want to remember the hug on the back deck as our last.

She's tearing up again.  So am I.

Then, I assume from somewhere deep within, she gathers herself and leaves me with, "Killian asked me if I thought you could beat this thing.  And.  I told him that of all the people that I've ever met in the entertainment business—the good, the assholes, the bitches, the fakes, the climbers, the poisonous snakes, the has-beens, the emotional vampires—that you were the only one I'd never count out."  She gets in and starts her car.

I stand there, hands in my pockets, hearing her words echo through my mind.

She rolls her window down. "Please, take care of yourself, Shawn."

I nod, not knowing if I can do it or not.

She backs the car out of my driveway and onto the road. I watch as her headlights travel away until I can no longer see them.

I head back inside.

Thirty minutes pass, and I sit on the living room couch and stare into the fireplace. I've thrown a few extra logs on tonight, and they have blazed into a hot, orange-red feast before my eyes.

She's gone.

My new cell phone rings. Corie sent me a text message checking in on me about twenty minutes ago, but I haven't answered it yet. In fact, my phone has been steadily beeping for the past five minutes, but I'm not in the mood to write anyone back right now. I know Jo well enough to know that none of the beeping is from her. I should probably turn the volume off, but I'm too wiped. I might just sleep on the couch tonight.

The phone keeps ringing.

"Shut the hell up!" I yell at it.

After a few more rings, it stops.

Ten seconds later, it starts again.

A thought occurs to me. Perhaps, she's had second thoughts. My breathing picks up. Maybe she's reconsidered! I sprint across the living room to the kitchen counter, where my phone is charging. I see the screen.

It's Killy.

I unplug the phone from its charger and answer.

"Shawn, have you been on the internet or been watching TV?"

He sounds uptight, like something is wrong.

"No, Jo left a little while ago, and I—"

"So you haven't heard?"

"Heard what?"

He pauses.

Now my mind is racing. The fog and lethargy from the evening have dissipated in seconds. Was Jo in a car accident? Is she okay? Did the police find my kidnappers? Are we being invaded?

"Killy, what is it?"

"Michael Hunnie is dead."

# 17

As I hear David Killian's words, I think of two things: the last time I saw Michael Hunnie in person, which was at the Audies, and his voice crying out to me from the hallway outside of my recording cell. I think all people do this when they learn that someone has passed away; *When was the last time I saw him or her? Let me try and remember what his or her voice sounded like.'*

I did hear him, right?

Of course, I did.

I did.

Nobody believes me, but I know what I heard!

I don't know if Michael was killed when we were in that hellish place, but I know someone injured him enough to silence him. Now, he's dead. This could prove that I have not been making up my kidnapping. Killy's obviously shaken, or else he wouldn't be calling me.

"What do we know?" I ask as I scroll through my texts. One is from Killy, and the others are from Corie. Nothing from Jo.

"Well, it's not what you think. I got off the phone with Jeff right before I called you. Now, this doesn't go anywhere beyond you and me, got it?"

Jeff…Jeff…Oh, right. Jeff Ayers. Michael Hunnie's agent. "I understand," I say. Of course, I plan on telling Corie everything Killy is about to spill. Corie's last text said that he was coming over. Based on the time, he should be here in another fifteen minutes.

"You know that cabin retreat I told you about when you were in the hospital? Well, when Hunnie didn't show up for work today and didn't answer his phone, Jeff became concerned. Hunnie had not returned to celebrate the 4th of July, but he's done this a few times before when he wanted to soak up the solitude for another few days. However, he's never missed coming into work on the 6th and checking in with Jeff. So, Jeff called the local police, and they sent a car out to Hunnie's cabin." Killy clears his throat.

This isn't going to be good.

"Hunnie's vintage 1964 Land Rover was still parked in the dirt driveway. They knocked on the door, and there was no answer, so they busted it down. Inside, they found Hunnie and an unidentified woman, both naked, both dead, in the master bedroom. Hunnie was on the floor next to the bed, and the woman was sprawled on top of it." Killy pauses. "It looked like they overdosed on heroin. Cops found needles, syringes, rubber tubing, lighters, the works. Nothing will be official until the forensics and toxicology reports come back, but it appears the most famous audiobook narrator in the world had a taste for the same junk you do."

"Were there any other marks on his body?"

I hear Killy exhale. "Shawn, let it go. There was no kidnapping, and Hunnie wasn't with you—wherever you were for that week in L.A. Now, I called you for a couple of reasons. One is that this is a sad day for the community, and I wanted to make you aware before you heard or saw it somewhere else. The story is going to go live within the hour. Two, as tragic as this news is and as horrible as the following is for me to say right now, I hope that this news closes the door on your incident. You imagined it, man, and now is the time to put it all behind you. Don't think about it anymore. We've got you clean, and no one knows about you falling off the wagon. We want to keep it that way."

"But don't you think I should talk to the police and tell them what I know."

"And go from grieving colleague to a person of interest? Are you out of your fucking mind?"

"Go with me for a minute on this, Killy. I tell you that I was being held captive by two psychos and that I heard Michael Hunnie break out from the cell next to me and call out directly to me in arguably the most recognizable voice in the entertainment world today. Then, I see a being—I don't know who the hell it was—race across the open doorway. Within seconds, there is some kind of loud noise. I swear it sounds like a gun going off, but now I'm not sure. Either way, I continue to scream back to Michael, but whatever just happened has made it impossible for him to communicate back to me. Then, I hear him being dragged away. And now, a month later, he's found dead in an isolated cabin that is not too far from L.A. with a woman and drug paraphernalia very similar to what was used on me. C'mon, something doesn't sit right here. Did Jeff ever know Michael to do heroin?"

"He says he didn't know anything about the heroin but that Hunnie did have a certain liking for the white powder years ago. I guess Hunnie's favorite thing to do was to sniff a line off of his girlfriend's stomach and then lie down, put a line on his perfect beard, and have his girlfriend sniff the powder up with a straw—called it 'vacuuming the carpet.'"

"I don't think that Michael Hunnie just started shooting up with a random woman in his getaway cabin, Killy. He just won his ninth Best Male Narrator award. You saw him at the Audies. Did he look like someone in distress?"

"I also saw you there," Killy says. "You were fine at that point. We don't know what Michael had going on in his personal life, and, obviously, neither does Jeff."

"This doesn't add up, and you know it. Too coincidental. Also, didn't Hunnie have surveillance cameras at the cabin?"

"I asked Jeff, says no.  Michael didn't feel they were necessary.  I guess Jeff pushed him a bit on the subject, so Michael took him out there and showed him the place.  Shocked the shit out of Jeff.  Rustic with nothing of any real value inside to steal, so Jeff dropped the subject.  For all the rumored daily pampering in his palatial estate, I guess mister Hunnie liked to rough it for a month every year."

"How long have they been dead?"

"Jeff said they told him not longer than three days.  Rigor mortis had set in, but the muscles had not started to relax again yet.  So, it wasn't a month ago, if that's what you're thinking."

"Killy, those two guys are still out there!  They had something to do with this."

"No, they aren't, Shawn."  He pauses.  I know he's making sense, but this is too much for me to handle right now.  "Look, this is a tragedy.  Hunnie was a legend, but you have to realize that you had nothing to do with what happened to him.  Is it a bit coincidental?  I'll give you that.  But, Shawn, Michael's death is a separate incident and not related to your relapse.  Okay, man?"

"Jo ended it with me tonight."

"I know."

"How?"

"Spoke with her just before I called you."

"Why?"

"I called her and told her what I just told you about Hunnie."

"But you said that what you had to tell me was just between us."  I know, I know, I'm a hypocrite because I'm going to tell Corie.  But, still.

"And it is.  But, I also told her so that she wouldn't be taken by surprise if you reached out to her about it.  Then, she told me that you two are done."

I'm a bit perturbed, but I really can't blame him.  I made a mess, and he doesn't want to clean up another one.  "What did she say about Hunnie?"

"She was sad to hear the news, but she agreed with me that it had nothing to do with your relapse last month."

I take it in.  Maybe I could call her?

"Don't call her, Shawn.  She was still broken up about her visit when I spoke with her.  And, just so you know, because I knew you'd tell him everything, I called Corie too."

"I didn't plan on—"

"Yes, you did.  And it's okay.  He's on his way to your place, right?"

"He is."

"Good.  I want you surrounded by people who have your back right now.  If he wasn't able to make it over, I was getting on a flight out of LA tonight to come see you."

I want to be angry with him.  I *am* angry with him.  But I shouldn't be.  He's doing everything he can to protect me right now so that I can continue to function, recover, and still have a career.  The person I'm angry with is myself.  Angry because I fell off the wagon and blew up my relationship with Jo.  Angry because I can't prove that I was kidnapped.  And now, angry because there seems to be proof that puts a major hole in my claim that I was held captive and forced to narrate a book written by one of my two captors.  Killy is right.  This should be the evidence I need to put the supposed incident in the past.  But yet, my mind is ablaze with the possibilities.  What if after Hunnie was dragged away, they kept him in another location for almost another month until they shot him up with heroin and placed him back in his cabin to make it look like he overdosed there.  It's a possibility.  But, what about the woman?  That's where it gets complicated.  If indeed it was only a 2-man team that kidnapped me and Hunnie.  It would be stretching things thin for them to make someone else disappear without a trace.  The more I think about it, the more unlikely it seems.  Maybe Michael had his demons like I did, and they finally turned on him and his lady friend.

"Thanks, Killy," I say. "I'm sorry. Been a rough night and a horrible stretch for me."

"I know," he says. "But you're going to get through it. You see Dr. Baker tomorrow morning, right?"

"Yeah. Nine a.m."

"I'll call tomorrow night, and we'll start talking about upcoming projects. Don't be surprised if something from me arrives at your place tomorrow afternoon."

He ends the call, and I'm alone with my fire again. The crackle and pop seem to be in sync with my thoughts as each sound corresponds with a flash of memory from my time in captivity.

As Lady Macbeth said, *'You must leave this.'*

And I reply, "Oh, full of scorpions is my mind, dear wife." There is no one but myself to hear me perform the line, no audience to marvel at my words, not *one soul* in my house for me to share the moment with. She's gone. I am alone.

I rub my temples and try to focus on my session with Doctor Baker tomorrow. His office is a few minutes away in a posh residential strip close to downtown Carmel. I know, it's not in L.A., or in Santa Monica for that matter; it's in Carmel. There's a back door that celebrities can access from a hidden hallway off of one of the shoppe's service entrances. I appreciate the privacy and know that Roman I. Baker never has appointments back to back so as to protect the identity of his clients. He's going to get an earful tomorrow—Jo, the breakup, and Hunnie's death. I close my eyes and go through a few cycles of the breathing exercises he taught me.

Five minutes later, I walk out onto my second floor's terrace above the garage and wait until I see the lemon headlight beams of Corie's Volvo appear as he turns the car into my long driveway. I can think of only one thing…

Who was the woman with Michael Hunnie?

*2 Weeks Later...*

# 18

## Carmel-by-the-Sea

It feels good to be back in my booth—hasn't been easy. I swear, sometimes I feel more comfortable in my booth than I do in real life. Maybe I don't trust myself in situations that I cannot completely control. Wow. That statement either means I'm getting better at knowing my limitations or that I am unhealthy and not living life.

Well, no time to think about which it is.

Today is my fourth day in a row of trying to narrate a new thriller by debut author and former pilot John Armbrewster, yet another military thriller writer who cannot write dialogue and has a hero leading a team of operators into harm's way. Will anything happen to the hero? Hell no. This is the first book in the series, and Johnny Arm has a 3-book deal. The hero's name? *Jack Armstead*, a *pilot* turned ghost agent. I know, I know, another pilot writing about a pilot. Bor—ing. Mind you, I am in the corner of those who have served—my grandfather is a Vietnam vet, and my father almost died serving in the first Gulf War. However, as a narrator, I have my favorite genres to narrate, and then there are the genres I narrate to keep the lights on in my house.  Now, Corie, my activist and peace-loving, peace-marching fellow narrator, well, he *loves* narrating military thrillers.  He also loves the type of video games where, in his words, the sole purpose is to *'blow shit the fuck up.'*  Go figure.  As Doctor Baker told me, *Do not spend precious time trying to figure other people out or change them.  Attempting to achieve* self-awareness *and make changes are already mountains most human beings never climb.'*  As always, the virtuoso poet-psychologist Roman I. Baker illuminates.

Anyway, it's not the book that is making it a challenge to record.  Sure, I don't care about Jack Armstead.  I don't care about his secret mission.  I don't care that the author was a former pilot and is being lauded by his fellow military thriller authors for "writing what he knows" (with *gusto!*).  I care even less that I have been honored with a lengthy e-mail from John Armbrewster that started with, *'I guess we should get to know each other since you'll…'*  I stopped there and deleted the message.  And I don't care that Killy got me this gig to get me back in the booth narrating thrillers.  But, none of these sentiments of mine are preventing me from performing the book.

No, the real problem is the environment.  As soon as I sat down in here four days ago, the smells of the cell came back to me—the lingering stench of my flushed feces while I attempted to eat or narrate, the musty odor of wet socks, the tea that they gave me, the crusty urine in my jeans, and so forth.  I had to run out of the booth and meditate for an hour before I could return.

Then, after reading:


Jet Encounter

by John Armbrewster

Read for you by Shawn Frost


I heard Wolverine's voice saying, *'Nice opening, bubba.'* And I had to leave the booth again.

Nights have not been that different.  I have dreamed about my captivity for a week straight.  This comes on the heels of not dreaming about my experience for the two weeks prior; at that point, Dr. Baker and Killy thought I had reached a major milestone.  And that was the moment when Killy presented me with the new thriller.  *'Time to get back up on the pony and ride,'* he said.  Throw in the occasional nightmare about Jo and what could have been, and there you have it.

Remember when I told you that Corie enjoyed narrating military thrillers?  Well, after I sprinted out of the booth yesterday and cried on my couch for a good ten minutes—what triggered it?  Ace pilot Jack Armstead said:

## "Looks like this will be a converging affair, boys."

The walls of my basement booth disintegrated, and I was back in the cell reading the overview of *Narrator*, learning about bestselling author Stacey Groff's book *Converging Affairs* and narrator Robbie Bernstein.  After my crying spell, I called Killy, and it was then that he informed me that Corie had been responsible for getting the Armbrewster book into my queue.  Corie had initially agreed to do the book and the sequels, but then an insane deal, for more money than Killy had ever heard of, was struck for Corie to perform a 5-book erotica series titled 'The Deep Series'.

Book one: *Deep Lay*

Book two: *Deep Play*

Book three: *Skin Deep*

Book four: *In Deep*

And the series finale: *Deep [H]er*

And so, Corie, whose pseudonym is 'Raphael' when he records erotica, had reached out to Armbrewster's agent and publisher to see if Shawn Frost would be an acceptable replacement for him on the series.  Apparently, Lieutenant Armbrewster replied, *'Roger.  C. Woods punching out.  S. Frost new wingman.'*

Sometimes, I want to kill Corie.

But not today.  I know him well enough to see that he was trying to help me get back on my feet and probably thought that I could breeze through *Jet Encounter* while he narrated stories of a deeper nature.  Sorry, couldn't help throwing that in there.  No, no, don't make fun of Corie.  Multi-million-dollar careers have been forged by narrating erotica.  One of my fellow finalists, Crassus Dynasty, actually teaches a course in audiobook narration at the University of Southern California, and he always has a class period devoted to this subject.  In any regard, the point is, Corie and I talked about me getting back in the booth on the night he came over after Jo had broken up with me and we had learned that Michael Hunnie had died.  Right, about that.  The woman he was found with was a prostitute named Sally Meeks, street name Sharon Trixie, who had a record of drug abuse.  Footage had been found of Hunnie's Land Rover pulling up to the street where Sharon worked, Sharon getting in, and Hunnie driving off with her in the passenger seat.  Well, that put a perilous gash in my story, and Killy, Corie, and Jo—never heard directly from her, only through Killy—considered the issue closed.  I admit that the news helped me get past some of the trauma, but there is a part of me that still believes I was down there—and that Michael Hunnie was down there with me.

And what about *Narrator?*  How could that novel be so real to me, and how could I recall so many details about the book?  Dr. Baker's theory (and Killy's) was that my creative mind had concocted it during the week-long bender.  After all, I had envisioned an entire counseling session with Dr. Baker when, in truth, I was getting loaded with Calliope.  I suppose it's possible, but two things continue to make me uncertain.  One: I never thought up *anything* when I was doing heroin in New York City—and this was during the peak of my creative powers, which I have never been able to reach again.  Two: The sensory memories I have are so strong that it seems improbable to me that I could not have experienced them in real life.  The counterpoints that Doctor Baker presented are equally valid, although, like my points, ultimately unable to ever be verified. Counterpoint One: It has been so long since I created anything that an overwhelming volume of water broke through my metaphorical Hoover Dam and flooded my mind. Counterpoint Two: The sensory memories *are real* because I *did* experience them—just not where I think I experienced them.

I exhale, looking at the page I finished before going on this tangent of thoughts.

Get moving, Frost.

Today has been better.

And it has. I'm halfway through the book.

Here we go, back to invincible Jack, endless military acronyms, long-winded gear descriptions that read like gratuitous product placement ads, and enough wooden dialogue to build a Hobbit empire.

Seriously, stop. Leave your personal feelings out of it. Commit to the work. As I used to say in the theater, *"Leave your personal problems in the dressing room because there's no place for them on the stage."* Wish I could have followed my own advice back then—might not be in this booth right now telling the puffy-clouded ballad of Jack Armstead.

Manage your focus!

I take a bottomless, cleansing breath, then go into my routine.

I take a sip of water.

I put one drop of Ice Drops into my mouth.

I dab my stick of Burt's Bees a few times on my top lip, then my bottom lip.

I turn the page.


Armstead knew that the top brass at the Pentagon would never allow the CINCPAC to officially acknowledge his team's presence. They were just along for the ride. A few members of Armstead's team were ex-Marines and used to this dismissive treatment.  The biggest and burliest, an ex-Marine nicknamed "Bear," reminded Armstead of the unkind acronym formed from the word "MARINE"—My Ass Rides In Navy Equipment—any time they were guests of the U.S. Navy. Armstead thought of his own call sign, "Wolf," and knew there were many, many enemy sheep to be slaughtered in the coming days.  He peered down with a steely disposition at his new, thousand-dollar Garmin D2 Delta PX 51MM watch—specially ordered for this mission—which had a titanium band and features such as:

It takes me half a page to finish reading the features on the watch.  I flip the page, go through my routine, and pick it back up with:

It was 0400.  Time for coffee and then time to take a shit that even Bear would brag about—crazy jarhead.  Then, it would be time to take matters into his own hands.  Time to kill without hesitation.  There was a knock on his stateroom's door.

"Enter," Armstead said.

The door opened, and the monster figure of Bear approached him.

*I was just thinkin' about ya*, Armstead thought.

"Wolf, the team is up."

"Good.  Thanks, Bear," Armstead replied.  "I'll meet you for chow in five."

"Fuck yeah," snorted Bear, and the big moose left.

Armstead checked his Garmin once more. *Yeah, definitely time to take matters into my own hands—been shackled with*

My breathing picks up, and my chin starts to vibrate. I close my eyes, trying to calm myself. It makes things worse. Visions start to appear.

Shackles.

Chains.

Straps.

Wolverine pulling up a chair.

I roar in pain and anger as I bust open the door to my booth.

A few steps across the basement floor, my knees buckle. I reach for the back of my leather couch but miss, and I fall to the carpeted floor.

I shout, "It was real. It happened. Why won't anyone believe me?"

Now, I'm shaking, and I can't stop.

I continue to shout. "Why did they have us both down there? Why? I was Big Boss's favorite narrator. Michael was Wolverine's. Were we both recording the same thing? Did Michael record anything?"

I shut my eyes and moan in pain as I hear Michael Hunnie scream in my brain, *'Shawn! Shawn! Get out of here! They're never letting us out!'*

I slam my fist on the carpet. "But they did let me out," I say. Somewhere near Killy's posh neighborhood. I have a flash memory of me avoiding the gate guard, climbing over one of the walls to access the neighborhood, and sprinting down the street toward Killy's mansion—the Tom Cruise scene of my life. "Why did they let me go?" I bellow.

As if in answer to my question, I hear Michael's last, desperate effort, *'Shawwwwwwn!'*

Whether or not any of it actually happened, I can no longer say. But it is real to me, and it is affecting my work and my life.

I open my eyes and can't see anything but a blurry mess of the ceiling. I blink, trying to focus. My effort to see starts to pay off, but just as the metaphorical seas part and I'm able to make out one of my ceiling fans, I'm hit with the sound of Michael's body being dragged down the hallway. Every muscle and body function that is responsible for speech seems to overtake any awareness of reality, and I yell, "Michael! Michael!"

There is silence in the house. I feel lightheaded…like I'm about to…

My eyes flutter open. The basement light is bright, and I squint in reflex to the burning, yellow flash. I carefully start to test my body, starting with the toes and moving my way up. Nothing seems injured, and I thank Jo for convincing me to carpet the floor last year. I rub my eyes in slow circles, and after a minute or so, I'm able to see without pain.

I sit up and put my back against the couch. The booth door is still wide open. I look at my watch. Two hours have passed.

I lick my lips and try to generate enough saliva in my mouth to allow for a smooth swallow. I fail. My mouth is dry, and I feel the lethargic effects of being dehydrated. My mouth, throat, and body yearn for the metal water container that is inside my booth. But my thoughts override my ability to move my muscles.

You have a serious problem, Frost. You can't narrate thrillers.

I hang my head, and the tears start to build once more. I try to make an angry, Michael-Phelps-Olympic-revenge-swim face, but I am defenseless against the overwhelming pressure of the oceans behind my eyes.

I weep.

And, while I weep, the thought occurs to me: If I am unable to narrate thrillers, then *what will* I be able to narrate?

My work centers me and gives structure to my life. My work *is* my life. The audiobook narrator gig was supposed to position me to get back into my first love, playwrighting. Now, I'm moving backward from that dream instead of toward it. What does one do when one cannot continue in one's *backup* job?

This starts a sobering progression of thoughts that continues until my eyes dry, and I ultimately arrive at a final, exacting, and horrifying question with a potential answer that is so devastating I can barely say the words aloud.

"Will I *ever* be able to narrate anything again?"

# PART III

## Editing

*2 Years Later...*

# 19

## Carmel-by-the-Sea

I sit in my darkened booth and read the final page of *Billy the Bad Apple*, a children's story about a main character named, oh yes, *Billy* King—a one-time bully turned nest defender of a huddle of down-and-out third graders. It is my forty-second children's book in the past two weeks; I average four a day now. Even after all this time, they're still the only thing I can handle.

I also narrate "naked" these days. No, not *that* type of naked. Narrating "naked" means narrating without headphones. Yeah, gave them up. Reminded me too much of, well, you know. And I found that with the conditions I've got set up in my booth, I didn't really need them anymore. Not that narrating these children's books has brought out the performer in me, but I do feel more freedom to act without wearing my headphones. However, I still keep my pair in the booth. Why? Because they were specially made for me and have a picture of Princess Leia on the outside of each earphone. Corie got them for me for Christmas years back, and I can't bring myself to remove them from the booth.

So, there they sit on one of the three shelves in a custom rack I had put in around six months ago. Next to them is a framed picture of everyone on the stage who was a part of the first Broadway play I wrote and directed. The rest of that shelf has pictures of my family, Jo, Corie & Matt, my high school teacher…and one of Killy—a glamour headshot that he put in the booth himself when I wasn't looking. Slick bastard. Couldn't take it down. The second shelf has four essential theater books that I would not part with under any circumstance: *Putting It Together*, *The Norton Shakespeare*, *The Fervent Years*, and *Write That Play*. Killy thinks I'm torturing myself by having them in there, and I see his point, but they continue to give me comfort—if not for who I am now, then for who I used to be…and who I might be again one day. The last shelf? I leave it empty on purpose. Makes me think that my life is not over—still more to discover, more to do. Killy thinks it's a waste of space not to fill it. Corie thinks it means I'm incomplete. Maybe I am.

Maybe I always will be.

Anyway, I'm sleeping, finally, without nightmares. Well, at least some nights. But still, I'm not ready to narrate anything other than books about people under the age of twelve or animals that talk and probably need psychological help. Read: dog psychic—there's no escaping it. And, yes, there's even the occasional book about the inanimate object that, with magic dust, comes to life and attempts to deliver a veiled political statement to the masses. And I get them from both sides of the aisle, folks. They remind me of my theater days when a colleague who had learned a life lesson felt compelled to write the dreaded one-act show to enlighten the audience.

Un-dramatic. Doesn't work.

Okay, back to the final page of *Billy the Bad Apple*:

**Billy knew it was time to be honest with Jacob.**

I stop. I cannot find "Billy's truth" to save my life. All I hear in my head when I record is a melody of *"Bill-ee is a lie-urr. Bill-ee is a lie-urr."* When I narrated thrillers, it was so easy to find the main character's truth and get to an honest place where I could take ownership of the work and perform it. Lately, I feel no connection to works with characters like Billy King, King Billy, wink. I'm not in it. I'm not there.

I want to trash it, but I can't. It's my job to bring it to life.

Speaking of thrillers, Killy tried, once a month for the past three months, to send me a new thriller. I politely declined. *"Hell, let me get you a coach or a director—Fraley, Miles, Heller, Huber, Graham, Pratt, Rosenblat, Ruben, Rooney, Hudz, Rapkin, Musselman, anyone!"* I said no. My ex-girlfriend, Jo (yes, we're talking again), thought I was nuts for both turning down the thrillers and for refusing any coaching or directing. She's hard to argue with, and she could be right. Maybe I should take the leap. Regardless, it remains a challenge for me not to be with her. She's dating a fellow actor named Alex, and I guess it's pretty serious. I'm happy for them, but I still miss her. I don't think I'll ever stop missing her. However, on a friendship-only basis, we talk at least once a week. She still hasn't been back to my house, and I haven't been over to her place. Well, she's not even there anymore because she lives with Alex now. When we talk, it's on the phone or at a café in Carmel near Dr. Baker's un-fuck-Shawn's-mind center. I think about her all of the time. Mostly, I wonder what my life would be like if we were still together. Me? Single, no current prospects. Just my work.

My psychologist—have I mentioned him lately? Doctor Roman I. Baker of the starched collared shirts, jeans, and Vans? Well, I'm still seeing him, and the illustrious good doctor told me that my decision to steer clear of the thriller genre has been one of pure strength and self-awareness—and Killy should have stopped asking after the first rejection. But Killy would give a recovering alcoholic an ice-cold beer if he thought he could make some money off it. I know, I know. It's a touchy subject because I'm a recovering addict. Proud to say I've been clean for over two years now since my stay at Laguna. When I bring up Jo in my sessions with Bake, he just listens. He knows we're talking again.

Corie and Matt—they're married now, beautiful ceremony—threw me a Shawn's-been-clean-for-2-years pool party on their back patio that was attended by friends, old and new, who have been by my side for my entire career. Killy was there. My parents and sister were there. Jo came late, but she showed, which meant everything to me.

I rub my eyes. Back to Billy:


**Because his name was Billy King, and indeed *he had been* king of the neighborhood.**


Aw, shit. I'm listening to myself again. Big no-no.

Do the line again, Frost.

I do.

Anyway, at my party, there were fireworks, barbeque everything, sparkling water, soda, an ice cream bar, and about every kind of chocolate known to human beings. No booze or drugs. There were celebratory cigars, however, a vice I have maintained and one that Dr. Baker has permitted even though he says that my 1-cigar-a-week habit is killing me—just more slowly than my previous addiction. Killy's worried about my voice, but until I start sounding like Tom Waits, I'm fine. Everyone is still happy with my work. Perhaps the pitch of my voice has become a few notches lower, but...

Okay, I should quit smoking, and maybe I will, but that's a discussion for another time and another place. Where was I? Oh, right, Dr. Baker. Long story short, the golden-maned and golden-gray goateed Roman I. Baker trumped my ex-girlfriend and Killy: No narrating thrillers yet. But I'm getting close. I read a thriller novella in Dr. Baker's office, and it went fine. That was the event that prodded Killy and Jo to encourage me to get back in the game. I feel the pull too.  Killy said, *'If you can just do one, then that will go a long way toward earning the industry's trust in you again.'*  I have no doubt that is true.  I barely made it through the John Armbrewster fiasco.  When Killy told the powers that be that I couldn't finish the book for personal reasons, the cool-headed Johnny Arm unraveled, showing his true nature in an e-mail version of a B-52 strike on the small, seafaring, sleepy town of Shawn Frost.  Long story short, Corie came to my rescue and narrated *Jet Encounter* by staying up into the wee small hours of the morning for a week—and, from Killy's point of view, it was one of Corie's best performances.  However, it could not elevate the source material enough, and, after poor sales, ParkerWilson canned books two and three for Johnny Jet Encounter.

How did *Billy King* not get canned?  No—How did *Billy King* ever make it to print?  Perhaps, I'm about to find out.  I resume recording.

**But now King Billy had injured a former friend, and it was not okay...not criss-cross-applesauce okay.**

Billy, Billy, Billy.

Killy, Killy, Killy.

Killy's also been trying like hell to get me back on social media and to get me interviews.  Right before my relapse, I was making a post a week, updating my fan base on what I was up to.  Then, I disappeared.  There's been only one post since.  Killy got access to my account and pulled a Damon Lindelof.  He posted:

**Hey!  I'll be right b—**

Bottom line: Killy wants me back online—knows I might be getting close to entering the thriller world again.

*'Shawn, give them something.  You've got five million followers now.'*

*'I'm not making a post.'*

*'Let's set up an interview for you to keep your name out there.  I can call Daniela Acitelli and get you on Narrator's Cup of Joe.  I can try and have Chuck and Stacey work you in for a quick Q and A on VO Buzz Weekly.  Marc Guss from Voiceover Club has expressed interest in setting up an interview with you on Clubhouse—mainly just to see what in the hell you're up to.  I mean, everybody's curious as to what happened.  Been a few rumors, but I've controlled the narrative.  Hell, some people even wondered if you killed Hunnie and were hiding out.'*

*'I'm not talking to anyone.'*

*'What about the technical side of the house?  I can reach out to Dan Lenard and George Whittam and see if they'll interview you on Voice Over Body Shop?  C'mon, that's as safe as it gets.  You'd be talking about recording equipment and booth setup.'*

*'Can't.'*

*'For Christ's sake, at least let me get you in with Dave Fennoy.'*

*'I love him, but I just can't do it.'*

*'What about the theater?'*

*'What about it?'*

*'What if I can set something up with the American Theatre Wing?  Maybe get you on an episode of Working in the Theatre or at least an interview with Gordon Cox on his Stagecraft podcast.  What do you think?'*

*'HELL No.'*

And on, and on, and on.  We have a version of that conversation every month, and I know he means well.  I'm just not ready.

Lately, Corie has been down—missed out on a new series by Ivan Bacca, the thriller writer whose sales are red-hot and whose meteoric rise has shaken the industry crystal ballers silly.  Serves 'em right.  They hadn't seen the end of Nehemiah Stone coming two years ago either.  *You don't kill off a cash cow like that, dear boy,'* said one of the publishing oracle society's oldest members to Killy.  And, he was right.  Legendary thriller author M. Scott Sala hasn't had a hit since, eclipsed by the devious wit and superhuman writing stamina of Ivan Bacca—*three* novels a year! I like to think that because I stopped narrating Sala's books, it also had something to do with his fall, but that was for idiots like the crystal ballers to make proclamations about. I might have more thoughts on that later, but right now (I peeked ahead), Billy is about to confront Jacob.

Billy approached Jacob, the weight of his wars in kindergarten, first grade, and second grade weighing on his tiny shoulders.

I look back at the last page of *Billy the Bad Apple*. What can I say? The entire thirty-six-page story has been derivative. I've read the same plotline thousands of times now. The illustrations, however, are absolutely stunning, and I've probably taken longer to finish up this abortion of a book because I've been stopping every page to look at the pictures. Who cares? The publisher gives me a week to record each book, so I can look at pictures of Billy and crew for hours without reading a word and still come in ahead of the deadline.

The words are a blur as I fixate on the picture of Billy—crew cut, white T-shirt, cutoff jean shorts, and bright red Chuck Taylors—standing over his nemesis, Jacob Parker, the heir-apparent school bully after Billy had come to Jesus and found the light. Jacob is on the ground clutching his right leg that, moments ago, Billy kicked and sent poor Jacob down. I don't give a shit about Jacob. I don't give a shit about Billy.

Time to finish this turd so I can move on to…

…where in the hell is it? I lift a pile of papers off of my booth's desk.

Ah-ha! There it is. My next read: *Can I Tell You About Me?* by Tucker McGrady. There is some award sticker on the cover, but I don't bother to look at it. They've *all* got award stickers on them nowadays.

I turn back to *Billy* and bring the words into focus.  Sip of water.  Deep breath. Wrap it up already, Frost.  I hit record and start narrating.

"I just wanted to be your friend," Billy said.

"You broke my leg," Jacob replied.

"Sorry."  Billy began to sob.  He knew deep in his tortured soul that he had not broken Jacob's leg.

Jesus Christ.  Billy's family is going to be sued.

"I...I didn't want you to go on hurting them," Billy said, pointing at the group of misfits—kids who wanted to belong to something but didn't.  "Your leg isn't broken, Jacob.  Your leg is in pain.  But," Billy sniffled.  "I really think that *you* are in pain."  And Billy took his index finger and tapped on Jacob's chest.

Well, lookie what we have here: Billy was a God Damn Doctor Roman I. Baker, Ph.D. in the making.

Wait.  Who wrote this?

I flip to the front cover.

Oh, right, of course.  Tucker McGrady.

I forgot that this was a trilogy that starts with *Billy the Bad Apple*, weaves its way through *Can I Tell You About Me?*, and ends with *Billy's Graduation*—a book that is also somewhere in this booth.

I hit record once again.

And now Jacob began to cry. "You know what, Billy?" Jacob asked.

"What?" Billy said.

No!  You don't have to write every single response, Tucker.  *God.*

"I *am* in pain."

"I know.  I've been there before, and it *hurts*.  It hurts so darn bad."

A stocky playground aide the children had nicknamed Mama P. approached, and Billy knew what it meant.  Even though he had just taken down the school bully, he was in trouble—an outsider again, about to face the wilderness alone.  Jacob's leg would heal, he was sure of that.  But Billy King might not be around to see it.  Would he ever be able to attend Bickleberry Elementary again?  He didn't know.

The sound of the ambulance could now be heard.  Mama P. arrived, grabbed him by the arm, and began escorting him to the principal's office.

And as they exited the playground, to cheers, clapping, and a few boos, *King* Billy asked Mama P., "Can I tell you about me?"

And, we're done.

Instead of starting in on the second book in the playground bully trilogy, I decide to take a break.  I've gotten better at doing this in the past year.  When the triumvirate of Roman I. Baker, David Killian, and myself figured out that the only narrating I could handle were children's books, I became a workaholic, shouting, *'Next!'* inside my booth after completing each book for hours on end. Then, Bake and Killy noticed my weight loss, and I scaled back.

Nowadays, I take breaks. I ride my bike for at least five miles a day and walk my golden retriever Michael for at least two. Yeah, you noticed I named him Michael. Believe it or not, doing this has actually helped me. Originally, I thought naming him Michael would exacerbate my trauma, but when it was evident that, on a certain level, those memories—real or not, as I've come to conclude—were never going to go away, I found that I gained a measure of control and peace by being able to take care of Michael—raise him, walk him, feed him, take him to the veterinarian's office (where they love him), and show him love I didn't know I was capable of. Funny how animals can teach us things.

He's a year and a half old now and was probably the biggest ally that Killy and Bake had in getting me out of the booth during those initial marathon sessions when I began narrating children's books.

But, as you can probably tell, I feel as though a part of me has died reading them. No slight to the authors—well, maybe a dart or two to Tucker McGrady— but I know I'm mailing them in at this point, and it diminishes me as an artist. In my last session, I told Dr. Baker that I didn't know how much longer I could go on like this. He brainstormed with me other career options, but I came to the same conclusion I came to during my low point on the basement floor. I'm in my late thirties now and cannot see a happy future for myself that does not include either A) narrating thrillers or B) writing, directing, and acting in plays. Like the multiple-choice tests that I still hate, the preferred answer is C) both A & B, which brings me back full circle to the fact that I believe I'm ready to try a thriller again. I read the novella fine. Killy *loved* my performance, which is why I know he's been all over me the past three months. All Corie could do was get wide-eyed and nod while listening to my reading of the novella with me. When the recording finished, he hugged me and said, *'You're back.'*

How did I do it? My method was simple, and I'm going to use it when I try a full-length thriller. I would narrate for thirty minutes and then exit the booth. Michael lies on the basement floor right outside the booth while I record, so I would sit down on the floor and love on him for about five minutes. Then, I'd go back in the booth and record again, free of any worries. By the way, another ridiculous fear I had developed when attempting to narrate *Jet Encounter* was that someone would rip open the booth door and attack me. Having Michael outside the booth solves that problem. So, I would visit Michael every half hour until I had narrated for three hours. Then, we'd take a longer break where I would take him for a walk or go in my front yard and play fetch with the tennis ball, which is his favorite game to play. Oh, yeah, since my house is on a cliff, I had to have a portion of my property fenced in. Almost learned that the hard way on Michael's first day at my place—little fella ran toward the cliff face, and I caught him just before he and yours truly took a permanent dive.

Has Jo met my furry companion yet? Unfortunately, no. I thought about bringing him to the outdoor café, but the truth is he's still got too much puppy energy left in him. From what I hear, though, this should gradually go away over the next few years, and maybe then I'll try. Or, maybe, she'll have come back out to my house by then. As John Nash's roommate Charles from *A Beautiful Mind* once said, *'Nothing's ever for sure, John. It's the only sure thing I do know.'*

Sometimes, with what I've thought and heard, I think I am John Nash—without the math genius part, of course. Never been a fan of math.

I leave the booth, and Michael greets me with a wagging tail and kisses on my hand. I love this dog.

We head upstairs.

The kitchen stove clock says 4:13 p.m. as Michael and I enter, and I pull an ice-cold Coke from the refrigerator. I might be taking better care of myself, but I'm not giving up soda. Or cigars. At least not yet.

I refill Michael's water bowl, and he drinks greedily from it.  Guy can lap up an entire bowl in no time.

"What should we do, buddy?" I say, crouching down next to him.  "We already had our walk today.  Maybe another one?"

He continues to drink.

My cell phone rings from my bedroom—still don't take it in the booth with me, professionalism and all that.

"Be right back, big guy."

I jog toward the bedroom.  My smartwatch should be charged by now; if I'm taking a walk, you bet your rear end that I'm going to make sure I get credit for my steps in Noom.  Yeah, Jo got me started on the program.  Always looking to carve out some room for a snack after dinner.  Have to.  My defenses lower as the hours get later.

Have I lost any weight?  Let's talk about something else.

I pick up the phone.  It's Killy.  He never calls at this time because he knows I'm in the booth until at least five every day.

I answer while taking my smartwatch off the charger and start putting it on. "Hey, Killy."

"Shawn, thank God."

Why is he shouting?  He sounds out of breath.

"Killy—"

"I didn't think I'd catch you and was about to send Jo over."

"Send Jo over?  Why would you do that?  And why are you talking so fast?"

"Shawn, there's been a horrible accident.  It's Corie.  He's in surgery and might not pull through."

# 20

## Santa Monica

I'll never get used to the smell of a hospital, and I never want to. An optimist would claim that the sterile and temperature-controlled air signifies new life and healing. For me, every inhalation through my nostrils has a whiff of death in it. It doesn't help that this is the same hospital I was in before going to Laguna: UCLA Santa Monica Medical Center. On no occasion did I ever want to be back here, but here I am.

Corie was in week two of his three-week stay in L.A. to record two thrillers that are sure to be huge hits when they're released in November for the Christmas season, and the publishers wanted Corie to perform the books in their L.A. studio rather than in his home studio in Monterey.

As for the accident, like me, when he has the time, Corie likes to drive down to L.A. via the PCH. So, he had finished recording for the day and was heading southwest on Santa Monica Boulevard toward the Santa Monica Pier to have a late lunch at Maria Sol with an old friend. A few blocks southwest of the hospital, Corie's Volvo got t-boned by some 19-year-old in a Chrysler 300 who was heading northwest on 14th street. The authorities think he was texting near the intersection. Well, the kid passed away while I was in the air. Killy told me when I landed, and, to be honest, I was prepared for him to tell me that Corie had not made it. But, I suppose fate has other plans for my best friend at the moment. He's through the most important surgery—repairing a collapsed lung—but has many more to go. If there is one silver lining, it is that his voice will be fine. He'll be able to narrate again. Look, Corie was born to be in the booth. When we worked on an ensemble piece four years ago, I found him to be the most generous professional that I've ever worked with. If he can pull through this, I will be glad not only to have him alive but to know that he can go back to what he loves. Every narrator I know has nightmares about suffering an injury that affects his or her ability to speak. The fact that Corie's voice will be unchanged is a monumental win at this point. And, right now, everyone that cares about him needs a win.

I round the corner, and there's Killy, immaculate in dress, Adonis in the flesh. But today, worried in the face.

I give him a hug, and it's because I need it.

He says, "Hey."

I hang on as if my life depends on it.

"No change since we talked three minutes ago," Killy says. "Still in recovery."

I hold him for a few more moments and then break the hug. "Let's go see Matt."

It's been almost four hours since Killy's phone call. He got me booked on the first flight out of Monterey Regional for LAX, and my next-door neighbor, Diana, drove me to the airport and is taking care of Michael while I'm away. Tonight, I'm staying at Killy's. Tomorrow night and beyond, I'm going to stay at a hotel near the hospital.

We arrive in the waiting room, and Matt is so shaken up that he has trouble standing. I can see he's relieved to see me, but he looks, well, Goddamnit, he looks like someone who has almost lost the love of his life today. I go to him.

We hug, and he lets loose on my shoulder. "Matty," I say, giving him pats on the back. "Matty."

We stand there, and I hold him as long as he needs me to. I hear a few sniffles, and then we sit down as he rubs his eyes then blows his nose—you know, typical bawl your eyes out fare.

Killy is seated across from us and drinking a cup of coffee. He must have spied my longing look at it because he stands and says, "I'll be back with two more cups."

"Thanks, Killy," Matt says.

Killy's gone before it registers for me to say thanks. I'm just thrown off with how destroyed Matt is. It doesn't surprise me, but it's a whole other experience to see someone who is usually the most chill, uplifting, and happy soul you've ever met become an emotional pile of goo. It is unsettling.

And it is at this moment that I realize just how blessed I've been since my breakdown two years ago. Minus the occasional bad dream about my real or imagined captivity, I have lived a stress-free existence. Today is a reminder that life can end at a moment's notice. I am certain that I will get hit even harder when I'm alone in my room at Killy's tonight.

Matt and I talk over everything that has happened and what the doctors have been saying. There's nothing new, but it seems to give Matt some comfort or at least a measure of control by framing the situation in his terms. I have never been the world's best listener, but I make sure my phone is turned off and give my whole attention to Matt. Killy arrives with the coffee, and the hot, fresh-roasted liquid is a godsend. Everything is always better with coffee. Period.

Matt goes to use the restroom. Killy leans in toward me, his huge arms resting on his knees. "I am glad his dad is coming tonight."

"Agree.  Should be here in less than an hour now."

"How do you feel about staying until he arrives and gets settled in?"

"As long as Matt's good with it.  We know everything he knows, and there is nothing we can all do now but wait."

"Corie's a good guy, Shawn."

Killy never makes statements like this.  But then again, Corie should be in the Guinness Book of World Records as the first person to ever have zero enemies. Still, I'm thrown off.  Killy isn't emotional, but his words are full of emotion.  I've never had to react to him in this way before.  I could trump him a bit and say *the best*, but I decide to agree and appreciate the moment with my power agent as he shows a side of himself that I've never seen before today.  "He is," I say.

"Hell of a narrator too."

"Yeah."

"Like someone else I know."

This is the second time in all our years together that he's told me I was good at what I do.  The first was after I read the first Nehemiah Stone novel.  Once again, I'm thrown off.  "Thanks."

"You're sick of reading the kid books, aren't you?"

He may have been short on compliments and moral support over the years, but, pretty much since day one of working together, he has been able to read me better than anyone except my parents.  I think back to what he told me when he got me the kid book narrating gig.  *This is a* gift.  *Do you know how many strings I had to pull and favors I had to cash in to get you this opportunity?  The industry can't trust you right now; I can't take a chance on you with another thriller.  You are unreliable and are letting people down.  As your friend and agent, you need to fix whatever you have going on.  And so, this is it.  You're going to happily disappear for a year or two, narrating children's books while making a substantial amount of money, and then we'll talk about working you back into the genres that you were born to narrate.  Trust me, Shawn.'*  That was the first time that I ever realized that, no matter how successful I had been, Killy might bail on me in certain circumstances. And now, in a hospital waiting room with my best friend's life hanging by a thread, he has read me again. "Is it obvious?"

"Not in your performance. You still sound as welcoming as Mister Rogers, but not one of our conversations outside of the booth have any of the energy they used to—the scheming for upcoming deals, the thirst for industry gossip, the focus."

"Might not ever come back," I say, looking out the window at the Los Angeles landscape.

I once heard a fellow artist say that the reason he had been able to keep his confidence and conviction in his work during his lengthy career was that he would gaze out at L.A. once a night from his living room window—the bright, multi-colored lights blinking at him in the distance. And he would think: There are a few enemies out there, but there are even more people who love me and believe in me. And yet, the most important thing to remember is that everyone else out there isn't thinking about me *at all*.

I've tried this before, and it works.

Corie's never had to try it. His easy-going manner and devotion to the craft always transcended insecure worries about being loved. And because of this, I believe he is more loved.

"Remains to be seen," Killy says. "Don't mean to talk shop at a time like this, but I think you are ready to come back. And so does Baker."

"You talked to him?"

"I did."

I gaze back out the window. "Something to think about." In a recent session, Dr. Baker reviewed the ground we had covered years prior. I asked him, *How do I give up the fast, glamorous, and decadent lifestyle of more money than I could ever spend, power, artistic freedom, and people constantly kissing my ass?'* He replied, *Fortunately, in at least one regard—artistic freedom—and unfortunately in the other regards, this type of* fame *goes hand-in-hand with artistic achievement. Here's the real question you have to answer, Shawn:*

*How do you discover that creating and then seeing your creation come to life is* enough?' He brought up this early exchange because we were starting to explore how I might return to narrating thrillers or at least something different than kid books with characters like Billy King.

Killy puts a hand on my shoulder. "You need anything else?"

"No, thanks." I take a pull on my coffee cup. "This is perfect."

Killy continues to focus on me; I can see him out of the corner of my eye—like I could see Wolverine limping on his left leg as he returned from the hallway.

I glance at Killy. Talk about giving me a lesson in how to listen. The word *rapt* comes to mind.

"Corie's my best friend. Without you and him, I don't think I'd be alive, let alone still working in the business."

Killy nods, like a professor hearing a student add an intelligent comment to a classroom discussion.

"And you know what I'm regretting now?"

"About the friendship or about still working?"

"The friendship." I clear my throat, take a sip of coffee, then dab my lips with Chapstick. Sometimes my booth habits spill over into real life. "I don't like what I'm recording now, but I have to keep working." I go back to staring out the window. The hospital—ironically or mercifully, depending on your take—is only a few blocks away from where Calliope's apartment was. If someone overdosed, there was always a fighting chance they'd survive because the hospital was so close.

My thoughts swiftly move to *access to every illegal drug on the market is within walking distance.* Calliope's wasn't the only place I got my stuff from.

Focus on Corie, Frost.

"I don't think I ever told him in precise terms what his friendship means to me." I shake my head, partially to get the unholy thoughts about the numbing paradise that is ten minutes away out of my brain and partially because I have waited, once again, too long to give breath to my feelings. I waited to tell my parents and sister how much they meant to me. I waited to tell Jo what she meant to me. I just briefly told Killy what *he* means to me—it only took five-plus years. But, I have never expressed to Corie how lost I'd be without him. I don't know why it takes the threat of losing someone or losing something in life to illuminate that person's or thing's value. "There's a lot I haven't said."

"Corie reads more than words." Killy turns my body until I'm facing him; I believe the term among today's teenage crowd for what he just did to me is *'Square up, bruh.'* However, we're not sizing each other up. Killy wants my undivided attention in a paternal way. If anyone else had done what he just did, I'd be pointing a finger in a face and swearing—reaffirming my belief that if heaven is a place only reserved for those who have not uttered "fuck," then I will be nowhere near it. Seriously, when I stub my toe in the middle of the night, there's only one word that makes it feel better. Since Killy convincingly turned me, I'm focused on him. He says, "Subtlety plays in *life* too. He knows how you feel, Shawn."

I go to answer, but our peripheral vision seems to catch the movement out of the corners of our eyes at the same moment, and we turn to see Matt jogging with a snowy-haired doctor—Phil Donahue in a lab coat.

Their expressions don't look good.

And why are they jogging toward us? Oh, God, Corie's gone. I lost my chance.

They reach me, and Matt can't even speak.

Doctor…I look down at his nametag…Ryland says, "Mister Woods had a setback and is in surgery again. We'll know more in another hour."

Matt's legs start to wobble, two bowling pins teetering on falling over, and Killy grabs him right before he plunges.

# 21

Well, Corie pulled through that night. And the next.

And the next.

It's nine in the morning, and I will be able to visit him in a few minutes. Matt stayed late last night and is at home resting; he needs a few years of sleep after the past few days. Me? I didn't sleep that much the first night at Killy's, but as Corie's condition has improved, so has my sleep. The last few nights in the hotel have been fine—clean, quiet room, and I've walked a few miles on one of the fitness room's treadmills. There's an elliptical machine, which is supposed to be easier on my joints, but I'm not coordinated enough at six a.m. to stay on the thing.

I sit in the waiting room and drink from my cup of coffee. Whatever executive is responsible for selecting Barney's Boastful Roast as the coffee vendor for the hospital deserves a healthy bonus. I hate hospitals, but since Corie will be here for a while, I have come to look forward to my daily trips to Barney's. The tiny café, just off the main hallway on the ground floor, has become a refuge for me. Friendly baristas, muffins, newspapers—yes, some of us still like to read a paper version of the *Los Angeles Times*—and savory coffee. I don't mind sitting in the waiting room, but the café has a few tables and chairs, and I've made good use of them—especially in the long afternoons. The morning barista's name is

Sara—a lovely mom of two college-aged boys who lost her husband three years ago. Barney's opens at 5 a.m., but Sara starts work at 4. The first shift change occurs at 11 a.m., and a barista named Kemen, a senior at UCLA who is finishing his psychology degree, comes on until 5 p.m. They're both wonderful—cheery, chatty, empathetic, and competent as hell. My kind of people in a hospital coffee shop. Then, my favorite barista, Alicia, arrives and works until 11 p.m., when Barney's closes.

These are the things you notice when you're stuck in a hospital.

But wait, my friends, there's more.

A "wild card" barista (my name for the position) or "roving barista" (Barney's name for the position) named Leo shows up at 9:30 p.m. every night to assist Alicia with the mad, end-of-the-day-Barney's-is-closing-and-nurses, doctors, and-staff-members-are-freaking-out rush that continues until closing time. For that hour and a half, Barney's is a revolving door of hospital workers coming by to pick up their 4, 6, and sometimes 8-cup orders to get them through the night. However, they have all come to respect the hard rule that an 11 p.m. closing time means an 11 p.m. closing time. Alicia and Leo have their routine so down—I've watched it for two nights now—that when the digital clock on the wall behind the main coffee stand hits 11:00, Alicia turns the lights off and then pulls the metal gate across the entrance while Leo makes sure that no one tries to enter. Then, Leo locks the gate, and they head out. If workers miss the last call, then they are on their own, at the mercy of their wing's Mr. Coffee machine. Alicia goes home and then spends the morning working out before strategizing with her agent about roles she can audition for. Yes, sir, another actress trying to make it in Hollywood—and I want her to make it. I've only given her my first name and always pay with cash. Playwrights and audiobook narrators are afforded a little more anonymity than your top-line celebrity, and since I left New York, I am happy not to be recognized.

Anyway, after they close up for the night, Leo catches a few hours of sleep and is back from 4:30 a.m. until 6 to help with the large morning crowd. He is a machine. I asked him the other day how he does it since I never see him without his own coffee cup in his hand when he's working with Alicia at night. He explained to me that he's a semi-professional gamer and that he has international players counting on him between the hours of midnight and 3 a.m., so it works out perfectly. He simply goes home, puts on his headset, and disappears into the game until it's time to come in and work with Sara. He never drinks coffee in the morning and crashes hard at home before waking up in the late afternoon to eat, shower, and join a game by 6, where he claims he is *absolutely needed, Shawn,* until nine p.m. when he changes into his blue jeans and navy polo shirt with the red Barney's logo—the letters in red with three squiggly light brown lines rising from the open mouth of the "y"—over his left breast and "Leo" embroidered in red lettering over his right breast. This reminds me; I'm a big fan of the colors. The Barney's coffee cups are navy with three thin, red stripes near the bottom and the top with the logo in between. The plastic tops are light brown. Classy. Unique.

Naturally, I asked Leo what his long-term plans were. *'Other than becoming a professional gamer? Nothing. This is it. I love who I work with, love my job, and have security in it—no one wants to work my hours, but they're tailor-made for me. And Barney's knows this. That's why us rovers get compensated accordingly.'* Couldn't argue with that. In fact, I prodded the manager, Valentina, who shows up two times a day to make sure everything is running smoothly, about the Barney's business model. It's a two-pronged attack, and it's genius. The brick-and-mortar prong of the brand is exclusive to hospitals, which will never run out of customers. A bit morose, but it is what it is. The virtual prong is the online store, which is the only place other than the cafés inside the hospitals where you can order Barney's coffee. When I sat down with Valentina, I told her that I thought it was a bit risky since human beings are wired for association, and, let's be honest, smells and tastes are powerful prompters of memories. I haven't had a banana or a peanut butter and jelly sandwich in over two years. *'Other than the birth of a child, there are not a lot of good reasons that people are admitted to hospitals, and even fewer for people like me who are visiting people who have been admitted into these sterile palaces. Won't people associate Barney's coffee with traumatic experiences?'* At this, Valentina gave a knowing grin and replied, *'There is definitely logic to your point, Shawn. But, we are now in eighty percent of hospitals across the United States and have experienced tremendous growth the past three years. Our surveys tell us that this is for two reasons. One, hospital workers love our brand, and, two, customers love how they are treated by our staff. We take special pride in our training pipeline, which takes three months to complete, and every employee must attend our corporate training campus in Houston, Texas. It's really quite spectacular. They stay in our own hotel, have their meals taken care of by us, enjoy the classroom and training sessions during the day, and then the Houston nightlife if they so choose. So, a good portion of our online sales are to hospital workers; as a corporation, we also donate a percentage of our earnings to the hospital community—cancer research, medical school scholarships, nursing programs, fellowships, and so on. Another cornerstone of our training program is how to treat friends and family members who are at the hospital to visit loved ones. For our baristas, the job is more than just making coffee. It's about helping people who are going through a difficult time. So, believe it or not, another portion of our online sales are from customers in the hospital who were there to visit someone. Since our competitors are the coffee houses and cafés located outside the hospital—ever notice how many of them there are?—we try to beat their prices every day. We can't save someone's life, Shawn. Only the doctors and nurses can do that. But, we can try and make the visitor's experience as comfortable as possible. In terms of merchandising online, well, we only sell three things: our coffee—in a variety of quantities—our travel mugs, and our signature, large ceramic mugs. That's it, my friend. That's what Barney's is all about.'* I was, of course, impressed, but I had to know how they could keep their rover barista positions filled. Again, she was as smooth as silk, *'A lot of gamers out there, Shawn.'*

I rest my case. I'm a Barney's customer for life. (Yes, I already ordered coffee, two travel mugs, and two signature mugs).

But wait, there's more, and it's damned important.

Sitting at Barney's for the past few days has given me the first decent idea for a new play that I have had since leaving New York. The experience has reminded me where the best ideas for stories come from: observing everyday life. I have closed myself off too much. No, not in the booth, but pretty much all of the time outside of the booth. With the shadow of forty looming, I cannot continue to hide at my home, and I cannot continue to hide from my paper and pen. Maybe it was talking to Alicia and seeing how excited she was about chasing her dream of becoming an actress. Maybe it was Killy showing me warmth from some reservoir that has been hidden from me since he became my agent. Maybe it was the fact that I almost lost Corie. And maybe it was the cliché of a combination of all three. Or, maybe, it was me realizing that it was time.

"Mister Frost?"

I snap out of my trance and look up at the nurse who is calling my name. "Yes?" I say.

"You can come back and see him now."

I get up and follow her down the hall. Am I a little nervous to see Corie? Yes. The past few days, he's been out of it—eyes open for a second or a weak smile at most, and then he drifts off again. The important thing, as my mom and sister explained it to me on the phone last night, is that he knows I was there by his side.

Last night, however, Matt told me that Corie's talking a little. So, here I am on my way to see him.

The nurse ushers me in, and I see even more balloons, flowers, and cards on the table and underneath the table than I did last night. The arrangements have even spilled over onto the floor on both sides and are like vines, creeping toward the window on one side and the door on the other. Like I said, Corie is adored by the masses. The symbols of well wishes on the table and floor give the impression that thousands of people somehow squeezed into the room last night to have a candlelight vigil in his honor, even though he hasn't died. Also, if Corie did die, I can't see a vigil happening. A toned-down celebration of this man's spirit would be more in line with how he would want to be remembered.

Anyway, it doesn't surprise me to see these multiplying signs of love for him, but, nonetheless, I am glad to see them. I think I'd heal quicker if there were abundant gifts of sentiment that continued to fill up my room like *Robert* Frost said that the woods filled up with snow.

But, I'm a sentimental sucker, and I buy into that line of thinking in the same way that I buy into the infrared patches that my chiropractor gives me to relieve my back pain. Maybe you've heard of them—the ones that are imbued with Chinese herbs?

Well, I'm *that guy* who swears by them.

The nurse leaves as I arrive at Corie's bedside and take a seat in the room's one recliner. I reach out and place my right hand on his muscular left forearm. As I do this, I look at his other arm, which is in a cast that goes from his fingers around the seventy or eighty-degree bend in his elbow and ends just below his shoulder. The doctor said they'll cut the cast down to just below the elbow in a few weeks so Corie will be able to bend his arm again, but right now, they want it as still as possible to aid the healing process where the radius and ulna can fuse their respective bones back together. In the accident, both bones snapped in two.

I can't believe I just described this because I just shuddered thinking about it. I'd say the hairs on my own arms are sticking up, but I'm wearing a long-sleeved t-shirt—have been since the second day here. Hospital rooms are also incredibly cold.

Corie opens his eyes, apparently registering my hand on his forearm. Or the sudden *jerk!* my hand just made when I shuddered. Either way, the hand's fine now, and I'm giving his forearm a series of light *taps*.

"Shawn Frost," he says. "Can you narrate me out of this shithole, brother?"

I grin, and it's authentic. Only Corie could start off with a joke after almost losing his life. "You got it," I say.

"Thanks.  Thought you would have already done it after seeing me yesterday. Must be losin' your touch."

"All those damned kid books," I say.

He smiles, but I see that it hurts him to do it.  No more jokes, Frost.

"Ice chips, if you please?"

I take off the plastic top to the Styrofoam cup on his tray.  Then, using the spoon that was on the napkin next to the cup, I scoop out a few chips and carefully guide the spoon into his mouth.

He sucks on them and then chews for a good thirty seconds before swallowing.  "Bless you, Iceberg Productions."

I let another grin slip as he refers to me by a shortened version of my audiobook production company.  The full name is Shawn Frost Iceberg Productions.  Killy came up with it.  One, it's obviously a play on words because my last name is Frost.  Two, it plays on the fact that you only see approximately 10% of an iceberg (the part above the water)—90% is beneath.  *We'll have a graphic that has books above the water, and then your name in huge letters with a microphone underneath the water, which will say to business partners and audiences that reading the book on their own only gives them 10% of the entire experience; having* Shawn Frost *narrate it fills in the other 90% to give a completely fulfilling and enriching experience,'* Killy said when he pitched the idea.  I replied with, *'But, Killy, those proportions aren't righ—' 'Forget the proportions. Do you want people hiring you or not?  Do you want people listening to you or not?'* he interrupted.  I didn't have the guts to counter him, so we had the logo designed, and…as usual, he was right.  Corie's production company is called Deep Dark Woods Audio & Film, LLC.  The logo is a muscular, African-American lumberjack wearing over-ear headphones, whose features look exactly like Corie's, frozen in mid-swing with his red ax inches away from the vertex in the gaping triangle that he has already chopped out of the giant tree before him.  The forest is full and lush around the figure with the moon, high above the tree line, providing the only light in the portrait—a spotlight on the mighty lumberjack hard at work below. Needless to say, Corie could retire from recording and live off the logoed merch he sells at his online store.

Michael Hunnie's company was Honey Bee Listening. There was a bee— never mind, the whole thing is still too painful to talk about. Besides, I should be concentrating on Corie right now. Another curse that has been unfairly bestowed on us creative folk is that in the most serious and dramatic of moments, our brains will diverge to other realms upon hearing a single word or phrase. Case in point, Corie simply said *'Iceberg Productions,'* and my mind took that rocket ship to another solar system.

"How are you feeling?"

"More chips first."

This time I improve upon my lackluster first attempt, and I scoop out an entire spoonful of ice chips.

"Now you're talkin'," Corie says before he opens wide, and I put the spoon in his mouth.

He sucks and chews as I sit and watch.

There's so much I want to say, but he's alive. My best friend is alive, and the urge to pour my heart out has been replaced by my urge to enjoy his company and not overwhelm him. I didn't see this coming, but I suppose a lot of people who are ready to empty their emotions at someone's deathbed retreat when they realize that the person is going to make it. If I'm being honest here, I might end up retreating. Or at least retreating until he is feeling better and won't get worked up—in a good way—about what I have to say. If smiling is painful for him, then I can't risk stirring other emotions.

I'm not copping out.

I think back to what I told Killy the other day.

Okay, I might be copping out.

"Matty at home?" Corie asks.

"Sleeping. He'll be in later this morning."

His eyes get glassy. "There's a lot I never told him, Shawn. You know? What he means to me. Things I meant to say but always seemed to put off. Well, I'm gonna tell him today."

And now I feel lower than low. If Corie can push through, then I guess I can too. Here it goes. "I—"

I stop because we started talking at the same time; when I said, *'I,'* he said, *'He.'* I let him continue. "Told me last night about the kid who hit me." Corie pauses. "Was sad to hear he didn't make it."

He's being genuine. Only Corie Woods could feel sad for someone who almost ended his life. Told you he was a gem. I also think that he didn't hear me start talking at the same time he did. In fact, I'm sure of it because whenever he's noticed in the past, he—not me—has always been the one to stop and say, *'Oh no, you go ahead.'*

"Yeah," I say. "Parents are really hurting, I heard."

He closes his eyes. "I'm not going after them."

Now hold on just a minute there, sir. It's one thing to be humane toward parents who have lost a child—a child that almost ended your life due to his negligence. But it's another thing to not realize that because of this dead kid's mistake, your body is never going to be quite the same. I want to scream, *Take a look at your* body! *Matty and I, and, well, everybody almost lost you forever!'*

Instead, I say, "Are you sure?"

He opens his eyes, and I feed him another spoonful.

He closes his eyes while rolling the chips around in his mouth. "Kid already paid for his mistake," he gets out with a mouth still full of chips. He works them around some more and finally swallows. "I'd say the real culprit here was his phone, but we all still possess the ability to choose whether or not to use it while we're driving. So, I'm not suing the cell phone company either." He opens his eyes. "Plus, doc says I'll be healed and back to my old self—just going to take a while."

I'm not letting him off the hook that easy.

I give his arm another pat and say, "Well, don't worry about all of that now. Let's focus on getting you better."

"Amen to that."

I motion toward the ice chips with the spoon, and he waves me off. "Anything else I can do?"

He manages one more tiny smile. "As a matter of fact, there is."

I pat his arm again. "Anything."

"In my bag over there," he says, pointing to the familiar backpack I've seen him sling over his shoulder a million times, heading out of his house with me to go get coffee and take a walk in the park.

I hop up and walk to the bag.

"Bring over the book, will you?"

I open the bag, and underneath his favorite sweatshirt, I see the top of a hardcover book. I pull it out.

As I turn it over in my hands, I feel a lump in my throat. It is a book I know well, *Mission to Berlin*, the very first Nehemiah Stone novel by M. Scott Sala. The book that put me on the map. In a way, this book is my *career*.

But why does Corie have it with him?

I return to the recliner.

"Surprised?"

"Well, yes. Why is this in your bag?"

"Bought it the day I listened to you perform it for the first time. By a mile, my favorite book. It's never left this bag."

All those years, it's been in there. I don't know what to say.

"You're amazing, Shawn."

But, Corie always knows what to say. The tears are coming now.

He closes his eyes. "Read it to me, old friend."

It takes me a few moments to gather my composure.  Yes, I steal some ice chips while I'm doing it.  Then, after a few calming breaths, I begin.

As the words

## Nehemiah Stone was only alive

come out of my mouth, I see Corie grin as his head rests peacefully on the pillow. It is then that I realize that the words I had planned to say to Corie would have been inadequate, but he has now given me a chance to express them through a reading of a book that I never knew had touched him.  But then, like a thunderbolt, the plot comes back to me—Nehemiah's uphill climb in life for freedom, his drive to protect and serve those who cannot protect themselves, and yet, his inability to get close enough to the human beings that he comes into contact with, which would entice him to stay in one place.  The makings of the character that I still miss are all right there in this remarkable opening book.  After losing at the Audies for *The Paris Sanction* and my unfortunate departure from the world I loved afterward, I doubted I would ever narrate a thriller again.  Certainly not anything with Nehemiah Stone in it.  But, as I let myself become immersed in the text and welcome Corie's listening ears into the story, I realize just how much I have missed Nehemiah's company.

And, as the surroundings of the hospital room begin to fade, turning into the beautiful architecture of Berlin—spires and stone, steel and glass—as Corie and I travel there and witness the old-world charm with Nehemiah, it finally hits me.

After all of this time, I'm ready to give thrillers another try.

# 22

I leave the hospital four hours later. Matt is back with Corie, and I'll return sometime after dinner. Corie was in and out of sleep while I visited, but we made it through 6 chapters of *Mission to Berlin*, and I'm excited about getting back to tonight's pages.

I drop by Barney's, say hi to Kemen, and grab a to-go cup. I'll see Alicia later tonight when I come back. With the stress of the past few days, it feels good to have carved out a little routine and to have people that you know, like, and trust embedded within that routine. There's a book out, something or other about habits, that Killy made me read. Didn't work. I hid my bags of potato chips in the pantry and placed a bowl of fresh apples on the kitchen counter, the philosophy being that if the apples were the only thing visible in the kitchen and were readily accessible, then I would naturally pick up an apple when I got hungry for a snack.

I walked right past the apples and headed to the pantry for a month. Then, I thought I got smart and put the apples in the pantry and the potato chips in a bowl on the kitchen counter…

Never made it to the pantry. Bowls of chips disappeared in record time, forcing me to make more trips to the grocery store. Moral of the story: if you want to form the habit of spending more money at the grocery store, put apples in your pantry.

I take a sip of the wonderful, mild, early-afternoon brew from Barney's and leave through the hospital's main entrance. The warmth of the July afternoon engulfs me as I put on my sunglasses and stride down the sidewalk along 16th street. I love the weather down here this time of year—a dry mid-80s in the afternoon and cool mid-60s at night. With my long sleeves and jeans on, I'm a tad bit warm at the moment, but the coffee is magnifying the effects I feel from the perfect sun in the cloudless sky. L.A. in the summer. Nothing like it. If I wasn't in Carmel, I'd be here in Santa Monica.

I cross over Arizona Avenue and continue down 16th street. My legs have loosened up, and I'm feeling relaxed—emotionally drained but relaxed. Ahead, vehicles speed across my line of view on Santa Monica Boulevard. I'll cross over in a few minutes and continue down a few more blocks until I reach my hotel.

Unless that is, I want to make a quick stop at DK's Donuts & Bakery. I skipped lunch—never a good thing—and now my stomach is grumbling. I could have picked up something to eat at Barney's, but after the morning with Corie, I wanted to get some fresh air and *move*. I'm tired of my smartwatch vibrating, telling me it's time to stand up. I had been spending some time outdoors at the hospital's Harman Garden Plaza over the past few afternoons when I wasn't hanging around Barney's, but I want to get back to my hotel to rest and regroup before I visit Corie tonight. Plus, if I walk, then I'll be freeing up the necessary calories to enjoy a double-decker donut at DK's. It worked yesterday when I went there.

It's settled. I'm going.

I am a couple of hundred feet from the intersection when a car passes me, stops at the stop sign, and lets a passenger out before taking a right on Santa Monica Boulevard. I see that it is a large man, and he walks across 16th and waits at the corner, head on a swivel, checking the heavy traffic on Santa Monica Boulevard before using the crosswalk.

I cross over 16th as well, and in a few seconds, I am within a few yards of him. His back is to me, and I see that he's wearing black dress shoes, black dress pants with pleats, a black belt around a trim waist, and a white dress shirt that is smartly tucked in but angles out to his massive shoulders. Beyond him, across the street is the small parking lot ringed with stores: DK's, Chomp Eatery & Juice Station, Lee's Chinese Fast Food, Cellular Gallery, and good old reliable 7-Eleven.

Cars zoom past us as I pull up, even with him on his left. An imposing figure, maybe 6'4 or 6'5. He's got salt and pepper hair with a military cut and is wearing wire-rimmed designer glasses. Around his mouth is a thick, grey goatee. Sharp lad. He seems to notice me and takes a step to the right, putting a little more space between us. I see that he's wearing a shiny watch—can't see the brand— on his left hand as he pulls out his cell phone and starts scrolling, apparently in no hurry to make a dash for the other side. Me? My stomach is howling now, and I can see donuts on every car that passes.

There's a break in the traffic, and I decide to go and let my fellow walker take care of business on his phone while he waits for the next opening. But before I start to walk, I look at his profile one more time. There is something familiar about it. I don't know why. It just seems like I've seen him before somewhere. In the hospital?

I break off my stare, look up and down Santa Monica Boulevard one last time, and start to walk across the street. A few steps into the crosswalk, I hear footsteps behind me. I guess he decided to cross after all.

We make it to the other side, and I head left toward DK's. My mouth is salivating now as I can see the sign above the door—the gateway to ooey-gooey goodness. But, as I contemplate the fulfillment that shall soon enter my mouth and belly, I listen for my fellow walker's footsteps. I hear them, but they're getting fainter. Casually, as if I'm out for a Sunday stroll without a care in the world, I look to my right and see that the large man has continued straight on the sidewalk, heading toward 7-Eleven or beyond.  About to wish him well on his journey—this is what writers and actors do: we make up conversations in our heads and sometimes speak the lines in public where no one within earshot understands what in the hell we're saying—I notice that he has a slight limp in his left leg.

# 23

And suddenly, I'm not in the parking lot of DK's anymore. I'm in a cell studio watching one of my captors, Wolverine, limp in the hall. Could this man be him?

I go through my checklist.

Limp in the left leg? Check. Watch on the left hand? Check. Height and build? Check and check. Hair and beard color? It's not the same, but I have always assumed that he was wearing a brown wig and had dyed his mustache brown. So, it still could be him. The glasses are different, but now that I think of it, when I got a profile look at him on the other side of the street, his current glasses framed his face in a similar manner. That must have been the thing that got me thinking that I had seen this man before. Eye color? Damnit. I couldn't see his eyes. If I can get close enough to find out that he has blue or brown eyes, then we're still in the game. My God! I'm thinking about trying to get closer. Get a hold of yourself, Frost!

I look away and walk as calmly as I can toward DK's. I walk a little more to my left so that I can make a wider turn when I get closer to the store entrance and, hence, create more time to view him without drawing attention. A few more steps...

I start my turn.

He's still moving down the sidewalk toward the 7-Eleven.  Will he go in?  And if he does, what am I going to do about it?

What if he keeps walking past the 7-Eleven?  Do I follow?

I take my time making my turn and keep watching; his eyes are straight ahead, so he doesn't see me.

If it *is* him, then why in the hell is he here?  Are he and Big Boss following me?  Watching me?  My breathing picks up.  The nightmares are returning, and I'm helpless to stop them.

I reach the sidewalk that runs in front of DK's and slow to almost a standstill.  He keeps walking.  Phone time.  I step back into the shadows, almost right up against the store window, and reach in my pocket.

No phone.

I reach in the other pocket.

Nothing.

Shit!  I left it at the hotel this morning!

Okay, think Frost.  You can't get any video evidence, but there is something going on here.  It's too coincidental.

He's almost to 7-Eleven.

Think!

Then, it comes to me.  I have to confront him.  No, no, not in some kind of fighting manner.  I need to create an interaction with this man.

I need to see his eyes.

I need to hear his voice.

*'Hey bubba,'* rings through my head.  I would never mistake that tone.  If I can get this limping bastard to talk, I'll know whether it's him or not.

I have to close the gap, though.  If whoever dropped him off pulls over in the next 20 seconds and picks him up, then my plan is toast.

I walk into the parking lot.  There are people getting into their cars, and I believe that I can get away with walking faster toward him if I do it by maneuvering around parked cars. He shouldn't notice me because a lot of people move this way in parking lots. If I was to pick up my pace while continuing to walk along the sidewalk in front of the strip of other businesses, then I'd stick out for sure.

He's at the point of no return. I'm closing.

He goes past 7-Eleven!

I continue my pursuit. I'm within ten yards now; he hasn't turned around.

How do I do this?

I make what my contractor uncle used to say was a "field decision" and start to sprint.

A few paces behind him, I start yelling, "Sonofabitch! They just couldn't wait for me!"

He starts to turn.

I continue yelling. "I'm gonna be late now!"

I get a quick glimpse of his face as I bolt past him. God, it looks like Wolverine.

About three bounds past him, I enter the actor's studio once more—been years, feels unbelievable—and trip on the sidewalk.

Down I go, saying, "Agggghhhhhhh!"

I time the fall just perfectly so that I don't hurt myself too badly. I do skin up my palm, and the concrete did not feel good on the old hip. I can't think about it now. No pain, no gain.

I wait.

He takes the bait and approaches me. With the way I fell, he had to, or else he'd look like the world's biggest tool. I yell, "Oh, this day!" for good measure and shake my fists at the sky.

"Sir, are you okay?" he says.

What the hell? He doesn't sound *anything* like Wolverine.

I look up at his face, acting like I'm still pissed off at the world, which is my way of maintaining my composure.

His eyes are blue.

And the shape of his face is exactly like I remember Wolverine's. How I wish he had a mole or something that would have helped me confirm it. The wrinkles are still there on his forehead, though, so his age is about right.

I answer him. "Ever have one of those days?"

He gives a knowing smile. Damnit, his thick goatee throws me off, and I am unable to compare his smile with Wolverine's. In fact, Wolverine showed more teeth, and they were a disgusting brown color. A few of them were even crooked. This guy has a set of white, straight teeth.

"All the time," he says. He kneels down beside me. "Feel like anything's broken?"

I study his face while saying, "Don't think so. Tell you what, though, the way the day's going, I bet that's next." It's all there. The eyes, the way the glasses sit, the shape of his face. It really could be him!

"Need help getting up?"

Perfect, he'll have to grab me in some way, and I will never forget the kind of grip Wolverine had. And, while I'm at it, it's time to mess with him a little and see if I get a reaction. "Yeah, thanks, bubba," I say.

And I see it. It's him. If I wasn't looking directly at his eyes when I said it, I would have never seen the small flinch of recognition as he made eye contact in an instant, his head jerking ever so slightly back at my statement. One hand is already reaching for my hand, his other hand going for my upper arm. He can't stop now, or it would definitely signal that something was wrong.

Time to pile it on. Footwear and baby Jesus.

As he grabs my hand and upper arm—damn, it's a vise grip like I remember; his hands are huge—I say, "Jesus Christ, the hell with these shoes. Need to get me some GOD DAMN Wolverine boots. Know what I'm sayin', bigun?"

To his credit, he helps me all the way up but quickly releases me.

"Might need to," he says, avoiding my eyes now.

I put my left hand on my right shoulder and wind my right arm round and round. "Appreciate you helping me up. Gotta strong grip, man."

"Not a problem." He makes eye contact with me. "You okay now?"

The hell I am! "Yeah." I lift my right leg and then my left as if I'm testing them. "I can make it where I'm headin'. Just need to take it slow." I put out my hand, "Thank you…"

He gives my hand a firm shake. "Peter," he says.

"Shawn," I say back.

He turns and starts walking away down the street in front of me.

I follow.

We pass by a homeless shelter and its associated admin building. He's not rushing, but he's not looking back either.

I watch as he crosses over Broadway. There's a VFX studio on the left and a community-owned natural foods store named Co-opportunity Market Santa Monica on the right where I've been picking up odds and ends.

I reach Broadway. My hotel, a brand-new Hilton that was built on the site of a Food School that had shut down, is across the street on the left corner of 16th and Broadway. I walk right past it, continuing to follow him.

I've closed the gap, but he hasn't noticed. Another giveaway. He has not looked back once. If I had just helped out a stranger who had fallen down, you better believe that I would have at least glanced back a few times to see how he was doing. I think anyone would do this.

I can now see cars passing 16th street, driving along Colorado Avenue. Is he getting picked up? If so, I threw off his timing.

He makes a deliberate left and disappears out of view.

I walk fast and reach the point where he vanished. There's only one place he could have gone: straight through the front door of Santa Monica Bed &

Breakfast. I wait on the street for a minute, making sure he doesn't appear somewhere else. There is a small parking lot next to the B & B, but this is the only way in or out by car.

I give it another minute and then walk toward the front door.

I'm going in.

# 24

I enter through the teal-colored door, and a chime rings.

Where is he?

The small lobby has a paneled front desk that is painted white with a sculpted fireplace mantel on top. The floor is tiled in small salmon-colored, glassy squares. A wicker couch and chair with glass end tables gives the room a cozy vacation feel like you're one step closer to paradise. A ceiling fan blows overhead.

There is no one at the front counter. There are two exit doors off the lobby that I see. One of them is in the corner, at the far end of the front desk, which must lead into an office. The other is next to the coffee station, and I guess that is the door that leads to the rooms.

I approach the door next to the coffee station. The smell tempts me to make myself a quick cup, but a group of loud hosts arguing over something on the lobby's television set distracts me.

About to open the door so that I can continue my search for Wolverine, I hear, "Good afternoon, sir. May I help you?"

I turn around and see a bony, small man with a marvelous full head of white hair wearing a crisp, white t-shirt with a pocket standing behind the desk. I deliver a perfect lie. "Hi. Didn't know if anyone was here."

"Nature does call now and then," he says.

Too much information, but the guy's honest. I walk up to the desk. Time for lie number two. "I believe a large man just came in here." I show him the scrape on my arm. "I took a tumble out on the sidewalk a few minutes ago and wanted to thank him once again for helping me up. Guy stayed with me until he was sure I was going to be all right. You just don't see that much nowadays, you know?"

"Thank you for saying so. When social media came in through the window, common courtesy and decency flew out."

I hit the right spot. I don't agree with him one-hundred percent, but I pulled the right lever. Time for lie #3. "Can't argue with that, sir."

He warms to my lie. "Let me shake your hand, mister…"

"Boar. Kurt Boar," I say. Lie #4 feels good. Screw *Narrator*.

He grasps my hand and seems to squeeze for all he's worth. "Sweet Bill," he says. "Wife calls me that, and it's kind of caught on with everybody else, so I go with it. The old girl is off today. Fishin' or some such thing. Be back for dinner, though."

*Sweet Bill!*

We shake—an eyeball to eyeball shake at that. Why not pour it on? "Glad to know there's still two of us that believe the world is headed for the—" Hmmm. What would Sweet Bill predict the destination for the world is? I go with my instincts. "Shitter."

This gets a wicked cackle. "Have to spread the word. Gotta be more of us out there."

Great. Now Sweet Bill and I are activists.

Lie #5. "Deal," I say and rest my elbows on the pristine and polished counter. "Now, about that big fella?"

"Heard the chime ring, but, like I said, I was takin' care of other business." He winks at me.

Why do old men like to talk about the bathroom? Maybe I'll find out one day. "Got it." Now what do I do? I need to get through that door or find out what room Wolverine's staying in, at the least. "You have any rooms available?" I ask.

He gives an amused laugh. "You thinkin' of checkin' in?"

"Would love to, but no," I say, playing along. "This place is a gem, though. Your lobby is spotless."

"Pride myself in keeping a tidy house. That's another thing this new generation needs to learn."

I nod in agreement, lying once again. "How many rooms do you have?"

"Six."

I guessed it was somewhere around that figure. "Nice number of guests to host," I say, knowing absolutely nothing about the business.

"Get to know most everybody," he says.

I point to my wound once again. "Well, the gentleman who helped me up from this was around six-five maybe. Anyone like that staying here?"

"Matter of fact, there is, Kurt," he says. He slides over a few feet and opens up a ledger book. "I don't do computers. That's the wife's area of expertise. Me? I like something I can hold in my hands." He hoists the ledger book up. "This never needs to be restarted or runs out of power."

I nod in agreement. I mean, he's right.

"Let old Sweet Bill see here," he says, putting on a pair of heavy-duty glasses. "Yes, sir, a Mister Peter Canfield is in suite four."

Well, Wolverine is keeping his alias consistent. "I don't suppose you would be able to see if he's available to see me right now, would you?"

"Sure. Why not? Nothing happens around here all day. Most of our guests head to the beach—only see 'em around dinner time."

"Thanks," I say.

Sweet Bill disappears into a room at the far end of the front desk and comes out through the door in the corner. His t-shirt is tucked into the cuffed, tan shorts he's wearing. Black belt on with a flashlight hanging from a holster. Two skinny, white legs end in white socks pulled up around his calves and black tennis shoes with two Velcro straps on top. He strides past me. "Be right back, Kurt."

He opens the door by the coffee maker and vanishes. A few seconds later, I hear muffled knocking. Then, silence.

Is Wolverine back there talking his way out of seeing me?

I wait a minute more. The yelling on the talk show has ratcheted up another level, and one of the hosts is now standing, pointing a finger at the other three co-hosts. Who watches this nonsense? Oh, right. I do. "That's right. You tell her, lady," I say to the TV.

I wait another minute. My mind, as it typically does, goes to the worst-case scenario. Has Wolverine hurt Sweet Bill?

I decide that if he's not back in thirty seconds, I'm going back there.

I get to fifteen, and Sweet Bill returns.

No one is behind him.

"Well, I knocked, and after not hearing anything, I opened the door and checked inside. As the owner, I always have the right to do this. I just file it under the category of 'needing to make sure that one of my guests wasn't in danger.' It's all good. Never had a problem."

"Was he there?"

"Nope. I even checked his back patio. Each of our rooms has one. Nobody out there either."

A back patio. "Could someone leave your property that way?"

"Sure," says Sweet Bill. "There's a back gate. All of our guests are issued an access card that they can swipe to leave and enter."

Damnit. He's gone. "Thanks," I reply.

"I can be sure to tell him you stopped by."

A thought enters my mind. "Did he check in alone?"

"Yeah. He's the only one staying in the room. But—"

"But what?"

"Well, as I'm sure you can imagine, a few of our guests over the years have brought someone back with them on occasion. It's usually through the back gate to be discrete, which we appreciate, of course. Can't say for sure if Peter will be that type or not."

"I don't mean to prod." Yes, I do. "But do you know how long he's staying with you? I have to get going but might like to come back later tonight or tomorrow."

He waves a hand as if he gets asked this all the time. "He's not checking out until tomorrow."

"Good to know," I say. Then, another thought occurs to me, and I look around the room—up at the corners where the ceiling meets the walls. I don't see what I'm looking for. "Any security cameras?"

"Never needed 'em. What's the interest?"

Time for lie number…I forgot what number I'm on. "Just curious. You see them everywhere now. Kind of nice to not see them."

"Amen. Gotta hold the line on trust. We lose that, and we're done."

I extend my hand, and he takes it. "I might be back later tonight, but do me a favor and don't tell Peter that I was here. I might surprise him with a gift."

Sweet Bill gives me that good old boy my-word-is-oak shake and nod.

I leave Santa Monica Bed & Breakfast and head back toward my cookie-cutter Hilton. Cut your losses, Frost. You didn't identify Wolverine, but you did identify a character for your next play. I start whistling "Wedding Bell Blues" by The 5th Dimension.

I'll be returning in a few hours, and this time, I'm bringing someone with me…

I used to run the hundred in ten flat.

I'll be back with the whole fire department.

# 25

In one sense, I, Jo Mansfield, can't believe I am actually walking down the street in Santa Monica with my ex-boyfriend, Shawn Frost. In another sense, it seems like we were always destined to have one more moment like this together. I am either going to have my mind blown away by identifying—hence, verifying—one of Shawn's supposed captors from a few years back, or I am going to witness the utter demise of a broken, lost soul. My heart tells me the former will happen; my brain tells me the latter is more probable.

"The place is right there?" I ask, pointing at a sign that says: Santa Monica Bed & Breakfast.

"Tucked away, isn't it?" Shawn says.

"Could drive right past it."

"Right?"

He's amped-up, has been ever since he called me five hours ago.

My boyfriend, Alex, attempted to talk me out of going. He said that it sounded like Shawn was exhibiting the same exact erratic behavior from two years ago. *'He can't be trusted!'* I couldn't argue that with him; when Shawn told me that he had found the man he called "Wolverine" a few blocks from the hospital where Corie was recovering after almost losing his life, I thought, *You poor soul. The accident has triggered a relapse.'* Then, I became angry. Not with Shawn, but with David Killian.

Killian should have kept a better eye on him. This is not how things were supposed to go. When Shawn told me that he had been walking back to the Hilton every night, I almost screamed, *'Well, shit, David! Does that sound like a smart idea?'* But I didn't. No use venting my frustration with Killian over the phone to Shawn. And I'm probably being too harsh on Killian; Shawn is a 39-year-old man. In fact, I started to feel guilty. Guilty because I haven't reached out to Shawn enough. Some old feelings stirred when I saw him at his 2-years-clean party, and I realize now that I've been keeping more distance than I needed to— or wanted to. We were such close friends before, as well as lovers. The year-long run of my play in New York City was a highlight of my career but also a gut-wrenching withdrawal from the man I thought I would be with forever. The way it *ended.* And, now, here on the streets of Santa Monica, the way it's ending again.

If I would have known that he was walking to the Hilton every night, which is near the apartment complex where he was getting his fixes back then, I would have paid for a cab both ways every single day for him. But no one told me. I only heard from Matt, David, and Shawn when the accident occurred and once from Shawn over a day ago when things started looking better. I should have come down. I planned on it, but now, as I look at my ex-boyfriend in his long sleeves—hmmm…wonder why he's got a *long-sleeved* shirt on—I realize that I'm too late.

So, what did I do before I got on the plane? I broke Shawn's trust and called David Killian. I had to. Because I still care for Shawn.

Killian's plan is simple. I am to babysit Shawn through this investigation at the B & B, making sure that he doesn't cross any lines, and then walk him back to the Hilton under the pretense that we are going to sit down in his room and plan our next move. What is really going to happen? David Killian will be waiting out front with a paramedic team to take Shawn to the hospital to get drug tested. And, if our suspicion is correct and he tests positive, then it's off to Laguna again.

And it will be bye from me forever. I'll be done with him. Alex wanted me to cut it off on the phone, but no, Shawn deserves better than that. He needs to know that I was willing to give him another chance. Plus, he's so harmless. Nothing is going to happen at this place. Shawn couldn't physically hurt anyone. The guy is incapable of it.

Now, I'm not saying he is incapable of fighting. We all have that conditioning buried deep inside us from thousands of years of human evolution. What I *am saying* is that even if he did fight, he couldn't injure anyone. I've never said this to him, but I think he knows it.

"You ready?" Shawn says. He's holding his cell phone in his hand like it's a weapon.

I motion him toward the door. "After you."

We head inside. I hear a bell jingle and notice that there is no one at the front desk. Also, I am *surprised*. The room is exactly as Shawn has described it to me. I thought that when I saw that the lobby was not a tidy, bright, and welcoming space, it would be the first sign that he was out of his mind. Well, actually, I thought it would be when we walked here and found out that the place didn't exist. Yes, I looked online before flying down, but there have been places I have researched online only to find them torn down or abandoned when I actually visited—happens all the time when you visit big cities. And, no, I didn't call ahead. I wanted to show Shawn *some* respect, and if there is a 1% chance that he really is on to something here, I couldn't bring myself to interfere. And, as I said, I do my breakups in person.

The place is cute—clean and comfortable, but definitely has a woman's touch. I need to acknowledge that at least he was right about the description.

"Just like you said," I say, giving his arm a squeeze.

"I'll see if I can get Sweet Bill."

Now, I don't care if we find out whether this "Wolverine" character exists or not tonight. But I sure as hell want to meet Mr. Sweet Bill. Please, Shawn, tell me you didn't make him up.

I arrive at the front desk next to Shawn. "They don't watch the front desk too closely, do they?"

"Same as this afternoon."

He's about to yell out for someone; there isn't one of those handy little bells that you can ring. Then again, I thought the bell on the door was supposed to announce that the place had visitors.

A stately woman walks out of the office next to the front desk and approaches us. "Hi. Looking for a room tonight? Got one open."

She's professional. Black slacks, white blouse, cobalt-blue nametag with white letters that spell "Suzie."

Shawn starts right in. "Hi, Suzie, my name is—" he pauses.

What the hell? He looks over at me and then back to Suzie. "Kurt Boar."

Before I can do or say anything, he squeezes my hand. I can't wait to hear this explanation later.

"And I was here earlier this afternoon. I spoke with your husband."

She raises an eyebrow at him. "When did you speak with him?" Her tone is not kind.

Shawn looks confused but then answers. "It was this afternoon. His name is Sweet Bill, right? Can I please speak with him?"

"No."

Shawn looks to me, seemingly searching for answers. I have none, bud. He looks back at Suzie. "Why not?"

"'Cause he suddenly fell ill right before dinner tonight. Ole boy's in bed."

"Oh, I'm sorry," Shawn says. "He looked fine when I met with him."

"Well, he's not now. Can I help you get a room, or what's your business?"

"Did he say anything to you about meeting me today?"

"No."

I can see he's getting frustrated. This is going to be hard on him, but I've just got to ease him out of here and get him back to the hotel where Killian is waiting.

But, Shawn Frost is not one to give up, even though he may be in another reality right now.

"I'm sorry. I fell outside today, and a man who is staying at your bed and breakfast helped me. It was very kind. Long story short, I saw that he was staying here, and I wanted to drop by tonight and give him a small gift to show my gratitude."

"What's this got to do with my husband?"

"Well, I stopped in today because I wanted to thank him then, but your husband went to check his room, suite four, and he wasn't there. So, I'm back now, hoping to catch him."

Suzi still looks confused, but she goes over to her computer and starts punching keys. Shawn and I exchange a glance. Thirty seconds or so later, she merely says, "Uh-huh."

"What did you find out?" Shawn asks.

"There is no one staying in suite four."

"What?"

"Didn't you hear me? There's no one staying in suite four."

"Did he check out?"

"Looks like it. About an hour ago."

"I thought he was staying until tomorrow."

She glances back at the computer and scrolls up and then down with her mouse. "My records don't show that."

Shawn is starting to sweat. Time for him to go—for sure before she finds out his name is not Kurt Boar.

I say, "Hey—"

"Can I see your husband's ledger, please?"

Now, she gives him a look that says: *Mother hen is now about to protect her chick.* "How do you know about that?"

"He showed it to me this afternoon when I asked about the man in suite four. Sweet Bill said his name was Peter Canfield."

She gives Shawn an even colder stare. "Now, what's going on here?"

"What do you mean? I'm just trying to find this man and figure out what happened?"

"You're lying."

I take his arm. "We really should get—"

"I am *not*," he snaps back.

"Oh, yes, you are, honey. The man who was staying in suite four was Mark Massey."

Shawn peers over the counter. "Where's the ledger? It's in there. Sweet Bill looked it up."

Suzie does a quick survey of the space behind the front desk. When her eyes return to Shawn's, it is unclear whether she has seen it or not. "Don't see it."

"Well, can you look around, please?"

"Listen, I don't like what's going on here. I'm about to call the police."

Finally, I grab him harder and get his attention. "Let's leave her alone, okay. I want to talk to you outside for a minute." I sneak my eyes over to Suzie. Her hand is right next to the front desk's phone.

Shawn looks at me—frustrated, pleading, near-broken—and says, "Okay."

"Thank you for your assistance, ma'am," I say. "We won't be bothering you anymore tonight. Have a good evening."

She moves away from the phone, and we exit.

I'll spare you Shawn's profanity-laced rant on the way back to the Hilton. He's not himself. I still need him to think that I believe his story until we get him inside the ambulance. I will try my best not to tell Killian that Shawn told the B

& B owners that Shawn's name was one of the characters in the story he was forced to narrate in the recording dungeon.

"And why didn't she let me look at the ledger?" he shouts. It's the tenth time he's said it.

"I don't know, Shawn. Let's just get to your room, and we'll plan our next move." I've said that at least twice now.

We round the corner onto Broadway, and there is the ambulance.

"Oh, no," he says. "I hope everyone is okay." He says this every time he sees an ambulance. Like I told you, he may be the kindest man I've ever known.

We get to within five yards of the ambulance, and we hear the rich baritone voice of David Killian. "Shawn, Jo."

Shawn immediately stops, looking in all directions. "Killy?"

Killian appears from around the side of the ambulance.

"What are you doing here?"

Before Shawn can look back at me, the back doors of the ambulance explode open, and two huge orderlies jump out and grab Shawn. He's so shocked that he doesn't struggle or scream, and they get him inside in seconds. Killian closes the door.

Now, I can hear Shawn scream for me.

Moments later, his voice ceases, and I know that means that they have sedated him.

"I'm sorry," Killian says. "But thanks for working with us again."

"We should have done better," I say. "We should have looked after him."

He puts a hand on my shoulder, nods, but doesn't say anything for a few seconds—a man whose power reaches the world round yet couldn't reach his own prized client…and friend.

"A cab will be here in ten minutes to take you back to the airport. They've got your things from Shawn's room at the front desk. I already gathered his suitcase and checked him out."

"Will you call me when the tests come back?"

"Immediately."

"Okay," I say.

"This was never your fight, Jo.  He's a grown man."  Killian hugs me.  "Safe travels."

We break the embrace, and I hear the ambulance start.  I begin walking toward the Hilton's entrance.

The sound of a car door opening makes me turn around, and I see David Killian getting into the passenger's side of the emergency vehicle.  The lights start to flash.  He shuts the door, and the ambulance drives off.

I watch the bright flashing of its lights until the vehicle rounds a corner and disappears.

Goodbye, Shawn.

# PART IV
## Mastering

*3 Months Later...*

# 26

## Pacific Palisades

"**D**avid, I just emerged from a publishing rights war, the likes I've never seen in our forty years together in the business."

Greetings. My name is David Killian, and this is how major deals are made in the publishing industry. *This* is how you take care of your clients. I'm in my silk pajamas, resting comfortably on my couch with a flute of champagne—prefer to be comfortable when I work a major deal. The person I'm talking to on the phone? Rider Elizabeth Cross, the CEO of ParkerWilson Publishing and Queen Bee of the publishing world. I've never called her anything but "Liz." We started out together as copy editors in the basement of Doubleday when Reagan was president and rose together after that. To my knowledge, everyone else calls her Ms. Cross. Well, good for them.

Right about now, Liz must be pinching herself. Rumor has it that ParkerWilson paid high seven figures for a two-book deal with an unknown debut author. *Unheard* of. Crazy. Manuscript has the entire industry in a *frenzy* right now. Go figure, it's a psychological thriller about an audiobook narrator. Who would have thought, right?  For perspective, Penguin Random House gave Dan Brown four-hundred grand for his two-book deal when it acquired *The Da Vinci Code*—and he already had *three* novels in print.

"I heard about the manuscript."  Anyone who's anyone in the business has.

"I assumed so."

"*Listen To Me.*  Good title."

"We think so."

I pause.  The real conversation is about to start.  Liz isn't calling me to shoot the breeze.  Liz is calling me because she needs a narrator.

"What can I do for you, my friend?"

"I need a narrator for the book."

"Oh?"  I love playing dumb.  Now, usually, debut authors don't get to choose who narrates their books.  Veterans can work it into their contracts, but newbies are traditionally at the mercy of whom the publishing house wants and who is available to narrate.  But.  For a deal this big, the rules change.

"Yes."

"Who do you have in mind?"

There is a hint of hesitation before she says, "Shawn Frost."

"Really?  You think my guy is the perfect person to narrate *Listen To Me*?"  I ask.

"I don't know about *perfect*.  This book would have definitely gone to Hunnie if he were still alive.  But, the author's agent says she prefers Shawn Frost.  We've got some other options—a few big names have reached out—but, as a friend, I wanted to give you the first crack.  I'm sure you've heard.  We're fast-tracking the publication. Red hot.  Need to get it recorded and need to get it out."

She isn't telling the whole truth.  No surprise and I'm not offended.  I'd *be* offended if she didn't play the game with me.  The most valuable commodity I know of in this stage of dealmaking is *information*.  And information I have.  They *are* fast-tracking the publication, which I agree with—the idea is too good to sit on. If Shawn hadn't been crippled by his own trauma, I would have told him to write a novel like this. Just a matter of time before someone else did, and here we are. Here's where Liz is not being completely honest: Through my backchannels with the author's agent, I've discovered that the author wants Shawn Frost, and *only* Shawn Frost, to narrate the book. Important to know, wouldn't you say? Did I tell Shawn this? Fuck no. He'd lose it—start in on his conspiracy theories again. *They only want me? Don't you see it, Killy? I've been set up!'* or some such nonsense. "And that's why I'm speaking with the CEO of the grandest publisher in the land right now, correct?" Never hurts to boost her ego a tad during the proceedings. She was merciless as an editor and has graduated to mercenary as a CEO.

"Our entire industry is getting turned upside down, David. We need a hit, Goddamnit."

She is absolutely right on both counts, and when she curses, it's unsettling because of the way she slows down to emphasize the expletive. But I've got to toy with her a bit more. All part of the game. I've already delayed calling her back by a day, and I'm the *only one* in the business who can get away with that. "Bullshit, Liz," I say. "You've got the most enviable stable of *New York Times* bestselling authors in the business."

"Not enough anymore, old ally." Her response is so fast that it is as if she knew what I was going to say. One tough cookie to play the game with. And, she threw in "ally," like we're a team. Smooth move. I take a sip of champagne as I consider her statement.

She's right again. We're eating our breeding stock, and everyone knows it. A slight agreement here will build some momentum. She's horrible at taking compliments but secretly enjoys them. But, what I'm about to say will get her to the point. "Well, if anyone would know that that's the case, it's you, old friend."

"So, Shawn Frost. Is he..."

Told you.  But.  She's playing one of her high cards here, and I need to be very careful with what I say.  You better believe her pause is for effect.

"How should I say this—*reliable* these days?"

"Shawn's never been better.  Just finished up his second thriller in the past month.  He sounds incredible.  Energy and performance are at all-time highs."

And I'm not lying here.  I was convinced that life was done surprising me until a few months ago when Shawn Frost tested clean for every, and I mean *every* known drug on this planet.  My first surprise was when I tore down his sleeves in the ambulance and couldn't find any needle marks.  Then, the test results came back to the hospital, and I had to eat humble pie.  I apologized to Shawn and hired a private detective to look into the man who had been staying at the Santa Monica Bed & Breakfast.  This went a long way toward repairing our relationship, but the P.I. was unable to generate any leads.  The man paid with cash, so there was no tracing a credit card.  The ledger went missing and never showed up again.  The consensus was that someone took it.  Perhaps, it was the man who had stayed in suite number four; perhaps, not.  In fact, the only thing the P.I. ended up confirming was that Sweet Bill swears that he wrote the name Peter Canfield in his register.  Apparently, the man had checked in with Suzie and given her the name Mark Massey, which is, of course, strange and a red flag.  But this is California, and people do weird shit every day—partly why I love living here.  I'm never bored.  Stuffy, elitist, East Coast noses in the air, no thank you.  And it's *cold* there.  I'll take lax—okay, sometimes lazy—wealthy, West Coast nerds and divas any day.  And it's sunny and warm here.

In any event, when Peter/Mark was alone with Sweet Bill, he gave him the other name for his ledger.  And the ledger was a sore subject with the husband and wife because Sweet Bill refused to enter anything into the computer, so Suzie was not quick to try and find it after Shawn and Jo made their visit.  The one thing that gives me chills, though, is that Sweet Bill and the man had shared a cup of coffee later that afternoon after Shawn had initially stopped by, and it was soon after that drink that Sweet Bill started feeling ill. My money says he put something in Sweet Bill's cup. Not good. While they were having the drink in the lobby, the man told Sweet Bill that he was looking forward to seeing the man who had fallen on the sidewalk earlier in the day.

And that's it. The investigation started and ended there. Sure, a street camera and a camera outside of 7-Eleven had video of the man, but it only confirmed that the man was real and fit Shawn's description. There was no video available of the car that dropped the man off.

Since then, Jo has apologized to Shawn, and we are all in debt to Corie Woods for being the mediator in all of this—conducting most of the sessions from his hospital bed. I am proud and happy to report that he's back home, recovering quickly, and narrating again. As penitence for my well-intentioned intervention, I bought Shawn a year's supply of Barney's coffee and got him a 2-book deal narrating thrillers from the hottest hand in the market, Ivan Bacca.

And he has been supreme in both novels—even better than he was in the Nehemiah Stone glory days. No one is narrating thrillers as well as he is right now. *No one.* Did he have a close call over two years ago? Yes. Did we all think that he had relapsed again because of Corie's accident? Yes. Were we wrong? Yes. Why would a man who had imprisoned him to narrate a shit-tastic novel for a person named "Big Boss" show up two years later on the same street corner as Shawn? You got me. Do I think that, when he is on, Shawn is the greatest talent to ever sit behind a microphone and narrate? Absolutely, unequivocally YES. Have I told him this? No. Not the way I roll. When he *wins* Best Male Narrator, I will. Does anyone in the industry know exactly why he took a break from thrillers and was narrating children's books? No. I've played every misdirection card in the deck and then some. The waters have been sufficiently muddied so that the past is now in the past, and everyone is ecstatic that Shawn is back in the booth narrating top-notch thrillers. However, that doesn't mean that there haven't been rumors over the past few years, and that is what Liz is testing me on right now.

"Been rumors that he's relapsed. Now, I'm not saying that *I* believe any of them, but they *have been* floating around the industry for a while now—the children's books and all that. Something about an ambulance in Santa Monica too. You understand my position. Have to know we can count on him."

"Shawn's clean, Liz. Rumors are from envious colleagues and agents. You know how it goes." I'm telling her the truth—just not the *whole* truth. Welcome to the world of agents and publishing.

"Still haven't seen him post anything on social media in years, David. He used to interact with his fans pretty regularly. If he gets this job, we're going to need him to do that again."

"Shawn's been working, Liz. But, trust me, he'll be happy to help the cause." There. I got it out calmly. Truth is, she just hit one of my vulnerable spots. I'm livid with Shawn right now about his lack of social media presence. Guy's become a hermit—a Kenobi Bedouin in the desert of his booth. Yeah, I like *Star Wars* as much as my lost puppy of a client, Shawn Frost—I still smile when I think about Billy Dee at the Audies, seems like his appearance was centuries ago. Anyway, when this deal is signed, Shawn Frost is getting back on social media whether he wants to or not. And he's *going* on the interview circuit too.

"How's Corie Woods? Heard Shawn was pretty broken up about the accident."

So, I closed the door on the Shawn-Frost-is-unreliable-due-to-drugs line of attack and pledged his social media support. Now, she's opening up the third line while also trying to get my defenses to lower because she's showing concern for one of my other clients. Smart move. But I'm ready.

"Back home and narrating. Should be out of the arm cast soon, and then it will be some follow-up with physical therapy. I'm sure you've seen the numbers on Corie's titles. 'Exploded' is even an inadequate description."

"That's a relief to hear." She already knew all of this. "And Shawn?"

"Wouldn't you be a little off if your best friend almost died?" I shouldn't do the following, but why the hell not. She went there. "What if it was *me* who was in an accident?"

Now, she'll get down to numbers. Risking coming across as cold-hearted would not improve her position.

"You thought about a price for Shawn to perform the book?"

I know *she* has. "Oh, I've had a few numbers bouncing around inside my head for the past few days."

She lets out a quick blurt of a laugh. "I've heard that before."

Time to drop the hammer. Time to take the Lucas & Spielberg maneuver on Paramount Pictures for *Raiders of the Lost Ark* out of my negotiating toolbox. In short, I'm gonna sock it to ParkerWilson. Shawn usually gets fifteen to twenty-thousand per book, which is in the one-percent category of audiobook narrators. In his final year, Hunnie got twenty-five grand per title. But *Listen To Me* is something special. Every author's nightmare scenario was detailed in Stephen King's *Misery* over thirty years ago—a once-in-a-lifetime book written by a master. Everything after it on the same subject was merely an imitation of the original. Now, here comes *Listen To Me*, a book about every audiobook narrator's worst nightmare. Liz knows that this will be the first of its kind, which is why she outbid everyone for publishing rights. I would have done the same thing. It's already known as "that audiobook narrator novel" around ParkerWilson. In every other publishing house, it's known as "that *fucking* audiobook narrator novel" because they lost out to Ms. Cross. Boo-hoo. Go cry to someone else. The audiobook business is booming, and this title will be marketed as "Think *Misery*—only with an audiobook narrator." Jennie Masterson beat everyone to the first punch and has it made for life, regardless of how the second book in her deal goes.

But, I know how Liz is viewing the upcoming launch. She's thinking about it like a horse race: Jennie Masterson is the horse, and Shawn Frost is the jockey. Usually, you bet on the horse. However, for a debut author whose book is about an audiobook narrator coupled with the fact that the audiobook business is blasting off, you absolutely bet on the *jockey*.

Which brings me to Shawn's fee. He's the best there is, and this novel is the perfect vehicle to launch him to number one—the one that will be responsible for reframing his career when hall-of-fame time comes. There's already talk of the movie rights ballooning to over 15 million. Again, comparing them to *The Da Vinci Code*'s, which went for 6 million, this book is going to make more than a splash. This is a monstrous rogue wave ready to drench the market. Hunnie's twenty-five grand per book sounds like a lot, right? Well, it's not compared to what Liz's top-echelon authors are making. Like her legal thriller writer, Jacqueline Donahue, who makes twenty-five *million* a book—and doesn't even write her own books anymore. (I won't point out to Liz that she's missing out on bringing in new talent and new fans by staying with her breadwinners who sell fewer and fewer books each year and whose fans are *literally* dying off). Now, I'm not going to ask for any amount near the Jacqueline Donahue payday, but I want a few things for Shawn.

First, the money. I'm going to shock the socks off Liz in a few moments and ask for one million big ones. Of course, she'll say no, but what I really want is half a million. I'll fight all the way down, eventually acting like she's gotten the upper hand, seen right through me, and clobbered me as a has-been negotiator. I've lost my touch, I'm weak, and on and on. I'll hang my head and accept the negotiated fee of at least $500,000.

Second, at least a guaranteed role in the film for Shawn. I'll throw in that I want it written into the contract that he also gets an audition to play the main character in the film. Do agencies normally have a specific team member who handles anything to do with film or film rights? Sure. But, in my agency of one agent, that person is David Killian, and he is friends with every major studio head. Additionally, I have leverage since Shawn is the only person I know who is a critically acclaimed audiobook narrator *and* a Tony Award-winning writer, director, and actor. Who cares if he hasn't acted in years, talent is talent, and *no one* can match his resume. I know that the theater is where his heart is, but this will at least get him closer—even if he doesn't get the part. Am I reaching for outer space on this deal? Perhaps, but I owe Shawn after the ambulance fiasco. And, God, Jo is still a mess—think her boyfriend left her. Also, before you fall in love with the altruistic attitudes of David Killian, don't forget that I get fifteen percent from the deal. So, $75,000 for what will be a few minutes of negotiating with Liz and then the official contract paperwork that will fly back and forth between the publishing house and yours truly. Maybe, *maybe*, a week of work. That's the business, folks. When I was young and used to grind, I did a deal a week for low numbers. Now, I do a few deals a year and make sure they're big deals for big clients. And right now, Shawn Frost is about to be my biggest client ever so long as I can close this up and keep him out of trouble. It shouldn't be difficult. *I* make the magic happen and make the green bills multiply.

I'm the one who knocks.

"I thought about high-balling you with a ridiculous offer, which I might have done if it was another publishing house. But we've known each other for going on four decades now, and you're my friend—the best in the business. So, I thought, and I thought, taking into account every variable in this equation, and here's a number that seems more than fair to me, my client, and most of all, you." Pretty good build-up, right? I pause to let my words take purchase. "An even million dollars will be Shawn Frost's fee, Liz. And, we want a small percentage on the back end from the sales."

There is silence, and I count to three in my head. I know what's coming.

"David, have you completely lost your mind?  That number is ridiculous!  And a percentage on the back end?  This is an insult.  Sweet Jesus, what were the other numbers bouncing around inside your head?"

"All higher than the one I proposed."

"A million is *way* out of our price range on this."  She always says this as her opening argument.

"Are you certain?  My numbers tell me that it's fair market value for the revenue that Shawn Frost is going to bring into your house."  I've got some numbers I can share with her, but the real value in what I just said is that it has all the key phrases that executives like to hear.  She won't ask me what the numbers are.

"Well, my numbers are a lot different.  Sorry.  We wouldn't even be able to get close to that sum."

No doubt she has her lead deal lawyer listening in on the conversation.  No problem.  I've got mine too—sitting right next to me on the couch and sipping champagne.  When Liz and I are done tonight, we'll agree to something in principle and celebrate.  Then, the teams of contract negotiators and lawyers will move in and do the job of hammering out the details.  "I also want Shawn guaranteed three gross points on the film that will be made."  I don't want this, and getting points on the film's gross is nearly impossible to get, but it's something I can walk back.  This should get a reaction.

"What the *hell*, David?  Have you forgotten how this all works?"

Perfect.  Now, I can throw some numbers at her, and then we can start to negotiate.  "Not at all, Liz."  I make myself cough to give me a few seconds.  I want to make her think about my cough and not the outlandish request I just made.  An *author* wouldn't even get three gross points on the film that is made from his or her book unless they are Jacqueline Donahue and crew, but even they only get a point or two.  I get my coughing under control.

"Look, we know that this book is going to kill it.  It might not debut at #2 on the *New York Times* bestseller list like that flight attendant's book did a few years ago—also a first-time novelist who had a seven-figure deal, I might add.  It might not be 80 million copies sold like *Da Vinci*, but it's going to be huge.  Then, take the movie.  In 1990, *Misery* was made for 20 million dollars and brought in 61.3 million—a top 20 hit made out of a horror novel.  *Da Vinci*'s film rights sold for 6 million…but remember how much that film made?  760 million worldwide.  Now, last I heard, the film rights were still at the negotiating table but had crossed the 15 million dollar line.  So, with all due respect, my old friend, 1 million is pocket change from what the book and film are going to make."  This should bring out some numbers on her end.  She knows everyone is going to make a killing on this book and film.

"Well, none of that is a done deal for this book, and I don't deal in hypotheticals, David.  Here's what I'm offering.  I have been instructed by my financial advisors that we can probably do $300,000 for Shawn, which is twelve times the largest amount ever paid to an audiobook narrator.  This is a one-time, flat fee with no percentage on the back end and nothing from the film."

A bit higher than I expected her to start.  From my experience, whenever a publisher tells someone the sum that the financial advisors have told her, the amount they really have is approximately double that.  So, six-hundred thousand.  I look at my lawyer.  She nods; our number is there, which is always good to know.  Now, time to bring the deal into focus.  "Not a bad place to start.  Totally unacceptable, but now we can get down to business."

"David, I told you that's as high as we can go."

"I know what you *said*, Liz."  Now it's time to hit her with the more important numbers.  This is where information pays off.  "But, you're paying Jackie Donahue twenty-five million a book."

"That's a l—"

I keep going. "Well, I mean, Jackie doesn't *make* twenty-five million. You pay her twenty-five million, and she pays her ghostwriter two million. You pay the husband and wife 'dream team' fifteen million per book, and you pay the new 'king of the military thriller' ten million per book; I'm sorry, nine million per book, and one million to make sure that, even for a military guy, his social media posts all lean center-left. By the way, who's in charge of those? Those accounts are a master class in staying on point. Tweets are every hour, Facebook posts are every two, and Instagram every three. Worth it, though, right? Zero scandals, which always cost 'headache money,' which we don't have a lot for these days." I pause, knowing I've hit her and her deal lawyer hard. She won't even bother asking me how I found these things out—she knows I wouldn't tell her if she did ask. "You still listening, Liz?"

There's no answer. But she is no longer trying to call me a liar either.

"So, let's talk real numbers and conditions. We'd love the points, but you're probably right, three is too many. I know the head of Sony, Angelica Westover, the frontrunner for the rights, is one of your good friends." She's also a close friend of mine—and Shawn Frost's. "How about one gross point, the percentage on the back end of the audiobook sales, and 850,000 up front? That get us anywhere?"

"Zero points, percentage on the back end, and $400,000," she says. "And, David, let's maintain perspective here. Immense difference between what the *creator* of a finished novel should get and what the person who sits in a recording studio for a few weeks reading that already finished novel should receive."

"Put a poor narrator on this project and let me know how it goes." There's still some fight left in her. I know that the inside information I just hit her with hurts. She probably hates paying the right-and-honorable Jacqueline Donahue that much for merely being the figurehead of a declining brand. But Liz is not innocent in this either. I already know that *she's* going to get at least one gross point on the film; rank hath its privileges. The poor author probably won't. After all, she only *invented* the whole story; the movie—and audiobook, for that matter—doesn't even *exist* without the book. Regardless, the gulf between the two artists' pay remains substantial across the board in the industry. And, you'll get no argument from David Killian that an imbalance shouldn't remain between creator and performer. However, my job in this negotiation is to point out to Liz that the imbalance between Liz's top authors and the narrators that bring those books to life is too wide right now. Don't even get me started on the imbalance between a book and the film based on that book.

In any event, I moved the needle forward; giving up Shawn's points brought the price up to almost what I want. To be honest, the percentage on the back end doesn't matter much to me. It's usually never what you think it's going to be. Plus, I don't know how the audiobook is going to sell after ParkerWilson stops hemorrhaging money in the first few months to launch the sucker. The amount they paid to get the rights tells me that it will be substantial, but I want to preserve both Shawn's up-front, guaranteed money and his role in the film, and he's got a damn good shot at getting the lead, in which case we're talking *millions* more for him. So, I mention everything about how he is uniquely positioned to be the star of the film—his experience, credentials, and so forth. I name-drop Angelica Westover once again for good measure.

After hearing me out, Liz comes back with, "Zero points, percentage on the back end, and $450,000. I can also talk to Angelica about Shawn being in the movie."

My lawyer's eyes light up. We're close. "Very generous of you," I start. Time to play my last card. "I actually had lunch with Angelica yesterday." There is no way she checked on this because I had to pull some major strings to find out that Sony was the frontrunner, which I found out only ten minutes before the phone call. The lunch date was a total gamble on my part, but you don't get to where I am in this business without rolling the dice a few times. I laugh, "I don't know if I've ever heard her so excited about a book before. Remember how happy she used to get when you got a new Jackie Donahue book? Now, she doesn't even call me when J.D. launches a new one. Ah, I miss those innocent days." Now, I've reminded her of how close the three of us are and made her at least wonder about what we discussed yesterday. "Anyway, how does this sound? $600,000 up front, which is an absolute steal compared to what everyone else is going to get, including *you*, I drop the bit about the points and the back end, but I get it written into the contract that Shawn Frost gets at least a minor role in the film and a no-kidding, legitimate audition for the lead? Now, Liz, that's fair."

"Give me a minute," she says and puts me on hold.

I look at the deal from her point of view. She's had to come up $300,000; I've had to come down $400,000. Advantage: Liz. I gave away the back-end percentage on audiobook sales. Advantage: Liz. I gave away the gross points. Advantage: Sony Pictures Studios. If she agrees to working Shawn's audition and his permanent minor role into the deal, it's zero gain or loss for her. Advantage: maybe me, but she didn't have to give anything up. So, it looks like she's outmaneuvered me, but all I wanted was $500,000, which is astronomical compared to every other audiobook narrator deal in history, and a role for Shawn in the film. What I'm not telling her, though, is that, based on what I discussed with Angelica yesterday at lunch, I think I can get Shawn a point on the film anyway, whether he's in it or not. She owes me a huge favor from a screw-up years ago with one of Corie Woods's books that Sony made a film of—well, a *disaster* of a film anyway.

I hear background noise coming from the phone, like someone on Liz's end is shuffling papers. "David, you there?"

"Present and accounted for."

"I really appreciate your flexibility here. It's going to be a great book, and we'd love to have Shawn Frost onboard. I'm assuming the audition and minor role are deal-breakers, correct?"

"Yep."

"Okay, here's the absolute best I can do: $550,000 up front, and I'll talk to Angelica when we get off the phone about Shawn. I don't think a minor part and an audition for the lead will be a problem. She wants Spielberg to direct, which means he'll have a lot of control if it happens. But, for what you're asking, I think we'll be fine." Her statement hangs in the air for a moment. She's going to bring me into the picture now. Steven's an old friend too. "However, if we run into problems, I might need you to join the conversation at some point—definitely with Angelica, probably with Spielberg too. Will you be around tonight?"

*Will I be around tonight?* You bet your Sweet Bill ass I will. "Happy to help out if I'm needed."

Spielberg is the perfect choice for this film. Why? Because he's a master storyteller and this novel and subsequent film are all about storytelling. I can already imagine the experience for the viewer that he will be able to create. For instance, when the narrator is performing a scene from the book, he can dissolve into *that* scene, and the audience will get to "see" the scene. Then, he can dissolve back to the narrator reading in the booth. There are all kinds of possibilities to creatively tell the story and the story-within-the-story, and Steven will know exactly which ones to use and when.

I'm getting excited just thinking about it. I take a sip of champagne.

"So, do we have a deal?"

I know I said I wanted $500,000, but you never go lower if they offer more. And I need to act like she won. "I wish the offer was a little higher, but I understand your position, Liz. Shawn will be a little disappointed." This is a lie; Shawn is going to be ecstatic. Why? I told him I thought I could *maybe* get 75 grand if I fought hard, burned bridges, and used all of my tricks. In fact, it's time to use one of those tricks right now: make the publisher think that we are now a team that needs to get the most out of my client. "But, he'll get over it. He's got a job to do for you, and I'll make damn sure that he's ready to go. Gotta hand it to you, Liz—haven't lost your touch. You've been very gracious and easy to work with.  Off the record, one of the few left in the business."  I pause, just for a second.  "Yes, we have a deal in principle."

"Thank you, David.  I'll have the agreement drawn up and call you later tonight after I speak with Angelica."

"I'll be here.  Tell her I said hi."

The phone call ends.  Five minutes later, I receive a text from Liz.

J.D.'s salary per book—you sneaky bastard.  Won't even ask how you got it.  Part of me loves it.  Sure you don't want to work for me?  BTW, I'm getting 3 points on the you know what.  Talk to you later, you insufferable man ;)

I don't expect any major problems at this point.  A few more maneuvers, perhaps, but nothing major.  The book's fate was sealed by the bidding war price.  My lawyer, Gisele Rubie, pours two fresh glasses of champagne, and we toast.

She's wearing my robe; my fifth wife is out of town tonight.  Nothing new in the life of David Killian.  One is not supposed to mix business and pleasure.  I've made a career out of doing it.

I'll call Shawn tomorrow.  He won't be expecting me to phone him tonight.  Why?

I told him I was speaking with Liz tomorrow afternoon.

*1 Month Later...*

# 27

## Carmel-by-the-Sea

"Today is the day," I announce to Michael as I rub behind his ears with one hand and sip from my morning coffee in the other. We are sitting on a new, cushioned lounger on the back deck. Michael is licking one of his paws, and I am staring out at the endless sheet of Pacific blue. My golden retriever weighs sixty-five pounds, but he still thinks he is an eight-week-old puppy who is small enough to fit on my lap.

I don't mind, and I've never stopped him from sitting on me ever since he came to live with me. Hence, I can confirm that I have a sixty-five-pound lap dog who doesn't know how big he is. Seriously, the guy just wants to be around me—follows me everywhere.

Again, no complaints. Michael has helped save my life. Plus, he's helping to keep me warm on this cool November morning.

"Manuscript arrived yesterday, young man," I say to him. "Daddy's going to finish his coffee and then head downstairs to start the journey. You'll be joining me, I presume?"

He eyeballs me like only a golden can—big, brown, expressive eyes. I'm convinced he understands every word I say.

My phone vibrates on top of the glass end table next to the lounger. I set down my coffee mug and pick up the annoying rectangle that supposedly connects me to the world.

It's Killy.

When a person gets you over $500,000 for recording an audiobook, you answer the phone.

"Good morning," I say. "They having second thoughts about me performing the book?" It's a joke. At least, I hope it's a joke. The publishing house has a lot riding on the book and me as the narrator.

"Hell no. Don't even say that," Killy says. "How are you feeling?"

And because the publishing house is all-in, Sir David Killian is all-in. Kidding about the "Sir" part. Killy hasn't been knighted, but he does act like it since the deal for me to record the book was finalized. For that alone, he should be knighted. I'd knight him.

"I'm good. Just having coffee on the deck with Michael, and then I'll get in the booth."

"You read any of it after we spoke last night?"

Is he that nervous that I'm going to freak out? I've had double sessions with Doctor Baker since the deal was finalized three weeks ago. I know that *Listen To Me* is about an audiobook narrator who gets kidnapped, but I've worked through everything. Was it a little strange, and possibly coincidental, that I was one of the author's top choices to narrate the book? It was, but both Killy and Bake assured me that it was because of my talent and to not overthink it. Or, if I was set on obsessing over it, then obsess about the other high-caliber audiobook narrators and actors who lost out on performing the book to me. Apparently, Jeremy Irons phoned Rider Elizabeth Cross and said, *'I know where I would take the story if given the opportunity, Ms. Cross.'* Geesh. Corie explained to me that Killy and Bake were using classic reverse psychology—whatever that means—on me to make me feel grateful for the job and focus only on that. Well, all I can say is that it worked. Thankfully, Corie was not one of the losers—he wasn't interested in the project. Killy's handling another massive deal for him right now for another erotica saga. He won't make as much as I do for this one book, but Killy told Corie he's going to get damn close to my payday. I am convinced that nothing in this industry makes sense.

Do I still think about the guy whom I am convinced might have been Wolverine? A little, but Roman I. Baker talked me through some of my unresolved trauma regarding whatever happened to me a few years ago. He calls them breakthrough sessions, and I broke through some recessed memories that, unbeknownst to me, had become company that had stayed too long. Additionally, Bake presented the logic, or illogic, I should say, of the incident in Santa Monica. Even if I had been kidnapped almost three years ago and everything had happened just as I said it had, what would "Wolverine" have to gain by staking me out when I was visiting my friend who seemed to be on his deathbed? The supposed book that I read in my supposed captivity, *Narrator*, hasn't been traditionally published or self-published, and a tech wizard that Killy hired for me, bless his heart, hasn't been able to find any trace of the novel or my performance of it online, and he still checks once a week for Killy. I have nothing to worry about.

In fact, narrating *Listen To Me* is a final exam of sorts for yours truly. One last mental hurdle to leap over and prove to myself that I can narrate *any* kind of thriller again and be done with the event that may or may not have happened to me. I still have my days when I believe that it all did, but Bake's logic and Killy's conviction are powerful forces to the contrary.

And then there's Jo.

We've texted a few times since her tearful apology to me in my Hilton hotel room that I got back after passing all of my drug tests and a psych eval from Bake.

I forgave her. All the signs were there, and everyone just misread them. But, her words of atonement, starting with the phrase I hate, '*I own it,*' have not erased the event from my memory. The pain of her wrongful mistrust has dulled, but, whatever *we* were since she had returned from New York, which wasn't much but better than no contact, has never returned. I do know that she and Alex are done and that she's acting in a production of Pinter's *Betrayal* in Monterey right now, but that's it. I want to see the play—it's one of my favorites—but I don't know if I can.

Anyway, Killy is just being Killy and closing ranks with the publisher right now. He likes guarantees, even if he has to manufacture them. The one point that Doctor Baker agreed with me on, and Killy saw the light soon after too, was that, for my peace of mind, I needed to know that *Listen To Me* was not *Narrator*— a wolf in sheep's clothing as the saying goes. So, I wrote down from memory the plot and characters from *Narrator* and had Killy check. He did, or rather, had, someone check for him. No Stacey Groff. No Robbie Bernstein. No asshole Kurt Boar. As for the plot, it basically follows *Misery* beat for beat, with one exception that is enough for it to stand on its own and not have Mister King & Company come a-knockin' with a lawsuit. In fact, King has blurbed the book, and his blurb, "It's as if someone kidnapped Lindsay Crouse and made her read *Misery*, and then…well, you'll have to read *Listen To Me* and find out." will be on the front cover of the hardcover's dust jacket.

Because of the subject matter—an audiobook narrator getting kidnapped— I did not want to know too much about the novel ahead of time, which is why I didn't read it and check. I want my narration to be more spontaneous and rawer, which will produce a better overall performance. I need to feel like *I* am the narrator in the book, experiencing everything as it happens with no prior knowledge of the plot twists or outcome. I rarely do this for a book nowadays, but this is, of course, a special circumstance. But, as you've witnessed, that wasn't good enough for Killy, which is why he's calling me this morning to see if I've previewed any of the text.

After he called me last night, I did crack open the paperback proof copy that was delivered to me yesterday morning. The digital copy is already loaded on my iPad in the booth—annotated with notes from my research team (pronunciations, etc.)—and ready to go. The opening chapters that I leafed through were good. Plenty of intrigue, and I like the main character: Legendary Audiobook Narrator Lionel Goliath—I will definitely be able to get inside his head and bring him to life with authenticity. If ever there was a character whose "truth" I could discover, then Lionel Goliath is that character.

"Read some of it last night after we spoke. Didn't want to get too far for obvious reasons, but the main character is good. I know who this guy is, Killy."

"Knew you would," he says.

No, he didn't. But now that he knows I've read some and am invested, he feels relieved. I can hear it in his voice.

"You about to head down?"

He knows that I told him this at the beginning of the call, but Killy can't overcome his own nature to micromanage when a big deal has been struck. I've learned to calmly, nicely repeat myself instead of reminding him that I've already answered that.

"Going down right after I slurp up the rest of my morning Joe."

"On target, sir. Music to my ears. You'll call at the end of the day and let me know how it went, right? Want to keep the wolves fed."

What he means is ParkerWilson—Rider Elizabeth Cross, to be exact. They know I'm starting today too. I learned a long time ago in the theater that producers always play a heavy hand in choosing the stage managers for their shows. Why? Because the stage manager is a producer's eyes and ears—the known spy. And I never forgot that whenever I directed. Rider Elizabeth Cross fought to have someone direct my performance of *Listen To Me* in one of

ParkerWilson's studios in L.A., but Killy outmaneuvered her. Thank God. I have to do this one on my terms.

"You can count on it. I'll phone you when I leave the booth this afternoon."

"Around four, right?"

He can't help himself. Believe me, if there is anyone that I've got to keep fed and happy at this stage, it is David Killian. "Probably. Unless I get on a roll." Always have to leave myself some wiggle room. And when it comes to Killy, overdelivering is the only thing that brings about any kind of patience on his end. He'll agree with what I just said, and the conversation will end. He never wishes me any kind of luck. It is expected that I'll bring my best. And, for half-a-million George Washingtons, he is right to expect that I'll be able to reach and maintain the height of my powers in the booth.

"Got it," he answers. "Talk soon."

I don't even bother trying to say goodbye because the call has already ended. I set the phone down, and Michael moves his head so that his chin lies directly on my left knee. His eyes stare up at me as if he knows that our morning snuggle time is about to end, and he will soon man his post on the floor outside my basement booth.

I take a sip of coffee and then pet his head. "About that time, big fella."

He closes his eyes as I continue to rub *with the grain* across the top of his head. I'm a little nervous but, more than anything, excited to get started. It's been a long haul for me. I've hurt a lot of people by my mistakes, but they've been forgiving and are better than I deserve. I want them to be proud of this book when I'm done narrating it because they all contributed to making it happen.

I throw back the rest of my coffee. On another note, I have finished the first draft of a new play that was inspired by my time in the hospital with Corie.

But, more on that later. I'm going to slay my demons one at a time, and, right now, it's time to narrate my worst fear.

✳ ✳ ✳

I sit in the booth and bring up the first page. There it is: *Listen To Me* by Jennie Masterson.

Then, I go through my routine while saying it over and over again in my head.

*Listen To Me*

*Listen To Me*

*Listen To Me*

by: Jennie Masterson

Masterson…Masterson

*Listen To Me* by Jennie Masterson

I close my eyes for a moment. You can do this, Frost. Michael is right outside; nothing can hurt you now. You are an artist, a sculptor of speech, a narrator. You've come a helluva long way, and you're going to finish your comeback *right now*.

I open my eyes and start recording.


**ParkerWilson and Shawn Frost Iceberg Productions present**

*Listen To Me*

**by: Jennie Masterson**

**Read for you by Shawn Frost**


**For MJ, who took a dream and made it a reality.**


**"Beware the man of a single book."**

**—St. Thomas Aquinas**


I did it. I started. I know it sounds trivial, but I needed to nail the opening credits, and I succeeded. Dr. Baker explained that over the next few weeks, I would not have a constant, overwhelming feeling like I was conquering some adversary.  But, rather, my progress would be tiny, single victories that would stack up—out of sight—until there were too many to be ignored, causing my subconscious to yield to my conscious, and the growing pile would show up as plain as a snowcapped mountain against a peacock blue sky.

I wonder who MJ is?  Dedications always intrigue me.  One thing I always do—I admit, it's weird—when I read an ambiguous dedication like this one is to imagine who that person might be.  Hmmm.  MJ.  Michael Jordan?  Mary Jane Watson?  My mind went to those two names immediately because I'm a huge NBA fan, and Spider-Man is my favorite Marvel superhero.  Hence, from this point forward, in the world according to Shawn Frost, this book has been dedicated to Michael Jordan and Mary Jane Watson.  Therefore, I'm already a fan.

I read on.

Chapter 1

Somewhere in Wheeling, West Virginia

Lionel Goliath pulled his hairy arm out from underneath the silk covers and reached for the vibrating cell phone on his cherry nightstand.

I push stop on my recording equipment.  The line made me grin last night, and now, saying it aloud, I feel compelled to give a laugh to the invisible audience in my booth.  I chuckle and then say, "Well, folks, it's not every day that you start a novel with a line as sexually charged as that."  This reminds me, I'll look for opportunities to pause for an extra beat if I think the listener will need time to react—like after a funny line.  Again, this goes back to my theater days.  You have to give the audience time to clap or cheer after an actor or actress gives a great performance or delivers a wonderful number.

I continue.

The caller was Beryl Sterling, a woman who needed no introduction to Goliath or the world for that matter. Not when you're the most prolific author the globe has ever seen. Not when you are calling the narrator who has performed every single one of your audiobooks. Certainly not when that audiobook narrator is a lover who knows you on an orgasmic level that few others have witnessed or know the far reaches of. *And most certainly not*, when you are engaged to the narrator who is first among equals on the Mount Rushmore of audiobook narrators.

I flip the page, smiling as I do so. I have a focus I've not felt for years—even while doing the two Ivan Bacca novels over the past few months.

I go through my routine, taking comfort in my booth rituals and rhythms. I'm in the story now, and there is no stopping me.

The titans, Lionel and Beryl, are engaged. Will their relationship survive Lionel's upcoming abduction by Beryl's rival author Greg Ladd that happens in chapter two? I cannot wait to see.

# 28

I look at the digital clock in my booth, and it says 5:22.

I've been so immersed in the book that I've lost track of time. I know that I should give my voice a rest, but I'm churning through the chapters like the Xenomorph's acidic blood through the decks of the *Nostromo* in *Alien.* Instead of Tom Skerritt as Captain Dallas yelling, *'That crap's gonna eat through the hull.'* I hear him saying, *'That narrator's gonna read the whole damned book by dinner!'*

I'm in the middle of chapter 16, and Lionel Goliath is in the fight of his life with his psychopathic captor Greg Ladd. A third of the way through the book, I can now see why this debut novel initiated a bidding war.

Folks, it's *that* good.

I usually don't perform a debut author's work, but if this manuscript is any indication of what fresh talent is capable of producing these days, then maybe I should be. Do I sense the editing hand of ParkerWilson's deity-like developmental editor Esperanza Benoit, the woman with the magic red pen? Yes. This is a bona fide page-turner. But, what I find most impressive about the book is the detailing of Goliath's imprisonment from not only visual and visceral descriptions but also from a psychological standpoint. I've agreed with basically every dread the storied narrator has felt and thought about in the novel so far. I knew from my preparatory sessions with Dr. Baker that this aspect of the novel might trigger my own experience—whether it was real or not is inconsequential at this point. I experienced a trauma of some sort. Period. But, what *has* happened, instead of me getting thrown off by the similarities, is that I've actually grown close to Goliath by empathizing with what he is experiencing—more of a feeling like, *Wow—someone else is going through what I went through.* And because of this, I think my performance has risen to a place I am not sure that it has ever reached before. It wouldn't surprise me if author Jennie Masterson was a practicing or retired psychologist. Or, if not, then she did an exhaustive amount of research into the mindsets and actions of prisoners in captivity. Stanford prison experiment, 1970's, anyone?

I want to go on. I'm in a groove of flow that makes narrating feel effortless right now, but my awareness of how it feels to try and narrate the day after pushing it too hard is talking some sense into me as I pause to go through my routine. Unable to quiet this voice of reason, I decide to finish this chapter and call it an evening with my appetite whetted for tomorrow morning's pages. Plus, I'm excited to give Killy a keen report on the day's work. It could not have gone any better.

At this moment, we're learning about Beryl's evolving approach to her publishing house in the twilight years of her fabled career—specifically, in regard to a new novel she has coming out. As a publishing world gossip myself, I am enjoying each word and want to know every minute detail and how it will figure in with Goliath's battle for survival in the basement of Greg Ladd's house.

I finish the page I am on and then go through my routine. My water bottle is almost empty, which is another sign that it's about time to stop.

I advance to the next page...

...and read:


**Beryl had steered clear of the ever-present politics being played by William Morrow's major players—that was her**

mega-agent's job, to cajole the men and women who held the levers of power into thinking that the once-in-a-generation book deserved a commensurate price tag.

I blink and then can't see the screen—just an unending wall of searing, white light, threatening to burn through my eyeballs and exit the back of my head. I gasp, but then my mouth feels like someone has just sprayed expanding foam inside it, and I can't speak or breathe. Tremors, deep within my nervous system, activate, and my body starts to convulse in the booth chair.

*The words.*

They're my words…

The very ones that I came up with narrating in captivity.

I shake my head and rub my eyes. It cannot be! Clear your mind, Frost. You're trying to sabotage the wonderful day that you've had. Now, take a step outside the booth, pet Michael, and then come back in here and read the words again.

Shaking, I stand up. The booth's features are fuzzy, but I can make enough out to locate the door handle and pull on it. I exit the booth.

Michael leaps up and starts licking my face as I kneel down to embrace him. The booth door clicks shut behind me. I regain my full vision, and my breathing starts to normalize. My smartwatch says that my heartbeat is…

126 beats per minute! It's like I'm fighting a bad virus or working out!

I hang on to Michael, and his soft fur and unlimited licks continue to keep me sane.

Did I really just read that line? Or am I more tired than I thought I was and imagined the words I came up with in captivity? As my heartbeat lowers, I realize that I have pushed it too hard for the first day and am sure that what I thought I read is not really what is on the page. I give a half-hearted laugh and say to Michael, "This was bound to happen. In fact, I should have expected it."

I stand back up, and Michael looks up at me.  I know in my heart that he's worried about me.  "I'm going back in there," I say to him.  "But I'll be right back out, and we'll get some dinner and take a walk.  Okay?"

He wags his tail.

I turn around and re-enter the booth.

Without reading the screen, I scroll up to the previous page.  I'll go through my routine and then start the page over, knowing that the words will be different.  C'mon, Frost.  A woman named Jennie Masterson wrote this novel, and the story is *nothing* like *Narrator*.

I advance to the next page and rea…

Beryl had steered clear of the ever-present politics being played by William Morrow's major players—that was her mega-agent's job, to cajole the men and women who held the levers of power into thinking that the once-in-a-generation book deserved a commensurate price tag.

I stop.

The line hasn't changed.

Could it be just a coincidence?  What about what comes after the line.  I pause.  You're going to have to go back there in your mind.

I know it's risky, but I have to know.

I close my eyes and try to remember.

The first flashes against the black canvas of my memory start like the comic strip segue into every Marvel film.  There's the recording cell.  There's me.  There's the cot.  There's the toilet.  The corner shower illuminates and then disappears.  Then, I can see the table with the screen and microphone.  Now, Wolverine comes into view, but that image is interrupted by the scene of me falling down on the sidewalk in front of the man… The scene goes dark, and I'm back in the cell, this time at the table, wearing the vest and chained to the floor. I'm narrating. I listen in.

**Stacey had stayed out of the publishing house's politics— that was her mega-agent's job, to cajole the men and women who held the levers of power into thinking that the once-in-a-generation book deserved a commensurate price tag.**

I open my eyes. Okay, the part of the sentence before the em dash is not exactly as I said before, but it's damned close. I feel the butterflies rise and swirl in my stomach as I face the fact that the part of the sentence after the em dash is exactly what I narrated in the cell. There's no escaping it.

But, wait.

How about what comes after the sentence?

I close my eyes and try to go back again.

I return to the scene. What did I say after the part that I inserted on my own? What was the story? I search like a blind man tapping with his stick to see what is in front of him.

*Nothing.*

And then…

I've got it. The next line I remember narrating was:

**Kurt was being Kurt, and it pissed her off so bad.**

Then, the book goes on and on about Kurt's troubles as a publicist and the unfortunate sexual allusion to his "big stick." Then, we get a primer for a Stacey-Kurt sex scene. Terrible stuff.

I open my eyes. Okay, let's scroll ahead and see if any of that is in here. If it is, then I'll know for sure.

I scroll down.

There is nothing remotely close to what I read in the cell.  The paragraphs that follow my improvised words are all about Beryl's agent, Iris Schuller, and her epic battles over the years with the William Morrow brain trust.

No big stick.

No wand.

No, someone being someone and pissing someone off *so bad*.

I exhale.

What are the chances?

I scroll back up and locate the line.  Then, I copy it into a Word document. After entering the line down a few double spaces, I go up to the top and type the original sentence that I narrated with Big Boss and Wolverine.  The document looks like this:

Stacey had stayed out of the publishing house's politics— that was her mega-agent's job, to cajole the men and women who held the levers of power into thinking that the once-in-a-generation book deserved a commensurate price tag.

Beryl had steered clear of the ever-present politics being played by William Morrow's major players—that was her mega-agent's job, to cajole the men and women who held the levers of power into thinking that the once-in-a-generation book deserved a commensurate price tag.

I read them both over and over again.  And, as much as I try to convince myself that this word-for-word miracle of imitation could happen, I am filled with the inevitable, sick-to-my-stomach feeling and realization that, no, this is beyond the realm of random possibilities.

Then, the feeling escalates to a whole new level as I start to comprehend the result of this evidence.

All of it happened. Big Boss and Wolverine are *real*. I was kidnapped, drugged, forced to narrate a novel, heard Michael Hunnie's voice, and released by my captors near Killy's Pacific Palisades neighborhood.

And I now have the evidence to prove it!

I grab my water bottle and exit the booth, collapsing to the floor next to Michael.

I say, with growing conviction, "This is real. This happened. Killy, Jo, Corie, Matt—they *have* to believe me now."

And then, like a curtain being raised in a theatrical version of a whodunit mystery, I see a scene on the stage of my mind that I cannot believe. A scene that makes me shiver and blink, attempting to erase the vision. The vision does not go away—just becomes clearer, and clearer, and clearer.

Oh my God. A terrible thought just occurred to me.

How did I not see it before? It's so obvious. I can't believe I missed it.

No wonder they had me sedated.

No wonder they called me a liar and said I needed help.

I can barely get the words out, but I say, "They've been in on it from the beginning."

# 29

I attempt to stand but underestimate the effect that my mental state is having on my body. My legs bend like rubber, and my body crumbles to the floor. I sit there, stunned, but my brain is working so fast, I am unable to quiet the overload of information it is processing—new connections in the web of deception forming by the second.

"They might have known," I say. "There's too much that seems to add up, but I'm not totally convinced yet."

I pull my water bottle up to my mouth. There is one big swig left, and I take it. As I let the cool liquid sooth my throat, I begin to lay out the information that I have so I am able to see if it makes sense or if I am somehow having delusions brought on by the material I am narrating.

I try to get up, but every part of my body feels heavy—especially my arms and legs. You know when people say that their bodies are talking to them? Well, mine is speaking to me now. I decide to remain seated and think things through until I am physically able to move. It is clear to me that I need to get my mind right.

So, let's review the situation and see if I can make sense of it.

*Listen To Me.* It is clear that the line I improvised in the recording cell has made its way into the book. I don't know how it did, but two immediate theories come to mind.

One: The author Jennie Masterson is somehow connected to Wolverine and Big Boss. "Jennie Masterson" could be a pen name, and I need to find out if it is. Next, I need to see early drafts of the manuscript and see if it in any way resembles *Narrator.*

Two: Someone who had input on the manuscript is somehow connected to Wolverine and Big Boss. In this case, Jennie Masterson would be innocent, and a developmental editor or copy editor would be the best place to start. After that, it would be nice to see some drafts that have the editorial comments included. Almost everyone uses Microsoft Word and track changes, so it should be straightforward to access the files.

Beyond this, I'll need to consult my team and see if they have any ideas about how my line made it into *Listen To Me.* But, in order to proceed down that road, I'll have to clear them first, which leads me to my primary question.

Did my family, Killy, Jo, Corie, Matt, or Dr. Baker know about or have anything to do with my captivity and/or the writing of *Listen To Me*—and the push to have me narrate it?

Jo. The main thread that jumps out to me is that the night that Jo and I broke up, Killy and Jo talked on the phone. In fact, throughout this entire ordeal, Killy has stayed in close contact with Jo. I only have their words about what they said they discussed about me. What if they are lying? Then there is the fact that right after Jo broke up with me, she headed straight to New York City for about a year. I know she was in a play, but was it arranged because she was involved in something much, much bigger involving me? The timing seems a little too convenient.

Corie. Corie showing up the night that Jo broke up with me was like Noah Emmerich showing up with a six-pack of beer every time there was a possible hiccup with Truman in *The Truman Show*. He's my best friend and all, but looking back now, he always seemed to be around when there was a new development after I returned from my abduction. I have to admit that it could simply be that he is indeed the best friend a person could ask for, but I have to question everything right now.

Killy. Did he ever even talk to Michael Hunnie's agent? And what does it mean if he was lying and didn't? Why has he always seemed to be in contact with Jo when something involving me was happening or about to happen? Why, of all the places in the world, was I released by *his* neighborhood? And, let us not forget the ambulance fiasco outside of the Santa Monica Hilton. Do I really have the entire story about what happened? I know that I am the one who reached out to Jo, but, come to think of it, she was pretty neutral during the entire encounter, and I sure as hell didn't see *her* shedding any tears when the guys jumped me outside of the Hilton.

Dr. Baker. Bake has been involved every step of the way, and it always seems like he and Killy have spoken before anything involving me and the good doctor takes place. He could definitely be "in on it." What do I mean by "in on it?" I'm getting there.

Me. I absolutely lied to everyone about my whereabouts when I was visiting Jeffrey Calliope to get my drug fixes. But here's the main point: Did everyone know that I was lying and my whereabouts *before* I was abducted? This would change everything.

My family. They love me. I put them through hell when I almost overdosed in New York City, and I am certain that they never wanted to go through that again. Were they concerned and emotional when they visited me in Laguna? Absolutely. However, at times, their nods of understanding seemed more of the *'Yep, this is all part of the process to get Shawn recovered'* variety and not the *'Oh, my God, he's relapsed and taken us totally by surprise'* variety. I noticed their business-like attitude then, but, I admit, I never brought my observations to their attention.

Now, because of *The Truman Show*, I've accessed the film directory in my brain, and one picture appears that could tie all of this together. It is evident that my family, ex-girlfriend, agent, best friend, and others care about me and want me to not only live but succeed in my love—the arts. And it's because of this that the following movie stands out:

*The Game.*

I am Michael Douglas.

Is everything—from the abduction to me recording *Listen To Me*—part of some elaborate, risky, and creative intervention? I admit that I was pretty far gone when I was abducted and was not of sound mind and body while I was in that recording cell…

Was the basement recording cell a detox center of sorts?

Maybe they weren't shooting me up with heroin. Perhaps, they were trying some new way to get me clean and stay clean? It would make sense. I'm that dreaded word, "celebrity," and I was most likely on my way to an early exit from the world again. Killy would have access to the contacts and, hence, resources that were needed to make it all happen. Were Wolverine and Big Boss *nurses* or *doctors*? My gosh, was everyone—Killy, Jo, Corie, etc.—watching everything from Big Boss's camera?

WHOA.

Was *Jo* Big Boss? I've heard her lower her pitch and speak more from the throat before.

Was *Corie* Big Boss?

Was…

*Killy*, Big Boss?

Freaking out here.

But wait a second. Why the theatrics? And why have me narrate?

I sit, pondering what the possible answers to the last question could be. All I hear is the sound of my breathing and Michael's; it's like we're meditating together—me, with my eyes wide open.

An answer materializes out of the dark. Was Killy trying to push me through some barrier? Did he consult with Bake and realize that I was regressing after the loss at the Audies? Even I can admit that I was on a path to destruction. Was the plan all along to position me for a title like *Listen To Me*? But what about all the children's books? Diversify my recording portfolio? Show my range? That's the only thing that makes my theory beyond a stretch. I don't know how making me suffer through all of those books could be a cogent part of any rehabilitation plan. Although, on the other hand, I could not narrate thrillers during those years. But, that was due to the horror I experienced in the recording cell. So, if they were all in on it and the plan was to get me clean and push me to new performing heights, then this couldn't have been the master plan. And what about Michael Hunnie? Was he in on it too?

Then, another thought pops into my head. Did something go horribly, horribly wrong with their plan? Have they all been performing damage control for the past few years? Killy was on edge in those early months, and he's not a good enough actor to put up a false front. He was actually uncomfortable.

What about the possible sighting of Wolverine in Santa Monica? Was getting me checked in to the Hilton part of a test to see if I would relapse? Was Wolverine there to monitor me for Killy? Was Big Boss the person who dropped him off at the street corner? Oh, how I wish I would have been paying attention to who was in the car!

I close my eyes and search for any new connections or threads to form.

There are none. For the time being, I believe that I have exhausted every thought regarding this subject that my mind generated. My body no longer feels heavy, but my head throbs after such an intense period of concentration.

I owe Killy a phone call.  So, I'm going to take Michael upstairs, feed him, and let him out.  Then, I'm going to call Killy and Jo and invite them over.  I need to get everything off my chest and show them the document I created regarding the repeated line from *Narrator*.

I need explanations from them.

I need *answers* from them.

Am I afraid of what those explanations and answers may be?

Yes.

And, yet, I won't rest until I have them.

# 30

It is just past nine in the evening, and I open my front door.

David Killian and Jo Mansfield stand next to each other. The expression on their faces is of concern. Well, perhaps there is some anger bubbling under the veneer of concern. The last time I saw Jo, where she is standing right now, was when she broke up with me. As painful as that memory is, it is good to have her back at my home.

Michael is by my side, wagging his tail. Golden retrievers love *everyone*. Do not get one for a watchdog; I am convinced that Michael would lick a burglar's hand.

I invite my agent and ex-girlfriend in, and we sit on my living room's L-shaped couch—Killy and Jo on one side, me on the other. There is a roaring fire in the fireplace, and the *cracks* and *pops* from the fire sound like bones breaking as we settle in to discuss the past few years…well, everything. Michael lies on the floor in front of the fireplace—dog can sleep anywhere.

I calmly lay out everything that I thought of in the booth and provide them a printout of the section from *Narrator* that appears in *Listen To Me*. I end by telling them that I will be speaking to Corie later but wanted to talk to them first. They tell me that they have honored my wishes and spoken to no one about their visit to me tonight.

While I was speaking, they were courteous and took notes on the legal pads I provided for them. I've never seen Jo write so fast. She must have written ten or more pages worth. Killy was more surgical and summative in his approach. On at least three occasions, he held up his jeweled hand and asked me to repeat what I had just said. Other times, he'd lean toward me, and I would speak to his right ear more than to his face as he concentrated and then scribbled notes.

On a table next to where I'm sitting is a thermos of water and my special tea that I sometimes drink after a day of heavy recording. Both beverages came in handy as I just talked for around a half-hour straight. Orson Welles is known for many things, but, perhaps above all, he is remembered for his masterpiece film *Citizen Kane*—both as the director of the picture and as the lead actor in it. As the legend goes, the film almost never made it to theaters as William Randolph Hearst, the famous newspaper tycoon, fought to keep it from being released. But, in a closed room with the RKO Pictures brass, Welles gave what is generally known to the world now as his greatest performance, which was not recorded and, hence, will never be seen. Until this evening, I have never had my *Orson Welles performance moment*, but as I take a sip of tea and say, "Thank you for hearing me out," to Killy and Jo, I know that I have. Michael heard me rehearse my speech twice earlier; neither practice attempt came close to what I just delivered.

Killy takes a sip from his champagne flute. *If I'm flying from LA to Monterey at a moment's notice and you're not telling me anything other than the fact that you're suspending work on* Listen To Me *until we talk in person, then I am for damn sure bringing champagne for me and Jo,'* he said before leaving tonight. I don't blame him.

Killy sets his flute down—his "Time to get down to business" gesture. And with the setting down of the flute, his facial expression takes a hard turn toward pissed off. "Seriously? You had me fly up here to listen to this shit? You—" He flips a page of his legal pad. "—you think Jo. And Corie. And *me*...orchestrated a two-year-plus plan to have you kidnapped, observed while you were forced to read a book, shot up with drugs, released, rehabilitated, made to read kiddie books, followed, ambushed outside of a hotel, admitted to a hospital again for drug testing, all so we could, one, get you clean, and—" Killy laughs in disbelief, "—two, challenge you, and thereby emotionally manipulate you to reach your potential as a narrator by getting you the largest deal in audiobook narrator history to perform a book that has one line in it that you *think* was in the same book that you read in captivity, which we all supposedly knew about and arranged?" He throws the legal pad against the couch. It bounces off and lands on the floor. "Are you out of your *fucking* mind? No, no, wait a minute. I'm getting ahead of myself. Yes, you *are out* of your fucking mind. I—"

"David," Jo says. "I think it's better if I start."

I've never seen Killy lose his composure like that. But, I suppose if there was anyone who could make him do it, it would be me. Now, after what he just said, I don't know what to believe.

"What good is that going to do?" Killy explodes at Jo. "He's accusing you of the same damned thing!"

Jo takes a sip from her near-empty flute and then sets it down. "Pour us some more bubbly, David, and take it down a few notches."

Killy shakes his head while shrugging. Then he gives us both a patronizing smile. "Fine. Whatever." He refills their glasses, and Jo starts in. If Killy just gave me a death by beheading, then I expect Jo to tie me to a rack and cut out my organs one by one—a slow, painful death.

"I want to let you know, Shawn, that I had nothing to do with any possible scenario you just presented. And that is the truth. The times that David and I spoke on the phone were about concerns we had with you, but they were never to coordinate on some overall plan to get you clean or to up your performance. I can see how, the way you connected everything, it seems like a legitimate possibility, but from the bottom of my heart, where it's me and only me, I swear I was never a part of anything to deceive you or take advantage of your trust." She takes a long sip of champagne. Killy only buys the expensive stuff now.

When he was my agent in New York City, he was the definition of cheap. Well, times change.

Jo continues. "I know you're going to speak with Corie, but the only conversations we've had since the Audie Awards show, when you lost, were to brainstorm how we could help you. Corie loves you. He'd never do anything to hurt you." A tear escapes from her right eye and slides down her cheek. She is an actress and a damned good one, but this is not acting. I'm getting the real Jo here—the woman I fell in love with. The woman I cheated on, ruining the good thing we had.

She takes a breath and regains her composure.

Killy stares at her in disbelief—his own champagne flute frozen in his hand.

"All that being said, you've made a compelling case to me in regard to your abduction. Before, I thought it was just some wild tale that you cooked up during your bender. You didn't see me, but I cried the night the ambulance took you away from outside of the Hilton. Now, I'm not so sure about what happened to you when you vanished for that week. If, in fact, this selection," she says, holding up the piece of paper, "was from the novel you were forced to read while you were in captivity, then it is worth looking into." She stares directly into my eyes. "Shawn, you are an incredible storyteller, but this time, I don't think you're making anything up or adding your trademark brushstrokes of embellishment. I always supposed that one day I would return here," she says, looking at the ceiling the way people do when they say things like she just did, "but I am grateful that it happened now. I care for you. I trust you. And, I want to help."

Either they coordinated the good-cop-bad-cop routine before they got here, or I have just witnessed a major change in our relationship.

Then, she does something I never thought I would experience again. She walks over and hugs me. But, as soon as the smell of her hair and perfume start to awaken memories, the embrace is over, and she's headed back to the couch and her champagne. Let's just say that if she were a femme fatale and the plan was for her to distract me while her accomplice shot me with a poison dart, um, I'd be dead right now. It is clear to me, more than ever before, that I'm still in love with her. I want her back.

This is not the time to bring that up, though, so I take a long sip of tea. As if he senses the electricity in the air, Michael lifts his head—stares at Jo, then stares at me. Jo, and then back at me. I'm in my socks and reach out my right foot and rub his belly; he puts his head down and closes his eyes. I'll tell him all about what just happened later tonight.

Killy sets down his glass of champagne and picks up his legal pad from the floor. He flips through his notes. Jo and I lock eyes while he prepares his remarks. Jo has thrown us both for a loop, that is, if she is being genuine. If she is, I wonder if she is feeling what I'm feeling.

Look, all men are shit at one time or another, okay? I don't deny it. But she's had a serious relationship since we were a couple. She's been with another man. And I was with Jenna while we were dating. It's not the same thing, but the fact remains that we have both been intimate with others since we were intimate with each other. Has enough time and healing passed for her to give me another chance? It appears that I have her caring and support for now, and I know I need to be happy with that as a start.

Unless it's all a charade.

Don't push it, Frost. You are emotionally vulnerable right now, and that is when you've made your highlight reel of critical errors in life. Trust your feelings, but for God's sake, don't *act on them* at this moment. I need to be guarded.

Killy crosses his mammoth legs. "I sincerely hope that you have this all written down somewhere, Shawn. After hearing Jo, I'll get to where we see eye-to-eye in a moment, but your creativity is at an all-time high right now. If I didn't know myself and where I was and whom I spoke to since you relapsed, hell, I'd believe what you are saying. Seriously, get this into a book or a play or a screenplay—*anything* before the whole thing leaves you. I'll help you sell the shit out of it. You've got the magic back that I haven't seen since you left New York."

I know that Killy is somewhat patronizing me. But, he senses what I have sensed since I started working on my new play, which I still need to tell you about, and that is: I've found my voice again. My muse is speaking to me regularly after abandoning me for half a decade; I wondered if he had left me for good. But, no, he's back, and as Mike Greenberg once said every morning for seventeen years *'better than ever.'* God, I miss Mike & Mike. Nothing, my friends, *nothing,* lasts forever.

"Thanks, Killy," I say with some degree of uncertainty.

"Here's what I can say: I'm furious with you right now. Still don't know how you could believe the story you told us. But, for the record, I'm in the same boat as Jo. Had nothing to do with any conspiracy to get you clean. Had nothing to do with you recording *Listen To Me before* I was contacted because they were interested in you narrating the book. I have no idea why you showed up in my neighborhood after disappearing for a week. If I had rigged it, then I am an idiot for what you did to my clothes that night. And you know how I value my threads. I did call Hunnie's agent the times I said I did, and I'll call him again right now if it makes you feel better. Everything, and I mean *everything,* has been legit and above board between you and me." He pauses. "Any questions before I continue?"

He's gone from angry to serious, but I like Killy when he's serious. It's when I trust him the most. No, I'm not going to have him call Hunnie's agent. The gesture was all I needed. "No," I say.

"Okay. Now, in terms of your abduction." He exhales. "Man, I don't know. Jo believes you, and maybe I want to believe you. But I'm not there yet. After another look, what you've put together on this sheet has my attention. But, Shawn, *you have to be sure* if I am going to look into this. We've got the largest audiobook narrating deal in history, and I will not allow my client to jeopardize it on just a hunch or what he *thinks* he remembers. It is a fact that you had a relapse back then—tracks on your arm, puking on my jogging suit, rappin' about coke in the backseat. Right? It's hard to believe that you reading *one sentence* in *Listen To Me* has opened up the epiphany door. Does that make sense?"

Killy scares the hell out of me sometimes. And tonight, he's scared me twice—first, when he exploded like a volcano, and second when he just presented his viewpoint in his trial-mode manner that has led to millions and millions of dollars in deals over his career.

But, it is a good kind of scare that I feel, though, if that makes sense. I know I withered a bit when he tore into me, but I have to defend my truth. Right here. Right now. "I understand your position, Killy. But my abduction *happened.* I got tortured down there, and I need information."

He stays silent for a few moments.

Jo seems to be hanging on our every word.

Michael is sleeping.

I feel sweat coming down my neck.

"What's your angle?" Killy says.

This is what he usually asks before trying to talk me out of something. It won't work this time. I'm adamant about finding out the book's origins. I decide to go for the win, whatever the hell that means right now, and tick off the questions on my hand that I've been stewing about since I read *my* sentence in the booth. "Who is Jennie Masterson? Is that the author's real name, or is it a pen name? Where does she live? When did she query her agent? Who is her editor? Can we get an early draft of the manuscript? I want to—"

"Okay, okay. Hold on a minute," Killy says, cutting me off and raising his hands. "I can't make inquiries into all of those questions at once." He eyes Jo.

Why did he just do that?

"Let's start with one thing at a time."

"I'm not recording another word until I get answers, and why did you just look at Jo?"

Killy frowns. I can tell he doesn't like any of this. Tough. I am one-hundred percent sure that I was held in a recording cell against my will. "For heaven's sake, man, I looked at her because we're having a conversation."

"He's right, Shawn. There is nothing going on here between David and myself." She turns her attention to Killy. "You could find out who Jennie Masterson is fairly easy, right?"

I decide to believe her. Until she gives me a reason to doubt, I consider her to be on my side. Team Shawn!

Lord, now I sound like I'm watching the *Twilight* Saga. And…I realize that by thinking that, I just admitted that I did watch the *Twilight* Saga. The hell with it. I was and will forever be Team Edward. I'm an old soul. Jo was Team Jacob. Maybe we shouldn't get back together.

"Depends," Killy says. "Her agent is Trafalgar Simmons—a real asshole who is not happy with the financial arrangement I negotiated for Shawn."

"Why not?" I ask. "He got Jennie Masterson millions in the deal, which equals a nice payday for himself."

"This is off the record, but Trafalgar tried to talk Masterson out of hiring you." Killy takes a drink of champagne. "Thinks you're unreliable, overrated, and wanted an up and comer like Parker Barrett to perform the book." Another one of his patronizing laughs slips out. "Fuck, after what you presented tonight—"

"David, stay on topic," Jo orders. I love it when she's assertive. Get him, ma'am!

I also need to stay on topic. So, I ask Killy, "So, Masterson wanted me?"

"I didn't say that. I just said that she preferred you over Barrett."

"Still, that sounds a bit suspicious—a debut author not heeding the advice of her agent?"

"Happens all of the time. Authors get someone in mind, and they get tunnel vision. I wouldn't read too much into it."

"Do you know who the other narrators were who lost out on the book?"

"Doesn't matter. You got it." Killy pauses. "And. Are. Going. To. Keep. It."

"Not if I don't get some answers."

I stand and start pacing. Michael raises his head, watching me.

Killy takes another sip of champagne and then puts his flute on the end table. Jo doesn't touch her flute; she just gazes at me as I walk back and forth on the carpet. I'm not sitting down until I hear what I want to hear out of Killy. I give him a glower every time I turn around. I look ridiculous, but I don't know what else to do. I could always vacuum, I suppose.

Jo breaks the silence. "David, can we start with finding out who Jennie Masterson is?"

I stop pacing and wait for his answer.

"You really want to go down this road?"

"Killy, Goddamnit, you saw the piece of paper I handed you! Someone kidnapped me, and my words are in *Listen To Me*!"

I've never yelled at him. I just went Killy *on* Killy. No clue how he'll respond.

He exhales and puts his head in his hands. This is his gesture when he needs an extra moment to think. I will permit it for now, but if he doesn't help me, I'm taking matters into my own hands. Jesus, I sound like I'm performing a voiceover for a cheesy noir flick.

He picks up the piece of paper along with his flute of champagne. For the next minute, he sips and studies. Other than the fire, the only sound I can hear is his exhalation through his nostrils—another sign that Killy is perturbed and yet focused. He finishes off the bubbly and puts the empty flute and paper back on the end table.

He clasps his hands together. This is Killy's "I've come to a decision" posture. "So," he says, eyeballing me and then Jo, "you both want me to stick my neck out to see who Jennie Masterson is, is that it?"

"For starters, yes," I reply. What I *wanted* to say was, "You're in it now, up to your *neck!*" *The Guns of Navarone*, anyone?

Jo plays her card now and puts a reassuring hand on Killy's round, mountain of a left shoulder. It is hard to refuse her when she does this. Why? Because the gesture is not sexual in nature. It is genuine—not a ploy—but, dear me, if it was…what an effective weapon in someone's arsenal of persuasion.

Killy pulls out his phone. "I'm going to make a few calls from your basement. Sit tight."

Only David Killian could say that in another person's home.

"Okay," I say.

He gets up and moves past me—phone and legal pad in one hand, champagne bottle and flute in the other. Seconds later, I hear the door to the basement open and heavy footsteps descending the stairs.

I sit back down on the couch; Michael rests his head on the floor.

Jo picks up her champagne flute and gives me an understated toast. "Let's see what he comes up with."

"Thanks for helping me with him," I say. "Just when I think my relationship is solid with Killy, a feeling always comes over me that clouds that certainty."

She finishes her sip. "Why?"

"I think there are certain circumstances where he might bail on me." I shake my head and give a fatal laugh. "Like now." I exhale into my palms. "Like about every other incident over the past thirty-six months." Why did I say thirty-six months instead of three years? I have no idea.

"I can't argue with that fear. Remember, I was the one who fielded all of those phone calls when you were at your worst. But, that isn't the case this time. Trust me."

"How can this *not be* one of those times?  I just told him that I had a theory where he was Sean Penn, and I was Michael Douglas in some real-life version of *The Game*?  He's probably down there calling a psych ward.  There *is* no curtain for me to pull back, and I'm *not* going to meet the wizard."  I must admit that the everlasting actor's urge to take center stage almost made me jump off the couch earlier and say, *'Don't you raise your voice to me, Killy,'* and then yell, *'Did I have a choice? Did I have a* choice?'

"Enough of that," she says.  "David Killian isn't bailing on you."

"He's calling Laguna right now."

She laughs.  "Know why he isn't?"

I cross my legs, which is something I rarely do.  Then, I pull yet another line from the annals of performing arts out of my head.  "Enlighten me."  Sometimes I am such a nervous, parsimonious tool.

"Because David Killian makes deals and makes money.  And, at this moment, his job is to make sure that you fulfill the terms of the deal *he* negotiated for the both of you."

"Are you telling me he's down," I say, pointing at the floor, "in my basement right now helping me out?"

"*Yes*.  I could see it in his eyes before he got out his phone."  She takes another sip.  "Something is going on."  She sets her flute on the table and grabs her legal pad and pen.  "You up for reviewing everything?"

"You think *that* will help?"  I already know her answer.  She has always preferred rehashing issues several times when trying to make sense of them.  And I've always admired her method.  Her mind stays in an analytical loop while hearing the same data two or three times.  Eventually, she is able to come up with new connections and insights even though the information remains the same.  My mind problem solves in a similar fashion, but I'm much more of a visual person— says the playwright and audiobook narrator who attempts to give words pictorial life on the stage or in the listener's mind.

"It would," she replies.

We go over everything again, and I am in awe of her attention to detail. She misses nothing, and her questions are exact. Maybe I *can* trust her.

We finish, and my mind and body are exhausted, having probed traumatic topics and memories once more.

I finish our last line of thinking with, "And that's why I am certain that everything I told you about happened. How could my mind just make up those exact words in *Listen To Me?*"

We are both silent for a few beats. Then, she starts tapping her legal pad with her pen. I'm anxious to hear her take and any additional intuitions that she has gained from our review session, but I know to wait.

"Don't ask me how right now, but I think it is possible that Michael Hunnie was there with you."

"Oh, come on, Jo! You've got to tell me *how*. Michael Hunnie *not being there with me* is the only freaking thing that I have convinced myself of!"

"It's mostly a hunch. Call it actor's insight, call it whatever you want, but I feel unsettled on that issue and need to give your description of the event some more thought."

"But he was found with that prostitute. For Christ's sake, there was video evidence of him picking her up in his Land Rover!"

"I'm not challenging your truth, Shawn. Everything else you have said sits fine with me."

"That's easy for you to say, but now you've got me thinking that I'm wrong about Hunnie. My God, Jo, am I going to question *everything* all over again?"

"I don't think so."

How can she be so calm right now? My nervous system is at DEFCON 1.

"But what is it about the Hunnie situation that bothers you?" I ask her.

"Because it is inexplicable."

What can I say? It's a mic-drop, Sherlock Holmes moment that renders me powerless. I don't like her answer, but I am convinced that it is an honest one.

She puts her legal pad and pen down. "I'm sorry."

"For what? Turning my mind upside down?"

"No," she says, rubbing her eyes.

Uh, oh. What is this? I go from DEFCON 1 Shawn Frost to lump-in-my-throat Shawn Frost in seconds. Jo Mansfield still controls the switchboard that makes this possible.

"I'm sorry for not believing you when—God, it's embarrassing the number of times."

This is dangerous territory. I feel a truth serum coursing through my veins. Go with it, Frost. "No, it's not, Jo. I wouldn't have trusted me."

"You're letting me off easy. Don't."

I throw another log on the fire. It's a distraction to give me time to think. Tonight, I was prepared to talk about my theories of how my friends were in on my captivity and rehab. I was not prepared to cover old ground with Jo.

"You don't have to stay any longer. I'm grateful that you came down here tonight—didn't know if you would." I can't help it. I look into her eyes. "Didn't know if you'd *ever* be in my house again."

"Do you want me to go?" she asks.

I swallow. If you don't tell her how you feel, you'll regret it the rest of your life. "This was supposed to be our place together." I motion with my hands all around the room like some realtor. "We had it all worked out, remember?"

She nods. Her eyes are getting glassy, and I see orange flames dancing in the two elliptically-shaped reflecting pools.

"And then I ruined everything." I point at Michael. "He's tired of hearing me talk about it, but he continues to tolerate me. I'd have left me by now if I were him." I smile, but it is just self-deprecatory window dressing for the gnawing regret I still feel. The sadness. The loneliness. Beyond Michael, I'm alone all of the time. I'm alone when I wake up. Alone when I go to bed. Alone when I talk to strangers at the grocery store or gas station. Alone in every miserable room in this huge house by the sea. And, other than a few trusted characters in novels that I have performed, I feel alone in the one space where I'm supposed to *be* alone and be comfortable with it: my booth.

Come to think of it, most of the friendships in my life have been with imaginary people. I don't regret that. Those people are real to me. They were real when I created them for my plays, and I know that they are real to the authors who create them for their novels. I do not feel alone when I see Corie or Matt, but they live in Monterey and have their own life together. I was not a fan of many of the children's books that I narrated during my hiatus from thrillers, but there is an emptiness within me because I do not have children. And I know that that aspect of hollowness would not exist if I didn't want to have kids. I have plenty of friends in the industry who don't want to, and I support them—no law that says we all have to reproduce. To each their own, right?

And now I sound like Roman I. Baker, Ph.D.

And yet, I read that the average age of people living in Japan is around fifty, and getting older by the year. Not good. The United States? Around thirty-seven and holding steady. Should be fine.

And now I sound like someone from the Pew Research Center.

But. The incredible woman that is sitting on my couch, whom I am staring back at right now, is the person *I wanted to have kids with.*

As if that thought were a trigger that has just been pulled, my mouth opens in response, and I say, "Remember when we talked about how many kids we wanted to have?" As soon as the words reach both of our ears, I want them back. I can't do this to her.

"Shawn—"

"No, it was wrong of me to go there. I apologize."

"You don't have to."

I watch as she stands up and walks toward me.  Is she saying goodbye?  Did I mess things up all over again?  Is she going to…

She sits down next to me.

There are perhaps six inches of couch between us, and the luscious smell of her perfume hovers in the air between us.  I study her face, looking for any sign that it would be appropriate for me to kiss her lips, embrace her, tell Killy to get lost for a few hours.

"I haven't forgotten," she says.  "Until tonight, I didn't know how much I—"

She stops and looks toward the basement door.

I hear it too.

Killy is coming up the stairs.

# 31

"Ready for some answers?" David Killian asks as he shuts the door to the basement behind him and then passes through the kitchen on his way to the couch.

I answer, "Yes."

Whatever life moment that I was about to have with Jo Mansfield has passed. By the time David Killian opened the door, Jo had traveled back to the other side of the couch. I don't know what she was going to say or what we were going to do, and I have to accept the fact that I may never know.

She throws back the rest of her drink and gets her pen and legal pad ready.

Killy puts his phone, legal pad, and pen on the couch beside him. He left the champagne bottle and flute downstairs. It doesn't concern me at all; I know they are both empty.

"Ready to work, David," Jo says.

The moment between us may be gone, but she is still determined to help me. That has to mean something, right? I suspend my hope for continuing the conversation that Killy's footsteps interrupted but remain grateful for Jo's belief in me. Don't be a needy adolescent right now, Frost. Find out what Killy knows.

"First, I don't know if what I am about to tell you will put your mind at ease, Shawn. What I *can* tell you is that it certainly clears up a lot for me." He leans forward. "Jennie Masterson is a pen name."

My eyes glow. I knew it. The author is really a man. I doubt the name will be either Peter Canfield or Mark Massey, the names that Wolverine registered under at Santa Monica Bed & Breakfast, but you never know.

"I had to cash in a major favor to get that information because Trafalgar Simmons is going to great lengths to keep Masterson's real name a secret. But, he's not as smart as he thinks he is."

"Damnit, Killy, what is Jennie Masterson's real name? It's a man, right?"

"A man? What? No. Her real name is Nora Stewart. Some recluse who has been writing the story off and on for the past twenty years—ever since the audiobook business started to explode."

"It can't be," I say. "There is no way she wrote the exact words I narrated in that cell. No way in hell."

Killy exhales.

"Don't exhale like that!" I yell. "I know what I'm—"

"Shawn," Jo says, interrupting my outburst. "Let him finish."

I'm short of breath, and my hands are shaking. Suddenly, all I can hear is Big Boss's voice from the ceiling speaker, saying, *'Narrate it* exactly *as I have written it, Shawn.'* Then, I hear Wolverine yelling, *'Oh no, you don't!'* I close my eyes, and now it's Michael Hunnie screaming, *'Shawn! Shawn! Get out of here! They're never letting us out!'*

It all happened!

I open my eyes, ready to continue my rant, but the soothing voice of Jo stops me.

Her attention is directed at Killy. "Continue, David."

I look at Killy, and his eyes elevator down to my shaking hands. He glances at Jo. "Right." He looks me in the eye. "She dreamed of having Michael Hunnie narrate her book and was devastated when he passed away.  I guess she listened to the stories that he narrated every night before going to bed.  Told Simmons something cute like, *I've gone to bed with two men every night for years—my husband and Michael Hunnie.'*  Apparently, she wasn't even going to try and get the novel published, but her family—husband and two kids—talked her into it." He leans back.  "Believe me, man, I tried to look at this through your eyes.  If Jennie Masterson was a pen name for a man, then I'd be with you and would still be in your basement digging into this.  There might have been something to it.  Before I came up, I thought about what you told me tonight about the manuscript—everything that you've narrated so far and the rest of the book that you skimmed to see if anything else was familiar."

"And since there isn't, you're saying we've hit a dead end."

"Not trying to be mean, but a dead-end would occur only after we had a start, and, Shawn, we don't even have a start here."

"Is there an early draft of the manuscript that we can look at?"

Killy hangs his head for a moment and then locks eyes with me.  "I thought you might ask that, so I looked into it.  Good news and bad news.  Bad news is that there's no way we're getting our hands on an early draft.  Good news is that we don't need to.  My contact told me that there were no major changes from the manuscript version to the finished book that you're narrating right now."  He looks at both of us, and then his eyes settle on my eyes once more.  "To confirm this, the second-to-last call I made was to none other than Esperanza Benoit."

"Who is that?" Jo asks.

I reply, almost in a whisper with, "The woman with the magic red pen."

Killy doesn't wait to clarify.  "ParkerWilson's top developmental editor."

Jo nods.

In a defeated tone, I ask the fireplace, which is where I'm staring now, "And what did she have to say?"

"That she worked with Nora Stewart for about six months. Naturally, she wondered why I was calling her, and I told her that you were absolutely delighted with how much of a page-turner the book was—so much, in fact, that you were having a hard time narrating it because you wanted to see what happened next, which is a rarity for you. Then, I kissed her ass for another minute or so and slid in the final question: 'How heavy of an edit was it?' She said there were a few pacing adjustments but that the bones and details of the story that you are now narrating were probably ninety-five percent set when she looked at the draft that Simmons sent her. And this is why she got a deal for book number two. She thanked me for the call, and I know there won't be anything that follows. If there is, it will only be Liz Cross calling me to express her gratitude for our kind words to Ms. Benoit." Killy clears his throat. "Now, your logical follow-up question for me is: But what about Nora Stewart's agent, Trafalgar Simmons? How much did he have her change before he submitted it to Ms. Benoit? Remember how I told you that he thinks of himself as one of the intellectual elite? Well, he's also incredibly lazy—has a reader that he trusts and has used for years to weed out all of the manuscripts that are submitted to him. Her name is Cindy Shriver, and I've known her for years—hates Simmons, but her bank account cup runneth over because of him. She's the last call I made tonight." Killy pauses, rubbing his hands together. "Shawn, she said that the story that Simmons passed on to Benoit was the same one she had read before recommending it to Simmons. Now, to be fair, she didn't recommend any changes because she thought that the story was that good. Plus, she knows what Benoit likes, and Benoit is going to make her own changes anyway. However, she did confirm to me that Simmons hasn't changed; if a manuscript gets recommended by Cindy with no suggested changes, he doesn't make any before submitting. There's no smoking gun here, friends."

I have to hand it to him. Killy is thorough—especially when he has a stake in the game. And, right now, his money and reputation are tied up in me finishing my performance of *Listen To Me.* Jo sits in silence. Her expression toward me is one of disappointment—not disappointment *in me* but *for me.*

"Shawn," Killy says. "I haven't changed my position from earlier this evening. I don't think you've gone crazy. Something happened a few years ago, and I don't know if we'll ever truly know what it was." He gets up and comes and sits next to me. The couch sinks, and I almost tip over toward him. "Look, I'll even give you the benefit of the doubt and believe your claim that those are your words on that piece of paper over there. But how they made it into the book you're narrating, we'll never know. It has to be some kind of fluke." He pats my left knee with his massive right hand. "There's no place to go with this. Believe me, if there was, I'd look into it even further for you." He gives a long exhale. "As your agent and as your friend, you've got to let this thing go now. Finish this book, collect the dough, and let's get you into another Ivan Bacca thriller. And if you narrate *Listen To Me* like I know you are capable of, then you'll win this time at the Audies." He pauses again, seeming to contemplate something as he rubs his five o'clock shadow and stares into the dying fire. Then, as if he's just had his own epiphany, he gives my knee a quick, firm hit. "Actually, you know what I'm going to do for you when you finish this book? I'm going to get on the phone with M. Scott Sala and tell him to bring back Nehemiah Stone. Been waiting to do it for a while. Needed big-league leverage. And now that he hasn't even tasted *any* bestseller list in the past two years, it's time. Prequel, sequel, doesn't matter. Readers are very forgiving when it comes to getting more of their favorite character."

This is not what I wanted to hear, but I know that if I bring up anything else, Killy might reach his limit with me. Plus, there really is nothing else he can do. If I asked him what I want to ask him right now, the whole evening would unravel. No, I've got to do this on my own.

It's the only way I can ever fully trust Jo and Killy again.

I summon my strength, put steel in my spine, as some football coach once said, and give myself to the actor's studio once more. I lower my head. "You've done more than I could have ever hoped for, Killy. I," I look up at Jo and then Killy with tears in my eyes, really gotta sell this. "I need a day to get myself back together. A good night of rest tonight and another one tomorrow night." I wipe my tears and lock eyes with Killy. "I promise you, I'll be back at work on *Listen To Me* the morning after that. I won't let you down, and I'm going to make it my best performance."

Michael has come over and has his head on my lap.

"It just seems so real to me," I say, lowering my head again.

Killy puts his arm around me. "I know. I know it does. But it's all in the past now. You looked at the rest of the book and know that everything is fine."

I nod.

He drops his arm and rises from the couch. "I want to be the first person to listen to it. Forget what Ms. Cross said. Send it to me first. Okay?"

I raise my head. "Okay."

"I'll call you tomorrow, mid-morning. I'm staying in Monterey tonight. Call *me* if you need anything."

I nod in agreement again.

Jo stands up.

I want her to stay, but for what I have to do, she can have no knowledge of it. The way she stands and is looking at me, I have a feeling that she wants me to invite her to stay over, and she knows that she cannot initiate that discussion. The best I can do is what I actually do—doesn't always work that way with me. I give Michael a little love and then stand up.

I walk toward her and open my arms. "Thank you, Jo. For everything."

We embrace. I ask in her ear, "Can I call you at some point over the next few days?"

"Of course," she says.

We break our hug.  She knows from my question that I won't be asking her to stay the night.

Killy is already gathering his coat and Jo's.

I walk them to the door, and we say goodbye.  The evening could have gone a lot worse, but it is not how I envisioned it ending.

I watch as the headlights of Jo's car travel down my driveway.  It's like a bad dream happening all over again.  Part of me wants to listen to what they are saying to each other right now;  another part of me knows I couldn't handle it.  I have the same philosophy with audiobook reviews.

I take one last look, make sure the door is locked, and head upstairs.

Michael is waiting for me by the fire.

"C'mon, boy," I say to him.  "It's time to find out where Nora Stewart lives."

# 32

I pull my car onto the shoulder of the road, perhaps twenty yards from the paved entrance to a long driveway that snakes a quarter of a mile back to the four-thousand-square-foot log cabin residence of Nora and Marcus-John Stewart. Zillow and Google Maps are a beautiful thing.

I'm in the Sequoia National Forest, about four hours east and a tad south of my place in Carmel-by-the-Sea. It's eight p.m., and yours truly is making an uninvited house call this evening. Last night, David Killian and Jo Mansfield were at my home; tonight, I'm catching up with Nora and Marcus-John. I will be pleasant and open-minded, and if Marcus-John is under six-five, then I shall congratulate Nora on her incredible book deal, apologize for not contacting her ahead of time—I'll make up some story about miscommunication with Killy— maybe ask her about the evolution of her story, and then be on my way, satisfied that neither Nora nor her husband are the people I am looking for.

Or, at least, the people whom I think I am looking for.

Actually, if this visit doesn't yield anything, then it will be time to put the whole kidnapping business to bed and move on with my life. I will be able to trust Killy and Jo again. I mostly trust them now, but this is a final step I have to take. I called Killy this afternoon and said I would keep my promise and be back at recording tomorrow morning. The whole entertainment industry is about to go dark until early January, so I want to get the book recorded and then cash in on Killy's promise to get me a few more Ivan Bacca thrillers—and press Killy to put the heat on M. Scott Sala to bring back my beloved Nehemiah Stone. However, those aren't the things I'm most excited about. Why I really want to get this novel recorded is so that I can resume work on my new play. I know I promised details, but right now, I've got a couple to surprise. I wonder if their kids are home tonight. Why wouldn't they be? C'mon. Keep it tight, Frost. Yes, I'm totally ripping that line off of Sala—always wrote, *'Keep it tight, Stone'* when Nehemiah headed toward danger. Part of me hopes that I'm not. Another part of me hopes that I am.

Oh, and in case anyone is wondering, no one knows I'm here.

I turn off my GMC Yukon XL. Environmentally friendly? No. Is it the preferred vehicle of Nehemiah Stone? Yes. I bought it brand new and fully loaded three years ago—midnight blue exterior, gray leather interior, the works. In retrospect, I believe I was planning ahead—a first for me—for a family with Jo back then. Now, it sits in my garage for most of the time, but, and I hate to admit it because Corie gives me an exorbitant amount of lip on the subject, I love to drive it. Nope, not ready to go electric yet, my friends.

I zip up my black Columbia fleece jacket. My Yukon told me that the temperature outside was 53 degrees, and that's damn cold for California. I have since confirmed the temperature on my phone and further confirmed it on my smartwatch, so the temperature reading *must* be true. When he goes on his missions, Nehemiah is always wearing black, so I've once again been influenced by my fictional hero. I've got jeans on and my black Brooks running shoes. Cell phone is charged and in my jacket pocket now, and I have a Swiss Army knife in the front, right pocket of my jeans—no idea in hell what I'd use it for, but I feel better knowing it's in there.

Yep, no gun. Scared to death of them, and I wouldn't know the first thing about carrying a concealed weapon. Plus, if I did bring one, I'd be thinking more about the gun than about observing Nora and Marcus-John, which would defeat the whole purpose of my visit.

Also, I don't own a gun. So, there's that.

I close the door and feel the cool breeze immediately as if the mighty, soaring sequoias are whispering to me that I shouldn't be here. Other than the wind blowing through the forest, it is quiet—not a single car on the small road leading to the Stewarts' driveway.

I look to see if there is anyone around—would be a shame if I ruined the surprise before I ever set foot on the driveway. Oh, I need to lock my car…

…so, without using my previous thought to prevent stupid behavior, I hit the lock button twice on my Yukon's key fob. The lights flash, and the horn beeps. You know the drill.

Frost, you are the world's worst covert operator. Live it through the books, young man, but let the pros take care of things in the real world.

I shrug and can only hope that the Stewarts haven't heard my mistake a quarter of a mile away. I start my trek toward their lovely log home, taking a step onto the smooth asphalt, which smells like it has been recently surfaced…that familiar burnt aroma still hanging in the air. It is dark, but I don't dare use my phone's flashlight. I plan to stick to the driveway and take it slow. Five to ten minutes from now, I'll be ringing the doorbell.

"Well, you're committed now, Frost," I say as I walk down the driveway. There seems to be a dull, yellow glow in the distance, but I am unable to make anything out through the trees as the path starts to wind to the right. I assume that when I get closer, I may hear some sounds of civilization—a door opening or closing, human speech, or children playing outside. Maybe the dribble of a basketball if they have a lighted court or a dog barking—if they have one…wonder what breed they would have?

The woods feel incredibly close and impenetrable to me as the drive straightens for a bit before starting to come back left. The darkness adds to the effect, like I'm about to round a bend and be squeezed by the forest as it presses in from both sides and the canopy above lowers.

I shiver. I'm usually not out walking this late. On the back deck, enjoying a sparkling water with Michael on my lap? Sure. But I'm fine. I know what I want to accomplish. I know what I want to say and how I want to say it.

Actually, I'm scared shitless right now.

What would Nehemiah do right now?

He'd have guns. Next question.

I suddenly stop. My left arm feels like it brushed against something. That's impossible, Frost. You're in the middle of the driveway. What was it then?

I trace my right hand down my left shoulder to my elbow and then all the way to my wrist. I shake my head and blow air out my nose. You idiot; it was your smartwatch vibrating. I flip my wrist and look at the display.

Exercise ring closed.

"Well, would you look at that," I whisper to myself.

I start moving again. Then, perhaps after twenty-five more yards, the driveway bends to the left, and I can see lights up ahead and the rough outline of the cabin. The internet pictures don't do it justice. The place is huge. Instinctively, I leave the driveway and head a few yards into the woods. Now, I feel like an operator.

I take a few steps to see how much noise I'll make if I continue. The answer is *not much*. I proceed. The lemon beams grow brighter as I get closer and closer to the house. I can now see three lights on the garage—one at each side and one in the middle of the two garage bays. Both doors are closed. A gigantic front porch runs along the front of the house, and there is a light on next to the front door. I know from the pictures on Zillow that the place has a sizable basement— you bet your ass I want to see it—and the french doors open up on the other side of the house. The walkway leading from the concrete pad to the front porch is lined with half-a-dozen flickering orange lights, spaced evenly apart on one side.

The front yard is bright green and thick, like if I was to go across it, my footprints would show as if I was walking across damp sand.

I reach the last sequoia before the yard begins and take station behind it. Let's just wait here a few minutes and observe. Gather as much information as possible. Plenty of time to approach the front door and start the evening's masquerade. And, to my knowledge, I haven't been detected yet. Keep it tight, Frost.

I am shameless.

My patience pays off. After a minute of hearing and seeing nothing—not even a shadow crossing by one of the front windows—the front door opens…

And as I see who's standing there, I'm suddenly questioning my whole plan.

# 33

Aman who, judging by his relation to the front door, stands somewhere under six feet tall, heads down the steps and takes the lighted path to the sizable concrete pad. Is this the husband? If it is, then it will be the easier of two plans tonight. He did not say anything when he left the house, and there was no customary looking back at the front door on his way out. He simply opened the door, exited, and closed it behind him. I alternate my eyes between the man and the front door. Maybe someone will come out? Or, if it is the husband, then where is he going?

He stops in the middle of the concrete pad and stretches his arms up to the starlit sky. He's wearing jeans and a long-sleeved t-shirt with some type of work boots. I smile, wondering if the brand is Wolverine. Anyway, he's not going jogging. He turns toward the right-side garage door and starts whistling. I don't recognize the tune.

The garage door starts to open, and the light underneath the door grows until I can see a small, red-colored SUV, a hybrid of some sort. He starts walking toward it.

Shit.

Please don't get in the car and drive off. You'll see my car and then…

But, just before he reaches the vehicle, he turns and goes around the right-hand side. Then I hear, "Just tell me when you're out, babe."

It is the voice of a woman. Nora Stewart? Would a woman call someone "babe" who wasn't her husband? I don't know.

The man wheels out a heavy-duty mountain bike and, when he's clear of the door, yells, "Good to go."

Immediately, the garage door starts to close.

Damnit.

Car, bike…it doesn't matter. He's going to ride down the driveway and see my car in about two minutes.

I watch as he turns on a large headlight and mounts the bike. Well, I'm going to have to approach the front door as soon as he rides past me and goes out of sight.

He starts to pedal…

…and goes around the side of the garage!

I watch as his light travels into the woods, getting dimmer and dimmer the farther he gets away. A path!

I take a few cleansing breaths and gather myself. A stakeout is infinitely more stressful than what I imagined. How did Nehemiah Stone maintain his nerve through all of those situations? And how did M. Scott Sala keep the tension wired as tight as a guitar string? If anything, I now have a deeper appreciation for his craft. I always thought he was more than a serviceable writer, but now I'm convinced that he is a master.

The multiple questions running through my mind bring my current situation back into focus, pulling the curtain down on a vision, far in the future, of me attending a lifetime achievement award banquet to honor the craft and career of M. Scott Sala—I'm walking to the stage with the help of a cane, Killy is in a wheelchair and drinking scotch…

Right. The questions.

Is that her husband?  If so, where is he going?  When will he be back?  Is he even coming back?  If that isn't her husband, then who is he?  Who rides a bicycle with a headlamp off into the sequoias after dark?  Where does that path lead to?

I realize that I can't worry about any of those inquiries at this juncture.  It's time to act.  I pull my cell phone out from my jacket pocket.  Why?  I'm not quite sure.  It just makes me feel more like I'm in control.  I hold it in my left hand and pat the right front pocket of my jeans with my right hand.  Swiss Army knife all present and accounted for.

God Almighty, where did that come from?  As I take my first steps around the giant tree and toward the house, I remember.

*Jet Encounter*

by John Armbrewster

Read for you by Shawn Frost

Man, fuck that book.

In thirty seconds, I'm up across the concrete pad, up the porch steps, and at the door.  I ring the doorbell and then give a few knocks.

A light comes on inside, the foyer, I presume, and a woman's voice says, "Oh, what did you forget this time, babe?"

She opens the door and jumps back—her face as pale as a sheet of copy paper and her brown eyes as wide open as if she is Hooper at the end of the film *Jaws* when the shark busts through the cage bars.

Then, as if a force greater than shock takes control of her body, she breaks into the widest grin I've ever witnessed in my thirty-nine years of life—red lipstick and her straight, white teeth gleaming.  "Oh, my God!" she says.  I'd categorize her tone as Valley Girl…and I am her long-lost sorority sister.  It is hard to believe that she is the same woman I heard before the door opened, but it is.

"Good evening," I say and cock my head to one side in a semi-mocking, Shawn-is-trying-to-be-cute-and-get-laid posture.  "Nora Stewart?  Or, should I say, *Jennie Masterson?*"

She puts her hands on her hips in a playful way. "In-person," she replies.

And, for a moment, I am unable to reply. There is something familiar about her—like, I've seen her before even though I know that I haven't. Her hair is red. I'm talking Flamin' Hot Cheetos red. I would have remembered that. She's in her bare feet—nail polish that matches her hair—and around 5'6, a few inches shorter than Jo. Average height, so nothing that stands out in that regard. She's wearing a black tank top with black stretch pants that highlight her rail-thin form. Her arms are toned but with enough muscle to move past the categorization of bony. Hands? Long, delicate fingers with—you guessed it—red nail polish. And, because her fingers are so thin, the huge diamond wedding ring gives the impression that she won a Super Bowl rather than got married. Nothing in particular about her jogs a memory, but I have a sensation—my "Peter tingle"—coursing through my body that is still telling me I've met or seen this woman before. Or, perhaps a better way to put what my brain is currently doing is to rely on my old friend M. Scott Sala who once wrote that Nehemiah Stone's brain *"completed a facial recognition analysis of the beautiful woman he saw before him, and the words 'target not acquired' appeared on the display of his mind."*

"I'm—"

"Shawn Frost. My narrator! What are you doing here?"

And suddenly, all of the momentum and control of the situation that I envisioned on the drive over has vanished. I'm on the defensive and need to step up.

"I am." I give her a warm, God-damn-I'm-so-proud-of-you smile and say, "What am I doing here? You mean David Killian didn't call you?"

She gives me a puzzled look.

I roll my eyes—God, I miss acting. "Ah, that is *so* David." I've never called him David or referred to him as David since I've known him. I give a besmirched chuckle and add a few quick head shakes for effect. "Well, this is not going how we planned, and I'm sorry, I heard you call to someone through the door before you opened it. Are you expecting another guest? I don't want to intrude."

Her eyes look past me for a moment. "No, a neighbor just left before you got here, and I thought he might have left something." Her gaze returns to me, and her big smile is back. "I call everyone 'babe.'"

As soon as I hear the word *neighbor*, my adrenaline starts to pump. That wasn't her husband. Wolverine could be somewhere in this house.

"I saw him pedaling off into the woods as I was walking up."

"One-mile path between our houses. Weaves around the sequoias like a maze in a kid's activity book, but beats the four-mile drive by road." She pauses. "Speaking of roads. Why didn't you drive up the driveway? I mean, you didn't walk from Carmel-by-the-Sea, right?"

So, she knows where I live. Forget that line of thinking, Frost. That's simple enough to explain. She found out you were performing her audiobook and looked up your address online—just like you looked up her address last night. Now, answer her question.

I raise my left hand, twist it, and the display lights up on my smartwatch. "Need the steps. I'm Nooming right now and ate fast food on my way over. Still a kid—get in the car, and there's a magnet toward the golden arches." I grin, putting my hand in my jacket pocket. "Went over on my calories and am seeing if a little extra walking gets me back into the 'good' range. So, I parked at the end of your driveway and hiked up. Beautiful place you've got here."

She shows me her smartwatch. "I'm Nooming too! Trying to get in presentable shape for my book tour."

I give a nod of understanding, one Noom warrior to another, one artist to another. "And that's why I'm here," I say. "I'm having such a wonderful experience narrating *Listen To Me* that I *had* to reach out. So, I was ready to give you a call, but then I found out that you lived only four hours away. Imagine that. I told my agent that I was going to take a break from the booth and pay you a visit to express my gratitude. He was supposed to call you and tell you I was on my way over, but judging from your surprise, I see that he hasn't." Now, I give her the I'm-in-awe-of-your-talent smile. "I've never read anything like this book. Seriously, it's—

She touches my arm, and it's a sensual touch. "Before you go any further, please, come in!"

She ushers me in through the front door and closes it behind me.

Okay, where is he?

I start tapping my thigh with the fingers of my right hand. Being inside has made things much more real. There is a beautiful wooden staircase directly in front of me, and I anticipate either hearing or seeing her husband or kids at any second.

My God, what if her husband *is* Wolverine, and he walks around the corner with his arms around his two children—good old dad doting on his kids. *Then,* what do I do?

You can leave right now, Frost. Make up some excuse.

I hear the door's lock click.

Nope. You're in it now. *Get out of my freaking head, Gregory Peck.*

Nora strides past me, waving me down a long hallway. For a log home, the design is less of an open concept than I am used to seeing in *Architectural Digest.* Yes, I am a home design connoisseur. Jo and I had discussed what our dream home would be before I went off the rails.

From the pictures on Zillow, I wasn't able to form a layout of the house in my mind. I assume we're headed for the living room, but who knows. The hallway has three doors—one on the left and two on the right—and they are all closed. I pat the pocket with the Swiss Army knife in it again. Still there. I feel the smooth plastic on the back of my cell phone in my sweaty right palm.

Nora looks back at me and gives me a wink, then continues down the hallway.

Not going to lie. She is a knockout.

And she's sweet, which begs the question that has been running through my mind since her first words to me—actually, I posed it to Michael before I left, but he just looked up at me and wagged his tale.  I'm telling you, I understand my furry companion's gestures and moods, but, for the love of Lakers' players past and present, I wish he could talk.  This reminds me of a trend in audiobooks right now that I wish would stop: the dog psychic book.  Ugh, *enough*.  Anyway, the question:  If Nora is married to Wolverine, could she possibly know the truth about her husband?  From what I've seen so far, my answer is no.  Believe me; I know acting when I see it.

We reach the end, and the space opens up to a kitchen on the left and a huge, sunken living room on the right.  There is a football game on the mammoth big screen hanging from the ceiling in a corner, and a u-shaped couch faces the screen.  A wall of glass is to my left with lights on outside over a beautiful and spacious deck.  That I do recognize from the pictures.  And I also know that the walkout basement's french doors are right below it.  The woods beyond the deck are dark and imposing, as if I'm on a submarine traveling into the deep, and the sub's lights only illuminate so far ahead.

My eyes follow Nora as she enters the kitchen.

"A drink, Shawn?"

"Just water, please."

She turns around and gives me a pout.  "I've got the best narrator in the world in my house, and he won't even have a glass of champagne with me?"

My God, she's persuasive.  Maybe…

Just one…?

No!  Get your head in the right place, Frost.

"Gotta drive and gotta keep my voice lubricated for tomorrow's pages."

Voice lubricated?  What the hell is wrong with you?

I raise my arm and point at my watch.  "And, I'm already over on my damned calories."

She gives a frisky smile and says, "Ooooookkaaaaaayyyyy.  I guess I can't argue with those reasons."

Does she know that I'm a recovering addict?  If so, then I should be offended.  But I'm not.

"Go ahead and sit down on the couch," she says.  "I'll be back in a minute."

She disappears down the hallway, and I turn toward the couches.  Before I step down the two steps that lead to the sunken living room's floor, I see a door to my right.  I estimate that I am even with the stairway in the foyer.  The door must open to the stairs leading down into the basement.

I shiver as I walk past.  I want to tear open the door and fly down the stairs to see if there are two rooms down there, both with toilets.  However, I'm pretty good at remembering smells, and even though I'm on the first floor right now, the smells of the house do not remind me of anything my senses picked up while I was being held in the cell.

I step down into the living room and sit on the couch with my back to the wall so that I can see the TV off to my right, the living room and deck beyond the windows in front of me, and the kitchen off to my left.  No one is going to sneak up on me.

My hands are starting to shake. Relax, man.

What was once white noise coming from the TV becomes clear to me as I sit back and stretch my legs.  Southern California is playing Oregon, and the Trojans have the lead late in the second quarter.  Normally, I would have a tremendous amount of interest in the game, but right now, it is the TV itself that opens up another line of questioning.

Who was watching the game before I came in?  Nora?  Nora and her neighbor?  Nora's kids?  Nora's husband?  Were they all watching?  Is this a football family?

From my perch on the soft sofa, I anticipate that Nora went off to grab the family and that I'm about to meet them, which, as long as her husband is not Wolverine, will be a good thing. I'll visit with them all and then be on my way.

But what if she's calling her agent right now?

I pull out my phone. Better give Killy a heads up. He's going to flip out, but I can't worry about that now. I text him:

**At Nora Stewart's house. Told her that you were going to call her earlier and let her know I was coming over. That's the story if anyone contacts you. Sorry. I'll explain later. Be home tonight and back in the booth tomorrow morning.**

I silence my phone and place it back inside my jacket pocket. He's going to blow up my phone now, and I can't be distracted. As soon as I pull my hand out of my pocket, I hear footsteps down the hall.

Nora walks into the kitchen. She's carrying two cell phones in her right hand and a bottle of champagne in her left. She gives me a quick smile before setting the phones on the counter, but I sense that something is off. I can't tell what, but her demeanor strikes me as more of the "on guard" variety now. My thoughts return to the neighbor who rode out before I arrived.

Is she having an affair? Why does she have two phones?

And now my guard is up again.

She opens the champagne bottle and says, "Sure you won't join me?"

"I'm sure, but many thanks for the offer. Water would be much appreciated. A bit parched from my walk." I'm totally lying, but what else am I supposed to say? Why in the *hell* does she have *two* phones?

"Can't say that I didn't try to be hospitable when you go back to your glamorous life," she says, pouring herself a flute of bubbly.

You just offered alcohol to a recovering addict. Twice. "I will sing high praises about your acumen as a hostess—hosting with zero notice, I might add."

"I can settle for that, I suppose." She pours a glass of water from the refrigerator and then walks toward the living room with both drinks in hand.

Okay, I can't wait any longer. "Are your husband and two kids around? I'd love to meet them and brag some more about you and this once-in-a-lifetime book I'm narrating. Again, I'm so sorry you didn't know that I was coming. I feel bad about…this, like I'm imposing on you."

Man, am I struggling with words right now.

She hands me the glass of water and sits on the couch across from me with her back to the windows. She takes a sip of champagne and then waves her hand, "Nonsense. This is an honor. I'm sure there's a simple explanation about what happened."

Oh, there is. And he's probably screaming at me in a voicemail right about now.

"As for my family, my two girls—a freshman and a sophomore—are at a high school basketball game tonight and are going out for pizza afterwards, so you probably won't see them. My husband is around here somewhere," she says, laughing.

"Marcus-John, right?"

"The one and only. We've got a pole barn back about a hundred yards on our property. He loves to work there but doesn't always let me know when he's heading that way. And," she says, motioning toward the phones on the counter, "he forgets his phone a lot of the time." She takes another sip and shrugs. "What's a girl to do?"

I'd like to ask her neighbor "babe" that question. And, I want to search their basement. And, I want to see what is in their remote building—maybe ask, 'Pole barn got a basement?' But, at least the phone question has been answered.

"Oh, where are my manners or sense of occasion?" she says, standing up and leaning over toward me. She holds out her flute. "To *Listen To Me* and surprise visits."

We toast, and she sits back down. Cheering from the TV speakers turns our attention toward the game, and we watch as an Oregon player sprints down the sideline and enters the endzone. The Ducks take the lead. She grabs the remote control and turns the TV off. "Sorry for the distraction."

"You could have kept it on."

"It's better if it's off. I'll be a better host. Every time I watch, Oregon jumps ahead."

"USC fan?"

"Diehard."

"Graduate?"

"No. Bandwagon since I moved out here."

Her girls are in high school, so I put her age somewhere in the forties, but she could easily pass for younger than me. Drug relapses and a late-thirties belly will do that to you. How was I to know potato chips would become the vice that replaced my more sinister and harmful ones? But, remember, I'm Nooming; Shawn Frost is making a comeback.

"So, you're liking the book?"

"Very much so," I say. "Every audiobook narrator's secret fantasy is to narrate a book where the main character is an audiobook narrator. For every book I narrate, I try to form some connection with the main character, but for this book, I feel like *I am* Lionel Goliath. Superb character names, by the way."

She takes a drink and then sets down her flute. "Thanks. And thanks for coming all the way over here to tell me that."

"I usually have little to no contact with the authors I work with, but this book is special, and I told my agent that I had to come see you—especially before I finished it. Go figure, he doesn't call you. Well, I left him an unkind Voicemail when you stepped out of the room earlier. I'll call him when I leave your place and ream him out some more." I say it semi-jokingly so that she doesn't think I'm an egotistical asshole.

"Like I said, it's fine."

"Thanks for being understanding. And, talk about manners, I'm way late on congratulating you on your big deal. Seven figures. That's almost unheard of."

"I'm extremely lucky."

"Well, the novel is fantastic, which always seems to help one's luck."

"Thanks. How far are you in the book?"

Her surprised, carefree, and welcoming spirit has evolved into a *let's talk business* posture—akin to watching someone's smile disappear in slow motion at the mention of bad news. Well, then, let's talk business, Ms. Stewart. I take a sip of water and set my glass down. "I'm going slower than my usual pace, savoring every word, but I just reached the part where Beryl is talking about publishing house politics. Having witnessed many publishing wars over the years, I'm impressed with your knowledge of the industry and your diction—some memorable phrases in there for sure. In fact," I say, leaning forward, "a passage I just read has stayed with me all day."

She's got a good poker face. I'll give her that.

That is, if she's acting.

Time to see how good of a poker face it really is, though. If she has had anything to do with what happened to me, then I'll know it after I repeat these lines.

"Oh, you're not going to embarrass me now, are you? I have worried about what my words would sound like when I heard a professional read them for the first time. I even told my husband, *'What if they sound awful?'* No disrespect to you because you'll elevate whatever I wrote. But. What if some of my writing is poor?"

I throw her a bone first. "I'm a third of the way in, and the writing is beautiful. When you've had an editor like Esperanza Benoit give your manuscript her seal of approval, you don't have anything to worry about."

Some of her Valley girl accent comes back. "You really think so?"

"I know so. Now, here is the passage that had me thinking about what comes next in the story for the entire car ride over here." I take a sip of water and put the glass back down. I pretend I'm in my booth. There's only one exception. I'm going to use Stacey instead of Beryl, can always explain it away as a mistake if, indeed, Nora Stewart has had nothing to do with what happened to me twenty-nine months ago. There I go again counting months.

Stacey had steered clear of the ever-present politics being played by William Morrow's major players—that was her mega-agent's job, to cajole the men and women who held the levers of power into thinking that the once-in-a-generation book deserved a commensurate price tag.

I see a mix of awe, confusion, and recognition stream almost simultaneously across her face. She is speechless, which is good for me. It's not a sign of guilt, but it allows me to follow up my recitation with a question.

"Is everything okay?"

"Yes, that was incredible, Shawn."

I grin and give the self-deprecatory "bow nod" as thanks for a demonstration of my life's work. It's as close as I can get to giving a real bow at the end of a play, which I am hungry to do again.

"However, I have to ask, who is Stacey?"

Time to play dumb. "Stacey, who?"

"I think you said Stacey when you meant to say Beryl."

"Did I?" I laugh. "Sorry about that. And here I said that I had that passage going through my mind all day. Stacey. I must still have Gwen Stacy on my mind or something. You know, the one from *Spider-Man*? Peter Parker's one true love?"

"I haven't seen any of the films," she says. "My girls have, though. When it comes to Marvel movies, they're certifiable."

And I can't get a read on her! I feel if I probe any further, then I'll seem suspicious, which is not what I want. Now, the question becomes *How much longer can I make this glass of water last until I get to see her husband?*

Then, another thought materializes. If she's not in on it, and her husband is, then my presence here has put her in danger. Oh, God. Now, I'm concerned for this non-Marvel-watching writer-mom's safety.

What's your move, Frost?

Stay on the Marvel topic for a minute while you think. "I think you'd like the films. Fun as hell."

She's about to answer but stops as we both hear a noise.

I can't place it. Dull thuds, one after another, and getting louder. Where is the noise coming from? My eyes search the living room, the deck outside, and then the kitchen.

The kitchen!

I see a window open above the sink.

She watches me, and I state the obvious, "What is that noise?"

She swallows and stands up. "It's my husband coming up the stairs on our back deck."

This is it. I don't know what will happen next, but *this* is the moment I've been waiting for.

# 34

ora Stewart starts walking toward the sliding glass door off the kitchen. I stand up and follow; I am about to get the main answer I came here for. My hands are shaking again.

Heavy step.

Heavy step.

I access the picture of the back deck from my memory. There it is. Yes, there is a stairway at the far end of the deck, on the other side of the kitchen window. To get to the sliding glass door, you would have to walk ten yards or so, which means passing by the window. Judging by the height of the window and the closeness in level between the kitchen floor and the back deck, if I see his head and shoulders, then I'll know he's tall. I'm about to get a glimpse of him.

Heavy step.

Heavy step.

A pause.

He must be at the top of the stairs.

Step.

*Stehhhp.*

It sounds like a limp—a slight dragging of one foot.

Step.

*Stehhhp.*

Step.

He passes by the window. It's dark out, so I couldn't see what he looks like, but I was definitely able to make out a profile of his head and shoulders.

He's tall.

Nora gets to the sliding glass door just as a hulking figure appears in front of her. She's blocking my way, and the outside deck light is so bright that I can't see his face. He's huge, though. Towers over her.

I'm about three steps behind her when the door opens and his face comes into sight.

It is the man I saw on the street in Santa Monica. It's Wolverine. His hair has grown out some, but his goatee is still there. And those eyes. Those blue eyes.

You get one chance at this, Frost.

I swing for the fence.

Standing straight up, I give him the most menacing look that I am capable of. With my left hand, I point right at his chest. Then, I slowly start to reach down by my right hip as if I'm about to pull out a gun.

And it works.

His eyes open wide like a rabid dog. Suddenly, his eyes shift side to side, and then his head is on a swivel as if he expects the police to close in at any second. He's paranoid as hell. A stiff breeze from the deck carries the strong smell of alcohol toward me as Wolverine opens his mouth. "How did you know?" he yells at me and backs out onto the deck.

She takes a step back and then screams, "Marcus-John! No!"

He pushes her out of the way and rushes into the room. Nora's head hits the side of the kitchen counter, and she falls to the floor. She's not moving. I can see he has a revolver in his right hand—and he's raising it toward me.

I'm close enough to the kitchen table to grab a chair, so I do and throw it at him. If the shit works in the movies, it will work here.

It does. He fires, but because of the chair, the shot hits the kitchen floor. I don't waste any time and throw open the door to the basement and dive down the steps. A shot rings out above me. I keep sliding, my elbows, forearms, and knees taking a pounding on the wooden steps, but I reach the bottom alive.

I slide onto the floor and immediately roll left, out of view of the staircase, and it's a good thing I do because a shot hits the carpeted floor right where I was seconds earlier.

Damnit. My cell phone came out of my pocket and is on the floor at the bottom of the stairs. Can I grab it if I move quickly?

Another shot rings out, and my cell phone explodes. That answers that question.

Okay, I don't have a phone, but my decision to come down here has put me in a good position. I have options. If he comes down the stairs, then I'm bolting out the french doors, sprinting under the back deck, and taking off into the woods. If he comes in through the french doors, then I'm rushing up the stairs and heading out the front door. Either way, I'll be hauling ass to my Yukon.

First things first. I yell, "Nora, are you okay?"

My words are met with silence. Where is he?

I stand just to the right of the staircase in a large room. I flip on a light switch. The room has the distinct smell of an area where someone has recently been working out—a kind of sweet, scented sweat. There is a pool table, ping pong table, big screen TV, and bar with stools. On the far wall are the french doors. Across the stairwell is a dark hallway. I think I can see the outline of a few doorways, but I'm not certain. Is one of those rooms my cell? It's hard to believe because Nora and Marcus-John have two girls. The only thing that would make it possible is if Nora took the girls on a vacation during that time.

I hear a creak upstairs. "Pretty good position you've put yourself in down there, Shawn," Marcus-John says. His voice still sounds like the man I encountered in Santa Monica. I want him to sound like Wolverine.

"You're going to prison, you psychopathic fuck! How could you do that to someone? And who is Big Boss? He's going down too, *Wolverine.*"

Mocking me, he speaks for the first time like Wolverine. "Let's not get carried away now, bubba. Whatru packin' down there?"

I feel sick to my stomach. Hold it together. You can't crumble now. If you do, he'll be down the steps in two seconds and kill you. I take a breath while my knees wobble. At least he still thinks I've got a gun. Problem is, I don't know the first thing about them.

Think, Frost!

Then, it comes to me. I do know about guns. In fact, I know a tremendous amount about guns. I listen for footsteps while trying to concentrate on the armory that Nehemiah Stone had hidden behind a bookcase in his home. It won't come to me. I concentrate harder. Nehemiah's library comes into view, then I watch as the bookcase slides back and the door to the armory opens. I can see inside. On neatly arranged racks are every killing machine known to humankind. Rifles, rocket launchers, automatic weapons, boxes of ammunition stacked to the ceiling, knives in all shapes and sizes, and a row of handguns. What would he carry on a mission like mine? The weapon comes into view. Of course. Keep it simple. There it is. His favorite, which I've detailed to readers countless times over the years in the booth. A .40 caliber Glock 22—old reliable.

"Glock 22," I yell up. "Fifteen rounds, all with your name on them."

"Impressive, bigun," he says. "I thought you entertainment types shied away from the firearms?"

Why is he talking to me? If Nora is in on it, then maybe she's going to enter the basement through the french doors, or through another window or door I don't know about downstairs. Shit. I hadn't thought of that. But she did yell *no* at him.

"Is your wife okay?" I ask.

"Naw, naw, naw, don't you be worryin' 'bout her. She'll be visiting you soon enough." He starts to laugh. "You're dead, Shawn. You know you ain't never leavin' here alive."

Damn. So, she is headed down here. I'm trapped. Wait, he could be lying. She wasn't moving at all when I rushed down here. What could I do to throw him off?

I've got it. "Did you know there was another guy over here tonight before I showed up?"

There is silence except for the creaking back and forth of wood that is under significant weight. My guess is that he's rocking back and forth on one of the top steps.

I continue. "Yeah, heard her call him 'babe.'"

"Shut up!" he yells.

"I'm not shutting up, dick. You tortured me, and you tortured Michael Hunnie, and your time getting away with it is *up*." I throw in some Wolverine to mock him back. "I ain't makin' it up. No sirreee. You in big trouble, feller."

I hear something. Whispering? I can't tell. He speaks to me in his normal voice, "I think you're the one making shit up, Shawn. Hunnie wasn't down there. It was just you who we were screwin' with."

He takes a step down, and I get ready to run to the french doors.

Then, I hear Nora scream, "Shawn! Are you okay? What's he talking about?"

"Shut up!" he yells at his wife. "Come over here, where I can see you!"

Is he now yelling at me, or her?

"He's gone insane, Shawn!" There's a three-second pause. "Oh, Shawn! He's going to kill me!"

The stairs creak, and I get one foot in motion when I hear Marcus-John yell, in his normal voice, "Nora! Why you—"

There's a huge blast. Then, the house sounds like it's falling to the ground as Wolverine tumbles down the stairs. My mind tells me to run out the french doors, but the blast was so deafening, I stay put to see what in the hell just happened.

I watch as Marcus-John Stewart, aka Wolverine, comes to rest at the bottom of the stairs. He doesn't move. I make a fist, ready to plunge it into his face if he so much as opens an eye.

Then, I see his shredded t-shirt—tiny holes oozing with crimson blood. I've seen enough films to know that this was from a shotgun blast. I feel for a pulse. There is none. His handgun is on the carpeted floor, about five feet away from his body. I grab it, take one more look behind me at the lifeless hulk of my one-time captor, and head up the stairs.

I've only taken two steps when I see a bloody hand appear at the top of the steps. It shakes, looking for something to hold on to. This is followed by the weak plea of, "Shawn?"

I race up the stairs and find Nora Stewart lying on the floor next to a shotgun. Behind her are bloody streaks on the kitchen floor.

"Nora, where are you hurt?" I ask.

"He shot me. I was trying to protect us. He's a monster. So sorry," she says, fading.

I gently turn her over and see that she's been shot in the upper chest, near her right shoulder. She's lost a lot of blood.

"Phone," she says, pointing toward the counter.

I jump up and grab them. She takes the top one and drops the other to the ground. As she dials 9-1-1, I take off my jacket and apply pressure to her wound. After telling the operator her address and that she's been shot, she passes out. I stay on the phone while I do my best to stop the bleeding until, fifteen minutes later, I hear the sirens of the ambulance and police coming up the driveway.

It's over now.  It's finally over.

*2 Months Later...*

# 35

## Los Angeles

I sit in the conference room at the law offices of Rudolph Jay Bentwater, Attorney at Law. And let's just say that I am thankful that the black granite with speckles of jade conference room table is of Bruce-Wayne-mansion-like proportions. 'Tis a feast of lawyers at the banquet today, and, after two hours of the usual back and forth, attack, counter-attack, schmooze, betray, offend, get offended dance, I think we all see that the end is in sight.

I occupy the center chair of the table. David Killian is seated next to me on my left, and my attorney, H. Jefferson Montaigne, known to me and Killy as "Monty"—I know, I have nicknames for everyone—sits next to me on my right. To the left of Killy is his lawyer and current girlfriend, Gisele Rubie. To the left of Gisele is Rider Elizabeth Cross, CEO of ParkerWilson, and to her left is her longtime lawyer Zyta Brzezinski. The rest of our side is filled with paralegals who have been getting fresh coffee, taking notes, and whispering amongst each other whenever a big moment has taken place. Two of them were when Killy almost got kicked out. There is a rectangle of cushioned chairs that line the four walls of the room. Only one of the chairs is occupied, and the person seated in that far corner chair, behind our side, is Roman I. Baker, Ph.D., who has been nodding off for most of the morning.

Across from us are three estate lawyers, led by Rudolph Jay Bentwater, for Nora Stewart and her late husband Marcus-John Stewart, now also known as Wolverine. Nora is not present for the proceedings; she is at home with her two girls. Rudolph Jay Bentwater sits directly across from me and is flanked by Attorneys at Law Bryson Walker and Janice K. Ramirez. To Ramirez's right is Nora Stewart's, aka Jennie Masterson's, agent Trafalgar Simmons and his lawyer Gordon Geoffrey Wiley. The rest of the seats are filled by their paralegals, who have had their own mini-war going on with our paralegals—hoarding of coffee and courtesy mints, disgusted stares, and playing the home turf card every chance they get. The writer, actor, and director in me has been soaking in the entire morning, filing observations away for future works. A few times, Monty has had to tap my arm to bring me out of my daydreaming and back into the negotiation.

Paper coffee cups line our side of the table; large, navy-colored ceramic mugs with the initials RJB in gold lettering line their side. Legal pads, cell phones, and expensive pens are scattered across the table as if they've just been through a battle. There are a few laptops and tablets, but those are only in front of the paralegals.

Rudy Bentwater rubs his gray beard and then takes off his wire-rimmed glasses, placing them carefully on his marked-up legal pad. If he were on the stage right now, I'd say he's playing the part of the old gray fox, a warrior who has been to hell and back and is now ready to cut a deal. He tugs at his loosened tie with his meaty left hand, rubs his eyes with his chubby right, and then takes a sip of coffee from his steaming mug. "Look team, fellow professionals, defenders of the law, Ms. Stewart just wants the novel to go away at this point. She understands that if it gets published, she will be paid a one-time sum of $250,000 with no royalties and nothing when the book is optioned to a film studio.

Through our mutually agreed arrangement last week, she has already returned the $9,750,000 advance, and her relationship with her agent and ParkerWilson have both been terminated. There will be no second book. She understands that her previous contract allowed ParkerWilson to do this and that it is completely the prerogative of ParkerWilson to publish the book if it chooses to do so. However, if *Listen To Me* gets published, she feels like any profit that it makes will be poisoned and unholy money, even though the malicious men who were responsible for this novel are now dead. She is only guilty of being the front for them as a female author because the men wanted to remain anonymous and thought the book would sell better with a female author. Nora isn't a writer, and to be quite honest, she's not that much of a reader. Who can blame her? She's raising two *wonderful* teenaged daughters. And let me tell you," Rudy says, leaning forward, seeming to struggle with maintaining his composure. "Those are two....*great kids*." He leans back, and the I-can-barely-get-the-words-out emotional act is over. His facial expression morphs into a smug stare that says: *I dare you to not accept my terms and* hurt *these children.* Doesn't surprise me. When in doubt, pull the kids into it for leverage—an old lawyer trick as suave as the time-honored Broadway trick of turning up the stage mics to make the applause sound louder. Did I ever use it?

Undeniably.

Rudy continues, "We all agree that Nora is deeply embarrassed and horrified at what her late husband did—of which she had no knowledge whatsoever—and everything that his decisions have put her and her daughters through. I would remind you that the detectives and forensics teams have unequivocally cleared her of any wrongdoing. Marcus-John Stewart, also known as Wolverine, and Bob Croft, also known as Big Boss, acted together but separate from the rest of the Stewart family. Mr. Croft had no family—lived alone, was an only child, and his parents passed away years ago. As I've said before, this sweet woman, Nora Stewart, thought she was doing her husband and her husband's friend a service.

She was naïve. She thought it would be as simple as going on some book tours and making appearances on morning news and talk shows. I mean, that sounds *fun*, right? And it happens all the time. Ghostwriter writes a book, and an author makes the publicity rounds." He surveys his team, looking right and then left, and then back at Monty.

"From our perspective, the decision *to not* publish the book is the superior option and a win-win for everyone." He leans forward again. "So, let's get to it. Our final offer is to pay Mr. Frost *double* of what ParkerWilson has agreed to pay him. He must not record any more of the novel *Listen To Me* and what he has recorded needs to stay unpublished—better yet, erased. ParkerWilson has already agreed to pay Ms. Stewart's agent, Trafalgar Simmons, a flat fee of $2,000,000 whether the novel gets published or not and for Mr. Simmons's affidavit that he will forgo any lawsuit when Mr. Frost's memoir of the whole ordeal is published by ParkerWilson, narrated by Mr. Frost, and the film rights sold to a major studio. Mr. Simmons has also signed away his right to make any deals in the future on the subject in which he could profit from—his own memoir, documentary, interviews, etc. ParkerWilson will close the project for good, *then go* public with the story about why the book was canceled and control the exclusive rights to Mr. Frost's forthcoming true account. Ms. Stewart, who, I remind you, has already returned her advance, will receive a one-time settlement payment of $2,500,000 from ParkerWilson to forgo any lawsuit when Mr. Frost's memoir is published by ParkerWilson, narrated by Mr. Frost, and the film rights sold to a major studio. Ms. Stewart will also sign away her right to make any deals in the future on the subject in which she could profit from—her own memoir, documentary, interviews, etc. In essence, the same terms as Mr. Simmons has agreed to."

He shifts his gaze to me. "So, Mr. Frost gets 1 million dollars from the Stewart estate for not recording *Listen To Me*, the Stewart estate receives $500,000 for living expenses for Ms. Stewart and her daughters with zero opportunities to make any future money from the story;  the other million dollars will go to me and my legal team.  ParkerWilson, which has already recouped its seven-figure advance from Ms. Stewart, will own the rights to Mr. Frost's tell-all story about his harrowing experience, which, according to our estimates, should yield *billions* of dollars for the parties present across from me here today.  And, most importantly, *for the deal to go through*, Mr. Frost needs to paint a positive picture of Ms. Stewart as the woman who saved his life by killing her own psychopathic, murderous, and evil husband and highlight her innocence.  If these conditions are all agreed upon and met, Ms. Stewart and her daughters will be aided in changing their names and relocated to an unknown location to live out the rest of their lives in peace.  Once this has happened and they have been settled for six months, then Mr. Frost's memoir may be announced.  In forty-eight hours, I can have a draft agreement drawn up and distributed to all parties present today."  He makes one last survey of the entire room, and so do I.

His side:

The team is licking its chops—$400,000 for Rudy, $300,000 a piece for the other two lawyers; the paralegals look hungover.

Our side:

Rider Elizabeth Cross is smirking.  She wins either way.  Her lawyer takes a sip of coffee, and pats Ms. Cross's arm.

Killy is still hot about almost getting kicked out.  He stares down the entire other side of the table.  His lawyer is scrolling on her phone.

The paralegals are leaning forward as if my answer will determine whether they attack or shake hands.

Bake is still asleep.

Corie, Matt, and Jo weren't allowed in.  I'm still not happy about it.

Rudy puts his glasses back on.  "Ladies and Gentleman, do we have a deal?"

How did we get here?

Well, before I answer Kingpin Dealmaker Rudolph Jay Bentwater, I should explain. It's pretty simple when you boil it down.

As you know, Nora Stewart survived; her husband did not. Marcus-John Stewart and his best friend, Bob Croft, who lived a few miles away, were truckers—truckers obsessed with *audiobooks*. According to Nora, Marcus-John always deferred to Bob even though Bob was more introverted, which makes sense that Bob Croft was Big Boss and that he only communicated through the speaker attached to the ceiling of my cell. His voice? Yeah, Marcus John's phone still had two voicemails from Bob, and I listened to them. In one, Bob simply said, *'Hey, call me back.'* In the other, Bob said, *'C'mon over tonight. Let's have a drink by the fire.'* Even though it had been a few years—and I was drugged out of my mind for most of the time that I was in the recording cell—the voice sounded familiar.

Marcus-John and Bob would travel ten hours from Springville, California, to Elko, Nevada, where Marcus-John and Nora Stewart owned a hunting lodge. The men would vacation there two times a year—to hunt in October and to relax with peace and quiet in June. Nora and the girls would visit most summers, and, on occasion, Bob would bring a girlfriend with him. Yes, Nora confirmed that there were two suites in the basement of the hunting lodge—each with a toilet—but that they were still unfinished the last time she had been out there, which was a year before the abduction. She did not visit the cabin at all the summer when I was kidnapped or after that. The detectives checked her alibi. The girls were staying with Nora's mom in North Carolina during that time, but the Stewarts have always had a landline phone. When the investigators looked at the phone records during that time, they saw that most days, there were long-distance phone calls from Nora to the girls in North Carolina. Some days there were two calls spaced five hours apart, which would have made it impossible for Nora to be in Elko. The girls and Nora's mother confirmed the conversations.

Guess what happened to the lodge? Yep. Marcus-John told her a few months after that June trip that it had served its purpose as a rustic getaway but that it was too much to keep up and too far away. He wanted something closer. So, he handled the sale, and a couple looking to open a hunting bed and breakfast getaway bought the place and gutted it. Did the authorities find pictures with the couple when they went there to investigate? Yes. But, the before pictures they took of the basement showed a completely stripped and demolished space, which was why the price had been so low. Nora theorized that they had destroyed any evidence down there and made it look unrecognizable. When the authorities searched her own house, they discovered that all the pictures of the lodge from their family albums had been taken out. Where did they find the family albums? Behind a bunch of boxes in the pole barn. Because of cell phones, Nora hadn't even looked at the family photo albums in years.

Nora Stewart explained that she had overheard them talking about how they were fed up with trucking and wanted to retire. So, she believes that four or five years ago, they must have come up with the idea to kidnap an audiobook narrator, observe how he acts in captivity, release him, and then write a novel together about a famous narrator who gets kidnapped and escapes. And who did that narrator end up being? Me.

She claimed that her husband was obsessed with the novel *Misery*—owned hardcover, paperback, and audiobook versions of it. He also loved the film based on the book. In tears, she said that maybe she should have seen this coming— life imitating art kind of thing, but with a twist. Of course, I didn't hold her responsible. Just because I am a fanboy of *Star Wars* doesn't mean that I'm going to go and kill my dad.

Nora also provided a record of all of the audiobooks that Marcus-John had ordered over the years, and the authorities were able to get a record of Bob Croft's purchases too. Their favorite narrators? Me, Ray Porter, Johnny Heller, Corie Woods, Julia Whelan, Michael Hunnie, Scott Brick, D.J. Webster, Hillary Huber,

Jim Dale, Suzanne Elise Freeman, George Guidall, Dion Graham, Crassus Dynasty, and Simon Vance.

The recording equipment purchases showed up on Marcus-John's personal credit card. So, that checked out. Marcus-John and Bob had worked a number of odd jobs over the year for cash, and so that is how she theorized that the men were able to purchase the drugs and medical equipment. *Where* they got the equipment, she had no idea. Nora remembers the men returning from their June trip almost three summers ago in an unusually happy mood. From that point forward, they spent most of their free hours in Marcus-John's pole barn. Nora even said that the door would be locked when she or the girls walked over there. She never questioned what was going on because they were on the road so much. She admits that her marriage to him was basically over, but she was hanging on until the girls graduated high school. Then, she planned to divorce him.

Over a year ago, Marcus-John and Bob invited her out to the pole barn and presented her with a manuscript. She was shocked. Marcus-John had been excellent in English and had even acted in a few high school plays before dropping out to be a trucker, and he explained to her that the writing bug had finally bit him enough times for him to start. Bob was also a book nerd, and they wanted to see if they could write a book together after listening to thousands of audiobooks in their cabs over the years.

She bought their story and read the manuscript. It was surprisingly good. She did a little prying and found out that Bob was definitely the better writer of the two men. Nora said, *'This upset Marcus-John because he had more schooling in that area, but Bob was naturally gifted. I can see why he was the boss, behind the scenes, and why my husband was the one who actually met with Shawn.'* Not knowing anything about the events that had led up to the men drafting the manuscript, she decided to help them out, thinking that the chances of them actually getting an agent were slim to none, but what the heck. She even agreed to front for them as the author, and they all came up with the pen name Jennie Masterson. Jennie was her mother's first name, and Marcus-John and Bob thought Masterson just sounded cool. They had done their research, they claimed, and thought that a female author would sell better. She began querying for them. Nineteen rejection letters later, Trafalgar Simmons took the bait, and the rest was history. Around this point in her recollection to me and the police, she looked at me, sobbed, and said, *'Oh God, I'm so sorry, Shawn. Now I know why they wanted me to push for you and only you as the narrator for the novel.'* I was forgiving. It made sense to me too. Also, Killy confessed at that point that he had lied when he told me that others were in the running for the job. I forgave him too. I probably *would have* started spouting conspiracy theories if he had told me I was the only narrator they wanted.

Anyway, four months ago, Marcus-John found Bob hanging from one of the rafters in Bob's garage when Marcus-John went to check on him after not hearing from him for a few days. Nora now knows that it must have been the overwhelming guilt of what he had been an accomplice to regarding me, but at the time, it was just a random, heartbreaking discovery. There were no answers— only questions. One day Bob was alive. One day he wasn't. Since there was no family, the Stewarts had a private funeral and buried Bob in the woods on their property. Bob had listed Marcus-John and Nora as co-executors of his estate, and they sold the property a month later. A young family now lives in the house and were kind enough to let the forensics team and detectives search the house and property, but they didn't find anything. Bob had been a minimalist, and it had been Marcus John's job to clean out what little Bob had in his house and garage.

After Bob's death, Marcus-John started to hit the bottle hard. Nora said that he became even more remote, spending most of his days and nights in the pole barn. If there was any physical evidence left to prove that I had been kidnapped, the investigators reasoned that it had to be in the pole barn. There was a computer station in the barn, but all it contained was a Word document of fifteen thousand words titled *Down the Road and Under the Night Sky*—the start of a story about a trucker who gets kidnapped. It was the second novel in the two-book deal that they had signed with ParkerWilson. The rest of the initial search yielded nothing, which surprised Nora—surprised me. *'He was in there all of the time!'* she exclaimed. However, when the authorities returned with a machine called a Utility Scan Pro, or something along those lines, that had ground-penetrating radar—push the "I believe" button, folks, the stuff is beyond me—they were able to locate an underground compartment near the back right corner of the barn. Inside was a bag full of audiobooks narrated by me and a single shelf with two items on top: the *Narrator* manuscript, all 446 pages bound with rubber bands, and a flash drive. The manuscript was everything I remembered reading and had the sentence that I had improved in it. Killy and Jo compared it to the paper I had handed them that night at my house and couldn't believe their eyes.

What was on the flash drive? Only a handful of files. But…they were all edited versions of my recordings while I was in captivity. Happy Birthday to Big Boss, the bottom of the 10th in the Red Sox-Mets '86 thriller (found out Marcus-John was a huge Mets fan—a fair amount of Mets gear in the master bedroom closet), Kenyon's poem, the disses of my fellow narrators, Macbeth's soliloquy, the Most Interesting Man in the World, "Coke in the Backseat" and everything else. It was all there and was both entertaining and horrifying to listen to. Of course, there was also my complete, yet edited, recording of *Narrator*. Once again, Killy's and Jo's mouths opened at hearing my improvised line about Stacey navigating the perils of publishing house politics. I had butterflies in my stomach as we all listened to the passages that followed because that was when the supposed Michael Hunnie incident had occurred, and I could not remember if I had been recording when I heard the toilet flush or when I heard his voice or when I shouted *'Michael!'*. My head sank when we heard none of it. It had been edited out or had never occurred. Not knowing still bothers me.

The dates of the files were seven months after my prison stay. Clearly, Marcus-John and Bob had cleaned them up and edited the original recordings from a computer that was missing and presumed to be destroyed. Unfortunately, anything that Wolverine and Big Boss said or anything that Michael Hunnie might have said—a part of me wanted some of the recordings to be his of *Narrator* (I mean, why else would he have been down there?)—had been erased. The search team tore up the barn and then tore up the Stewart house looking for the computer. They found nothing. When given the choice to keep the *Narrator* manuscript and flash drive or have them destroyed, I surprised everyone and decided to keep them. They are in a wall safe at my house, hidden behind a framed picture I had enlarged. The picture is the only time Michael Hunnie and I were ever photographed together. It was at the Audies a few years ago, just after I had been interviewed by P.J. and Suzanne. I accidentally bumped into Hunnie, and he almost spilled his drink. Then, a photographer raised his camera, and we both smiled—two tuxedoed rivals caught in an authentic moment. The picture was taken in color, but I had the studio print it in black and white.

All this to say that when I showed up to their place a few months ago, Nora Stewart had no idea about the secret that her husband had been keeping from her. She was surprised to see me but was ready to keep the charade alive because her husband had finally retired from trucking and, even though he was torn up from the loss of his best friend, Bob, was already working on book number two. She was proud of him and ready to go on tour promoting his book. Shady business move, right? Happens more often than you think.

Who was the man that I saw leaving the house before I approached? You know, the one she called "babe?" That would be Ken Oakley, their next-door neighbor and family friend. Ken and Nora had been playing their bi-weekly battle of ping-pong downstairs while Marcus-John was in the pole barn working on the next book. Ken had been interviewed, and his story matched with Nora's. Now, what *type* of "ping-pong" they were playing down there...

That night? When Marcus-John saw me, he must have reasoned that I had figured out who he was and decided to take his chances by killing me and then maybe later claiming it was a home invasion. And, I have to be honest, with my past, he might have gotten away with it. **Previous Drug Addict Narrator Shows Up Unannounced At Author's Home** or some headline like that. Perhaps that was why he tried to kill Nora.

One, she was threatening him with a shotgun. I saw how hard her head hit the counter when he pushed her; she was right to try and protect us. He could have killed us both—get to that in a minute. She said he had physically hit her in the past, but that had been before the girls were born. I'm just glad she made it through—don't know how I would have gone on with my life if she had died because of me.

Two, even if she hadn't had a weapon aimed at him, he may have killed her anyway and blamed it on me. The fact is, though, he was drunk and, from Nora's perspective, seemed to grow heavier and heavier with guilt every day after Bob committed suicide. I'll never know how he would have approached things if I had not acted like I had found him out and had a gun underneath my jacket. But I don't regret it. I had to know if he was the man who had kidnapped me. Plus, he was carrying a loaded revolver on him after drinking; if that doesn't sound like paranoia, then I don't know what does. However, I have thought about what might have happened that night if he had just walked in through the door, given Nora a kiss, and greeted me with a handshake…

Oh, right, sorry, almost forgot. *Santa Monica.* Nora explained that Marcus-John was gone for that week from their house, trucking. A trace of his cell phone showed that he was in Santa Monica during the time I saw him. Only one street corner camera in that area was able to provide a fuzzy picture of him during that timeframe. Other cameras were out of position or not working. Technology giveth and technology taketh away. What in the hell was Marcus-John doing in Santa Monica? All of our best guesses were centered around the fact that his paranoia was growing, and he wanted to keep an eye on me. Clearly, he didn't expect to have an encounter with me, but because he did—making the mistake of getting too close to me—it proved to be the event that eventually triggered the catastrophe that took place at their house when I showed up and recognized him as *that* man. A trace of Bob Croft's cell phone showed that he was not there but trucking in Northern California, Oregon, Washington, Idaho, and Nevada. I asked Nora whom she thought the driver might have been that dropped him off. *'Uber, of course.'* Yeah, I felt dumb for not thinking of it. Were the cell phones' locations from three years ago able to be tracked? No such luck. Different phones, different providers. Oh, and speaking of technological surveillance and paranoia, for all of Marcus-John's growing obsession, the Stewarts didn't have and never have had a single security camera on their property. This would have made life so much easier to see the comings and goings over the years, but no such luck. And there aren't any cameras close by. The Stewarts live, literally, in the middle of nowhere.

Well, anyway, Nora almost died twice in the ambulance on the way to the hospital. I was held for questioning. I got a phone call off to Killy, and he arrived with Gisele and Monty around midnight at the hospital where Nora was having surgery. Over the following week, I saw David Killian turn into the most apologetic pile of mush I have ever seen. It was only when the two of us were alone but he humbled himself, and I forgave him. After all, how could he have known? And, if I hadn't gone to Nora Stewart's house, I would have *never* known. But I did. And I was finally able to fully trust everyone again, knowing for sure that they had not been involved in any way. And here's something else: Jo and I are dating again.

So, I have an important decision to make, and I have two options available. One: I can let Monty know that I accept the deal and therefore position myself to make more money than I have ever dreamed of by publishing my memoir of the past three years. But, if I go that route, my days of privacy are over. Is the money worth the sacrifice? Monty thinks so; of course, his payday will more than double.

Or, two: I can let everyone know that I am going to finish *Listen To Me*, and ParkerWilson will publish the book. No one will ever know what happened, minus the people in this room and the detectives and forensics teams who investigated and searched the Stewarts' property in Springville, California, and their hunting cabin in Elko, Nevada. In some weird and improbable way, life will go on as normal. Sure, Nora Stewart could try and make a story about all of this, but why would she? If she really wants it to go away and not draw attention to herself and her family for the rest of their lives, then she'll be quiet. Killy is for this option. *'Fuck 'em all. You'll never get another book like this, and I want you to win Best Male Narrator because of your performance of this book, not because of some bullshit sympathy vote for a less than worthy book you narrate after your memoir comes out. I owe it to you, as your agent, to tell you that once you publish that memoir, you'll never know for sure if you get awards after that because of your performance or because people feel sorry for you. And I know you, Shawn. As a competitor, it'll destroy you to not know.'*

Strong arguments on both sides—and everyone in the room except for Roman I. Baker is looking at me right now.

I tip back my cup of coffee, finishing it. A stressed-out junior paralegal, who has been tapped to play server for the occasion by Rudy's firm, runs to my seat, refills my coffee, and then re-takes his position by the coffee pot. This is ridiculous, but so was getting kidnapped.

Rudy raises his eyebrows at me. I clear my throat and speak. "I will be finishing the book. Period."

The place EXPLODES for thirty seconds. Legal pads are thrown, pens are raised as if they are knives, Killy laughs hysterically, Bake jumps out of the chair with a loud scream, not knowing where he is, Bentwater's posse points fingers and levies empty threats, Bentwater himself shoots off a string of expletives and slams his fists on the table, Rider Elizabeth Cross shrugs and takes a drink of her coffee. I wait it all out.

The room calms down, and Rudy's glasses are off again, and now so is his tie. He says, "Haven't you suffered enough? Why? Why would you want to do this to yourself?"

And, for perhaps the first time all morning, I get serious and speak from my heart. "Because I've *lived it*. No one can narrate this story like I can." I stand up. "I've *earned* the right to do this. And no one is going to stop me." My tone is strong and uncompromising. "I *need* to do this."

I walk out.

*2 Weeks Later...*

# 36

## Carmel-by-the-Sea

I sit down in my booth, and both my level of excitement and my level of anticipation have reached a zenith. After an entire afternoon and evening of waiting, it is now 9 o'clock at night, and I am ready to record the final three chapters of *Listen To Me*. I stopped recording at 11 a.m. earlier today. I could have wrapped up my performance this afternoon, but I peeked ahead and saw that the time in the book that the final three chapters take place is from 9 to 10 p.m.—the third to last chapter starting right at 9. In a ceremonial way, I proclaimed to my booth that I would return at 9 to finish. On special occasions, I have recorded sections of books at precisely the same time that the events in the books occur—dissolved into the world and brought out my best performance. For many reasons, *Listen To Me* warrants this kind of treatment and precision.

An overlooked aspect of narrating that I tell new narrators to focus on is creating an atmosphere for performance. Put yourself in a position that will enable you to go anywhere creatively that you want to or feel you need to. A position where you can respond to the material and take risks! If you are reading a horror novel, change your routine and set your working hours for between midnight and six am; pick a scary movie to watch each night before you enter the booth to record—narrate *scared*: your performance will elevate, and your listeners will be rewarded.

Smile when you say a word because the change in the shape of your mouth *changes* how the word sounds; in this case, you'll sound *happy*. Read the book ahead of time. If it's a whodunit, you need to know whodunit. You need to know all of the red herrings so that you don't draw attention to them during your performance. If you did, it would alert the reader and spoil the book. Now, to be honest with you, I'm breaking that rule tonight. I only read a few sentences of Chapter 36 to know what time it was in the story. I have no idea what is going to happen to Lionel Goliath, Beryl Sterling, or the villain Greg Ladd tonight. As a veteran narrator, I am trusting my instincts, and those instincts tell me to perform the ending of *Listen To Me* cold. If I'm affected by the story, then so will the reader. If I am surprised while reading it, then the reader will hear it, which should add to the listening experience. I will be able to create a genuine sense of immediacy that, no matter how many times I have tried in the past, I cannot generate if I've read the story ahead of time.

Use props! I'm living my advice tonight. Lionel Goliath is in his booth recording perhaps one of the greatest thrillers of all time. It is penned by the legendary master of thrillers and suspense, his former lover, Beryl Sterling. Goliath is dressed for the occasion: classic black tuxedo with a black bowtie. He's sporting a fresh haircut, thick, salt & pepper locks gelled and combed to Cary-Grant-like perfection. His face is a sheet of smooth, tight curves—a result of a straight-razor shave.

Guess who is wearing a tuxedo and had a haircut and straight-razor shave this afternoon?

Shawn Frost.

Normally, I would wear a t-shirt in the booth because a dress shirt is more likely to make noise whenever you move, but if Lionel Goliath can wear a tuxedo while narrating, then so can Shawn Frost.

My smartwatch and smartphone are charging upstairs. There will be zero distractions tonight.

My resolve is powerful; I am unstoppable. I haven't thought about a drink or a drug in ages. Monty has cleared all of the legal hurdles, and Rider Elizabeth Cross has the ParkerWilson publicity machine *humming*. The reading and listening world are about to see a promotion and launch of *Listen To Me* that, according to Killy, *'Will go down as the most unprecedented release in the history of publishing.'* Even bigger than Riley Cannon's *Dark After Midnight*, which I didn't think was possible. Jo and I are back together, she's forgiven me, and I am completely dedicated to her. I have asked to be alone tonight, and she is staying at her place. She knows I need to finish the book on my terms, and I am grateful for her understanding and support. And my terms are that I narrate these final three chapters, walk out of the booth a free man, embrace Michael, who has taken his station on the floor outside the booth, and go to bed for what I hope will be the best night of sleep in my life—all purple on my god damned smartphone's sleep app. Then, tomorrow, I'll wake up and call Killy, Jo, and Corie, tell them that I've finished, and have them over for a brunch like they've never seen before. It has all been planned. I told them this morning that I would finish the book this evening, and Corie and Matt joined Killy on a flight to Monterey this afternoon. Corie has been in L.A. recording a new military thriller, and Matt has been working on a new screenplay with Vanessa Taylor. They are all now staying at a hotel, eagerly awaiting my call tomorrow morning. And, at that magnificent brunch, I will deliver my final surprise and hand each of them a copy of the second draft of my new play, *Waiting Room*.

I will conquer this period of my life once and for all tonight and put the past three years in a crematorium and *incinerate* them. I had to do this. It was the only way I could ever become what I want to be again: a healthy, functioning, creative—actor, writer...*playwright*. I may also narrate, but I took myself out of what I truly loved years ago. Many thought I would never return. But, now, I am here in my booth, in my tuxedo, and am going to narrate a book that could have ended my life. But instead, I will end the book. I get the last word. I get the last say.

I prepare my space for recording and execute my usual equipment checks: Mic, shock mount, mic stand, pop screen, XLR cable, M Box 2, computer & Pro Tools LE 8 software—all good. Next, the irreplaceable and essential items for my routine. I put my metal water cannister, bottle of Ice Drops, and a stick of Burt's Bees in their usual places on my booth desk.

I take a deep breath and bring up the manuscript on my computer. I scroll down.

There it is.

Chapter 36

I pause, taking in the moment. I've earned it.

I've also discovered that *pausing* instead of raising my volume is a much more powerful way to emphasize words—both in narrating and in life. See what I just did there?

When you think about it, an audiobook is the oldest art form we have. It's as pure a form of storytelling as there is. Like film is to the stage, audiobooks are to stories told around the campfire. Corie is a fan of old-time radio, and he believes that audiobooks are the closest thing we have to them; I tend to agree. Why am I waxing nostalgic about these matters now? I suppose that finishing this particular book symbolizes the renewal of my place in the wonderful tradition that story is and continues to be. But, on this occasion, finishing my telling of *Listen To Me* is more personal.

I'm finishing a story that was born out of a larger story in which I was directly involved. A part of me will end when this book ends. But then, as Shakespeare so eloquently wrote in the final couplet of Sonnet 18, "Shall I compare thee to a summer's day?":

So long as men can breathe, or eyes can see,
So long lives this, and this gives life to thee.


Hence, so long as human beings are alive and have the ability to read or listen to this novel, then the book will continue to live on. If I do decide to publish my personal account of how this book came to be, then that story will live on as well. If I don't, then, perhaps, it will survive as a rumor, a secret story whispered by the handful of people who knew the truth.

I am being dramatic as usual, but I cannot help it. I am who I am. Drama is my life.

I think of the copy of *Narrator* and the flash drive with my recordings in the safe behind the framed photograph of me and Michael Hunnie. I feel Michael Hunnie's presence here with me in the booth. And, I never thought I'd think this, but I wish he *was* here, recording this with me right now.

I clear my mind, and the booth becomes absolutely silent. My house is empty; Michael is outside the booth; Killy, Jo, Corie, and Matt are in Monterey. I glance at the screen.

It's time.

Oh, wait! No, it's not. A little background, right?

Lionel Goliath has escaped Gregg Ladd's house. It was a gruesome battle, ending with Goliath launching one of Ladd's cigarette lighters at a gas line that had cracked open during their struggle inside the house. Goliath had pulled an R.J. MacReady from the end of *The Thing* and yelled, '*Yeah, fuck you too!*' and then threw the lighter at the gas line as he jumped out a window. The reader gets a picture of a stunned Gregg Ladd watching the gas ignite, which explodes the house. Goliath recovers in a hospital, has sex with Beryl Sterling in his hospital bed, and is eventually released.  Beryl finds out she is pregnant from the hospital encounter, and the two set their wedding date as Goliath begins performing Beryl's last novel titled *To the End of Time*.

But, Greg Ladd is still alive!  Apparently, right before the house was blown to smithereens, he was able to make a Six-Million-Dollar-man-like jump into the hallway bathroom's claw-footed tub, which protected him.  It also explains why Ladd's body was never found.  The local police captain's famous line, which took me four tries to narrate because I was laughing so loud, was, *'He must have been incinerated—burned right down to the ice'* (It was winter when the house exploded).  Again, another allusion to the 1982 cult horror film—have a feeling that Marcus-John Stewart had to have been a huge fan of *The Thing*.  Shit.  Who isn't?  Anyway, Greg Ladd is very much alive and very much in the mood for revenge.  And this is where, if I had continued narrating before, I would have realized that the end of the story is very similar to that of *Narrator*'s.  At the end of Chapter 35, Greg Ladd has abducted Beryl Sterling from her home and is taking her to Lionel Goliath's house for a showdown…and revenge.  And that is where I am at right now—no idea how it's going to turn out.  If it's like *Narrator*, then Goliath and Beryl are in for a terrifying fight but will ultimately kill Greg Ladd.  However, it is already slightly different from *Narrator* since Greg has kidnapped Beryl from her own home.  In *Narrator*, Kurt Boar was already inside of Robbie Bernstein's home, and he surprised Stacey Groff when she walked through Robbie's unlocked front door.

So, I haven't given the ending of *Listen To Me* too much thought because I know how the majestic ParkerWilson editor Esperanza Benoit works—always throws in a fresh twist or two in the end.  And I'm excited to find out.

I stretch my arms toward the ceiling of the booth.  Then, I bring them down and adjust my bowtie.  I smile up at my headphones on the shelf and consider putting on my Princess Leia buns for old times' sake but decide against it.  I'm a different narrator now.

Okay, all caught up.

And *now* it's time for me to begin.

I take a sip of water.

I put one drop of Ice Drops into my mouth.

I dab the lip balm a few times on my top lip, then my bottom lip.

I put the stick of Burt's Bees on the table, push record, and start narrating.

## Chapter 36

Lionel Goliath entered his booth at 9 p.m., prepared to finish, perhaps, his final collaboration with his soon-to-be wife and soon-to-be mother of his child, Beryl Sterling. So far, the novel had been one of her best—ambitious in scope, but lean, inventive, and packed full of surprises. If she pulled off the ending in spectacular fashion, he would have to give consideration to what the early reviewers had unanimously agreed upon: *To the End of Time* was Beryl Sterling's magnum opus.

The upcoming pages would require a subtle, nuanced performance. Because the book was a stand-alone, there was not a series character to revisit, which had saddened him when he started the book. Performing series characters was like wearing your favorite pair of jeans. It was like muscle memory. When you saw the words regarding a familiar character, you were right back where you left off. But stand-alones were a challenge. He needed to inhabit all of the characters. Give them breath. Give them life. But *To the End of Time* was also a thriller, which afforded him a certain level of comfort. All storytelling is manipulation, and thriller readers like to be teased, and Lionel Goliath enjoyed teasing them with his performance. But he had another ally in the process as well. He understood Beryl Sterling's intent and the context in which the story was written—namely, his kidnapping and miraculous escape.

*Focus on the content—on the page and not your voice. Remember to slow down. Relax. Put the reader in the moment so that they can imagine what things look like and how something feels. Embrace the emotional arcs, don't run from them.*

*Respect your audience.*

He wondered if new narrators would be surprised at his pre-recording self-talk. Perhaps. But, according to his agent, Gabby Emerald, this was what had kept him on top of the audiobook world—his uncompromising adherence to standards of excellence, his authenticity and adaptability.

After his recovery from the lair of Greg Ladd, he had immediately enrolled in both an acting class and a cold reading class. One's craft cannot ever reach perfection; it can only approach it. Hence, one can never take too many classes to help one's diction and performance. Even a Ferrari needs an oil change.

I allow myself a laugh.  I'm certain that Esperanza Benoit kept that paragraph in on purpose.  Perhaps to let Jennie Masterson realize once the book was released that *she too* had room to improve.

I continue.


However, in audiobook narrating, Goliath knew that there was a certain amount that was teachable and a certain amount that was a gift.  And his job this evening was to use all that he had been taught and all of the talent that he had been blessed with to bring Beryl Sterling's final novel to life in the ears of her loyal listeners.  Goliath took a sip of Traditional Medicinals Organic Throat Coat Tea, his favorite, and brought up the page where he had left off earlier in the day.  It felt right, him being in his sanctuary, his fiancé across town in her luxurious mansion.

He went to say the first word but suddenly stopped.

What was that noise?


*THUMP!*

What the hell was that?  It came from above.  My eyes lift toward the ceiling of the booth, and I listen for a few seconds.  I hear nothing and then laugh to myself.  Frost, only you could imagine the sound that a fictional character is hearing in a book and believe that something is making the sound in real life.

My eyes return to the page, and I go through my routine.


Goliath stopped rec—

*THUMP!*

I stop the recorder, and my eyes shoot back up to the ceiling of the booth.

*THUMP! THUMP!*

I sit motionless. The sound is coming from upstairs. What could it be? Did I leave the door to the basement open? Is Michael up there?

My heart is racing. It's as if the book and real life have joined together in a singular narrative.

I say, "Michael?"

There is no noise from outside the booth.

What is going on?

*THUMP!*

Okay, the sounds are real, and they are coming from upstairs…

In *my* house.

I stand up and slowly open the booth door.

Michael is not there.

I step out and survey the room. The basement door that leads to my backyard is closed, locked, and doesn't appear to have been tampered with. There's no one on the couches and no one hiding behind the bar. I walk around the corner. There's Michael, thank God. He's sitting at the bottom of the stairway, looking up at the door.

Where's my phone? I can check the cameras.

I head over to the coffee table, where I usually leave my phone. It's not there.

Damn it. I remember now. I left my smartphone and smartwatch upstairs to charge.

I walk over to the bathroom; Michael follows. I make a fist and then open the door.

No one is in there. I pull back the shower curtain.

No one.

Michael follows me, and we do the same for the bedroom and bedroom closet. We exit the bedroom.

No one is downstairs except for me and Michael.

We head to the bottom of the stairs and stop.  I look up and don't see any light around the door.  Did I forget to turn the lights on?  I can't remember, but I usually have them on when I record at night because I don't like going up the stairs and opening the door to a dark kitchen.

I give Michael a rub and then lock eyes with him.  I raise a finger to my mouth.  "Shhh, buddy."

We listen.

For a few seconds, there is silence.

Maybe I'm too much into the book.  Maybe I am hearing things.  Maybe I *can't* finish this damned thing.  But then Michael and I hear what sounds like moaning from the floor above, and I realize…

Someone is in my house.

# 37

My chin starts to vibrate. I am scared beyond all belief. Who in the hell is up there? And what in the hell are they doing in my home? If this is some kind of practical joke by Killy, Jo, Corie, or Matt, I will never forgive them. They wouldn't do this to me. Would they?

The moaning is louder. Whoever is up there, his or her moans sound like they are not born of pain but of trying to get someone's attention. Mine?

If the lights are indeed out upstairs, I need to let my eyes adjust to the dark before I enter the kitchen. I'll have a better chance to assess the situation if I can see—an old trick I learned from Nehemiah Stone. I turn all of the lights off downstairs and then return to Michael at the bottom of the stairs.

I stand next to him and let my eyes get used to the dark. Soon, I can make things out—Michael, the steps, the frame of the door above. I feel as ready as I'm going to be.

I kneel down and rub behind Michael's ears. "You stay here."

He wags his tail as I remove my dress shoes and tuxedo jacket and throw them to the floor.

I give him a hug and kiss the top of his head—and start to tiptoe up the stairs in my stocking feet.

Four or five steps up, I turn around.  Michael is at my side.  I purse my lips.  No one has ever stayed by my side like Michael has.  And, now, it looks like we're in it together.  I raise my finger to my lips again.  "Shhh."

We climb to the top of the stairs, and now we stand on the top step, right next to the door.  The sound of moaning is much louder now.

Who *is* that?

I look down at Michael and place my hand on the doorknob.  If I sense any danger when I open this door, I will shut it behind me and leave Michael on the stairs to protect him.

The moaning sounds like the person is trying to say something, but I can't make it out.  "Okay, buddy," I say to Michael, "here I go."

I turn the knob.

It is dark, but not as dark as the stairway.  My memory of how Nehemiah operates has helped me once again.  The door is now open six inches.

Nothing out of the ordinary.

12 inches.

Still nothing.

I open it a bit farther, and the hinges start to creek.  The moaning intensifies at the sound.

I open it farther still, and then I see a sight that absolutely horrifies me.

Tied up to a chair in the middle of my kitchen—around fifteen feet away—with a rolled-up bandana stretched across her mouth is Jo.

I take off for her, forgetting all about Michael.  I'm almost to her when her eyes get wide, and she screams behind the bandana.  It is then that I realize that she is seeing something behind me.

I turn my head in time to see a gleaming silver blade swinging down toward me, and I can't move fast enough to avoid the blow.  The knife sinks into my upper back, and I feel a searing ache.  My assailant screams and withdraws the knife.

I fall to the floor, looking up into the face of…

Nora Stewart.

Her eyes are glazed over and crazy. Her mouth is wide open as she screams again and plunges the knife down at me.

But I see a shadow appear on her right.

It's Michael.

I've heard him bark before, but this is the first time I've ever head the ferocious growl that bellows from his jaws.

He attacks!

Clamping his mouth around Nora's hand that holds the knife, Michael shakes his head back and forth.

Nora drops the knife and yells in agony. It all happens so fast. I try to get up, but blood is pouring out of the wound in my back.

Taking her other hand, Nora grabs a section of the coat of fur on Michael's back and lifts him off the ground. Michael continues to gnaw on her forearm, but she is now up on her feet and running with him toward the basement.

I reach over and pick up the knife.

Nora slams Michael on the ground, and he releases his grip. Then, she gives him a kick, and Michael disappears down the stairs.

"Michael!" I yell.

I hear him crash down the stairs and then hear whimpers before Nora slams the door shut.

I slide back toward Jo. My back is in agony, and I feel blood running down from my wound. Using Jo's right thigh for support, I stand up next to her with my knife pointed at Nora. "You psychotic fuck. Get out of here!"

"Just had to come over," she says. "Just haaad to come over to our house!" She now sounds nothing like the woman I've known for the past two months.

I look at the closed door to the basement and wonder what kind of shape Michael is in. I'll never forgive myself if he doesn't make it. He just saved my life. I yell, "If Michael dies—"

"You'll do what?" she says, pulling out a gun from a holster on her hip. She's wearing gloves. At first, she aims the gun at me and then drops her arm to her side. She winces and shakes her injured arm as if to loosen it up. Blood splatters everywhere. "A little different greeting from your dog than the last time I saw him," she says, examining her wound.

"What are you talking about? He didn't see you a week ago."

"I know. You don't remember? *Months* ago? The nice little lady who paid you a visit from PG&E, Pacific Gas and Electric?"

I remember the visit. I hadn't called anyone, but a woman showed up who said one of PG&E's plants had an accident, and she was going house to house checking homes in her grid—said there might be an issue with the electricity to my place. She'd received calls about power surges and outages and was here to look. She was knowledgeable and polite, but that could not have been Nora. The woman from PG&E was wearing a baseball cap, had blonde hair, bulky glasses, and was overweight. I remember it now. She had on a long-sleeved work shirt, khaki pants, and no wedding ring. In fact, I noticed her cracked nails as she examined some of my outlets. "No way that was you," I say. "That woman had just moved to California from Alabama."

She chuckles and then says in a perfect southern accent, "Pretty good disguise, huh? Had a fat suit on, which made me look heavuh. Remember how out of breath I was when we were playing with Michael outside? It was all fake, hun. I wadn't outta breath. But, I had to keep nudgin' him 'way from my pretend belly. Think he knew somethin' wadn't right der."

Shit. I try to remember where I took her in the house that day. She asked me where my fuse box was, and I took her into the garage. She examined the box—I'd never opened it before—and asked if there was a place in the house where I might be running too many watts. Well, to I-don't-remember-much-about-high-school-science Shawn Frost that meant: Where did I have a lot of stuff plugged in?

Then, a lump forms in my throat.

I led her downstairs…

And took her inside the booth.

She must have planted a listening device. How else would she have known I was finishing the book tonight and when to make the noise upstairs at exactly the same time *that event* was happening in the book? "You put a listening device in the booth, didn't you?"

Then, I remember how she looked when she made eyes with me just before she got into her car and left that day. It *was* her!

That's why she looked familiar when I first saw her at her house.

She gives a small clap. "The device I put in there is connected to the internet, so we'd listen on this little guy," she says, pulling a cell phone from her pocket. "Different phone, different name, different plan. Kept it hidden in the woods." She hoots, "Ha! Took it all straight from the *Narrator* story notes—notes *you* read. Remember Stacey's novel *Converging Affairs*?" She grins. "The electrician?" Her grin widens. "The bug placed in the booth? Ha! It was all right there in front of you."

My body starts to shake in anger. I motion with my knife at her and then at Jo. "Did you plan this way back then?"

"No. Just wanted to hear you narrate the book and see if you could get through it—little bonus entertainment for me and the hubs. And you were doing *so well* before. But, our one mistake was when you stopped recording that day. We just figured you were tired. Should've known it was more than that. Now, I curse myself because I didn't put another listening device in the house. Marcus-John wanted me to, but I said no. A lot of celebs have their places regularly swept for bugs, and I didn't want to take the chance. I figured if you had your place swept, then they wouldn't sweep inside your booth with all of your equipment in there." She raises the gun and puts the tip of the barrel underneath her chin. "But, after my lawyers failed to stop the book from coming out, and I knew they would parade me around on a book tour and pay me nothing, then, well, you put me in a corner, Shawn. I thought about what I could do to make tonight special, and when you finished your session this morning and announced to the booth that you'd be back to start at nine, and I knew what part you were on, you gave me the perfect opportunity for some real theater tonight. By the way, you talk to yourself a lot in your booth. Sure you're okay?" She points the gun at Jo and then puts the tip of the barrel back underneath her chin. "We had the best time listening to you. And when Goliath hears the noise above? Your lady here freaked when I hit the floor with the sledgehammer I brought in! Made a good *THUMP*, didn't it?"

This woman is certifiable. I've never had anyone sweep my place for listening devices. Guess who will be having that service performed in the future?

Wait a second. Speaking of surveillance…

My cameras!

"You can stop this whole stupid thing right now, Nora. It's over. I've got cameras all over this place, including a few in the front, one right above the front door, in fact. You're on camera and won't get away with any of this." I give her a smirk.

She laughs.

I immediately go back to feeling uneasy.

"Remember when you invited me over to your house for tea a week ago? Remember how Jo was here? And we all sat and poured our hearts out to each other? I told you that I understood and respected your decision to record the rest of the book and that I would be happy to tour with you, promoting it? Remember how Jo hugged me at that point? Said I'd still be fine playing the role of Jennie Masterson. The hell with my dead husband, right? He had turned my life upside down, and now I was going to get some recognition, even though I wouldn't be making as much money. I had had a change of heart, and it was the right thing to do. Then, we started talking about kids and dogs. Remember when you handed me your phone to show me pictures of Michael when he was a puppy? 'Got a whole slew of 'em in there, Nora.'" She pauses. "Ringing a bell?"

My eyes start to close…

Shit. I know what she did.

"Acted like I was enjoying the pictures, but what I was really doing was turning off all of your cameras. And," she says, shaking her head slowly back and forth, "I don't think you turned them back on, did you? Kind of absorbed in narrating a certain book, right?"

Jo asks me, desperation in her voice, "You turned them back on, didn't you?"

She's still gagged, but I understand her words. She isn't going to like my response.

I look down at her, regret in my eyes. "No."

Nora cackles. "Oh, look at the acting. It's so beautifully awful."

We turn our attention to her, and she aims the gun at me and bobs and weaves toward us and then bobs and weaves backwards, laughing. "You ruined everything, Shawn. And you're both going to die for it."

Jo shouts something at Nora from behind her bandana, and my girlfriend's eyes are not of fear but of hatred.

"Cool it, bitch."

She's going to kill both of you. Think, Frost! She's a sociopath, and sociopaths *always* want to explain themselves to their victims before they kill them. They're egomaniacs. It's in every novel you've ever read with a villain like this wacked-out person in front of you. She's already proven that with her story about disguising herself and the dystopian, theatrical staging of the situation you're now in. You've got to buy time. Challenge her. Diminish her. The knife is your prop. *Act!*

I rub the edge of the knife's blade against my cheek like I'm shaving with it. "So you put a bug in my booth and listened to me? Big. Deal. Marcus-John and Bob did all the heavy lifting, and they're both dead. You got in over your head, Nora." I point at her with the knife like I'm a teacher calling on a student. "I feel sorry for you."

She takes aim at a glass vase full of flowers on my kitchen counter and shoots. The glass explodes, and the water and flowers spill onto the counter and floor. "I was in over my head? *I* was in over my head?" she yells. "You've got a lot of nerve. You have no idea!"

She's focusing on the remains of the vase, and I move to just behind Jo and start to cut the ropes binding Jo's wrists. I make no effort to hide what I'm doing. I even start whistling a cheerful little tune.

She sees me out of the corner of her eye but still focuses on the vase. "Go ahead. Cut her wrists loose. You won't have time to get to her feet."

"*What* don't I have any idea about?" I ask. "Those two guys would have gotten away with everything if you would have just told me that your husband was out of town delivering a load when I showed up at your place." I smile. "You were bangin' that guy that rode his silly bike off into the woods, weren't you?" I cut through Jo's ropes, and she brings her hands up and unties her bandana, then goes into a coughing fit.

Nora's eyes dart over to me.

I've hit a nerve, but she's not saying anything.

I point at her again with the knife. "Norrr—uh? Norrrrahhhhhh."

Jo starts to lower her arms to the ropes around her feet, but Nora turns and fires her gun.

A piece of floor tile about a foot to the right of Jo's chair shatters.

"Put your hands on your knees, sweetie."

Jo does.

"You're so blind, Shawn."

"About the fact that you're a raving lunatic?  Guilty."

She hoots.  "Ah, what the hell?  You're both going to be dead in a few minutes.  I'm going to shoot you and Jo afterwards, and then I'm dumping your bodies over your back railing.  Nice big plunge into the Pacific.  Then, I'm heading downstairs to collect my listening device and end Michael's life.  After that, his body is going for a swim too.  Blood should attract some sharks—maybe a big Great White.  Who knows?  I won't be here to see.  I'll take some of your expensive stuff, and it will look like a robbery."

"Your blood is kind of everywhere," I say.

She points the gun directly at me.

Jo screams.

Nora says in a menacing tone, "You. Let. Me. Finish."

I put up both hands in the well-known "okay, okay" gesture.

"No one's ever going to know it was me."  And now it is she who uses her gun to point things out to her two-student class.  "All this beautiful Redwood.  I've got enough gasoline cans in my car to make this place go up in seconds.  It will be fun watching the bonfire from my rearview mirror as I drive away.  But, if anything does remain, like some of my hairs or blood, then I've got the perfect alibi.  Remember how I 'cut' my finger on a knife in the kitchen when I was slicing up one of the fresh oranges I brought over during my visit last week?  Remember who else was with us?  The detective, right?"  She pauses.  "Remember how you kept Michael in the basement because the detective was allergic to golden retrievers.  Never barked, though, did he?"  She smiles.  "Think he remembered me from my fat suit day?"

"Gotta pretty big bite mark on your arm right now," I say, motioning with my knife.  "Might be hard to explain."

"I'll drive straight home, dress the wound, and…who am I going to call, Shawn?"

It hits me. When she was at my house, she told me about the golden retriever she had rescued and how nice it would be to get together with me and Michael sometime.

"You've got it, don't you?" she says, smirking. "I'll call the pound, and they'll come out, and, unfortunately, good old Roy will have to be put down. Can't have a dog like that around, threatening me and my girls."

"I feel bad for your girls," Jo says, defiant 'till the end.

"Why?" Nora asks. "They hated their dad. They *love* me."

"What about Jo?"

"What about her?"

"They'll search her place and find traces of you."

Jo lowers her head.

"No, they won't," Nora says. "You want to tell him, or should I?" she asks Jo.

Jo says nothing.

"She was out for a walk, and I simply picked her up. Said I was in town for brunch tomorrow. Yeah, you said that aloud in the booth this morning too. 'I'll have 'em all over for a celebration brunch tomorrow like they've never seen!' Wasn't that the way you put it, Shawn? Anyway, I told Jo there had been an accident and that David Killian wanted me to pick her up. I knew from watching her house before that she takes runs at night." Nora turns her attention toward Jo. "Got right in the car, didn't you, my sweet? Didn't even feel the poke of the needle until it was too late when I acted like I dropped the keys on the floor of the back seat. No street cameras either, Shawn. Ah, technology never works when you need it anyway." Nora points her gun at me. "You're lucky your girl weighs around what I do. Wouldn't have been able to carry her into your house otherwise. I wish you could have seen her face when I woke her up in the kitchen."

"I'm going to kill you," Jo says.

"No, you're not. There's only one thing that could have possibly derailed my plans tonight, and I would have known about it before I picked up Jo. If that one thing had happened, I would have had to kill both of you quickly, canceling this stage production. But it didn't happen." She shakes her injured arm again as if to wake it up. Once again, blood flies in all directions. "You should thank me for tonight, Shawn. I gave you one last acting opportunity."

"There's plenty that could have gone wrong and might still go wrong tonight. There wasn't just one thing," I say.

"Nope. Just one. After you visited my house and turned my world upside down, it took me a while to figure out how you knew my identity. Trafalgar Simmons, that piece of filth, was told not to tell anyone my identity until after the book came out. But the sonofabitch has a big mouth. And I figured there was only one other person who knew who Jennie Masterson really was. That longtime reader of his. Well, let's just say that yesterday, someone paid her a visit at her home outside of Modesto and then took her for a little ride into the woods a few hours away. No cameras at her place. Again, I've done a lot research the past few months. Even if there were, I was in a different car and had my fat suit on again." She takes a step forward, and she squints her eyes. "She's buried in a shallow grave but will probably be found. Doesn't matter to me. No one saw us leave in my car, but they wouldn't have anyway because I pulled the same routine I did with Jo. The only difference is that I let Jo stay in the front seat—looked like she had dozed off. For the poor agent's reader, I put her in the trunk after giving her the needle." She points at Jo with her gun. "You're lucky you didn't get what was in *that* syringe."

It's silent for a few beats. Then, I hear more whimpering from downstairs. Michael. At least I know he's still alive.

My confidence has been shaken, to say the least. Nora Stewart is someone who plans ahead. I look at the distance between us. I'll never make it to her before she shoots me. I need to think of something else. What? Jo's feet are still bound to the chair, but her hands are free, and she can talk.

Talk.

I've got to keep Nora talking. She's overconfident and thinks she has time. I have to play on that. It's the only move I can make right now. Compare her to her husband and Bob again but act defeated.

"You are horrible, Nora, but we can see that you've thought things through. However, everything you've done here is still second rate compared to what your husband and Bob did."

"You still don't see it, do you? You're just another stupid actor with no common sense or imagination."

Well, you heard her. Act, Frost.

I work myself up until tears pour down my cheeks. "Don't say that." I lower to one knee next to Jo and make the knife fall out of my hands and onto Jo's lap. Jo wraps her hand around the handle. Good. When I get my chance to move against Nora, Jo can cut her feet loose and join the battle.

I rub Jo's right hand with my right hand and the back of her neck with my left hand. "We just want to live. Those two men put me through hell. Isn't that enough? Why are you trying to best them? You said Marcus-John was abusive. Can't you see you've won?"

She exhales and rolls her eyes. "How do you *stay* with someone like this?" she asks Jo. "If you wouldn't have come back to him, you'd never be in this situation. Now, you know why I came at him with the knife first. Didn't I whisper in your ear as he was coming up the stairs that he wouldn't put up much of a fight? Gotta admit, though, I didn't think his dog would attack, but as you know, with my rescue of my dog, I don't leave anything to chance."

Will Jo start acting too now? I'm counting on it.

"You're right," Jo says to Nora, shaking her head. "I should have stayed away. He really is pathetic." She motions to me with the knife. "What, Shawn, you want *me* to protect *you* with this now? She's still holding a *gun*."

I cry harder and lower my head.

She shifts her attention back to Nora. "But, you know what, Nora, I'm still not sure he was ever kidnapped. I've heard some of the evidence, and it's a bunch of bullshit. He was somewhere in L.A. on a drug bender."

I raise my head and grit my teeth as I look at Jo. "It *did* happen. Those two guys kidnapped me!"

Nora laughs. "If I let this go on, *she* might kill you for me, Shawn." And with that, she aims her gun at my coffee pot on the stove and shoots. Glass shatters and falls to the countertop and tile floor—like the old video opening of George Lucas's THX company logo. And right now, I wish it would reassemble into some invincible, horrible glass monster and slice up Nora Stewart.

"Counting my shots?" Nora asks. "That's three. Still plenty in my magazine for the two of you and Michael."

I turn my tearful rage at her. "I hated that coffee pot anyway. And Marcus-John and Bob never gave me enough coffee when I was in *that cell!*"

She lowers the gun and taps it against her jeans. "Okay, you are both wrong and stupid."

"What?" I say.

Nora smirks at both of us. "I was Big Boss."

# 38

I struggle to breath as Nora Stewart's words fill my ears. How is that possible?

Jo lets out a laugh. "Now, I've heard it all."

Nora raises her gun and shoots Jo in the lower left leg.

Jo howls in pain as blood splatters on the rope, chair, and floor. It's not gushing out, but I don't take any chances. I move to the other side of the chair and kneel next to her again. I remove my cummerbund and tie it around her wounded leg. Then, I leave my right hand around the Achilles tendon on her left leg. I pat her left knee with my left hand to distract Nora while I move my right hand down against the top of Jo's left running shoe. I give a quick downward push, and Jo signals that she knows what I'm asking her to do by raising her leg. I continue to push down while pretending to study my cummerbund handiwork. If I can get the shoe loosened, then I will have something to throw at Nora. I continue to apply pressure while Jo continues to raise her leg.

"Shut your mouth," Nora says to Jo…and then starts to *sing*. *"A wound for him, a wound for her. Who dies first? I'm not so sure."*

I look up at her, genuine fear on my face. She won't leave her words at that, but when she is done explaining herself, she *will* kill us. Time to abandon the tear parade. I look at Jo. "You okay?"

She winces in pain and says, "Fine."

I know the pain must be excruciating for Jo to lift her leg, but she continues to do it.

We both look at Nora.

She has the end of the gun barrel underneath her chin again.

Go ahead and fire, bitch!

"It's really simple," she starts.

Okay, get ready to go after her Frost, because when she finishes, she's taking you and Jo out.

"First off, and I can't believe you didn't figure this out, Shawn, Marcus-John and I had the agreement that he would always refer to the unseen person upstairs as a man. Didn't you ever consider that he was lying?"

To be honest, I didn't. Am I going to admit it to this fruitcake? Nope. Plus, that was Bob Croft's voice I heard in captivity. Nora Stewart is not Big Boss.

"This way, we could always frame Bob Croft if anything ever went wrong. Now, I wanted that person to be referred to as *Narrator*, but Marcus-John and I got into a heated argument after he punched you. And, if you remember, when he came downstairs, he slipped and said Big Boss upstairs was mad at him. He was supposed to start referring to me as Narrator, but then you asked if everything was okay between him and Big Boss, and he decided to go with it. Looking back, it was probably the better move anyway. Kind of fit in with the whole country boy slang thing he was presenting. You thought two good old boys had you captive down there, didn't you?"

"You're lying. I heard the voicemails that Bob left Marcus-John, and that was Bob's voice I heard through the speaker in my cell."

She smirks. "I can do Bob's voice perfectly. Practiced for hours." She now points the gun barrel at her throat. "The average male voice is around twenty percent lower in pitch than a female's. So, to lower my voice, I had to relax my upper body, speak more from my throat, and speak slower and quieter. Bob's voice was also a bit raspy, so I learned to hold my breath and exhale less air, which helped to create what's called a vocal fry that makes your voice sound rougher. Lastly, I practiced a lot of belly breathing and trained myself to use my diaphragm, which helped me speak with a deeper voice. Ready to hear good old Bob?"

I watch as she starts to swing her arms back and forth. Then, she yawns a few times. After a few deep breaths, she looks me in the eye and says, "Narrate it *exactly* as I have written it, *Shawn.*"

Pure horror. It is the voice of Bob Croft—the voice that spoke to me from the ceiling of my recording cell. It is *exactly* that voice. How did I not consider this possibility? I search my memory… Well, I did think about Jo lowering her voice and possibly being Big Boss, but that was back when I believed that she might be in on the kidnapping. After hearing Bob's voicemails, I never even thought about Nora as a possibility.

"Impressed?" she says in her normal tone but doesn't wait for me to answer. "I've been a writer all of my life. Not only did you like my voice-change demonstration, you *loved* that little tune I just came up with, didn't you?"

I'm still in shock and just gaze at her.

Nora sings the line again. *"A wound for him, a wound for her. Who dies first? I'm not so sure."* She taps the barrel of the gun on her chest and says, *"Talent,"* then places the end of the barrel back underneath her chin. "Wrote a dozen manuscripts and submitted them to agents in my early twenties. Rejection letter after rejection letter. Do you know how that feels? Naaahhh, you wouldn't. So, I gave up and became what my parents wanted me to become: a nurse. And I was good. Damned good. Makes sense to you now, right? How I was able to acquire all of the medical equipment? Did it a long time ago, though, when I was in Alabama. Poor hospital, never good with inventory, and I had a different name back then. Gathered everything up and then tendered my resignation. Surprised that the investigators never looked that far into my past, but it had been almost twenty years since I had been a nurse, so I guess they ruled that out. Been a substitute teacher and a stay-at-home mom since. Anyway, I moved out west. Go west, young woman. Go west! Met a cute trucker—thought I could entice him to help me carry out my dream of being an author. Marcus-John took the bait, and he gave me two girls. Wouldn't trade them for the world. The tranquilizers and heroin? Well, I guess Marcus-John was good for that—a lot more going on at trucker stops than people want to know about. Well, as you can guess, he wasn't happy with his job, and when the time was right, I told him my full plan. Sucker went for it. If he hadn't, then he wouldn't have been around any longer.

"But he did, and I told him my idea about kidnapping our favorite two audiobook narrators and seeing how they would act in captivity. We'd study them, and I'd use our research in my design of the novel." She pauses.

I know why. My mouth is open.

"Yes, Shawn. Michael Hunnie was there with you. He was Marcus-John's favorite. You were mine. What threw us for a loop, though, is that we figured *you* would be the problem child—the one who would resist. Thought Hunnie was mush. Were *we* ever wrong. He wouldn't record a damned thing! Now, we didn't have him next to you for your entire stay. In fact, the only days he was next to you were the day before he broke out and the day he did. We had threatened him by telling him that we would kill you if he made his presence known. He told us that he didn't believe that we had you captive as well, and said that if we could prove it to him, he would cooperate. My idiot husband didn't tie him down well enough either day, and Hunnie broke free and flushed the toilet like he had the day before. Thank God you were drugged then. But Hunnie did it again, and this time you were awake and recording. As you know, Marcus-John sprinted over to Hunnie's room, opened the door, and, well, you heard the rest."

I want to cry. Michael Hunnie was *there*. Keep it together, Frost. No time to grieve now. I continue to work on Jo's shoe. I've got Nora deep into her story, and I can keep her going. "Was that you who ran past the open door?"

"Indeed.  I was in my disguise, so I knew you had no clue who I was."

"I heard a shot in the hallway."

"There was a handgun, like this one," she says, raising her gun for a second, "on the hallway table.  Hunnie grabbed it, and if I hadn't jumped on his arm, he would have aimed it at Marcus-John, and then we would have had a big problem.  But his shot missed everyone, and I put him to sleep.  Hubby dragged him down the hall, and we made other plans for Mr. Hunnie."

"But there is no way you were able to kill him.  He was seen picking up a prostitute in L.A., and then the two of them died in a cabin in Utah.  I checked the distance.  Hunnie's cabin was six and a half hours from your hunting cabin in Elko and six hours from L.A.—no way you could have managed that.  Also, your home phone records from Springville proved that you were home and not at the cabin in Elko during the week that I was abducted."  I feel my confidence returning.  "Imitating someone's voice is one thing, but there is no way you are Big Boss."

"When did you smarten up?" she says, laughing.  "But, you're still wrong. Elko is a ten-hour drive from Springville.  When you look at the phone records, you'll see that there were many days where it was possible for me to drive there and back and still make the phone calls to my mom to check on my daughters.  I made sure to stay there a few days where I could make those phone calls five hours apart to make it look like I was there the whole time.  Also, I never stopped for gas.  I had can after can full in the back of my car.  Some of those cans are in my car in your driveway right now.  We had a stockpile of them in our pole barn and a stockpile in our garage at the cabin in Elko.  I was there, all right, Shawn— watchin' you piss yourself and talkin' to you in my deep, manly voice through the speaker."

Okay, she might be Big Boss.  Who gives a fuck right now?  I'm struggling to get the shoe loose.  Jo is really lifting up hard.  Hang in there, baby.  I'm going to get us out of this.

"Now, as for Mister Hunnie. First, after his attempted escape, we spent a few days breaking him. Then, we threatened to kill his parents and sister. This made him, shall we say, suddenly open to suggestion—also threatened to damage his vocal cords, and that really got his attention. So, we finished with you, and then kept you drugged up. While Marcus-John watched over you, I drove a drugged Hunnie down to his cabin in Utah. There, we got in his Land Rover, and he drove us to L.A. A few times, we pulled off the road into a remote location and used the cans of gas to fill up his vehicle—the cans were way in the back and hidden under a large blanket—so there is no footage of us ever stopping at a gas station, and no chance for him to make a stupid cry for help. I'm also guessing that when they got the footage of him picking up the prostitute, they overlooked the blanket covering the cans of gas—Hunnie had those windows tinted anyway.

"So, I hide under a blanket in the back seat while he pulls up and picks up the prostitute. My husband and I wanted *that* on camera. Once he gets outside of L.A., I come out from underneath the blanket and put the ho to sleep. We do our gas routine and eventually pull back into his cabin in the wee hours. And that's when I surprise him. I put him to sleep just as he turns off the ignition. I take them both inside and shoot them up with heroin laced with fentanyl. This kills them, making it look like a classic overdose case. By the way, I'm wearing plastic over every part of my body, so there's no trace of me. And, I covered up any trace of my car or me ever being in his driveway. Then, I drive home, go to bed, and then pick the girls up two days later from LAX. My husband is the one who dropped you off near Pacific Palisades." She simulates doing a mic drop with her gun and says, "Boom."

Jo's ankle is almost out of the shoe. I frown, looking at the cummerbund, and raise my right hand up to it. I then use both of my hands to adjust the cummerbund as if I'm redressing the wound. My heart is racing. I'm ready for war—just one last point to make before I grab the shoe, and it's on. I don't care what her explanation is. She could tell me she's secretly a foreign agent sent in to disrupt our supply chain system, and I wouldn't give a shit.

"But you're forgetting Bob Croft," I say.

"Saved the best surprise for last," she says, giggling.

I lower my right hand to Jo's shoe and resume working.

"Would you believe me if I said that he wasn't in on it at all? Ha! I had your investigators completely fooled. Naturally, it was all by design. Bob Croft didn't know *one* thing about what Marcus-John and I were doing. He was never a part of it but was the perfect person to set up. The only things that I told the truth about were that he visited the lodge in Elko with Marcus-John and me and had brought a girlfriend with him on occasion, and he died four months ago, and he loved audiobooks like my husband did. But, everything else I told you and the authorities was made up. Perfect, right? Well, I had to have a backup plan if anything ever went wrong." She waves the gun at both of us. "I'm not going to prison. So, as the stakes got higher—especially when my literary agent made the huge deal with that mega-bitch Rider Elizabeth Cross, I put my plan into motion.

"First, I started an affair with Bob. By that time, he had already made us the executors of his estate in case anything ever happened to him. I told him a lie that Marcus-John and I were basically done and that, after the girls had graduated high school, I wanted to run away with him. He believed it all. Then, when the time was right, I killed him. Sex was his leverage point. Got him drunk and led him out to his garage. Told him to get ready for the kinkiest sex he'd ever had. Got naked—except for wearing rubber gloves, told him the wonders they would help me perform on his cock—teased him, threw a noose around his neck, tightened it, teased him some more, handcuffed his wrists and ankles—*over* his clothes so that there wouldn't be marks—and secured his wrists *behind* his back, started to give him head and worked in a little spontaneity with the gloves, then stopped…walked around him, told him to lie down on the ground…gently so as not to hurt his hands. I tied one end of a rope to a tractor and one end to the cuffs around his ankles. Asked him if he felt helpless. Said he did. Gave him a little more head and then walked around behind him, told him I was going to sit on his face for a good while. Instead, I pulled on the noose, watching him shake until he died. Zipped up his pants, took off the two sets of handcuffs, untied the rope from the cuffs and tractor, threw the rope coming off the noose over a rafter, stood him up on a ladder while I tied the end of the rope off to the rafter, and then kicked the ladder over. And there he hung, right where my husband found him a few days later. It crushed him. He had no idea about the affair or that I was setting Bob up to be 'Big Boss.' Next, I took all of the pictures of our Elko cabin out of our photo albums and destroyed them. Then, I hid the albums in the boxes in the pole barn. Not only had I now set up Bob, but I had also set up my husband in the event that he was ever found out. There was absolutely nothing that tied me to any of it—as long as I controlled the narrative."

She smirks.

"The night you came to our home, Shawn, I had to think quickly. First, you were right, I was having an affair—well, still am—with Ken Oakley. Marcus-John proved to be weaker than I thought he would be. It all started when we killed Hunnie. It was the first murder he was a part of, and he thought things had gotten out of control. I already knew what it was like to kill and get away with it—made a doctor and nurse disappear from that hospital down in Alabama. Did such a good job of it, I was only questioned once, and that was mostly to see if I was okay. Both cases went cold, and the bodies were never found." Nora breaks into a little song, *"But I know where they're aaaat."*

Okay, she *is* Big Boss. Doesn't matter: Jo's ankle is out of the shoe!

Nora kisses the barrel of the gun and continues. "Then, when Bob died, Marcus-John started drinking heavily, and I knew I might have to take care of him soon. And so, when you showed up that night, Shawn, I seized the opportunity. When you were downstairs—great move, by the way; I was thinking of killing you both—I got my shotgun out and yelled to you like he was trying to kill me. Boy, did I surprise him. As soon as I started shouting, he turned around, and I blasted him. I just didn't think he'd get off a shot, but something in me tells me that he had just put two and two together." She shrugs. "I'll never know, and if he had killed me, then things would have all turned out differently. But he didn't kill me, Shawn, and now, because of you, I've had to give up my writing for a second time. *Listen To Me* is my book. *My* book! And you were going to read it and make millions off *my* hard work. And, also because of you, everyone thinks that my husband and his trucker friend wrote the book. They didn't! Every word of that novel is *mine*. Well, except for the part you improvised that I never caught. So, I guess I made two mistakes."

I grasp the heel of the shoe and squeeze. I've got a solid grip. Fear, horror, and adrenaline course through my body. Everything comes down to this. If I screw up, Nora Stewart *is* going to kill us and get away with *everything*. I take a breath…

And let it out.

Nora squares her shoulders to us and says, "But, I won't be making a third mistake."

I rip the shoe off and throw it at her as she raises her gun. It's enough to distract her as I leap at her. She shoots, but the shot misses me.

With an animal instinct coursing through my veins that I have never known before, I grab her arm that's holding the gun, and we wrestle to the ground. She bites into my shoulder, and I feel her gnaw and gnaw through the flimsy cotton tuxedo shirt, blood soaking it along with her saliva. I play dirty back and dig my fingernails into her wrist and forearm. She releases her mouth from my shirt and shouts in pain.

I look at her hand, and because of my digging, her grip around the gun is loosening. Then, I see an Adidas tennis shoe SLAM down on Nora's palm, inches from where my hand is. I look up. It's Jo!

Nora howls in pain, but using an incredible range of motion and gymnast-like agility, she kicks Jo, and Jo falls to the floor.

"The gun is free, Shawn!" Jo yells.

I see it, inches from Nora's hand. I let go of her arm and grab the gun.

She jumps on my back and starts clawing at my face. I feel a set of gashes streak my left and right cheek. She's going to go for my eyes. So, with her on my back, I drive my legs backward, trying to smash her against the wall.

I feel us hit the wall, or what I think is the wall. But instead of stopping, I hear wood splintering and realize that I have backed us up against…and now through…the door leading to the basement. I feel us floating for a moment through the air. I'm falling back…back…

*SMACK!*

We land on the stairway—her back and head taking the full weight of my body. The gun flies from my hand.

We slide down the stairs.

When we reach the bottom, she is moaning in pain. I roll off her looking for the gun. It's a foot from her right hand.

She reaches for it. As I leap for the gun, I realize that I won't be able to beat her to it. The best I'll be able to do is grab her wrist and try to prevent her from shooting me. The odds of that don't look good.

I want to apologize to Jo. I want to apologize to everyone I've ever hurt. I want to—

Michael's head appears in my line of vision, and his mouth closes around Nora's hand just before it reaches the gun. His hind legs are dragging, but he hangs on and shakes his head from side to side.

I seize the gun and, with no hesitation, point it at Nora's chest and shoot…and shoot…

…and shoot.

Her body lies lifeless—gaping holes, oozing blood, littering her torso.

Michael lets go of her arm just as the lights come on over the stairway.  I look up…

And see Jo limping down toward us.

*1 Year Later...*

# EPILOGUE

## New York City, March

I, narrator Shawn Frost, am back at the Audies. I missed last year because Jo and I were recovering in more ways than one from the nightmarish evening at my home; tonight marks my return to the beloved awards ceremony that recognizes the highest levels of achievement in the Voice Arts industry.

My longtime friend, the Executive Director of the Audies, Mariel W. Sissel, started off the program with a bang tonight by recognizing me with a standing ovation that lasted over a minute. Not a dry eye at my table, which includes Jo Frost, my wife of 6 months now, David Killian, his lawyer and fiancé Gisele Rubie, Corie Woods, Matt Woods, my mother, my sister, Dr. Roman I. Baker, Ph.D., my larger-than-life lawyer, H. Jefferson Montaigne, and the CEO of ParkerWilson Publishing, Rider Elizabeth Cross.

Who isn't at my table?

John Daniel Frost, my father.

Dad had a heart attack two weeks ago but is recovering at home and doing better each day. The man has never slowed down a day in his life. He does not know the meaning of the word "no" when people ask for help. I can only hope that this scary event will encourage him to slow down and enjoy the golden years, which he so richly deserves to live in comfort and peace.  I will miss him most tonight but am comforted by the fact that my high school drama teacher, another man who saw something in me that I didn't, is at my childhood home right now with Dad, watching the program together as it is streamed online.  My golden retriever, Michael, is also not here, but he has fully recovered from his broken leg, and a friend of mine is staying with him at our new home in Greenwich Village.

And we've now arrived at the moment of the evening for me.  The award for Best Male Narrator.  If I don't get it, I'll be fine.  I already won in the category of best thriller/suspense for my narration of *Listen To Me*, and that's enough recognition for me.  However, Killy wants Best Male Narrator for me, and so does Jo.  I don't know how I feel about it, mostly because I know the truth of everything that has led up to this moment.  I know about Michael Hunnie.  I have wondered many times what would have happened if he had not resisted in that doomed basement.  I might not be here.  In fact, I am convinced that Michael Hunnie and my dog Michael are the reasons I'm alive today.

When I finally finished narrating the novel's final chapters, I had an experience I am not likely to ever have again.  After years of trying unsuccessfully, I was able to actually bring my own life experiences, my *feelings* to the performance.  I was not a reader and not a failed playwright, actor, and writer who happened to be an audiobook narrator.  I was floating.  I was in the booth; I was not in the booth.  I was a narrator.

Mariel reads the names of the nominees, and my name is last.

There is a pregnant pause, and Mariel soaks up the torture she is inflicting on the nominees.  The guest presenter for Best Female Narrator was Oprah Winfrey, but it looks like Mariel wants to announce this award all by herself.  Then, she speaks.

"To present the award for Best Male Narrator, please join me in welcoming to the stage, Mr. Steven Spielberg."

As soon as I hear his name, the overwhelming feelings of surprise and joy radiate from my battered core. Not because it seems incredibly coincidental that the man who is directing the film based on the novel *Listen To Me*, which I have an audition for in two weeks, will be presenting this award, but because of what this man's work has meant to me.

I see him now. The applause is just as loud as it was for Oprah. He's walking up the stairs. He's walking across the stage. I cannot believe this. He stops at the podium, where he is greeted with a hug from Mariel. He gives a slight bow. I would run to the stage right now and kiss his shoes. He smiles and motions for quiet, but the applause roars on.

The only person who would top this man as a presenter for my category would be William Shakespeare—I'm a playwright, remember—but since he is unavailable, then the man whose films stirred something inside of me when I saw them in the cinema or on TV, long before I saw my first play, is perfect. I am working on what I want to express to him when I have my audition for *Listen To Me*, and seeing him in person tonight is a wonderful inspiration for that. I'll need to sit down immediately after the ceremony and write.

The applause starts to die down, and Steven says, "Can we pretend that she just introduced me as the director of *1941?*"

The place lights up with laughter, and Spielberg laughs too. I've seen *1941,* and love it.

He continues the jest. "So, I'm very glad that you liked the film," More laughter. Killy is going to fall out of his seat, "but it's time to present this prestigious award."

He pauses just like Mariel and then takes his time opening the envelope!

"And the winner for Best Male Narrator is…Shawn Frost."

And the standing ovation starts. There are hugs from everyone at my table. My world is a blur. I find my way to the stage and head up the steps where Spielberg and Mariel await.

Then, I cross a line off my bucket list and give Spielberg a hug. And it's a damned long one. When we break, he gives his signature laugh and says, "Okay, okay," and then shakes my hand and says, "Congratulations." He steps into the shadows, and then Mariel and I embrace for an eternity. She whispers, "Proud of you. Don't know if there'll ever be another book like it. And if you tell anyone that, I'll disown you." She gives me a kiss on the cheek and hands me the award. I face the crowd.

They're still on their feet, and the people at my table in the back are acting like they all have red ants in their underwear.

Finally, the applause dies down.

I've given speeches after winning major awards, but that was a long time ago, and that was a different person speaking than who I am today. I've prepared a speech, and I start to reach in my pocket but then pull my hand back.

I adjust the microphone.

I take a breath, hold it, and then exhale.

I close my eyes, a thousand thoughts run through my mind, but when I open my eyes back up, the thoughts stop.

"Mariel, Steven, members of the Audio Publishers Association, my fellow nominees, my wonderful colleagues and collaborators, my dear friends and family, including Dad and Ray, who are watching at home, years ago, I left New York City, only a few blocks from where we are right now, as a confused and broken kid. I didn't know if I would ever have a moment like this again in my life. Mostly because I didn't know if I would even have a life. The statistics were, and still are, against me. Addiction is real. I didn't know if I could beat it. But I vowed that if I ever did reach the podium and microphone again, I would call out the doubters, celebrate my comeback, and make a few optimistic—and probably brash—proclamations about the future trajectory of my career."

I look down and rub the fingers of my right hand in a few tight circles on the podium's smooth wood. I look up.

"However, since I made that imprudent promise—a child's promise—to myself, *fate*, or whatever else you want to call it, seems to have intervened. Everyone here knows the events that led me to narrate this book. Once again, I've cheated death, but I do not wish to make a mockery of my moment. When I started narrating, I thought that performing audiobooks was a sitzprobe for one day returning to the theater—a hyphen to my *real* work. I was a writer. An actor. A playwright. Not a narrator. Narrating was the way back to my true calling, my first love. Narrating was the way back to *art*."

I stop, unaware of where I'm at for a moment, lost in the brief thought about a younger man with the whole world ahead of him. I give a pained grin. I still love that guy, but I realize that I am no longer him.

"I was mistaken. Narrating…is art. Narrating…*is* the show." I pause, fighting back tears. "I discovered that I am not just a creature of the theater. I am also a narrator. Neither profession is a hyphen to the other. Instead, for me, they will now forever be separated by a semi-colon. Playwright; narrator. Narrator; playwright. For I plan to spend the rest of my life being both."

And then, just as I expect my eyes to water and my speech to fall apart, I find peace—warm, focused, and relieved inner peace—and hit my stride.

"We all have our favorite narrators." I pause, surveying the crowd. "Guides who take us on unimaginable adventures in the fragile, exciting, and mostly unknown realms of our minds. And then, there are our real-life narrators." I look toward my table in the back. "Guardians who help us make sense of life's challenges, disappointments, and complexities and light the way home for us during the darkest moments in the stories of our own lives."

I pause once more, taking a long breath in. I let it out.

"Mom, Dad, Sis, Ray, Killy, Corie, Matt, Jo, and my dog Michael, I am yours. Thank you for not giving up on me."

There's an applause, and I use the seconds to breathe, maintaining my composure.

The clapping fades, and the room is silent once more.  I swallow.

"Lastly, I would like to dedicate this award to *my* favorite narrator…the late Michael Hunnie."  I look up to the ceiling and close my eyes.  "Rest in peace."

Then, I face the audience one last time, and it *may be* the last time from this stage—no guarantee that I will ever be called up here again.  I embrace the moment and, with a smile of gratitude, say, "Thank you."

*2 Months Later...*

# New York City

The limousine pulls up to the sidewalk, and a colossal chauffeur, we're talking Dave Bautista size here, gets out and puts on a cap that looks ridiculous on his huge head. Nonetheless, he struts around the corner and opens the door for me.

"Good evening, Mr. Frost," he says.

"Good evening."

I get in and enjoy the soft jazz music and the comfortable leather seat that I sink into. It's the kind where, once it has you in its grip, you never want to get up. I see that there is a bottle of lime-flavored sparkling water set in the cup holder for me, and on the tray next to the seat is a plate of ginger snap cookies—both my favorites.

I am about to be driven to the opening night of my new Broadway play, *Waiting Room.* Against all odds, I've returned to my first love, the theater. Jo is already there. I offered her a role, but she chose to be my assistant director. I feared the collaboration would end in disaster. Most couples don't work well together in the entertainment industry, but we've proved to be the exception. Teaming up has worked out better than I could have ever dreamed it would. Perhaps, it's because we're both not acting. You know the story: one person starts getting all of the roles, and the other one fades from the spotlight. Lighter fluid and matches.

I've also been able to finally channel my competitive drive. I'm now chasing excellence, not awards.

But Jo. She has an eye for everything, has eliminated numerous headaches, knows the cast, and, most importantly, knows the theater. The fact that she is an accomplished actress has helped a great deal as well. The two of us, alone in the theater, performed an early draft of the entire play, and the experience guided the early editing process. Working together has also kept me away from my demons. Whenever stress has enticed me to wander, she's been right by my side. Have arguments come up?  Absolutely.  But part of our growth as a couple has been when those disagreements surface, we don't act like we're "on stage" with each other.  Instead, we have real discussions.  And we've discovered something else together throughout the process of putting on this play: Any project we do in the future will have to have both of us attached.  If that means fewer projects, so be it.

However, so as to avoid re-entering the theater for the wrong reasons, we both re-read *The Fervent Years* and *Write That Play* to see if they still resonated with us—that the magic was still there.

It was.

Kenneth Thorpe Rowe's words in the latter work have been echoing through my mind since I read the book again, and they are streaming across my thoughts right now:

*The love of the theatre is age-old and inherent.  If some cataclysm were to wipe all existence of the theatre from the face of the earth, it would not take long for human nature to evolve it again.  Take drama from a people and they will create drama themselves.*

For me, my journey started when I was seven.  I wrote the script to a gladiator play and coerced my sister into acting it out with me in our family's living room.  I made the costumes, built the set, gathered various household items to use as props, and even used my tape recorder to play classical music during the show.  On some level, everyone starts this way, and I have to believe that the younger generation, born and raised on streaming video, can still find enjoyment in strenuous recreation like going to the theater.  And I have no doubt that some members of the audience tonight will be from that younger generation.

*The audience.*

Is everything too pre-digested these days?  If *yes*, what happens to societies that lose the spirit of collective consciousness?  Jo and I hope to never find out.

A theater audience likes to work, and I am going to put them to work in a few hours.

And yet, I still can't look away from the big screen. Spielberg is supposed to be in the audience tonight, as is the head of Sony Pictures Studios, Angelica Westover. The audition went well…I got the part of Lionel Goliath. Filming starts in 6 months. Of course, the CEO of ParkerWilson, Rider Elizabeth Cross will be in a premium seat this evening, and, last I heard, Monty was a maybe.

Corie and Matt are coming tonight along with Killy and Gisele—now, as of last week, Killy's sixth wife. *This is the one, Shawn,'* he said to me up at the altar before Gisele came down the aisle. For no good reason, I believe him this time. My parents—Dad is well enough to travel now—and sister will also be attending, and so will Ray Jarold.

Oh, almost forgot. Bake will also grace us with his presence tonight.

What can I say? I'm grateful.

They never gave up on me. I'll have my whole team with me tonight.

*Waiting Room* was conceived, although I didn't know it at the time, the day I walked into Barney's to get coffee while visiting Corie in the hospital. It's a three-act play with three characters and three settings. The description underneath the promotional poster in the *Times* reads:

*A man whose best friend is about to pass away befriends a barista at the hospital's coffee shop—starting an unlikely friendship and ending in the most powerful love story of our time.*

The main character's name is Wayne, who is based on me, and whose experiences are loosely based on my experiences at Barney's. The coffee shop in my play is named Barry's. The barista's name is Tia and is based on Alicia. The dying friend's name is Carl, and he is, of course, based somewhat on Corie.

Guess who is playing Tia?

Alicia.

She was ready to give up acting when I called her. If life can give me a second chance, then she deserves a first chance. Her performance in rehearsals has exceeded all expectations. *Waiting Room* will put her on the map. Her next play should make her a household name. She owed me nothing when I walked into Barney's for a cup of coffee. What she gave me was comfort, friendship, and understanding.

*Waiting Room* is a play about the love that grows between Wayne and Tia. It's also a play about forgiveness between Wayne and Carl—saying goodbye and how matters can change in an instant. Second chances and making sense of life when it seems impossible to do so.

I admit it. I am nervous about opening night. It's been so long since I've had one, and anxiety has been building in me all day. I believe we're ready. We've workshopped the play to death. I've re-written the final act more times than I can count, but it's now *all* heart, and I'm proud of it. I even re-read Adrienne Kennedy's *A Movie Star Has to Star in Black and White* and got some fresh ideas for the hospital room scenes that I was able to put in during the final workshop. You don't write plays; you re-write plays. The entire process has also reminded me that we can always strive to treat people better—especially before it's too late.

Our press agents have papered the house, and we should have a friendly audience. All I can hope for are friendly reviews on social media tonight when the theater audience exits and the thumbs start tappin' away on the phone screens. Then, we'll run the gauntlet as the shows tomorrow and the next day are the ones that the majority of critics will be attending. We were offered the choice to have the play open in L.A. because of the source material that inspired *Waiting Room's* creation, but I said no. The *New York Times* would have sent a critic to review the play, and if the review was bad, we might not be where we are tonight.

But, it's more than that. I want to give the audience a good time. I want to delight. As one of my favorite actors, David Pittu once said, *"I want to be entertained. I know the world is a terrible place, but make something beautiful out of it."* Did

I mention that David will be in the audience as well?  He's coming, and I want to give him and everyone else what they want and deserve from a Broadway show.

The driver-side door opens, and my giant chauffeur gets in and closes the door.  He starts the car, and I expect us to join the bustling traffic and roll toward the theater at any moment.

Instead, the jazz music cuts off, and I hear the electronic mechanism that opens the tinted, sliding window between the front seat and the cab.

"Everything okay?" I ask.

"Yes, sir," he says.  "Just wanted to offer you a little something to relax you, take the edge off.  You'll find it in the compartment next to the ice bucket."  With that, I hear the mechanism engage again, and the window slides shut.

The soft jazz plays again.

I look over at the ice bucket and see the small compartment he's talking about.  Leaning over, I push a button, which releases the door to the compartment.  The door releases slowly until it is all the way open.

Inside is a small glass bowl of white powder and a blue plastic straw.

I whisper to myself, "Coke in the backseat."

"Did you find it, sir?" the driver's voice says over the intercom system.

"I did."

My breathing becomes shallow as I stare at the bowl.

One sniff…?

No one will ever know.

*Coke in the backseat, coke in the backseat…*

It's been so long…

*Coke in the backseat, coke in the backseat…*

I'm breaking…

Then…a symphony of Stephen Sondheim's lyrics start up and wage war with the grotesque lines already running through my head.  I've leaned on Stephen before, and, somehow, he and the theater gods must know that I need him right now.  Spielberg got me through my childhood and to the Audies; Sondheim will get me back to the theater.

But the pull toward the bowl is strong.  A jolt of intense power and transcendent escape is only a few feet away.

Just one sniff…

My heart is racing—smartwatch's readings have to be going berserk.  I'm returning to Broadway.  I…

I don't know if…

Sondheim's words grow louder…

And LOUDER.

And now, they're drowning out the other lines, *decimating* the hideous song.

My resolve is returning.  My confidence is growing.  My emotions are *stirring*.

And all at once, the other song disintegrates.  It is quiet—a beautiful silence.

Then, from some far-off horizon of peace and tranquility, I hear:

*Anything you do,*
*Let it come from you.*
*Then it will be new.*
*Give us more to see…*

And I realize that if I reach toward that straw and bowl, I will never give anyone *anything* more to see from me.

I slam the compartment door shut and open my bottle of lime sparkling water.  I yell, "Sunday in the park with George!"

"Sir?" the voice says over the intercom.

I roll down my window and open the compartment—eyes on *fire*.  In one quick move, I grab the glass bowl and THROW IT out the window.

A few seconds later, I hear it shatter.

My hands are shaking, and tears are welling up in my eyes.  I roll up the window and shout, "No thanks!"

He replies, "Very well," and the limousine starts to move.

Smooth jazz fills my ears.

I take a long drink from my sparkling water and then take a bite from one of my ginger snaps.  The sweet taste calms my nerves, and I feel stronger with each crunchy chew.  Tears of joy release down my cheeks.

Soon, we are in the middle of New York City traffic—congestion, drama, and people rolling toward different destinations and destinies.

Perhaps, Harold Clurman said it best:

*Everybody is so clever in New York…Ability, even talent, flashes at every turn and corner of the city.*

We turn a corner, and I see the lights of the theater ahead.

# AUTHOR'S NOTE

Thank you for reading or listening to *Narrator*. As an independent author, my success greatly depends on reviews and referrals. If you enjoyed the book, it would help me out if you left a quick review and then passed on the recommendation. If you would like more information on upcoming books and discounts, please sign-up for my email list through my website (landonbeachbooks.com) or follow Landon Beach Books on Facebook, Twitter, or Instagram.

*Narrator*. This novel is a project that I have wanted to take on for a long time. The seeds were planted decades ago when I read Julio Cortázar's short story "The Continuity of Parks" and saw these four films: *Vertigo, Play Misty For Me, Misery,* and *A Beautiful Mind.* In fact, after seeing *A Beautiful Mind* in 2001, a twenty-year brainstorming session commenced—the creation of a soup containing those 5 main ingredients along with my life experiences as a writer attempting to navigate the entertainment business. And so for twenty years, I stirred the soup. What I wanted to write was a psychological thriller, set in the entertainment industry, that was new and had never been done before. There were many taste-testing sips of the soup over the years, but nothing that made me stop and say, "Yes, it's ready." The final ingredient was added 3 years ago when my life forever changed: I contacted the unrivaled Hall of Fame narrator Scott Brick and asked if he would be interested in performing my 3 independently-published novels at the time. He read *The Wreck*...and said *yes*. As we collaborated on the production of those three books, I realized what my long-gestating story could be about and set to work on it.

The research I did to bring *Narrator* to life was fun, exhausting, and eye-opening, and through it all, I have come to have a monumental amount of respect for how difficult it is to narrate audiobooks well. If you want to follow in my footsteps and learn all that is involved in the process—from the time the manuscript arrives with the narrator until the moment you, as the consumer, listen to the final product—search away on YouTube! My job, of course, was to take the job of a narrator and dramatize it in a, hopefully, thrilling fashion. Like he has for my previous books, Scott Brick is responsible for bringing my vision of *Narrator* to life for audiobook listeners around the world, and he was generous enough to give an early draft a read and advise me on the technical aspects of audiobook narration. I am grateful for his time and expertise. However, I did take some artistic liberties to suit the needs of my plot and characters as my profession is to entertain. Hence, Scott is not responsible for any of the novel's potential shortcomings. If there are mistakes, they are mine. A few books that stood out during my research phase of writing the novel were: *Write That Play* by Kenneth Thorpe Rowe, *The Fervent Years* by Harold Clurman, *Putting It Together* by James Lapine, *Character* by Robert McKee, *Bring on the Empty Horses* by David Niven, *Dropped Names* by Frank Langella, *Awake in the Dark* by Roger Ebert, and *The Norton Shakespeare*.

Many thanks to MB, EL, SB, AB, CB, DB, JB, TB, CG, JG, CM, DM, MM, RR, NS, and JT, who all provided helpful comments on an early draft of the manuscript. To my fans: I hope you enjoyed this psychological thriller, and I continue to enjoy corresponding with you via e-mail and social media. I have a few more books coming out this year that I think you will like. Lastly, many, *many* thanks to my wife and two daughters for helping me to achieve my dream. Until next time…

Happy Beach Reading!

L.B.

If you enjoyed *Narrator*, expand your adventure with *The Wreck*, the first book in The Great Lakes saga. Here is an excerpt to start the journey.

# THE WRECK

Landon Beach

# PROLOGUE

## LAKE HURON, MICHIGAN
## SUMMER 2007

The Hunter 49's motor cut, and the luxury yacht glided with no running lights on. Cloud cover hid the moon and stars; the water looked black. A man in a full wetsuit moved forward in the cockpit and after verifying the latitude and longitude, pushed the GPS monitor's "off" button. The LCD color display vanished.

Waves beat against the hull, heavier seas than had been predicted. He would have to be efficient or he'd need to reposition the boat over the scuttle site again. The chronometer above the navigation station read 0030. This should have been finished 30 minutes ago. Not only had the boat been in the wrong slip, forcing him to search the marina in the dark, the owner—details apparently escaped that arrogant prick—had not filled the fuel tank.

He headed below and opened the aft stateroom door. The woman's naked corpse lay strapped to the berth, the nipples of her large breasts pointing at the overhead. A careful lift of the port-side bench revealed black wiring connecting a series of three explosive charges. After similar checks of the wiring and charges in the gutted-out galley and v-berth, he smiled to himself and went topside with a pair of night vision goggles.

A scan of the horizon. Nothing.

He closed and locked the aft hatch cover. Moving swiftly—but never rushing—he donned a mask and fins, then pulled a remote detonation device from the pocket of his wetsuit. Two of the four buttons were for the explosives he had attached to the outside of the hull underwater, which would sink the boat. The bottom two were for the explosives he had just checked on the interior.

He looked back at the cockpit and for a moment rubbed his left hand on the smooth fiberglass hull. What a waste of a beautiful boat. How much had the owner paid for it? Three...Four-hundred thousand? Some people did live differently. With the night vision goggles hanging on his neck and the remote for the explosives in his right hand, he slipped into the water and began to kick.

Fifty yards away he began to tread water and looked back at the yacht. It listed to starboard, then to port, as whitecaps pushed against the hull. He pressed the top two buttons on the remote. The yacht lifted and then began to lower into the water; the heaving sea had less and less effect as more of the boat submerged. In under a minute, the yacht was gone. He held his fingers on the bottom two buttons but did not push them. The water was deep, and it would take three to four minutes for the boat to reach the lake bed.

At four minutes, he pushed the bottom two buttons, shut the remote, and zipped it back into his wetsuit pocket. He treaded water for half an hour. Nothing surfaced.

He swam for five minutes, stopped, scanned the area with his night vision goggles, and swam again.

After an hour of this, he pulled the goggles over his head and let them sink to the bottom. He continued his long swim to shore.

# 1

## HAMPSTEAD, MICHIGAN
## SUMMER 2008

The sand felt cool under Nate Martin's feet as he walked hand-in-hand with his wife down to the water. A bonfire crackled away on their beach behind them—the sun had set 30 minutes ago and an orange glow still hung on the horizon. The Martins' boat, *Speculation*, bobbed gently in her mooring about twenty yards offshore.

They parted hands and Nate stopped to pick up a piece of driftwood and toss it back toward the fire. Brooke Martin continued on and dipped her right foot into the water, the wind brushing her auburn hair against her cheek.

"Too cold for me," she said.

Nate took a gulp of beer before walking ankle deep into the water beside her.

"Not bad, but colder than when I put the boat in," Nate said.

"Glad I didn't have to help," Brooke said and then took a sip from her plastic cup of wine.

"Not up for a swim?" Nate joked.

"No way," Brooke said.

They started to walk parallel to the water, with Nate's feet still in and Brooke's squishing into the wet sand just out of reach of the lapping waves.

Four zigzagging jet skis sliced through the water off the Martins' beach. Two were driven by women in bikinis and the other two by men. They weren't wearing life jackets, which usually meant these were summer folk who spent June, July, and August in one of the beach castles smoking weed in mass quantities. These four were probably already baked.

One girl cut a turn too close and flew off.

"Crazies," Nate said.

She resurfaced and climbed back aboard. Her bikini bottom was really a thong and her butt cheeks slapped against the rubber seat as the jet ski started and took off.

"Should they be riding those things this late?" Brooke asked.

"No," said Nate, "but who is going to stop them?"

They continued to walk as the sound of the jet skis faded. A quarter mile later, they reached the stretch where the larger homes began. The floodlights on the estates' back decks illuminated the beach like a stage. The Martins turned around.

When they arrived at their beach, Nate placed a new log on the fire and sat down in his lawn chair. Brooke sat down but then rose, moving her chair a few feet further away from the heat.

"What are your plans for tomorrow?" Nate said.

"I think I'll lay out. I looked at the weather report and we're in for a few good days until rain arrives," Brooke said, "then I'll probably go to the bookstore." Her voice trailed off. She gathered her thoughts for a moment. "We need to make love the next four nights."

"Okay," Nate said.

"You could work up a little enthusiasm," Brooke said.

He had sounded matter-of-fact. "Sorry. It's just that scheduled sex sometimes takes the excitement out of it. We're on vacation. We should just let it happen."

"So, you get to have your strict workout regime everyday, but when I mention a specific time that we need to make love in order to give us the best chance at conceiving, it's suddenly 'We're on vacation'?"

She had a point. He thought about trying to angle in with a comment about her obsessive need to clean the house the moment they had arrived earlier today, but as he thought of it the vision of his freshly cut and edged grass entered his mind. If they really were on vacation, as he had put it, then the lawn being manicured wouldn't be so important to him. Damn.

"What is your plan for tomorrow?" She said.

A switch of topics, but he knew she was circling. "I'm going to get up, take my run, and then hit the hardware store for a new lock for the boat."

"What happened to the lock you keep in the garage?"

"It broke today," Nate shrugged.

"How does a lock break?"

"I put the key in, and when I turned it, it broke off in the lock."

"You mean our boat is moored out there right now without a lock?" Brooke asked, while shifting her gaze to the white hull reflecting the growing moonlight.

"Yep."

"Do you think someone would steal it?"

"Nah. The keys are in the house. If someone wanted to steal a boat worth anything, they'd go down to Shelby's Marina and try and take Shaw's *Triumph*." Leonard Shaw was a Baltimore businessman who had grown up in Michigan and now summered in the largest beach mansion in Hampstead. Once his two-hundred foot custom-built yacht was completed, he'd hired a dredging crew to carve out a separate berth in the marina to dock the boat. With the dredging crew working mostly at night, locals and vacationers complained of the noise and threatened to pull their boats out of Shelby's. Nate was glad he had avoided the hassle by keeping *Speculation* moored off of his beach.

Brooke swiveled her eyes between Nate and the boat. "Why didn't you get a new lock today?"

He moved behind her and started to kiss the back of her neck. *We're on vacation, relax, baby.* "Is that a hint? Do you want me to swim out and sleep on board tonight?"

"Of course not," Brooke whispered back, enjoying the foreplay. "Are you trying to get a head start on tomorrow night?"

"No. Just trying to enjoy *tonight*," Nate said. "Can we concentrate on that?"

She leaned her head back and he kissed her lips.

Ten minutes later, the fire started to die with two empty lawn chairs sitting in front of it.

# 2

Sun rays peeked around the edges of the horizontal blinds in the Martins' bedroom window. Nate opened his eyes and looked at his watch, eight o'clock. He was normally up by six. Brooke was snoring, and he eased out of bed and lifted one strip of the blinds. *Speculation* was in her mooring. He smiled and dropped the blind back into place.

After putting on a pair of shorts and a tank top, he grabbed a pair of socks and his running shoes and exited the bedroom. The hallway was dark as he made his way to the kitchen. He pressed "start" on the coffee pot, and the coffee he had prepared the night before began to brew as he put on his shoes.

The past year had been a revolving door of pain, uncertainty, and disappointment. They had been trying to conceive for six months when his father died. Only last month had it felt right to try again. He hadn't been himself in the classroom either. His ninth grade physical science lessons at W. M. Breech High School had wandered aimlessly, his tests were rote memorization, and the usual passion he brought to each day had been missing; his students let him know they knew it.

His mother had lasted in the beach house until Christmas. The original plan had been for Nate and his older sister, Marie, to share ownership when their parents were unable to handle the upkeep, but Nate had bought Marie's half and the house was now his and Brooke's. His mother had left in January to move in with his sister in St. Petersburg.

He pushed the brass button on the doorknob and closed the door behind him. After wiggling the knob to make sure it was locked, he hopped off the small porch onto the stone walkway, went past the garage, and followed the dirt driveway until he was parallel with their mailbox. After stretching, he looked at his watch and started to jog down Sandyhook Road.

Each lakeside house had some sort of identifying marker next to its mailbox. A red and white striped lighthouse carved out of wood. A miniature of the house painted on a three foot by three foot board. A post. A bench. Something with the owner's name and the year the house had been built on the marker. This five miles of beach, once sparsely populated with neighbors in similarly sized residences, was now dominated by beach mansions that looked more like hotels than houses. The lots were owned by lawyers, congressmen, real-estate tycoons, government contractors, Detroit businessmen (of the few businesses that remained), and a few others who had money. Some were migrants from the already overcrowded western shore of Michigan. White collar Chicago money had run north and was moving around the Great Lakes shoreline like a child connecting the dots to make a picture of a left-handed mitten.

The sun flickered in and out of Nate's face as he ran under the oak trees spanning the road. He thought of the advice his father had given him when he was searching for his first teaching job: "Make sure that you buy a house east of the school so that when you go into work you'll be driving west, and when you come home from work you'll be driving east. That way, you'll never be driving into the sun. Just a simple stress reliever that most people don't take into consideration—that is, until they rear-end someone for the first time." As with all of Nate's father's advice, it had sounded too simple but ended up being right.

Last June his father had been diagnosed with stomach cancer. Three months later, on an overcast September day, Nate had buried him.

Brooke heard the back door close and rose from bed. She turned off their box fan and opened the bedroom blinds. The entire beach was motionless, and their boat was still moored, surrounded by flat water. The aroma of coffee drifted into the bedroom as she put on her robe.

By the time she reached the kitchen, Nate had already filled his mug and was headed down to the water. She poured herself a cup and started a bacon and eggs breakfast.

The sand parted with each step as Nate walked toward the water. Bordering both sides of the Martins' property was a wooden fence; the spindles were flat, painted red, and held together by wire with a metal rod driven into the ground every fifteen feet or so. The fence was not only a "beachy" way to mark property lines but served its primary purpose of trapping sand. Nate took off his shoes and set his mug down by the end of the northern fence line. He began to walk south.

The water ran over his ankles and then receded. It was cool and felt good on his tired feet. The beach looked abandoned. No more than twenty yards from where he started, Nate stepped down with his right foot and felt something sharp. He stood, balancing on his left leg as he inspected the bottom of his right foot. No apparent cut. No bleeding. He rubbed in circles and the pain went away. As he stepped back down onto the wet sand, he saw something sparkle in the place he had stepped before. Glass? A toy left behind by some toddler? As Nate picked the object up, he saw that it was neither. He submerged the object, wiping the wet sand off it, and then dried it with the bottom of his tank top. He held the object a foot in front of his face and studied it. In his hand was a gold coin.

* * *

Brooke saw Nate returning from the water. Assuming that he was coming in to complete his morning routine of running three miles, taking a walk to the water with his coffee, and now eating breakfast and reading the newspaper, she rose to unlock the sliding glass door from the deck. However, he walked right by the deck and headed for the garage. She unlocked the door anyway and refilled her cup. She took a seat at the worn kitchen table, which she wanted to replace but didn't as it had been in the family since Nate was a child. She had plans to redo many parts of the house, but Nate was adamant that the table remained and that the bedroom he stayed in as a boy not be changed. When his father was alive, Nate would have coffee with him in the morning and read the paper at this table. Brooke would still be sleeping and his mother would be cooking breakfast. He had remarked to her that at times he still felt like a visitor, expecting his father to pull up a chair and start a conversation with him about the old days and family stories he'd heard over and over again.

Brooke finished the paper, breakfast, and her cup of coffee and Nate had not come in yet. What was he doing? His bacon, eggs, and toast were cold. She grabbed the coffee pot and headed to the garage.

Nate heard the garage door open as he stared at the coin through a magnifying glass, mesmerized by it.

His wooden writing desk sat in the middle of black carpeting that covered one-quarter of the garage's concrete floor. Two bookcases that he had constructed from odds-and-ends left over from the addition that his parents had done a few years ago rested against the wall behind the desk. Favorite authors had taken up permanent residence on the top two shelves of the first bookcase, and the remaining three shelves were full of paperbacks, read according to his mood at the time he had purchased them. On the top shelf of the second bookcase rested a pair of fins and a mask that he used when cleaning off the bottom of his boat. His father's dive knife was next to the mask.

The shelf below the diving gear contained books that Nate had almost worn the covers off: a Marine Biology desk reference set, half-a-dozen books by Dr. Robert D. Ballard from the Woods Hole Oceanographic Institute, a few by Jacques Cousteau, and five years' worth of magazines from his National Geographic subscription.

The bottom shelves contained books about Great Lakes ports, navigation rules and aids, and boating regulations. Next to one of the rows of books were rolled up charts and a navigation kit. Nate had taught himself how to navigate and routinely took *Speculation* out overnight.

Brooke arrived at Nate's desk and refilled his coffee mug. "Are we rich?" She asked looking at the coin.

"Very funny," Nate said, "I found this on our beach this morning."

"Is that gold?" Brooke asked, more serious now that she had a better look at the coin.

"Maybe. I don't recognize any of these marks or the language that is engraved on it." He put the coin and magnifying glass down and pointed to the bookshelf. "Hand me that book."

Brooke reached up to the top shelf and grabbed a heavy, hardcover book. She looked at the title—*The Golden Age of Piracy*—and tried to hide a grin.

Nate knew her expression meant: *only you would have a book like this, Nate.* "Thanks," he said, laughing at himself with her. "I'm glad to see that I'm still a cheap source of entertainment for you."

She giggled back, and then kissed him on the cheek.

Nate began to leaf through the book.

Brooke set the coffee pot down and picked up the coin and magnifying glass.

After checking the appropriate pages, he closed the book and looked up at Brooke. "Nothing in here that resembles the markings on this coin." He took a drink of his coffee.

Brooke passed the coin and magnifying glass back to Nate. "I can't make out anything on it either." She picked up the coffee pot. "Well, I'm going in to take a shower and then head out to do a little shopping. Your breakfast is cold, but it's on the table if you still want it," she said. "I looked down the beach this morning and I think the Gibsons are up."

Nate was once more absorbed in the mystery of the coin and only grunted in reply.

"I wonder if anyone will make us an offer on our place this summer," Brooke wondered aloud.

A few Hampstead locals had hung on to their homes, repeatedly declining offers that were made for their property. In some cases, it was enough money to bankroll them for a decade. The ink on the paperwork transferring ownership of the house from his mother to Brooke and him hadn't even dried yet when they had been approached. It was over Easter weekend, and they were at the beach house furnishing it with some of their own things. The doorbell had rung, and after five minutes of polite conversation, Nate and Brooke had said no; the prospective buyer and his trophy wife had stormed off.

Some of the mansion owners had even tried to sue the cottage owners, claiming that the cottages detracted from the beachfront's beauty. They wanted the locals out. Most of the locals wanted the castles bulldozed.

Nate set the coin and magnifying glass aside for a moment. "You think that the local kids have all the lawn jobs sewn up yet?" His father had once told him of an unofficial lottery held at the town barbershop to determine who would be allowed to apply for the summer mansion mowing jobs. It had been one of their last conversations.

"Probably," said Brooke.  "I've felt stares at the dime store from Judge Hopkins and Sheriff Walker.  I know they're wishing we would just sell our cottage already."

"How wrong is that?" Nate said.  "The town leaders turning on the townspeople."

"What do they gain by us selling?"

"New mansions mean more opportunities for their sons or daughters to mow a summer resident's lawn," Nate said.  "And if their kid does a good job, then maybe, just maybe, they'll get invited out for a summer party."

"Funny how some people get fooled into thinking they're moving up in the world," she said.

"If they only knew that they look like the person who walks behind a horse and picks up its droppings."

He couldn't help but laugh at the scene he was now picturing.

"What?" Brooke said.

He continued to laugh.

"Naaayyyyte," she said, poking him with her finger.

He gathered himself.  "I started to envision some of the people we know who want to break into that circle walking behind the Budweiser Clydesdales at the Fourth of the July parade picking up piles of shit and waving to the crowd.  Agree?"

"One hundred percent.  Oh, the pictures you paint, Mr. Martin," Brooke said.

"You're the only one that can see the pictures I describe, sweetie."

"When are we getting our internet connection?" Nate said.

"They can't make it out until next week."

"Damned cable company.  We're supposed to have cell phone reception out here next summer too.  I'll believe it when I see it."

She kissed him and then left the garage.

He picked up the coin again and then looked out the window at the spot on the beach where he had found it. Where had it come from? Were there more? He put the magnifying glass and coin in the top drawer of his desk and reshelved the book. He stood with his hand resting on the dive gear for a moment. *Let's have a look.*

He entered the house through the sliding glass door and could hear the shower running as he walked down the hallway and grabbed a towel from the linen closet. He exited the house and as he stepped off the deck, he noticed that the blinds were now open on the lakeside windows of a house two down from them. No doubt the owner had his binoculars out and was watching to see what Nate was up to. The man spent more time prying into other people's lives than living his own. The beach mansion owners had one complaint that held weight: the locals were nosey.

Nate passed by the stack of unused wood in the sand and made his way to the water. The lake was placid and the sun had risen far enough to see the sandy bottom. He positioned himself at the approximate point where he had found the coin. He looked back toward the house to make sure it had been found on his property. It had.

After strapping the knife to his right calf, he pulled the mask down past his face so that it hung by its strap around his neck and rested on his upper chest. He entered the water holding the fins above the surface and probed the bottom with his toes for more coins as he walked out up to his waist. Feeling none, he put his fins on and pulled the mask over his head. He spit into the faceplate, rubbing warm saliva all over, and then dipped the mask into the cold water. After securing it to his face, Nate verified his alignment with the spot on the beach where he'd found the coin and dove under.

The water's temperature was probably in the high fifties, and Nate kicked to warm his body, seeing nothing on the bottom at first. Then, his own anchor auger, wire, and buoy appeared. He surfaced next to *Speculation*, took a deep breath, and dove to the bottom to test the auger. Holding onto the steel pole, he pulled from side to side, then up and down. Neither motion moved the mooring. He checked the wire which ran through the auger's eye to the buoy and back to the eye: they were secure.

A few summers back, he had applied for a job as a navigator on a yacht out of Shelby's. The local paper had advertised that a crew was needed for the vessel's summer voyage up Lake Huron to Mackinac Island, down Lake Michigan to Chicago, and then back to Hampstead. Perhaps "applied" was too strong a word. Thinking that mailing an item like a resume would be too formal, he had shown up at Shelby's to inquire about the job. The marina owner, Kevin Shelby, had finally opened his office door after Nate's third stream of knocking. Shelby had a cigarette and cup of coffee in one hand and was running the other hand through his greasy hair. There had been an open bottle of Baileys on his small desk.

After hearing Nate out, Shelby had said, "Fuck if I know. I've never even heard about the cruise, you sure you've got the right marina?"

And that was the end of his career as a navigator—and possibly berthing his boat there.

Nate swam under *Speculation* and after seeing that the hull was fine, he surfaced and kicked further out until the water was approximately ten feet deep. He took a deep breath and dove.

He traced the bottom and swam in a zigzag pattern out to a depth of twenty-five feet. Odds-and-ends were scattered across the sand: rocks, a tire, a rusted can but no coins. He surfaced. The sun hid behind a cloud making the water darker as Nate treaded. A breeze had started and *Speculation* wandered around her mooring. Where did the coin come from? Nate rotated in a slow circle watching the waves and hearing the distant cry of a seagull.

The sun came out from behind the cloud and the khaki colored bottom illuminated under his black fins. He dove and kicked back toward shore while hugging the lake bed.  Had he hoped to find something?  Sure.  Did he really think that he would?  No.  At least he knew the boat wasn't going anywhere.

As he dried off on the beach, Brooke emerged from the house.

# ABOUT THE AUTHOR

Landon Beach was born and raised in Michigan but now lives in the Sunshine State with his wife, two children, and their golden retriever. He previously served as a Naval Officer and was an educator for fifteen years before becoming a full-time writer. Find out more at landonbeachbooks.com.

www.ingramcontent.com/pod-product-compliance
Lightning Source LLC
Chambersburg PA
CBHW061207190726
48288CB00001B/96